She kissed him gently and then with more intent.

He leaned over and returned it. "Do you want me to stop?"

"No." She opened for him and suspected the way he plunged his tongue inside her mouth was an imitation of lovemaking. He made her feel shivery and hot at the same time. When he looked into her eyes, he pulled the covers down to her waist, and then he lowered his head and dipped his tongue between the hollow of her breasts.

She drew in a ragged breath, but before she could even think to stop him, he ran his tongue all along the inside seam of her shift. He was very wicked, and very hard to resist.

Glowing Praise for
Vicky Dreiling's Novels

What a Wicked Earl Wants

"Wonderful! Top pick! Four-and-a-half stars...Rife with the Regency's penchant for gossip, scandal, and matchmaking, *What a Wicked Earl Wants* is a delightful romance featuring a rakish hero, an innocent widow, corrupt villains, and a secondary cast of characters who add dimension, wit, and tenderness to the plot...Readers will find this a real pleasure to savor."

—*RT Book Reviews*

"Absolutely loved it...I can't wait until the next one in the series!"

—Maryinhb.blogspot.com

"With amazing characters and a story line that kept me turning the pages, *What a Wicked Earl Wants* is another winner from Ms. Dreiling."

—UndertheCoversBookblog.com

"I fell in love with [this] book. Who wouldn't with the romance, society, reputations, and extremely dreamy high society men?"

—ReadingwithStyle.blogspot.com

A Season for Sin

"A master of the genre."
—Library Journal

"*A Season for Sin* is a short but sweet glimpse into Vicky Dreiling's new series. Filled with intrigue and seduction, readers are sure to enjoy this treat and the prospects of what's to come."
—FreshFiction.com

"A delectable teaser...absolutely delicious."
—RomanceJunkiesReviews.com

How to Ravish a Rake

"Dreiling secures her reputation as a writer of charming, matchmaking romances with engaging characters...her cast of quirky, unconventional characters sets her stories apart. Fans of marriage-of-convenience love stories have a treat."
—RT Book Reviews

"A guaranteed delectable indulgence!...Vicky Dreiling is fast becoming an absolute must-buy for Regency fans."
—Affaire de Coeur

"Five stars! Packed with a delectable plot, charming characters, clever banter, humor, scandal, and lots of love, this story is a winner."
—RomanceJunkiesReviews.com

How to Seduce a Scoundrel

"Regency matchmaking, rakes, rogues, innocence, and scandal: oh what fun! Dreiling knows how to combine these ingredients into a delightfully delicious, wickedly witty slice of reading pleasure."
—*RT Book Reviews*

"5 stars! This was an enchanting tale that had me grinning from ear to ear. The chemistry between Marc and Julianne was flammable and only needed a spark to set it off."
—**SeducedbyaBook.com**

"The scenes between Julianne and Hawk are lots of fun; they have great physical chemistry and razor-sharp dialogue."
—**NightOwlRomance.com**

How to Marry a Duke

"Sexy, fresh, and witty... A delicious read! Better than chocolate! Vicky Dreiling is an author to watch!"
—**Sophie Jordan,** *New York Times* **bestselling author**

"A terrific romp of a read!... Vicky is a bright new voice in romance."
—**Sarah MacLean,** *New York Times* **bestselling author**

"Dreiling's delightful debut combines the rituals of Regency courtship with TV's *The Bachelor*...the inherent charm of the characters (especially the dowager duchess) keeps the pages flying until the surprising conclusion. Dreiling is definitely a newcomer to watch."

"Engaging...charming...the cast is solid as they bring humor, shenanigans, and deportment, but the tale belongs to the duke and his matchmaker."

"A witty, nourishing romp of a romance...impossible to put down...Dreiling mesmerizes as she brings an era to life. She fills the pages with laughter, sensuality, and charm. *How to Marry a Duke* is an irresistible ride readers will return to again and again."

Also by Vicky Dreiling

What a Reckless Rogue Needs

Book 2—The Sinful Scoundrels Series

By

VICKY DREILING

FOREVER

NEW YORK   BOSTON

Copyright 2014 by Vicky Dreiling
Excerpt from *What a Devilish Duke Desires* copyright © 2014 by Vicky Dreiling

Forever
Hachette Book Group
237 Park Avenue
New York, NY 10017

www.HachetteBookGroup.com

Printed in the United States of America

First Edition: March 2014
10 9 8 7 6 5 4 3 2 1

OPM

Forever is an imprint of Grand Central Publishing.
The Forever name and logo are trademarks of Hachette Book Group, Inc.

The Hachette Speakers Bureau provides a wide range of authors for speaking events. To find out more, go to www.hachettespeakersbureau.com or call (866) 376-6591.

The publisher is not responsible for websites (or their content) that are not owned by the publisher.

To my late father, Benny Gregory. Miss you, Daddy.

Acknowledgments

Many thanks to Michele Bidelspach for your insightful comments. You're an amazing editor.

To Lucienne Diver for all the guidance, fantastic ideas, and fun, too. I know how lucky I am.

To everyone at The Knight Agency—you guys rock.

To Kati Rodriguez for knowing exactly what I need before I know it. You continue to wow me with your ideas and suggestions.

To all the team at Forever Romance for the fantastic covers and great ideas.

Huge thanks to Carrie Andrews—best copy editor ever!

Most important of all, I wish to thank all the readers who let me know you enjoy my books. May the Magic Romance Fairies be with you.

What a
Reckless Rogue
Needs

Prologue

Eton, December 1798

Colin Brockhurst, Earl of Ravenshire, was only eight years old, but he knew bad things could happen.

He sat on a hard bench with the other boys waiting to go home. Normally, the boys were boisterous and bawdy, but under the stern eye of the headmaster, they fell silent, save for the occasional sneeze and cough. Most everyone had already left for Christmas holidays, including his friend Harry. Each time the door opened, frigid wind swirled inside, and even a warm coat and supple leather gloves were insufficient to block the miserable draft.

Footsteps stamped outside again, the sound a prelude to the door opening. Colin held his breath, but someone else's father arrived. Where could his papa be? His chest felt hollow inside, but he mustn't let on that he was scared, because the older boys would taunt him.

The door opened, letting in a cold blast of wind, and another boy jumped up, this time to leave with a servant. Colin's stomach knotted up. He hoped it was Papa who came to the door, not a footman. The hollow place in his chest made him feel alone and scared, but he clasped his hands together and forced himself to hold all the fear deep down where no one could see it. He had to do it or the older boys would sniff it on him like day-old sweat and make his life hell when the term started after the holidays. He'd learned to duck the older, bigger ones and use his fists to defend himself when he couldn't get away.

Sometimes he welcomed the fights, because it let him pound out all the fury and frustration inside of him. Two years ago, his papa had told him the angels had taken Mama to heaven. He'd been old enough to understand that she'd died and wouldn't come back, no matter how much he'd prayed for a miracle.

Now it was getting later, and there were only three boys left, including him. What would he do if Papa died and no one came for him? Would he have to stay at school all by himself? Papa had told him there was nothing to fear, but he had to clasp his shaky hands together even harder.

He must be brave. That's what Papa had told him when he first came to Eton. Colin made himself hold all the scared feelings inside, even though his chest hurt.

The door opened again. Colin held his breath once more and let it out in a whoosh when he saw his father. He grabbed his satchel and jumped to his feet.

"Are you ready to come home?" his father said, smiling.

He nodded. Papa's hand on his shoulder made him feel safe, and he hadn't felt that way in a very long time. They walked out, and a few snow flurries swirled in the air. He tried to catch one on his tongue as they walked down the steps to the waiting carriage. He climbed inside, and Papa gave him a woolen rug to keep him warm. The carriage rolled off, and the clatter of the horses' hooves along with the motion made him sleepy. Papa put his arm around him, and he sagged against him.

It was dark when Papa woke him in the carriage and took him inside the inn. He was so very tired he didn't remember anything until Papa woke him the next morning. After he washed and dressed, Papa took him downstairs for breakfast. Colin's stomach growled like a dog, and he ate every bite of his eggs and toast. Papa laughed and mussed his hair.

Then a man called a *porter* took their bags to the waiting carriage. Colin climbed inside, and after Papa sat beside him, he took a deep breath. "There is something I must prepare you for."

Colin stiffened. When grown people said things like that, it meant something bad.

"There's no need to be afraid," Papa said.

He held his breath anyway.

"You have a new mother," Papa said.

He let out his breath, but he was confused. "Where did she come from?"

"I met her while you were at school. She is my wife and your stepmother," Papa said. "She will live with us."

He didn't want a stepmama. He wanted his mother.

"All will be well, son."

He didn't believe it. Nothing would ever be well again. His mama had died and left him.

"You will meet her today," Papa said.

Colin felt as if the bottom of the carriage had dropped away.

Chapter One

London, 1821, The Albany

Colin awoke with an aching head and his tongue as dry as the Arabian Desert. He must've drunk enough claret last night to fill the bloody Thames.

He sat up on the edge of the mattress, only to realize he'd slept in his boots. A ray of sunshine speared through the drapes, blinding him. He shaded his eyes and turned away. The remnants of his drunken spree sat on a chest: two glasses and three bottles.

For a disoriented moment, his woolly brain refused to cooperate. He scrubbed his hand over the stubble on his face. Two glasses? In the bedchamber? Had someone else been here?

When the door opened, he stood to face it. A red-headed woman in a rumpled green gown entered. He vaguely recalled meeting her backstage in the actress's dressing room at the theater the previous night. "What happened?" he asked, his voice croaking.

She huffed. "I should think it bloody obvious."

Oh, Lord. "Did we...?"

"Are you daft? You were so foxed I couldn't wake you," she said. "I had no one to help me undress."

Relieved, he blew out his breath. Given his inebriated state last night, he doubted he would have been sensible enough to use a French letter. "Sorry, Lila," he said.

She rolled her eyes. "My name is Lottie."

"Of course. How could I forget?"

"You were drunk as a sailor," she said. "That's how."

He felt as if a carriage had run over him. "I must beg your pardon, but the landlord doesn't allow women in the rooms."

"That didn't trouble you last night."

Someone banged on the door, startling him. He met Lottie's gaze. "Stay here and be silent," he said.

She scowled. "What? You mean to hide me?"

"Well, yes. Please be quiet," he said under his breath. "The landlord will fine me if he discovers you here."

The knocking sounded again, this time more insistent. Colin's temples throbbed as he walked to the door. "I'm coming," he called out.

"Not likely," Lottie said, snickering.

He halted at the ridiculous double entendre and glanced over his shoulder. "Go back into the bedchamber. You can't be seen here."

She leaned against the door and grinned. "Tell the landlord I'm your sister."

He huffed. "I'm sure he's heard that before."

Her raspy laughter grated on his nerves. In a thoroughly bad mood, Colin strode across the small parlor and yanked the door open.

His oldest friend, Harry, stood there. "Sorry to wake you, old boy, but it is almost noon."

"Thank God," Colin said, ushering his friend inside. "I thought it was the landlord."

Harry blinked as he clapped eyes on the actress. "Oh, I say, bad timing."

"Don't worry," Colin said. "Lila is just leaving."

"Lottie," she said in an exasperated tone. Then she turned her attention to Harry. "You're a looker."

Harry took her hand and bowed over it as if she were a grand lady at a ton ball. "*Enchanté*."

Colin located his purse and handed her a shilling. "This should cover the cost of a hack."

She scowled. "You wish to be rid of me?"

"Not at all, madame," Harry said, ogling her décolletage.

Colin released a loud sigh, rummaged in the purse, and produced another shilling.

She lifted her brows. "Is this all I can expect after staying the entire night?"

"You had the use of a soft bed," Colin said.

She put her hands on her hips. "I had to keep my gown on."

Harry eyed the voluptuous actress's charms. "I suppose it's more expedient that way."

"He left his boots on," Lottie said with a sniff.

Harry shook his head. "Bad form, old boy."

Colin gave Harry a pointed look. "Is there something you wanted?"

"Yes." Harry took a letter out of his pocket. "This was mistakenly delivered to my rooms earlier this morning."

Colin took the letter and regarded Lottie. "I wish you many standing ovations."

She donned her cloak. "I certainly didn't get one last night." With that riposte, she marched out the door.

Harry burst out laughing and collapsed on the cast-off sofa.

"Stubble it," Colin said. He walked over to the table and broke the seal on the letter. "How much do I owe you for the post?"

"Nothing. You paid mine the last time," Harry said. "Who sent you a letter?"

"I don't know. I haven't read it yet."

"Aren't you a slow top today," Harry said.

"I've got the bottle ache." He set the letter aside and rubbed his temples. He'd suffered a lot of bottle aches lately.

"Where's your man servant? He could make you a concoction."

"It's his half day." Colin added coals to the dying fire. Afterward, he walked to the kitchen, pumped water into a kettle, and returned to the parlor. He measured leaves in the teapot and set the kettle on the hob. While he waited for the water to heat, he opened the letter and scowled.

"Well?" Harry asked.

His nostrils flared. "It's from my father."

"What does he say?"

"He requests my presence at Deerfield Park." Colin rose, slapped the letter on the table, and started pacing. "Damn him."

Harry lifted his brows. "Is something wrong?"

"There definitely is something bloody damned wrong. My father wants to sell Sommerall." Colin gritted his teeth at the thought of strangers taking possession.

"What about the entail?" Harry said.

"Sommerall was intentionally left out. My grandfather intended the property for a younger son, but my father was the only male issue." His parents had lived there until his mother's death, and then his father had abruptly moved to his grandfather's nearby estate, Deerfield.

Colin walked to the window and pushed the draperies aside. Sommerall had been his boyhood home for six years. No one had occupied it since then. He'd always assumed his father would grant him the property.

"When do you leave?" Harry asked.

He gave his friend a wry look. "At my earliest convenience."

"Sorry about the property. Perhaps you could persuade the marquess not to sell."

"Right," he said, the one word full of sarcasm.

"How long will you stay?" Harry asked.

He shrugged. "Long enough to find out what prompted my father's decision." He meant to change his father's mind, and he had just cause.

When the kettle started shrieking, he rescued it and poured the hot water.

"Will the Duke of Wycoff and his family visit for the house party as usual?" Harry asked.

"I doubt it. For all I know, the duchess and her eldest daughter are still in Paris."

"They returned six months ago."

He poured tea over a strainer into two cups and handed one to Harry. "How do you know this? Oh, never mind, your mother and female cousins would have told you."

Harry sipped his tea. "You know my mother's drawing room is famous for scandal broth. My cousins know everything about everybody. You do know Lady Angeline jilted Brentmoor over a year ago."

"I heard." That was all he knew of her situation, although he couldn't figure out how she'd gotten tangled up with that roué. He didn't want to know. Their families were close, but he'd had a falling out with Angeline years ago. His father had blamed him for supposedly breaking her heart at her come-out ball, but it was the exact opposite. When he'd requested a dance, she'd turned him down flat and accepted an offer from someone else. To be fair, he'd been nipping from a flask with friends and she'd been disgusted. Ever since they'd been like oil and water. They didn't mix well.

Harry set his cup aside. "Supposedly the broken engagement is the reason she fled to Paris last year."

He wasn't surprised. Crying off an engagement was serious business. The scandal sheets had reported it, albeit with poorly disguised names. He'd never understood why her father had approved the marriage in the first place. Brentmoor's sorry reputation was well known, after all.

Harry frowned. "Why would the marquess sell Sommerall?"

"That's the thousand-pound question." Colin clenched his jaw. He considered his father's decision an insult, but he wouldn't voice the words.

"The marquess will come around," Harry said.

"This is no idle inclination on my father's part."

"Do you think he's bluffing?"

"No, he's serious, but so am I."

"What are you planning?" Harry said.

Colin lifted his chin. "An offer he can't refuse."

* * *

Suffolk, Sommerall House, two days later

The carriage slowed six miles from Deerfield Manor and rounded the circular drive of Sommerall. Mercifully, the weather had held. When the vehicle rolled to a halt, Colin collected his hat and stepped out. The crisp autumn breeze chilled his face as he inhaled the fresh country air. It was invigorating after the filthy, choked skies of London.

He directed the driver to wait and strode off. His boots crunched in the gravel as he walked toward the sandstone house built in the early part of the eighteenth century. The darker blue hues in the sky signaled impending twilight. He was glad he'd arrived before all the light waned, as he wanted to inspect the condition of the property. When he met with his father, he intended to report any initial needed repairs. If he expected his father to consider his request, he must show that he had made a preliminary investigation.

He felt above the lintel for the key, but it wasn't there. Frowning, he tried the door, but it was locked tighter than a virgin's legs. There was nothing for it except to question his father about the missing key.

Colin tramped through the grass to the back of the house. The lower windows might have afforded him a view inside, but he couldn't see much from this vantage point. Colin gritted his teeth, but frustration wouldn't change a damned thing.

He walked west along a path that had probably once been well worn, but he couldn't be certain. His father's house was a mere six miles down good road, but there were reasons he seldom returned to Deerfield.

In the distance, a swing hung from a tall oak. Perhaps his late mother or father had given him a push, but he would never know, for he recalled very little of his childhood.

The papery autumn leaves crackled beneath his boots as he strode onward. Long shadows reached out from the barren birch trees. The property was far smaller than Deerfield Park, but it was excellent land. He envisioned workers in the now-fallow fields, but there was no rush. He was thirty-one years old and not ready to settle down.

The capes of his greatcoat snapped in the biting wind, but he was determined. In the distance, he saw the marble domed roof and the four Ionic columns of the mausoleum. When he reached it, he gripped the rail of the balustrade and looked down the flight of steps. Twenty-four years had elapsed, but all he had left of her was her grave and vague snatches of childhood memories.

His chest tightened. He couldn't recall the last time he'd visited his mother's grave, and it shamed him. He had no eloquent prayers, no memorabilia of his mother. Only a hollow place inside that had remained empty. "You will not be abandoned or forgotten," he said in a hoarse voice.

Colin turned and strode away. He'd be damned before he let his father sell the property where his mother was laid to rest.

By the time he reached Deerfield Park, the sun had set and the Tudor house that had belonged to his family since the sixteenth century was shrouded in darkness, save for the lanterns that the servants carried. When he stepped out of the carriage, a blast of freezing wind chafed his face. A footman with a lantern led the way to the horseshoe steps while the others unloaded his trunks.

When he entered the foyer, he handed over his hat, coat, and gloves to Ames, the butler who had been with the family all of Colin's life.

"My lord, may I be permitted to welcome you home?" Ames said.

"Yes, of course, Ames," he said, handing over his greatcoat. Then he smiled and retrieved a small snuffbox from his inner coat pocket.

"For me, my lord?" Ames said.

"I happened upon it and know you like to collect them. This one was made in India."

"I could not accept it, my lord. I'm sure it is quite valuable."

"Of course you can. I would be disappointed if you did not accept it."

"Very well," Ames said. "Thank you for the gift, my lord. I shall put it in a special place where it will remind me of you. Now, your room is prepared, and your valet will unpack your trunk as soon as possible. The marquess, marchioness, and all of the other guests are in the blue drawing room."

He paused at the mention of other guests, but of course, he would not question the butler. "Thank you, Ames." He'd hoped to speak privately with his father straightaway, but obviously he'd have to wait until tomorrow. His boots clipped on the marble floor as he strode across the great hall.

Feminine shrieks startled him. "Colin!"

Bianca and Bernadette, his twin half sisters, ran down the stairs. When they threw their arms around him, he frowned. "Wait, who are you? What have you done with my little sisters?"

Bernadette rolled her eyes. "You're silly, Colin."

"I'm afraid to blink," he said. "You might get even taller right before my eyes."

Until this moment, he'd not realized how much he'd missed them. They were mirror images of one another, something that often took others aback. Early on, he'd learned to distinguish them by a small beauty mark. Bernadette had one on her left cheek, while Bianca's was on her right cheek.

Bianca looked up at him. "How long will you stay?"

"A thousand years," he said, making his sisters laugh.

"We have a dog now," Bianca said. "We're supposed to keep Hercules in the kitchen with the servants."

"Hercules? He must be a big dog."

"No, he's not very big," Bernadette said.

Bianca giggled. "Papa said he's ugly."

Colin laughed. "Are you still speaking twin gibberish?"

"We gave that up ages ago," Bernadette said. "Next spring, we'll be sixteen and ready for our come-out."

His chest tightened yet again, this time with guilt. He would know about their upcoming debut if he'd made the effort to see them more often. God only knew what else he'd missed in their lives. Regardless of how difficult his relationship was with his father, he shouldn't ignore his sisters.

"We're not nearly as tall as Penny," Bianca said. "Here she comes now."

Penelope was here? He looked up at the landing where

a thin, tall girl with reddish blond hair stood. She lowered her eyes and turned toward the corridor.

"Come with us," Bianca said, taking his arm. When they gained the landing, he saw the back of a tall brunette in a brilliant green gown. His appreciative gaze slid down to the woman's rounded bottom. When the brunette turned, she looked somewhat familiar, but the candlelight in the corridor was dim.

As he drew nearer, recognition dawned. The candlelight burnished her brunette hair and shed a mellow glow over her stunning creamy complexion. He felt as if she'd knocked the breath out of him. Hell, she'd literally done it when he'd tried to give her a chaste kiss beneath the Christmas mistletoe a few years ago. She'd always had a sharp tongue, and he'd remained wary of her with good reason.

Angeline curtsied and regarded him with a shrewd smile. *"Bonsoir, mon ami."*

Their relationship had always been closer to adversary than friend, but he'd not seen her in a long time. There was no question that she'd grown even more beautiful.

Angeline offered her gloved hand, and he bowed over it. He flicked his eyes quickly over her generous bosom. Colin mentally reminded himself to keep his gaze a very safe distance above her low neckline. "I suspect you've had more than a few Parisian admirers."

Her one-shoulder shrug was all Gallic. "The French have a proverb: 'Beautiful grapes often make poor wine.'" A sly expression flitted through her green eyes. "So I avoid the grapes and drink the wine."

"Clever," he said.

Angeline clapped her hands twice. "Girls, repair to the drawing room. The marchioness is expecting us."

He offered his arm to her. "Shall we?"

"I don't know. You look as if you're facing a prison cell rather than a drawing room."

He said nothing, but he'd always dreaded visits to his father's home. He'd been at Eton when his father remarried, and on his infrequent stays at Deerfield, he'd never felt he belonged. It wasn't as if they were estranged; it was just circumstances. He'd always felt a bit awkward here, and as a result, he didn't visit often.

They entered the drawing room to the delighted exclamations of Angeline's mother—the Duchess of Wycoff—and his stepmother, Margaret, the marchioness. He noted the proliferation of gray in the duchess's hair, and the fine hair on his neck stiffened. The scandal must have created a great deal of vexation.

"I daresay they make a handsome pair," the duchess said.

Colin winced. When they were children, their deluded families had concocted the idea of a match between them, all because they were born only a week apart. But that had happened when they were mere babes, before his mother's death and his father's second marriage.

"Unfortunately, Colin and Angeline are about as compatible as two spitting cats," the marquess said.

"Chadwick, please mind your words," Margaret said. "Oh, look what you've started. The girls are hissing at each other. Bianca, Bernadette, you will cease."

His father had spoken the truth. Beyond the annual house party and the spring season, Colin and Angeline had done their best to avoid each other over the years, though they had not been entirely successful. Despite her outward civility this evening, he knew her capacity for causing trouble, and he could not afford to be distracted. The fate of Sommerall hung in the balance.

He escorted Angeline to a chair and headed for the sideboard. Five minutes in her presence had been enough to send him to the brandy decanter. Admittedly, a goodly portion had to do with her womanly figure. A shrew she might be, but she was also the sort of woman men mentally undressed. At that thought, he poured himself two fingers, and then his gaze veered to his father. *Show him you're confident and unconcerned.*

The Marquess of Chadwick returned his look with an inscrutable expression.

"Welcome, Colin," the Marchioness of Chadwick said.

He bowed. "You look well, Margaret."

"I'm very glad you came." For a moment, she looked as if she would say more and then seemed to reconsider. Her abrupt silence didn't surprise him. They had always been ill at ease with each other, although unfailingly polite. Her late father had been in trade, but she'd been educated as a lady. Colin assumed his father had married her for her wealth, but he did not know for certain, and he most certainly would never ask.

Margaret faced Angeline. "Thank you for bringing the girls to the drawing room. Left to their own devices, I fear they would spend all of their time in their room engaged in idle gossip."

"What gossip could they possibly know?" the marquess said in a gruff voice. "They aren't even out in society yet."

The twins immediately adopted cherubic expressions. Colin bit his lip to keep from laughing.

Margaret regarded her husband with lifted brows. "You seem to have forgotten the letter they wrote to the king six months ago."

Colin regarded his sisters with mock gravity. "Why did you write to the king?"

The marquess released a loud sigh. "Your sisters advised him to adopt a slimming regimen."

Colin's shoulders shook with laughter. The poor king's girth was the subject of many caricatures.

"Thank goodness Ames intercepted the letter before it went out with the post," Margaret said.

Colin leaned against the sideboard. So his sisters were still scamps. He found himself glad, perhaps because soon they would be entering the adult world, before he'd even gotten a chance to catch up on their burgeoning adolescence. The fault was his, and he'd meant to do better, but somehow intention led to procrastination. In London, it was all too easy to get caught up in the clubs, the races, the fencing matches, and the loose women who pursued him.

The Duke of Wycoff approached and clapped Colin on the shoulder. "I wasn't certain you would attend."

He wouldn't have done so if not for his father's letter. From the corner of his eye, Colin saw his father watching and retrieved the decanter. "Brandy?" he asked the duke.

"Don't mind if I do," the duke said. "It's been an age since we last met."

"White's last spring, if memory serves me right." Colin handed him a brandy and sipped his own drink. His father always stocked the finest brandy and port. "I take it Landale could not attend?" Colin said.

"My son did not wish to travel, given that his wife is in a delicate condition."

Colin smiled a little at Wycoff's old-fashioned reference to his daughter-in-law's impending childbirth.

Wycoff inhaled the brandy's fragrance. "It has been two years since the last house party. I confess I missed the shooting with Chadwick."

There was a reserved air about Wycoff that had never been there before. He didn't mention Angeline's broken engagement and subsequent journey to Paris with her mother. It wasn't the sort of topic one spoke of openly, but Colin felt it simmering beneath the surface. One thing he noticed was that Wycoff avoided looking at his eldest daughter. Colin found it odd and told himself he was imagining undercurrents. Deep down, he suspected there was something brewing beneath the surface, but he'd no idea what it was. Perhaps that was for the best.

Wycoff drew in a breath. "Still chasing the lightskirts?"

"Am I supposed to answer that?"

The duke laughed. "Sounds like an affirmative to me." He cleared his throat. "I try to be discreet."

The duke raised his brows. "It's not working."

In an effort to change the topic, Colin said, "May I freshen your drink?"

"No, thank you," Wycoff said. "I'll join your father on a comfortable chair and try not to doze as I'm wont to do."

Colin bowed and watched the duke walk away. Angeline attempted to intercept him, but he ignored her. Colin frowned. It seemed odd to him, but he shrugged it off.

He meant to remain at the sideboard, but Margaret sought him out. "Angeline has agreed to play the pianoforte," she said. "Perhaps you would be so kind as to turn the pages for her."

Short of claiming a sudden case of the ague, he could hardly refuse. "Yes, of course," he said, and strode over to the instrument where Angeline removed one of her gloves. He'd forgotten her long slender fingers. Then again, why should he remember them? He shook off the odd thought and stood there waiting for her to begin playing.

"Will you set up the sheet music?" she said, fumbling with the other glove.

"Yes, I will." He frowned. "Are you vexed?"

"Of course not," she said.

He suspected she was lying. "What will you play?"

"Grimstock," she said, handing the sheets to him.

He leaned over her shoulder and placed the pages side by side. "How appropriate considering you are looking rather grim," he said under his breath.

"I haven't played in ages. I fear this will be excruciating for me and everyone listening."

"It's a bit late to decline now."

"I will play when I am ready," she said in a testy voice.

"As you please, but there's no need to snap at me. I might add that the sooner you play, the quicker the misery will be over."

"I do not play that badly," she said.

He clasped his hands behind his back and said nothing.

"I am competent," she said.

"Of course you are," he said, trying very hard not to laugh.

"You are perfectly horrid and so is my playing," she said.

"At long last, something we agree upon." He'd forgotten the ease with which they sparred with one another. It was like verbal chess.

"Do not torment me," she said. "I might avenge myself by playing more than one piece."

"In that case, I am overwhelmed by your talent—at least for the duration of this one exhibition."

She pressed the ivory keys lightly. "I must concentrate."

When he turned the page, she leaned forward a bit and pressed a discordant note, but she managed to recover.

After a few moments, he said, "I saw you speaking to my stepmother."

Angeline kept her eyes on the sheet music. "The marchioness enumerated your many positive qualities."

He smiled. "Did she now? What did she say?"

"Hmmm. She said you drink like a fish and have a string of previous lovers who are permanently heartbroken over losing your affections."

"Margaret would never disparage me."

"So you deny you're a rake?" Angeline said, her tone challenging.

"My reputation is somewhat embellished."

She looked at him from the corner of her eye. "I rather doubt it."

"Why should you doubt me? You've no proof."

"I'm well acquainted with the type," she said. "I imagine you've heard."

He leaned over her again and straightened the sheet music. "I'm not Brentmoor."

She played a wrong note and grimaced.

"Sorry." He shouldn't have said that. It had probably

been a painful experience for her. "You're fine, keep playing."

"That's rich. Encouragement from a rake."

He was tempted to defend himself, but it wouldn't change the truth. Good God, he'd gotten so foxed in his rooms he'd passed out with his boots on and forgotten the actress he'd taken home. But in the world of London, there were rakes and there were disgusting scoundrels. He'd never sunk so low as the latter.

The duchess raised her voice. "Angeline, you must focus."

Angeline's mouth thinned as if she were struggling with her reaction. The duchess was a formidable woman, with a very strict interpretation of the proprieties. That brought to mind Brentmoor.

Colin could not fathom how Angeline had gotten involved with that roué. He wondered why Wycoff hadn't put his foot down with his daughter. Why hadn't he forbidden her to have anything to do with a known libertine? It made no sense.

Granted, he was a rake, but he kept his distance from virtuous ladies, mostly because he prized his bachelorhood.

Angeline faltered again.

Colin marked the way she winced and figured her mother's reproof had rattled her. But he found it odd. Angeline had never been a wilting flower. When she played another wrong note, he leaned closer and said, "Relax, my stepmother is distracting the duchess as we speak."

Angeline was more than a little flustered, and Colin's presence did not help. "I do not need your reassurance."

"I'm merely practicing being a dull, respectable fellow."

She continued playing. "Is that like putting on an old coat to see if it still fits?"

"I'm simply wanting for temporary amusement."

"Then I must be boring you," she said. "There is a dearth of real amusement tonight."

"One thing about you hasn't changed," he said.

"What is that?"

"You never want for a clever retort."

Or a strategic defense. She regarded him with a cynical smile. Truthfully, she had dreaded encountering Colin, but it was foolish of her. He'd likely heard plenty of rumors about her misbegotten and short-lived engagement, but she had a low opinion of dissipated rakes like him and cared nothing for his opinion, good or bad.

Liar. You hate that he knows you were brought down low.

She had hoped to avoid attending the annual house party, but her mother had insisted that she begin entering English society again in order to "repair" her reputation, though this gathering hardly counted as such. The notion of repair was laughable. The only way she could redeem her reputation would be to make a respectable marriage, and that was highly unlikely.

Even though she yearned to start over, to change what had happened, there was no going back. She couldn't retrieve her youth. Time had marched on like an obedient soldier, until one day she'd awakened to discover she was thirty years old and on the proverbial shelf. That had played a large part in her foolhardy courtship with Brentmoor.

Angeline played the last notes and reached for the sheet music, but Colin gathered the pages in a neat stack. When he turned to her, she was struck anew by his dark curly hair and brown eyes with amber hues that could melt butter in freezing temperatures—or more likely, a lady's objections.

Any lady but her.

Why was so much beauty wrapped up in a she-devil package? Perhaps he wasn't being fair. They had not spoken in ages, but given her acerbic remarks tonight, he doubted she'd changed.

She snatched her gloves. In her haste, she dropped one.

He retrieved it. "You seem a bit flustered. I hope I did not make you vexatious."

"You flatter yourself."

"There you are wrong. I have my faults, but excessive vanity is not one of them."

She covered an obviously feigned yawn. "I shall refrain from asking about your other excesses."

"Angeline," the duchess said, "will you play again or do you intend to dawdle?"

The rosy flush staining Angeline's face spoke volumes, but she recovered quickly and popped up from the bench. "I shall dawdle. I do it so well."

The twins marched over to the pianoforte and set up their sheets. Colin took the opportunity to escape Angeline. "Pardon me while I turn the pages for my sisters."

"How very charming of Ravenshire to turn the pages for the twins," the duchess said. "He shows his care for his sisters."

Angeline made a concerted effort not to roll her eyes. She'd always struggled to keep her thoughts from showing on her face, but it was particularly difficult when her mother made a big to-do over the simple act of turning pages. The duchess had obviously chosen to forget Colin's dissipated reputation, but Angeline had not.

She turned her attention away and spotted Penny hunching her shoulders in the window seat. "Excuse me, Mama," she said, and hurried off before her mother could detain her further. Penny smiled a little when she sat beside her.

"Are you enjoying seeing the twins again?" Angeline asked.

"Oh, yes. They are quite vivacious," Penny said. "Unlike me."

Angeline squeezed her sister's hand. "You have many talents, Penny. You play very well and your watercolors are beautiful."

"Thank you," Penny said, "but I wish I had the gift of conversing easily. I always think of something clever to say after I'm alone."

"Better to think before you speak," Angeline said. "I learned that the hard way, but let us not dwell on our faults. The grounds at Deerfield are beautiful. Perhaps we could go for a walk this week if the weather holds."

"I would like that very much." Penny bit her lip.

"What troubles you?" Angeline said.

"It is of no consequence," she said.

"You know that you can tell me anything." She worried that her mother might have inadvertently let something slip about her broken betrothal in front of Penny this evening. Angeline knew she couldn't protect her sister forever, but she did not want to reveal the circumstances while they were away from home.

Penny clasped her hands in her lap. "Bianca and Bernadette were speaking about our come-outs next spring, and all of a sudden I realized that I would be among an enormous crowd. I just know that I'll be a wall-flower."

She hugged Penny. "Sweet sister, you will do very well."

"You will be there," Penny said. "I could not possibly make my debut without you."

"You mustn't worry." But even as Angeline spoke, she wasn't entirely certain she would be able to attend. While a few of her mother's steadfast friends had called upon them in Paris, there were more than a few English ladies who had cut their acquaintance. She dreaded broaching the topic. Her sister was sensitive, and Angeline saw no reason to worry Penny months ahead of time, but Angeline was concerned. She prayed her scandal would not touch Penny, because that would hurt far more than Brentmoor's duplicity.

Colin bid the guests good night as they retired for the evening. The marquess had not moved from his spot on the sofa. As usual, Margaret was straightening the cushions, something she ought to leave for the servants. Then she pulled a stool over to her husband.

"Margaret," the marquess said in a warning tone.

She hesitated. "I thought you might wish to put your feet up now that the guests are gone."

Colin sat in a winged chair and leaned forward. "If you don't want it, I'll take it."

"I'll keep it," the marquess said.

Good Lord. His father was like a child. He hadn't wanted the stool until he realized someone else did.

Margaret curtsied. "Well, I'll leave you to your discussion."

"You may expect me in half an hour, Margaret."

Colin brushed at the nonexistent lint on his trousers. Did his father have to announce his intention to bed his wife in front of him?

After she left, the marquess polished off a brandy and regarded him with amusement. "Did you think I've become so ancient that I've lost my virility?"

He turned his head aside. "I don't want to know your intimate business."

"Are you blushing?" Of course he wasn't, but damnation, no man wanted to know about his father's marital relations. "I'm here because you requested my presence to discuss the sale of Sommerall."

The marquess clasped his hands over his slight paunch. "You are curt this evening. Perhaps you have forgotten who supports your lavish lifestyle."

His quarterly funds hardly counted as a "lavish" lifestyle, but Colin refused to be distracted. "I stopped at Sommerall earlier today. Are you aware the key is missing?"

"It is not missing," the marquess said. "I retrieved it some time ago to keep vagrants out."

Colin nodded. "I'll come to the point. I want Sommerall."

The marquess huffed. "For what? You spend all of your time in London. The property has remained unoccupied for years. The furnishings and paintings are covered with sheets. God only knows what sort of nests are in the chimney. The place needs to be occupied. I see no reason to let it rot when I have an offer."

Colin clenched his jaw and reminded himself to hold his temper. A row would serve no purpose. "I have a plan—"

"Not tonight." The marquess groaned after he moved his feet off the stool and stood.

Colin's eyes widened. "Are you unwell?"

"Of course not," the marquess said. "Go on now. I'll meet you in my study after breakfast."

"If you will listen—"

"Tomorrow," the marquess said.

"I only want a few minutes of your—"

"You will meet me as directed," the marquess said.

His father had always insisted upon having control of everything, including the last word. Colin gritted his teeth, stood, and bowed. "Good night," he said.

After Colin left, the marquess winced when his knees creaked. Little wonder. He'd tramped all over the property with Wycoff earlier today. He'd always been active, either riding or walking along the property. He personally inspected repairs and drainage issues. Only a fool would allow others to make the decisions, and he was no fool.

He was doubly glad that he was as fit as ever, as he didn't want anything to interfere with the shooting. Every autumn, he and Wycoff had a fine time shooting birds— or rather attempting. Aiming their guns at birds was a better description. They rarely ever bagged one, but that didn't matter. He enjoyed spending time with his oldest friend. He thought about inviting Colin, but the marquess knew it was time to teach his son a lesson. That was the reason he'd requested his reckless son's presence at the house party.

The marquess sighed. He had heard more stories than he could count about his son's debauchery, gaming, and dissipation. He should not be surprised. After all, he'd been quite the rakehell in his day, but he had decided it was past time that Colin settled down. Once the marquess made a decision, he stood by it.

He'd known his threat to sell Sommerall would infuriate his son, but he'd been fairly certain that Colin would have made excuses to avoid the house party and Angeline. The pair had never gotten along since her come-out. Margaret had told him in confidence that Colin had reserved the first dance, but there had been a dustup when he'd shown up late and foxed. That was years ago, but they had remained estranged all these years. Seemed ridiculous to him, but what was he to do about it?

But now his old friend Wycoff was worried about his eldest daughter. She'd gotten herself in a tangle over jilting a beau, and Wycoff worried about her future. The marquess sympathized, as he had his own problems with Colin.

Reason told him that Colin wanted Sommerall because his mother was buried there, God rest her soul. The marquess assumed his son wanted the property badly or he would have stayed in London to continue his typical rakehell pursuits.

His son had a plan. No doubt it was quite inventive. Colin, for all of his reckless ways, was shrewd. The marquess was interested to see exactly what his son had devised in such a short period of time. Of course, he would not make matters easy on Colin. In truth, matters could take a wrong turn, but he figured he had a decent chance of succeeding.

He chuckled softly, remembering how his own father had given him a blistering lecture many years ago. God knew he'd been as wild as the proverbial March hare in his day, but like his father before him, the marquess intended to force his son to leave behind his raking for good.

Chapter Two

The next morning

Colin had just sat down with a plate of baked eggs, bacon, and a roll when he heard his father shout outside the dining room. "I'd better investigate," he said.

Naturally, everyone at the table followed him into the great hall, where the marquess stood holding the funniest-looking puppy Colin had ever clapped eyes on. It was a wrinkly pug with a black snout.

"Bianca, Bernadette!" the marquess roared.

The twins padded into the great hall with widened eyes. Colin suspected his sisters had perfected their innocent expressions.

The pug wriggled in the marquess's hands. "Be still, animal."

"Oh, Papa," Bianca cried. "You found Hercules."

"In the water closet," the marquess shouted.

Angeline walked up beside Colin. "Oh, dear, your father is overset," she said under her breath.

Hercules licked the marquess's hand.

Colin covered his grin at the affronted expression on his father's face.

"This animal is an abomination," the marquess said.

Colin approached his father and tried to ignore the distinctive odor of urine. "Father, are you all right?"

"Do I look all right? This sorry excuse for a dog ruined my boots." He looked over his shoulder. "Ames!"

The butler strode into the hall.

"Throw this disgusting canine into the dustbin," the marquess demanded.

"Nooooooo," the twins cried out simultaneously.

Margaret gathered the girls in her arms. "Hush, Papa will not throw Hercules in the dustbin."

"Oh, yes, I will!"

Fat tears welled in Bianca's and Bernadette's eyes.

Colin folded his arms over his chest, knowing his gruff father wouldn't be able to withstand their tears. Doubtless the twins knew precisely how to manipulate him.

Ames held out his hands for the dog.

The marquess narrowed his eyes at his daughters. "He stays in the kitchen. I do not want to see him above stairs ever again or he goes. Do I make myself understood?"

Bianca and Bernadette ran to the marquess and hugged him. "Oh, Papa, thank you," Bianca said, sniffing.

Bernadette brushed her finger under her eye. Colin was fairly certain it wasn't a tear, but he must credit his sisters for their theatrical performance.

The marquess patted his daughters awkwardly and addressed Ames. "The water closet floor needs to be cleaned."

"Yes, my lord."

The marquess sat on a chair, removed his boots, and

signaled a footman. "The smell will never come out. Burn them."

"Yes, my lord."

The twins volunteered to take Hercules to the kitchen. Colin suspected they would sneak the pug to their room at the first opportunity.

"Colin, we will meet in my study in thirty minutes," the marquess said.

He inclined his head and thought his father looked rather undignified as he walked up the steps in his stockings.

Precisely thirty minutes later, Colin rapped on his father's study door.

"Come in," the marquess said.

When he entered, his father continued writing. "Be seated," he said.

Colin jiggled his leg, an old habit. *Be calm; be confident.*

The marquess sanded the paper, folded it, and applied a seal. When his father opened a new letter, Colin forced himself to relax his jaw. He understood his father's silent message: patience.

He did not expect this interview to be easy. His father would likely interrogate him, but he was prepared.

The marquess set the letter aside. "You requested this meeting. I will hear you out, but I am disinclined to make a gift of the property simply because you are my son."

Colin lifted his chin. "I understand. However, I am willing to take responsibility for all needed repairs."

The marquess folded his hands on the polished desktop and regarded him with a patronizing expression. "I received an excellent offer. The prospective buyer is willing to make the purchase and see to any needed repairs. It will cost me nothing, but I will certainly gain from the sale. You probably do not have sufficient funds for renovations."

Colin had expected this argument. "I understand that I would have to make a considerable investment."

The marquess huffed. "You mean *I* would have to make the investment."

"Only if you wished to contribute," Colin said.

"Well, how else would you finance this venture? Beyond your quarterly funds, you have no other source of income."

Colin knew that he would shock his father. "I've made investments in shipping."

The marquess snorted. "So you're literally waiting for your ship to come in."

This is business. Keep your emotions out of it. "I've been investing a considerable portion of my quarterly funds since I was twenty-one."

The marquess stared at him in a stupefied fashion. "You jest."

"No. I figured money was the key to my independence."

"You did it in the event I cut off your funds."

Colin smiled a little. "You did threaten once or twice."

"With good reason," the marquess said. "That affair de coeur with Lord Ogden's wife could have ended with you planted six feet under."

He'd been only twenty when Lady Ogden had seduced him, but he didn't want the conversation to veer off into a blind alley. "First things first. I will take care of estimates for the repairs. If I find that it is currently beyond my means, we could draw up an agreement in which I repay you for the cost of any required loan." Surely his father would not object.

The marquess tapped his fingers on the polished surface of his desk. "It may well require the services of an architect and all manner of workers. Why should I contribute funds when I have a perfectly good offer?"

"I understand, but I'm more than willing to make a partial payment now," he said.

The marquess narrowed his eyes. "You failed to answer my question."

"The primary advantage is that it keeps the property in our family." Surely he would not sell when his mother was buried there.

The marquess steepled his fingers. "You intend to occupy the house soon?"

"First I intend to inquire about the best men to provide estimates for the work."

The marquess stood and looked out the window. He was silent for a long moment.

Colin restrained the urge to speak. His father would reveal his concern in his own good time. Interjecting at this point would be foolhardy.

The marquess turned around. "Suppose I approve this plan. Will you personally supervise the renovations?"

Colin frowned. "I certainly intend to make inquiries on the progress."

"I see."

"Whatever it is that concerns you, I'm sure I can provide a solution."

"What happens if there is a problem while you're in

London? Do you expect me to take the reins while you're carousing?"

"Of course not. I plan to journey to Sommerall once a quarter."

"And the remainder of the time? Are you willing to give up chasing lightskirts, gaming, and swigging spirits to oversee renovations that might take years to accomplish?"

He doubted it would take years, but he recognized that his father was testing him. "If a problem arises while I'm in London, I will make the journey home."

The marquess shook his head. "The answer is no."

Colin was taken aback. "I'm willing to make concessions."

"I, however, am not. Your responses to my questions were unsatisfactory. You have no real interest in Sommerall."

"Of course I have an interest in Sommerall or I wouldn't be here," he said.

"Precisely," the marquess said.

Colin winced. "I realize that I've been distant of late, but I will remedy the situation."

"Forgive me, but I have doubts. As I recall, the last time you came home was Easter, and you departed before a sennight. If it were only the one time, I would make an exception, but you've kept your distance from all of us for years. Now you expect me to award Sommerall to you when you haven't earned it. Based upon your notorious behavior, I think it would be foolhardy for me to trust you. You are unwilling to supervise the work, and that tells me you have no intention of leaving behind your wild exploits in London."

"I will make the journey—"

"My answer stands. If you were truly interested in Sommerall, you would personally see to the work, but you've no intention of mending your rakehell ways. I know you've become a two-bottle man, and before you accuse me of spying, I assure you I'd rather not know. Unfortunately, gentlemen are competitive and like to rub it in a man's nose when his heir spends much of his time engaged in disreputable pursuits."

For pity's sake he was thirty-one years old and getting a lecture, but he decided to pacify the marquess. "Father, I know I can—"

"Enough. You're unwilling to commit to this venture. Under the circumstances, you give me no choice but to sell Sommerall."

Colin clenched his teeth, imagining spending months alone in the countryside. But if he didn't agree, he'd lose Sommerall forever.

He walked over to the hearth in an effort to calm himself. The worst possible thing would be to let his frustration show, and he couldn't let Sommerall pass out of his hands.

"Is there anything else?" the marquess said.

Colin took a deep breath and faced his father. "How much is the pending offer?"

"Even if you have sufficient funds to make the purchase, I won't sell it to you. Obviously, the property doesn't mean enough to you to make the necessary sacrifices."

"My mother is buried there," he said, struggling to keep the tone of his voice even. "How can you sell Sommerall?"

"I've already stated my reasons for selling it and won't repeat them. The meeting is adjourned. Close the door on your way out."

Colin was breathing like a racehorse. "You cannot sell it."

"You've no say in the matter," the marquess said. "You've shown insufficient interest in Sommerall and your family. I regret having to say no, but based on your actions, I find it difficult to believe you care about anything except gambling, drinking, and wenching."

He wanted to deny it, but he couldn't. "Tell me what you want, and I'll do whatever you require."

"Very well. You need to prove to me that you have matured and are ready to settle down."

"That's the point of allowing me to—"

The marquess cleared his throat. "You will give up your dissolute pursuits and choose a wife."

A strange sensation gripped him as if the floor had shifted beneath his feet. "A wife?"

"You heard me. A female, preferably a respectable one."

What the devil? Colin frowned. Had he heard correctly? "I think I should focus on renovating Sommerall first. Marriage can come later."

The marquess took a pinch of snuff and sneezed into a handkerchief. "You'll continue along the same rakehell path. One day you will thank me."

Not bloody likely. "Do you mean to drive me away?"

"Do not be tiresome, Colin. It is past time you give up your wild ways."

He took two steps toward the door with every intention of leaving Deerfield, but his father's voice stayed him.

"I know you don't like me ordering you about, but my own father curbed my wild ways. You may not believe me now, but I'm doing you a favor. When a man has a wife and children, he leaves behind his selfishness because his family means more to him than dissipation. In your case, enough is enough."

"I intend to wed in the future," he said.

"You're thirty-one years old, the perfect age for marriage. You will adjust your mind to your new responsibilities."

He turned around. "We're out in the middle of the country, for God's sake. Do you wish me to wed a maid?"

The marquess picked up another letter and broke the seal. "If you require assistance, I imagine your stepmother or the duchess would be happy to help you."

He'd walked right into a trap.

Colin clenched his jaw as he strode out of the house. He was shaking with hot anger and left the house without a hat or greatcoat. He barely felt the cold. When the sun speared through the birch trees, he squinted. Ahead, there were mounds of fallen brown and orange leaves, but he took no pleasure in the autumn scenery.

He strode faster and faster along the leaf-strewn path. His blood must be boiling a thousand degrees or more. How dare his father demand he marry? For God's sake, it was the nineteenth century, not the fucking Middle Ages.

He felt as if he would explode at any moment. In the distance, he saw two laborers hacking at a huge tree limb on the ground. All he knew was that he needed to smash something to control the rage racing through his veins. His breath frosted in the air as he strode faster and faster, his fists locked tight. When Colin reached the laborers, they pulled on their forelocks and looked at the ground.

"Stand back," he said in a growl.

He jerked off his coat, threw it on a lower limb, and untied his cravat. The two laborers' eyes widened as he rolled his sleeves up to his forearms. Colin's nostrils flared as he hefted the ax and brought it down in a giant arc. Splinters flew. He pressed his boot on the limb for leverage, gritted his teeth, and pulled the ax out with a groan. Then he stepped back and swung the ax over his head again. He grimaced as he pulled it out and swung it again...and again...and again with a guttural roar each time. Chunks of bark flew everywhere. One more swing cracked the limb in two.

"Colin!"

The feminine cry startled him. Salty drops of sweat stung his eyes as he spied Angeline running toward him. "Hell," he muttered.

He let the ax drop and wiped his eyes on his shirt-sleeve. He glanced over his shoulder at the two laborers. "Go on," he said gruffly. They pulled on their forelocks again and retreated as if they'd just witnessed a madman. He certainly felt like one.

The cold wind picked up, blowing through the damp linen of his shirt. He gritted his teeth.

Angeline reached him. "You'll make yourself ill in nothing but that thin shirt," she said breathlessly.

"Angeline, leave. I'm not fit for company." He picked up the ax again. "Go," he said.

"No, I will not leave you in this condition. Obviously you are in a state."

"For the last time, please leave," he gritted out.

Her eyes widened. "You're furious."

"If you have any sense, you will leave. Now go." God, why did she of all people have to witness his ire?

"You cannot stay out in the cold in that thin, damp shirt. You will make yourself very ill and worry your family."

His nostrils flared. "Please go before I say something I regret."

"Go ahead, but you'll not stop me." She unrolled his left sleeve and then his right. He looked at her from beneath his damp lashes. Her plump breasts rose and fell with each visible breath. He made himself look away. She might be comely and curvaceous, but she was trouble.

When she lifted her lashes, her eyes grew huge as she looked at the dark hair showing through the V in his shirt.

"What is it?" he asked. He rather hoped the husky sound of his voice would scare her off.

She cleared her throat and appeared to be looking over his shoulder. "You cannot go about with your cravat undone."

He huffed. "That's rich." He'd gone about with far fewer clothes on many occasions, but he thought better of mentioning that in her presence.

She lifted her chin, stepped closer, and closed the three buttons of his shirt. Her scent was familiar—something flowery. That thought reminded him. "Don't. I stink of sweat."

She flipped his shirt points up. "My nose will survive."

He watched as she pulled the two long tails of linen to an even length. Then she hesitated.

He winked and deftly wrapped the cloth round his throat. "Perhaps you could tie a knot?"

She managed on the third try. "It looks awful. I would make a terrible valet."

"A lady valet?" He envisioned a naked woman undressing him. "Brings to mind a number of possibilities."

She drew her large paisley shawl closed. "Mind your tongue."

Naturally he thought of several wicked uses for his tongue, but he pushed that out of his thoughts.

She looked up at him, her green eyes full of questions. "What possessed you to wield that ax?"

"Never mind."

"You looked enraged."

He retrieved his coat from the limb but said nothing.

"What were you angry about?"

"An unpleasant conversation."

"So you walked out without hat, gloves, or greatcoat?"

He had no intention of explaining anything to her. "I'm made of sturdy stuff."

Her gaze slid over him. "Yes, I noticed."

"Like what you see?"

Her eyes narrowed. "I should have known you would say something indelicate."

"I warned you I'm not fit for company." If she had any sense, she would have fled after seeing him hacking that tree limb.

"Really, you must change into dry clothes as soon as possible."

"I'll do." He started to slide his arm through the sleeve of his coat when she stepped forward to help him.

"I can manage." He didn't want her help. He wanted her to leave him in peace.

"I insist. Now lift your arm."

He knew she would persist, so he allowed her to help.

"Your shirt is damp with perspiration, and the coat only traps it."

"Angeline—"

"No, I refuse to listen to your arguments. You'll catch your death out here. You must return to the house immediately."

"It would be ungentlemanly of me to make you stand in the cold," he said. Truthfully, the brisk wind was more than a little uncomfortable, but he'd be damned before he admitted it.

"Your nose is red," she said.

A slow smile tugged at his mouth. "So is yours."

When she took his arm, he matched his pace to her slower one. They strode past the folly, and a gust of wind blasted them. He couldn't completely hide his shiver and regretted leaving behind his outerwear now. Next time he would just throw something into the fire. Of course, he hoped there wouldn't be a next time, but he was rather pessimistic about those chances.

She pushed her bonnet ribbons out of her face. "Something is clearly wrong. What happened?"

"I do not wish to discuss it." *Especially with you.*

"It might help to talk," she said. "Sometimes just airing your grievances helps you see matters more clearly."

Oh, good Lord. The one thing that drove him to drink was a woman who wanted to talk about feelings. But he knew enough about women to realize she wouldn't leave it alone. "My father and I had a difference of opinion." *That is all you need to know.*

"You quarreled," she said.

Her persistence irritated him. "You need not concern yourself."

"Is this about Sommerall?" she asked.

He halted. "How did you know?" he demanded.

She lifted her chin. "If you wish me to answer, you will avoid using a harsh tone."

"I beg your pardon," he said. Damnation. He did not want her poking into his affairs.

"It is quite obvious that you've had a nasty shock."

This was an unfamiliar side of her, but to be fair, she was no stranger to difficulty. "I'll sort it out." But he was far from confident.

"I overheard my father mention that someone was interested in purchasing Sommerall," Angeline said. "It has been unoccupied for many years."

"I beg your pardon, but this is not a matter I wish to discuss." *Leave me alone.*

"Oh, my stars. You do not want the marquess to sell."

"Angeline—"

"That is why you're so angry," she said.

He halted. "Of course I'm furious. My mother is laid to rest there."

"Surely you can persuade your father not to sell. I would think he would cede the property to you."

He shook his head and started walking again. "He will—if I do his bidding." They skirted around the thick, gnarled roots of an old oak. "I want the property, but that is insufficient for my father."

"What did you propose?" she asked.

"To take care of all needed renovations, but we could not agree on the terms."

"I don't understand. What is it that your father wants?"

"Proof that I'll honor my commitment." His father's lack of trust burned deep.

"The only way to prove you will abide by your obligation is to allow you to begin," she said. "I fail to understand why this is a problem."

He glanced at her. "My father proposed a different way for me to demonstrate responsibility."

"What is it? Clearly you find it abhorrent."

He laughed without mirth. "Marriage." He should have kept that between his teeth, but his head ached with the anger still infusing his blood.

She stopped him. "That is ludicrous," she said in an outraged tone. "Forgive me, but your father goes too far."

"I share the sentiment, but it matters not." His breath misted in the cold wind. "My father owns the property and can do what he wants." His father intended to manipulate him like a marionette.

"Marriage does not assure responsibility. We both could name dozens of irresponsible people who are married," she said. "The king, for example."

"My father's demands are unreasonable. Where am I to find a bride in the middle of the countryside?" he said. "It's not as if I can pluck her like an apple off a tree." He didn't want to marry now, and by God, he certainly didn't want to wed under duress, but he didn't want to lose Sommerall.

They walked in silence for a while, and then she said, "There is the little season in London."

"It will look as if I'm desperate." He huffed. "Considering the circumstances, I suppose I am."

"You are hardly desperate," she said. "Dozens of ladies in London would leap at the opportunity to marry an earl."

"I'd no idea you were so romantic."

"Oh, yes, I'm waiting for my shining knight in rusty armor." She regarded him with raised brows. "And you?"

"A local milkmaid."

"I'm tempted to say you'll find a way, but that will not help," she said.

He hesitated, but plunged in anyway. "Why did you break your engagement with Brentmoor?"

She didn't respond immediately.

"I beg your pardon," he said. "Obviously, it is a painful topic, and I intruded."

"It could have been far worse," she said.

He frowned. "How so?"

She met his gaze. "I might have married him."

I might have married him.

Angeline marched into her room, yanked the ribbon loose beneath her chin, and slapped her burgundy velvet bonnet on the bed. She'd owed him no answer at all, but the words had spilled off her tongue. Had she learned nothing?

Upon seeing the maid's wide eyes, Angeline took a deep breath and slowly released it. "Marie, will you help me with the spencer?"

"Yes, my lady."

Angeline lifted her chin while the maid helped her out of the tight sleeves. "Thank you, Marie. That will be all."

After the maid left, Angeline sat on the edge of the bed. Why had she responded to Colin's question earlier? She ought to have upbraided him for his impertinence. Unfortunately, his question had caught her off guard, and she'd blurted out the words. She'd likely piqued his curiosity, but she'd no intention of satisfying it.

Angeline realized she was overreacting, because she was sensitive about the subject. While his question had been impertinent, she had commiserated with him. She understood all too well how it felt to have a parent dictating one's decisions, but she swore that when this house party ended, she would move into the dower house where her grandmother once lived. There would be a dustup, but she could not continue to live like a child in her parents' home. She was thirty-one years old and determined to live independently for the rest of her life. It would not be easy, but she would live comfortably on the trust her grandmother had left for her.

After all that had happened to her, she'd known that marriage was out of the question. She knew how others would view her, but that was nothing new. Angeline intended to make what she could of her life.

A tap sounded, and her mother opened the door. "Angeline, why are you sitting here? I expected you in the drawing room over an hour ago."

"I just returned from a walk."

Her mother's lips thinned. "Gather your sewing basket and join us in the green drawing room."

Like all ladies, she'd learned the art of needlework at a young age. She was in no mood to sit for hours with her embroidery, but she knew it would be rude if she did not put in an appearance. There was no need to rush, however. "I will join you after I finish this chapter in my novel."

The duchess arched her slim brows. "Directly, Angeline."

When the door shut, Angeline inhaled sharply at her mother's command. To be ordered as if she were a young girl set her teeth on edge. It was one more reason to seek her independence. No matter how much she loved her mother, Angeline could not spend a lifetime beneath her thumb.

Perhaps she would have been better off if she had married Brentmoor, even despite his betrayal. She certainly wouldn't have wanted for independence. Doubtless Brentmoor would have ignored her in favor of his married mistress. She pressed her fingers to her temples as if she could push the awful memory out of her brain. Of course, she could not have married him after what had transpired. Truth be told, it would have been horrible. Ironically, they had both left England after the scandal erupted. He'd fled his creditors, and she'd fled the gossips.

There was no point in antagonizing her mother by procrastinating any longer. She retrieved her sewing basket and walked to the landing. When she saw her father, she hurried her step. "Papa, wait."

He frowned. "Is something awry?"

"Oh, no." She smiled despite his harsh expression. "I was hoping we might—"

"Your mother is expecting you in the drawing room," he said, and turned away.

Her hand trembled, and she dropped her basket. She knelt, and her eyes blurred as she retrieved the needles and embroidery thread. He'd taught her to play chess and vingt-et-un. They used to read together and discuss books. They had been close, until the awful day she'd broken her engagement. She'd disappointed him, and now he barely spoke to her. A familiar ache settled in her chest. Her father's rejection hurt one hundred times more than Brentmoor's betrayal.

Angeline dashed her hand beneath her eyes and rose. She took a deep breath, knowing it was critical that she appear unperturbed in the drawing room. The last thing she wanted was to alert her mother, and she most certainly did not want to worry Penny, who knew little about the awful events that had led the duchess to take Angeline to Paris.

She lifted her chin and squared her shoulders. Out of necessity, Angeline had learned to keep her head high, even in the face of condemnation and worse.

When she walked into the drawing room, she greeted everyone and decided to sit with Penny and the twins. The duchess regarded her with lifted brows.

Angeline smiled. "Forgive me for being late. I accidentally dropped my basket."

"You are here, and that is all that matters," the marchioness said.

Angeline brought out her sampler and threaded a needle. Her mother insisted that keeping busy helped to lift one's spirits, but for Angeline, needlework left her with too much time to dwell on the past. She preferred vigorous walks, because she felt free from all the constraints in her life.

"You are quiet, Angeline," Margaret said.

"Forgive me. I was lost in thought."

"What were you thinking about?" Bianca asked.

Angeline smiled a little. "That I have not spent time with a needle recently and need to practice my skills. What are you embroidering, Bianca?"

Bianca held up her sampler.

Angeline blinked. She couldn't make out whether the embroidery represented a tree or an animal. So she settled for an innocuous reply. "Oh, how...unique."

"It is Hercules," Bianca said. "I thought I should *immaritalize* him."

Bernadette elbowed her sister. "Immortalize, you silly goose."

Penny clapped her hand over her mouth, but a giggle escaped her. "Sorry, Mama," she said, lowering her chin.

The marchioness smiled. "Do not fret, Penny. Last week, Bianca embroidered a skull and crossbones."

"It was only a jest, Mama," Bianca said, her eyes twinkling.

"You would do better to embroider a proverb," the marchioness said.

"I don't know any," Bianca said.

"Of course you do," the marchioness said. "A stitch in time saves nine."

"What does that mean?" Bernadette said.

"Do not put off something, for it will only be more difficult later," the marchioness said.

Bianca shrugged. "You could wait and do it all very fast at the last minute."

Angeline's shoulders shook with laughter as she pulled the needle through her sampler. The twins never ceased to amuse her. She realized she felt better already. Matters with her father were difficult now, but she mustn't give up. He only needed more time to forgive her. She had to believe that in time she would reconcile with him.

"Penny, what are you embroidering?" Bernadette said.

"A leaf pattern on a handkerchief."

Angeline looked at her sister's work. "The whitework embroidery is very pretty, but you have always had a gift with a needle."

Penny blushed. "Thank you."

"Everyone has a talent," the marchioness said. "Angeline has an expertise in converting old-fashioned rooms to fashionable rooms."

Angeline smiled. "I fear it is my only real talent. My needlework is only average at best, and I'm surprised Hercules did not howl when I played the pianoforte last night."

"But Colin was much taken with your playing," Margaret said with a sly smile.

Oh, no. Surely Margaret wasn't bent on matchmaking. Angeline focused her attention on her needlework. "I'm fairly certain he felt obliged to turn the pages."

"He rather looked as though he were enjoying it."

"I must say you looked as if you were enjoying his conversation as well, Angeline," the duchess said.

God help her. If Margaret and her mother kept this up, she would have to put a stop to it. Otherwise, she and Colin would find this house party even more of a trial. She wondered if she ought to warn him and decided to do so only if Margaret and her mother became even more obvious.

The marchioness looked at Penny's needlework. "Your stitches are perfect."

"A thing worth doing is worth doing well," the duchess said.

"My girls would do well to remember that proverb," the marchioness said.

"Yes, Mama," the twins said in unison.

"Why do I suspect you will both forget the moment something else catches your fancy?" the marchioness said.

Angeline liked Margaret very much. She had a witty way of managing her high-spirited girls. Even her scolds were gentle but effective.

"Mama, may we take Hercules for his walk now?" Bianca asked.

"I can see very well you are wild to be out of doors." The marchioness turned to the duchess. "Do you mind if Penny joins them?"

"Not at all," the duchess said. "The exercise is good for their health. Do remember your bonnets and wraps, girls."

The twins and Penny retreated. High-pitched giggles echoed outside the drawing room and eventually dissipated.

"Angeline, do you wish to join them?" the marchioness asked.

"I think I shall take my sketchbook and walk," she said. "The scenery is so spectacular this time of year."

After she quit the room, the marchioness sighed. "She is better now, but we shall endeavor to enliven her spirits with walks, drawing, and conversation."

"She is restless," the duchess said. "When she begged me to allow her to make over the principle drawing room at Worthington Abbey, I could not deny her. She was excited, and we all saw her talent, but when it ended, she looked lost. Now she spends much of her time walking the grounds and drawing. I confess I worry."

"She will recover her high spirits," the marchioness said. "Angeline is strong, never forget that."

The duchess set her dish of tea aside. "Hopefully we have weathered the worst."

"I do believe the scandal has already faded," the marchioness said.

The duchess sighed. "It has faded because my daughter has not made an appearance in London society since breaking her engagement."

The marchioness set her own cup aside. "She is beautiful and the daughter of a duke. That and her marriage portion will pave the way."

"I'd always hoped she would make a brilliant match."

"I hope she finds love," the marchioness said.

"In our day, parents arranged the marriages," the duchess said.

"Yes, my father wanted to elevate our family," the marchioness said. "I was frightened half to death."

"You were educated as a lady," the duchess said.

"I learned the nuances from you, my dearest friend."

The duchess smiled. "More important, you found happiness with your husband."

"I am blessed to have married a man I grew to love," the marchioness said. "I wish it for Angeline. She deserves the ultimate happiness."

"I agree, but I would fail my daughter if I did not council practicality," the duchess said. "If she is fortunate, there will be affection, but you know my concerns."

"All will work out. I am sure of it."

"I received a letter from my son today," the duchess said.

"I hope Lady Landale is well."

"My son's wife is nearing her confinement. I shall have a grandchild soon."

The marchioness leaned forward. "Why are you not rejoicing?"

"I dread telling Angeline when the baby is born."

"She will be happy for her brother and sister-in-law," the marchioness said.

"Yes, she will express outward happiness for her brother and his wife, but it is only natural to wish for one's own fulfillment. In her situation, she may find the news a reminder of her recent troubles and her lack of a husband."

"I cannot credit it," the marchioness said. "She is better off without that deceiver."

"I agree, but we want our daughters to find happiness in marriage."

"And our sons," the marchioness said, "though Colin is not my natural son. I wish that our relationship was not so...guarded."

"Nonsense, you did an admirable job, but he was eight years old when you married Chadwick. He spent much of his time at school, and you were ill for a long time after losing an infant. You had to regain your strength. Colin's life was no different than that of any other boy at Eton."

Margaret clasped her friend's hand. "You came to nurse and comfort me."

"You were rewarded with two lovely, spirited girls."

"I am blessed," the marchioness said. "I only wish those same blessings for all of our children." She sighed.

"I do wish Colin and Angeline would form an attachment."

"It has been my dearest wish all these years," the duchess said. "I suppose we were too obvious today."

Margaret laughed. "I fear so."

"It is so frustrating," the duchess said. "It would be a brilliant match."

"I would council leaving the matter to Providence," the marchioness said, "but I suspect Chadwick has taken matters into his own hands."

"What do you mean?" the duchess said.

"I saw Colin storm out of the house earlier, and when I confronted my husband, he said that he had everything under control. I'm sure he made a muddle of things. Chadwick is as stubborn as a mule, but I shall speak to him. If he presses too hard, I fear Colin will leave and never return."

"Surely he would not do such a thing," the duchess said.

"If Chadwick goes too far, I fear a permanent break. I know that Colin has sowed wild oats, but I will never forgive myself if I do not intervene. I feel a responsibility."

"Be that as it may," the duchess said, "there is only so much you can do."

"I have more than a little influence on Chadwick," she said. "He will listen to me."

"You are so amiable, Margaret," the duchess said, "but you do have a backbone."

"No, I have an interest in seeing my family happy."

Chapter Three

Angeline strode with great purpose through the woods. Once away from the confines of the drawing room, her lungs expanded, allowing her to really breathe. It was a ridiculous notion, but she felt liberated nevertheless.

The birch branches stretched out shadowy elongated limbs. With each gust of wind, the branches shed spectacular copper and gold leaves. She shaded her bonnet rim and hurried her step when she saw the folly up ahead. Usually follies were nothing more than ornamental curiosities, but this one formed a Palladian bridge across the stream. After reaching it, she leaned against the rail, opened her sketchbook where she'd placed her pencil, and started drawing. The angle, however, wasn't quite right. She decided to walk through the covered part and try from the other side of the bridge.

Heavy footsteps startled her.

When Colin emerged, she had to suppress a groan.

She'd hoped to avoid him after sticking her nose in his affairs and revealing a bit about her own.

"Am I disturbing you?" he asked.

Of course he was, but she favored him with a brief smile. "You remembered your hat, coat, and gloves this time."

"One chill is enough for today." He closed the distance between them.

His height, easily over six feet, struck her anew. She knew he was fit; she'd seen the evidence when he'd chopped that huge limb with an ax. But how he managed it was beyond her, given the rumors about his rakehell exploits.

"I saw you hurrying along the path with your sketchbook and figured you would come to the bridge," he said.

She wondered what he wanted. "What made you so certain?"

"It is picturesque and therefore worthy of your best efforts."

"How would you know? Perhaps my best efforts aren't worthy at all," she said.

Naturally he laughed.

Her snippy barbs usually drove men away. Granted, men were not begging to court her. She winced, recalling the offensive way dozens of Frenchmen had treated her. She did not even want to know the rumors that must have precipitated their insulting entreaties.

"Do you not wish to capture this grand bridge? It will probably be here long after we are gone," Colin said.

"How utterly macabre." She drew a few lines for the bridge columns and shaded in the arches. His presence, however, interfered with her concentration. "Is there a reason you followed me?"

"Well, yes."

After making a few broad strokes, she glanced at him. "I cannot recollect you ever willingly seeking me out, other than the time you tricked me into standing under the mistletoe."

"You can't blame a fellow for trying to steal a kiss."

She rolled her eyes. "Colin, you want something. Spit it out."

He laughed. "Such language from a lady."

"Do try to recover your sensibilities. I've no smelling salts to revive you."

He grinned. "A gentleman in distress? The possibilities boggle the mind."

"Yours perhaps."

He laughed. "I heard you have a singular talent for renovations."

"I have some experience," she said. "Does this concern Sommerall?"

"Yes. I wish to approach my father again with a plan based on what needs to be done to make the house habitable. If you are amenable, I would welcome your assistance."

"You seem to have forgotten your father's decree that you must marry in order to take possession."

"Of course I haven't forgotten." He regarded her with a quizzical expression. "What about you? I would imagine your parents are urging you to wed."

Apparently, he was unaware of her damaged reputation, but she would not discuss that with him.

"My first task is to persuade him to let me determine what renovations are needed for the house. He's more likely to agree if you're involved."

"Perhaps your father has already looked into the condition of the property."

"To the best of my knowledge he has not returned to the house since my mother died."

The marquess might have finally decided to sell the property in part because there were too many sad memories attached to Sommerall, but that was many years ago. His decision had probably been far more practical. The chances of Colin leaving behind his London lightskirts and taking up residence at Sommerall were negligible. "I doubt offering my assistance will sway your father's decision," she said. "You cannot be unaware that men do not take a woman's opinion seriously."

"I take you seriously or I wouldn't have asked," he said.

"You asked because I'm the only qualified person available."

"Well, that, too," he said, grinning. "Do say you'll agree."

She narrowed her eyes. He was trying to charm her into doing his bidding. "Why should I help you?"

"Margaret said you took great pleasure in overseeing the renovations at Worthington Abbey. I thought you would enjoy lending your expertise."

"Your glib responses tell me you really do not care about returning Sommerall to its former stately beauty."

His smile faded. "If I did not care about the property, I wouldn't be here."

She didn't want to involve herself in his concerns. "Colin, we have never gotten along. We are here only because of our families. To be frank, you are asking a great deal of me, but I have no incentive to help you. Furthermore, I'm not certain it is wise for me to involve myself in this venture. Your father has by no means approved the idea."

"All I want for now is to make an inventory of the work that needs to be done. I think it is a reasonable plan that he will approve."

He was a rake with plenty of experience enticing women to do his bidding. Granted, she did not think he was even remotely attracted to her, but he'd already tried to charm her. She'd fallen for a charming rake once before, and she was wary of Colin. He would likely take advantage of her knowledge and probably abandon the project as soon as he grew bored. When that happened, she would feel the weight of responsibility because she'd gotten involved.

"You are reluctant," he said, "but I would appreciate any advice or assistance you're willing to give. I don't want the property to pass out of my family."

She remained unconvinced. "Were you concerned about Sommerall a fortnight ago?"

"A fortnight ago I'd no idea my father intended to sell."

"Do you plan to reside there?" She knew he wouldn't give up his carousing in London, but if he tried to lie, she meant to call him on it.

"Eventually I will take possession, but at the moment, my pressing concern is to keep my father from selling."

"*Eventually* sounds rather vague."

"I'm a bachelor and intend to live in London until I decide to marry. What difference does it make?"

At least he'd been honest. "Are you set to inherit?"

"It was always understood," he said.

"You assume it will be yours." He was the sort of man who expected that everything would come easily, because no one had ever made him earn what he wanted. Then again, she could say the same about herself before this past year.

"I'm his only son. There is no one else to inherit. What else am I to think?"

"Perhaps you should turn that statement around. Given your reputation, what was your father supposed to think?"

He glared at her. "You imply I'm unworthy?"

"I did not mean—"

"Of course you did or else you would not have dared to question me."

"You requested my assistance. I have every right to know the circumstances before making a decision." If he truly cared about the property, he would have done something about it years ago. No doubt he'd not given a thought to Sommerall until he'd found out his father meant to sell it. Worse, he wasn't likely to occupy the house. It would remain empty, perhaps for years. After all, she'd heard plenty of stories about him.

"If I thought you were sincere, I would offer my assistance," she said. "But I have trouble believing you really mean to renovate Sommerall. You just don't want to lose it on principle."

His eyes narrowed. "You have missed an important point. The circumstances are clear. Unless I can prevent it, strangers will possess the land where my mother is buried."

"Colin, I understand—"

"No, you do not. Apparently, I'm the only one who cares."

Her heart beat rapidly. "Colin, I did not mean to insinuate—"

"I apologize for disturbing you. Rest assured I will not do so again." He made a curt bow and strode past her with fisted hands.

He could storm off for all she cared.

His words rang in her ears. *Unless I can prevent it, strangers will possess the land where my mother is buried.* She shut her eyes and told herself to keep her distance. She could not afford even the slightest transgression, and getting involved in his concerns could lead to trouble.

She mustn't fall for his emotional appeal. God help her, she'd done it once before. It had ruined her life and wounded her family. She clutched her sketchbook to her chest as if it were some sort of shield. Why was she even having second thoughts about helping him?

Apparently, I'm the only one who cares.

The truth dawned on her. He'd been embarrassed to ask for her help. Because they had never gotten along, he'd probably figured she would turn him down.

His mother was buried at Sommerall, and so he'd made himself ask, because he had no other choice. She knew more than a little about having few choices.

He thought no one cared.

She turned and ran after him. "Colin, wait!"

He strode onward, but she pumped her legs faster. By the time she caught up to him, she was so winded she could hardly speak. "I-I'm s-sorry."

His nostrils flared. "I do not want your sympathy."

She knew how it felt to be the object of pity. When she finally caught her breath, she said, "Forgive me for my callous response. I do care for your sake. If you still wish it, I will assist you to the best of my ability."

"Why? You clearly are suspicious of me."

Something hot welled up inside her. She swallowed hard, knowing she'd treated him as if he were the man who had betrayed her. "I beg your pardon. My suspicions were unfounded."

She could feel him looking at her and hoped he would ask no questions, because she still couldn't speak about the events that made her grieve for her former carefree life.

"You are not obliged," he said, his voice rumbling. "No doubt you would prefer to occupy your time with something else."

"Such as tea and embroidery?" she said with a huff.

He clasped his hands behind his back. "I suppose those are things ladies enjoy."

"It's a dead bore if you want to know the truth."

He smiled a little. "Are you certain?"

She met his gaze. "Yes, I'm certain." She would much rather help him than stitch for hours, but that wasn't the main reason. Regardless of what he'd done in the past, he deserved a second chance. God knew she'd give anything for one, but it was impossible.

He flexed his gloved hands twice. "Thank you."

The gruff tone of his voice said far more than his words.

While he did not return to the ancestral pile often, Colin knew his father's habits well. The marquess adhered to the old adage that the early bird got the worm. Colin usually adhered to the mattress and pillow until the sun rose high in the sky. Nevertheless, he had requested Horace, his valet, to awaken him at the ungodly hour of six o'clock. Horace, being no more of a lark than his employer, grumbled as he shuffled into the room and opened the drapes. "God's toenails," Horace muttered as sunlight flooded the room.

Colin groaned. "Go away, Horace."

"My lord, you requested that I awaken you for an early meeting."

"You are mistaken," he mumbled as he flopped onto his stomach and pulled a pillow over his head.

"No, my lord. You were quite clear last night that I should not allow you to go back to sleep."

"I rescind my order," Colin muttered into the pillow.

Horace hovered over him. "My lord, you said it was imperative that you meet your father early before church."

It was Sunday, the Lord's day. Colin had forgotten. This was hardly a surprise, given that he had not set foot inside a church since his last visit home for Easter holiday. He knew if he did not catch his father early, he would have to wait until Monday. Colin did not want to delay. He must prove to his father that he was serious and worthy of the property.

Grumbling under his breath, Colin condescended to allow his valet to shave and dress him for the day. Upon reaching his father's study, Colin tapped the door lightly. "May I have a moment of your time?"

The marquess signed a paper and glanced up from his spectacles. "I am not working."

Colin blinked. "I beg your pardon?"

"It is the Lord's day. Margaret insists that the family rest on Sunday."

"Ah, I see."

"I am officially *not* working."

"Right. You are resting while sitting. It is a marvel your eyes are open."

The marquess narrowed his eyes. Then he signed a paper and set his pen aside. "Is this a special occasion?"

Colin frowned, wondering if this was a trick question. "I beg your pardon?"

"You are up before noon."

"I am dressed for church." So far, lightning hadn't struck.

The marquess broke the seal on another letter. "What is on your mind, besides Sommerall?"

"I wish to inspect the interior of Sommerall House."

"Have you found a bride?"

His father knew damned well he hadn't, so he ignored that question. "I wish to make an inventory of all needed repairs. Angeline has offered her assistance since she has experience with renovations and architectural... stuff." His ignorance was appalling. Thank God Angeline had agreed to help him.

"Well, that is generous on her part," the marquess said, "but I'm not altogether certain what you expect to gain from this expedition."

"I think you know," Colin said.

The marquess folded his hands on the desk. "Enlighten me."

"I wish to demonstrate to you that I'm concerned about the state of the property," he said, "and I am willing to finance the majority of the repairs."

"But you've no idea of the cost," his father said. "What if you do not have sufficient funds?"

"If I find more capital is needed, we can discuss the possibility of a loan."

"*We?*"

"Only in the event it becomes necessary," Colin said. Desperation made him wild to agree to just about anything, except to marry on a whim.

"You waste my time," the marquess said.

"Father, marriage is a sacred vow. It is not a step that a man should take lightly."

"I'm happy to hear you recognize the significance, but you've made no attempts to find a wife."

He gritted his teeth. "I will apply myself to the business of choosing a bride next spring during the London season."

"I'm not inclined to listen to promises you may or may not keep. The answer remains no."

He forced himself to stay calm. "I am more than willing to wait to occupy Sommerall until I wed, but meanwhile, I wish to see what needs to be done. Surely you cannot object."

"As a matter of fact, I can and I will," the marquess said.

"Give me three months to find a bride," Colin said. It galled him to think of having to make such an important decision so quickly—a lifetime one at that—but he couldn't let Sommerall pass out of his hands.

The marquess drummed his fingers on his desk. "Have you requested your stepmother's assistance to find a bride yet?"

"No, but—"

"You have not made any efforts to abide by my conditions for gaining the property. The answer is an unequivocal no."

Colin would not give up easily. "Very well, I will consult Margaret." How she would find him a bride mystified Colin, but he had to make the effort.

The marquess stared at him, his eyes piercing into Colin's. Colin wanted to shift and look away, but he refused to let his father win.

The clock chimed, and the marquess rose. "It is time for breakfast."

"Father, if you will give me a few more minutes, I will explain my long-term plans."

"I've made myself clear and have no intention of rescinding my decision." The marquess rounded his desk. "Shall we repair to the dining room?"

Colin thought about strangers trampling over his mother's grave, and it made him ill. He had nothing to remember her by except a grave, one that ought to be revered. All these years, he'd taken for granted that the property and his mother's resting place would be there when he was ready to face them. He'd thought he had all the time in the world. Now he was in danger of losing what little he had of his mother.

His hands fisted. There were things he needed to know, things that no one had ever spoken about since his mother's death. He would not give up, no matter what, because she deserved more than to be forgotten. She deserved to be remembered.

Colin made a point of walking alongside Angeline to church. His father had suggested they walk since the weather was clear. Colin slowed his pace so that he could speak to Angeline privately. "You will no doubt be delighted to know that my father refused," he said.

Angeline glanced at him. "Why?"

"The same reason," he said.

"Do not give up," she said. "We will think of some way to change his mind."

He wagged his brows. "You don't happen to know any respectable single lady friends who might wish to wed me?"

She'd not heard from any of her friends since her broken engagement, but she would not tell him that. "Do you think I would recommend a friend marry a notorious rake like you?"

"Perhaps I could reform."

She snorted.

Once they reached the church, both families filled the pews in the front, designated for the marquess, his family, and his illustrious friends. Colin would have preferred sitting in the last row of pews where he could close his eyes and nap through the sermon. Alas, he was out of luck and found himself jerking to attention after Angeline thrust her elbow into his side.

He leaned closer to her and whispered, "I will exact revenge."

"You may try." She regarded him with narrowed eyes. "I would not advise it if you wish me to assist you."

Why was his only hope of help coming from the shrew?

After a nudging from the marchioness, the marquess invited Reverend Quimby and his wife to dine at Deerfield that evening. Colin escorted Angeline and sat between her and Mrs. Quimby. That lady continually tittered about her good fortune to be seated next to *such* a handsome gentleman as Lord Ravenshire. Angeline reminded herself not to roll her eyes, but it was difficult when Mrs. Quimby monopolized all of Colin's attention. Meanwhile, Angeline was stuck making polite conversation with Reverend Quimby, who spoke at length and in minute detail about his plans for a spring garden. By the time the trifle arrived, Angeline was fighting the urge to yawn.

At long last, the marchioness led the ladies to the drawing room while the gentlemen enjoyed their port. Angeline smiled when Bianca persuaded Penny to play a duet with her on the pianoforte while Bernadette turned the pages.

Mrs. Quimby approached with clasped hands. "Lady Angeline, we have yet to have a coze. Shall we repair to the window seat?"

"Of course."

After they were seated, Angeline turned to Mrs. Quimby. "I understand you are new to the neighborhood. I assume Mr. Quimby came into the living recently."

"Yes, we have been here only three months," she said. "We were in Hampshire previously. Mr. Quimby's second cousin has a lovely property there. Are you acquainted with Baron Overton?"

Clearly Mrs. Quimby wished to brag about her connections. "No, I am not," Angeline said, tapping the toe of her slipper.

"Harwell is a very fine property, indeed," Mrs. Quimby continued. "In fact, I just had a letter from Lady Overton this week."

Now would be a good time to excuse herself, but when she attempted to speak, Mrs. Quimby interrupted her.

"There is another property near Harwell, though not as grand. Do you know Woodham Hall?"

"No, I do not." The woman's conversation was boring in the extreme.

"A young man has inherited the property. Lady Overton said he is quite handsome or so I have heard. Oh, dear, his name is escaping me. How could I forget?"

"There is no need to fret," Angeline said. "I'm sure it will come to you."

The marchioness hurried to the window seat. "Angeline, will you play for us?"

"Of course." She would do anything to escape Mrs. Quimby's dull conversation, but she must be polite. "Thank you for the coze, Mrs. Quimby."

As Angeline walked away, she looked at Margaret. "Thank you for rescuing me."

"Mrs. Quimby means well, but she has a tendency to prattle," Margaret said.

Angeline thought that an understatement as she sat at the pianoforte. Tonight she was relaxed, and as a result, she made fewer mistakes. She'd never had the discipline to practice and had never concerned herself about it. Ladies were expected to have accomplishments such as playing, singing, sewing, and dancing. She'd never taken any of it seriously. Instead, she'd delighted her father by playing chess with him and discussing philosophy, but those days were over. Each time she thought of it, another little piece of her heart crumbled. She wished there were a way she could redeem herself, but she held little hope of that.

At least in one respect, she'd proved her mother wrong. No amount of strict adherence to proper womanly behavior would ever land her a husband. Her mother would swoon for the first time in her life if she knew Angeline's plans for the future, but a spinster existence was preferable to becoming dependent upon her parents or her brother and his wife. She could well imagine her family's reaction, but it was her life. Eventually, they would reconcile themselves to her decision.

When the gentlemen joined the ladies, Angeline willingly abandoned the pianoforte. She grew a bit alarmed upon seeing Mrs. Quimby hurrying in her direction. Once again, Margaret intervened by inviting Mrs. Quimby to exhibit her musical skills. The reverend's wife exclaimed at some length over the great compliment the marchioness had bestowed upon her by asking her to play. "Of course I will oblige and hope that my meager talent is satisfactory," Mrs. Quimby said, her voice overly loud.

Glad to be free of Mrs. Quimby, Angeline decided to join Colin. He was leaning against the sideboard, looking every inch the bored aristocrat, with snowy white cravat and brandy in hand. His tight trousers were molded to his thighs and other manly attributes no lady should ever notice—or admit to noticing.

Angeline noticed. Heaven above.

She had better direct her eyes elsewhere. "Why are you looking so glum?" she said.

"You will find far more congenial company than me this evening."

He meant to warn her off, but she wanted to know what had transpired when he'd spoken to his father.

Colin poured another brandy and gulped it down.

Angeline wrinkled her nose. "Isn't brandy meant to be savored?"

"So is a victory, but alas, I am defeated."

She stepped closer. "Your father refused?"

"How very perceptive of you." He set the glass aside.

"He still insists you marry."

"Yes. However, I met with Margaret. She agreed to speak to my father, but I am far from encouraged."

"You mustn't give up," she said. "He will capitulate after Margaret tells him to be sensible."

"Perhaps you're correct. I am not, however, holding my breath."

"Did your father disapprove of my involvement?"

"No, he thought it generous of you, but he dismissed my offer to check out the interior of the house. Unless Margaret can persuade him, I'm doomed to lose Sommerall."

"I think Margaret will turn the tide," Angeline said. "For what it is worth, I am anxious as well to get started. I need a real occupation for a change."

He smiled a little. "As opposed to your feigned ones?"

"I have never been content to bask in quiet contemplation while busying myself with a needle. To be honest, I am going mad after only a few days."

"You prefer to walk and be active," he said.

She preferred to use the brain in her head. "It is the one time I am unconstrained by society's expectations of females."

"When have you ever followed rules, Angeline?"

Her face burned. "Excuse me."

He caught her arm. "It was meant as a compliment. You are unconventional, and a rarity among women because of it."

"You cannot be unaware of what that cost me."

He closed the distance between them. "I have every confidence you can rise above it," he said under his breath.

A complimentary sentiment, but it would change nothing.

When he searched her face, she was drawn to his golden brown eyes and felt the pull of his will. She wet her dry lips and only succeeded in drawing his gaze to her mouth. The music and the voices in the drawing room receded. She felt as if he were mesmerizing her. When his thick black lashes lowered to her breasts, she felt as if he'd managed to touch her with his gaze. Her heart hammered in her chest, and she felt breathless.

This was madness. She was caught up in a rake's seductive game in a drawing room where both of their families and the local vicar all sat in plain view. She had to break this spell he'd cast over her. God help her, she could not afford this madness, and yet, when he took her arm, she acquiesced because something inside of her yearned to be closer to him, to let the masculine scents of sandalwood and something unique to him envelope her. In that moment, she had more than an inkling of what she would be giving up if she chose independence. But she knew it would be highly unlikely she would have a choice. She would revel in this stolen moment and allow herself the pleasure of Colin's escort.

He led her to the window seat and lowered his head. "Unless something changes in the next few days, I'll likely depart."

"Why?" she said.

He shook his head. "I can't bear to stay and watch my father sell Sommerall. It's better if I go before matters erupt. I have my faults, Angeline, but I won't make a scene or disrupt the house party. I never should have come in the first place." He blew out his breath. "I knew it would come to this, but I held out hope anyway."

"No," she said under her breath. "You mustn't give up."

"He said no more than once. I won't beg, Angeline. It is an insult to me, and frankly, if he does sell Sommerall, I won't be returning again. I can't bear it."

"But what of your family?"

"I don't know. I just know that I won't let any man, not even my father, dictate my life."

"I beg you to reconsider. You will regret not fighting for what is rightfully yours and for your family."

"Thank you for agreeing to help me. I'll slip out now."

When he strode out of the room, she was tempted to follow and encourage him. But to what end? All she had were empty words, and she knew firsthand there was no comfort in them. She couldn't change yesterday, but she could attempt to influence the marquess through Margaret. Yes, she did want to help him transform Sommerall because it excited her, but she also felt badly for Colin, even though she probably shouldn't. She would *not* care under any other circumstances, but his mother was buried at Sommerall. It clearly wounded him to think of strangers possessing the land where she was laid to rest.

Angeline approached Margaret and took her aside. "I understand the marquess is hesitant to allow Colin to make a survey of the interior of Sommerall House. You know that I have some expertise, and it occurred to me that it would not be in anyone's best interest if it was ignored much longer."

"To be honest, I have worried about it, too," Margaret said. "He can't bear to return there. I know it would be very distressing for him, but you are right. Something needs to be done."

"There is a catch," Angeline said.

Margaret rolled her eyes. "Oh, yes. Chadwick is convinced he can reform Colin by forcing him to marry. I asked him if he thought I could conjure up a bride. He laughed, and then I got angry. What foolishness."

"If there is a structural defect such as with the chimney or the roof, the damage could potentially cost a fortune," Angeline said. "The house has been unoccupied a very long time. I recommend looking into it straightaway, especially since the marquess is considering selling it. We all have seen estates that crumbled due to neglect."

"I'm so glad you came," Margaret said. "You have convinced me. I will talk to Chadwick tonight. It is past time something be done about Sommerall, and really he should not try to force Colin into marriage."

"For now, I suggest keeping the focus on the survey of the house," Angeline said. "Let him consider one issue at a time."

"Yes, that should work. You know men can only think in a straight line," Margaret said. "They are easily confused by related topics. We have to introduce them one at a time and then explain the various relationships." She paused and looked thoughtful. "I've often been tempted to draw pictures for Chadwick."

"Well, it's probably best that we continue to allow the gentlemen to believe they are the stronger of the sexes because of their brawn," Angeline said. "We had better keep our superior intellect a secret."

"Yes, but they are far more malleable than you might realize, but you'll discover that after you're married." Margaret patted her hand. "Thank you, dear. You've been more helpful than you know."

Angeline crossed her fingers in her skirts. "I hope so." She paused a moment and said, "Chadwick is a very lucky man to have you for his wife."

Margaret visibly swallowed. "Thank you, dear. I daresay I do not deserve such a compliment, but I will cherish your words all the same."

Angeline knew a bit about Margaret's background. It could not have been easy for a woman whose father had been a shopkeeper to marry into the world of the ton and to be a stepmother to an eight-year-old child, but Margaret was a special lady.

Chapter Four

*C*olin meant to instruct his valet to pack his trunks after breakfast. There was no point in staying any longer. He would briefly explain his reasons to his father and begin the journey back to London today.

He sipped his tea and heard an odd chewing sound under the table. Then he noted that the sausages on his sisters' plates had somehow disappeared. When he lifted his brows, Bianca and Bernadette regarded him with innocent expressions. No doubt they had been feeding the dog beneath the table.

When breakfast concluded, the marquess cleared his throat. "I have an announcement to make."

Everyone regarded him quizzically, with the exception of the marchioness.

"After much contemplation, I have decided that it is time to make an inventory of the repairs needed for Sommerall House."

Colin stared at his father. All around him voices

buzzed. What had precipitated his father's sudden change of mind? Then he realized that Margaret did not appear the least bit surprised.

She must have intervened on his behalf. Why did that make him feel guilty? She had been kind to do it, and he had never done her a kindness. If anything, he'd kept his distance. He should thank her, but he suspected she neither sought nor wanted gratitude from the likes of him. Her motivation for helping likely had less to do with his wishes and more to do with keeping the peace at the house party.

The marquess held up his hand. "I have not finished. My son wishes to manage the work. After consulting with Wycoff, he and I agreed that Lady Angeline's expertise would prove helpful. To ensure that the proprieties are observed, a maid will accompany them."

Margaret cleared her throat. "We cannot spare Marie or Betty, so I am promoting Agnes to chaperone. She is the newest of three scullery maids and can be spared. She will busy herself dusting and helping to clear away any items that are beyond use or repair."

"Can we help?" Bianca asked.

The marquess frowned at his daughter over his spectacles. "No, you may not. I have another task in mind for you. That task is to walk your ugly dog and make sure he stays below stairs—"

"Papa, please do not say Hercules is ugly," Bernadette said. "You will hurt his feelings."

The marquess snorted. "As I was saying before I was interrupted, that dog is only allowed in the kitchen. Either you abide by my edict or the dog goes in the dustbin."

"Chadwick, do not overset the girls," Margaret said. "They are fond of Hercules."

The marquess shook his head. "I expect—"

A pitiful animal whine sounded beneath the table.

The marquess's eyes bulged as Hercules trotted out and sat next to his chair. The pug lifted his snout and whined again.

"Papa, Hercules is showing you his affection," Bernadette said.

"Who let this ugly dog out of the kitchen?" the marquess demanded.

Hercules promptly ran back under the table.

The marquess leaped to his feet and lifted the tablecloth. Hercules scampered out and the twins gave chase.

"Come back here, you sorry excuse for a dog," the marquess shouted.

Hercules kept running, apparently thinking it was a game.

The marchioness rose. "Chadwick, the girls will catch him...eventually."

Bianca and Bernadette were giggling as they chased the dog.

Hercules ran into the water closet.

"Damn dog," the marquess shouted.

"Chadwick," Margaret said in a shocked tone.

"Pardon me," he said gruffly. Then he stomped over to the water closet door. Hercules sprinted past the marquess. "Ames!" he shouted.

The butler hurried his step. "Ah, I'll get a maid to clean," Ames said, and rang the bell.

"Why has our home turned into a spectacle?" the marquess demanded.

"My dear, it may have escaped your notice, but our home has always been a spectacle of one sort or another," Margaret said.

Colin leaned closer to Angeline. "Notice the dog is smiling."

"And so are you," she said.

After Angeline went upstairs for her cloak and bonnet, the marquess beckoned Colin to join him in his study. "I wish to make it clear that this is only a preliminary measure. With Lady Angeline's help, you will make an inventory of everything that needs to be done."

"I understand, and I am ready to begin," Colin said. He tamped down his excitement, but this was real progress.

"I am not finished," the marquess said. "My original condition still stands. You must find a bride or I will sell the house."

His father had given in on the inspection, and Colin figured he could maneuver around his father's insistence on marriage, too. "It is quite possible the repairs will take many months," Colin said. "I will focus on making the house habitable and then I can begin my search for a wife when the spring season begins." He thought a minute and added, "It would be best if I had a home before acquiring a bride."

The marquess rolled his eyes. "There are two hundred rooms at Deerfield. You could take your pick. You will not divert me. You have six weeks."

For God's sake, not again. He meant to placate his father. "I intend to start a family in a few years." Forty sounded like a ripe, old age to give up his bachelor life.

"I have an offer for the house and have no intention of waiting for you to make up your mind," the marquess said. "If I do not insist on marriage now, you will continue to chase courtesans and actresses. All of the repairs will be for naught, because you will spend all of your time in London and let Sommerall fall to rack and ruin again."

"I need a few months to find a bride," Colin said. "It is a reasonable request. After all, it is a lifetime decision."

"You have precisely six weeks. That is my condition. You will either abide by it or I will sell the property. Now, you will excuse me. I'm off to shoot birds."

Colin gritted his teeth. Somehow he had to circumvent his father's ludicrous marriage requirement.

After Agnes climbed up next to John, the driver, Colin helped Angeline inside the carriage and sat with his back to the horses, facing Angeline. What the devil was he to do about his father's decree? The man was unreasonable. He knocked the roof with the cane he only used in the carriage. A few moments later, the vehicle rolled off.

"Something is wrong," Angeline said, raising her voice to be heard above the horses' hooves. "You were elated earlier."

"I do not wish to shout at you."

"Very well." She stood and swayed as the carriage turned.

He was on his feet in an instant. When the carriage hit a bump, he grabbed her arm and pulled her down on the seat beside him. He inhaled the scent of roses and freshly ironed linen, no doubt from the petticoat. The scents of a woman. Dangerous.

He would hold his breath—or breathe through his mouth.

Her bonnet was askew and her skirt was hiked up, revealing her silk-clad calves. Very long, slender calves. He imagined matching long thighs. No, he would not. This was Angeline—the shrew. He was *not* attracted to her. But she'd agreed to help him, and he needed her advice.

She tried to pull her skirts down, but obviously she was sitting on half of them.

"Don't worry, the skirt isn't going anywhere," he said.

"It will wrinkle," she said, squirming.

"Good Lord. Stand up and I'll hold your waist while you pull down the skirt."

"You will do no such thing."

He grinned. "I promise I won't squeeze."

Her glare could torch a man—in all the right places.

"Up you go," he said, placing his hands on the natural curve of her waist. Lord, she had a narrow waistline. As she pulled at her flimsy skirts, she revealed a deliciously rounded bottom. Naturally he imagined his hands on her derriere, and his groin tightened.

After she finished pulling and wiggling to his delight, he took her hand to steady her as she gingerly eased onto the leather seat. "Thank you."

"My pleasure," he said, grinning.

She narrowed her eyes.

"Is something wrong?" he asked, all innocence.

She sniffed. "I meant to ask you that question. You were happy at breakfast, but something transpired afterward. You were in a state again."

He released a gusty sigh. "My father still insists I marry."

"I think he is testing you," Angeline said. "It is an unreasonable demand. You might as well ignore it."

He met her gaze. "There is a new problem. He gave me six weeks to find a bride."

"That is outrageous," she said.

"Yes, but my father is adamant."

"He did, however, approve of the renovation," she said. "That is a big step."

"Do you not see the problem? I might spend a fortune and lose the property because I have no bride. All of my efforts might be for naught, except to beggar me."

She shook her head. "The marquess knows that it is impossible for you to find a suitable wife out in the middle of the country. I think you should set it aside and focus on the house. Once he realizes you are serious and industrious, he will likely extend the time frame for you to find a bride."

"And if he doesn't? I can't take that risk."

"What else can you do?" she said.

He looked at her. A long moment elapsed. If he married Angeline, all of his troubles would disappear in a snap. But good Lord, Angeline?

She met his gaze, and they both looked away. Had the same thought occurred to her?

After an uncomfortable silence, she said, "I do not envy you."

"Your parents aren't pressing you to marry?" he asked.

"I'm not besieged with suitors," she said. "Frankly, I'm relieved."

He didn't believe her. "Oh, come now. Every woman wants to marry. That is what ladies do."

"I'm not every woman, and I have no intention of marrying."

"That sounds like pride talking," he said.

"No, it is me talking."

"You can't live independently."

"My late grandmother left me a fortune. It is in trust, of course, but I can live comfortably enough at the dower house."

"You can't be serious," he said. "You would prefer to live as a spinster rather than marry?"

"That is my plan," she said, "whether you believe me or not."

"You are joking."

"No, I am not."

"I doubt Wycoff will approve," he said.

"I am thirty-one years old, as you well know. I do not need his approval."

"Every lady I have ever met views marriage as the Holy Grail."

"Not this lady," she said.

"Do you realize what you're missing?" he said.

"Such as intemperate and adulterous rakes, rogues, and roués?"

He looked astounded. "You are serious."

"We need to concentrate on the work that needs to be done. If you worry about the marriage issue, you are likely to feel overwhelmed. Think about accomplishing one thing at a time," she said.

"Did someone give you that advice?"

"I came to that conclusion myself." She turned her attention to the window, letting him know she would not elaborate.

She clearly did not wish to discuss her decision, but he thought it odd. He suspected her decision was born of pride and perhaps fear. No doubt her engagement to Brentmoor had caused her more than a little grief.

He still could not fathom why she'd gotten involved with Brentmoor. The man was well known for high-stakes gaming and multiple liaisons. She could not claim ignorance of his character. Perhaps Brentmoor had convinced her that he'd turned over a new leaf and reformed, but that also brought to mind another question: Why had Wycoff allowed the man to court his daughter? The duke was no fool.

Was it possible she'd carried on a secret romance with Brentmoor? He mentally shook off the thoughts. Whatever had occurred was none of his affair.

Granted, he'd led a rake's existence for years, but he'd only dealt with sophisticated women. He never went near the innocent belles or single ladies; he avoided anything that might result in getting a leg shackle. At any rate, he wasn't one for a grand romance. He'd leave that nonsense to radical poets and besotted swains.

More than anything, Angeline needed real occupation. Last night, she'd tossed and turned in bed. She would be here for only a month. When the house party ended, she would return to Worthington Abbey and make the announcement to her family. There was no doubt in her mind that her mother and father would disapprove, but there was nothing they could do to stop her.

It would be far better to move into the dower house as soon as possible, but thoughts of Penny worried her. Her sensitive sister would be overset, but Angeline would make sure that Penny knew she could visit at any time. There would be much to accomplish. She would have to hire a cook and a few servants. Perhaps she would even buy a gig and learn to drive it. It wasn't the life she had always envisioned, but she would make the best of the situation.

She could well imagine her mother imploring her to make one more attempt during the spring season, but Angeline had no intention of exposing herself to society again. She knew exactly what would be in store for her, and she refused to play into the hands of the gossips.

She worried about her father's reaction the most, but eventually even he would come to terms with her decision. Unfortunately, ever since the debacle with Brentmoor, he had all but avoided her.

It would be better for all of her family if she lived quietly and independently in the country. Her mother and father would take Penny to London in the spring, and while it hurt to know that she would never be able to see her sister at her come-out ball, Angeline knew it was for the best. She'd learned she was strong enough to withstand many things, but she could not bear the thought of her poor reputation hurting her sister.

Sommerall, one hour later

Colin carried the heavy hamper. "Cook must have packed enough food for an army. Honestly, I don't know what she was thinking."

"The fresh bread smells wonderful," she said, "and I smell biscuits." She reached inside. "They're still warm," she said, popping one in her mouth.

"You're like a greedy child sneaking a biscuit," he said.

"We both used to steal biscuits when we were children," she said.

He huffed. "I don't remember anything of the kind."

"You ought to remember. We were nine years old, and I stole two biscuits, but you got caught with your hand in the jar. As I recall, you got your hand rapped for it."

He glanced at her from the corner of his eye. "Now I remember. You escaped all punishment. I was a gentleman even as a child and took your rap on my hand."

"Hah," she said.

While John took the horses to the barn, they walked up the steps. When Colin turned the key, Angeline had the oddest sensation that she'd done this once before with him. The feeling was so strong she felt as if it had truly happened.

He ushered her inside, and there was a familiarity just at the edges of her thoughts, although she couldn't point to anything specific. They would have been young children at the time the marquess had closed up the house. Most likely she was imagining something that had never happened, and even if it had, there was no significance attached to it.

Colin removed his gloves and ran his finger along the marble hall table. "Dust," he said with a frown.

"After so many years, the dust should be much worse," Angeline said. "Obviously, someone has cleaned it before, though not regularly."

Agnes set her basket on the floor and applied a feather duster to the table and the gold-framed mirror above.

"We can set our gloves here and hang our wraps on the pegs," Angeline said, removing both. "Thank you for persuading me to accompany you. Painting screens, embroidering, and playing the pianoforte seem so frivolous. Helping you restore Sommerall will give me a sense of real achievement. I feel invigorated already."

"I never realized that ladies might grow bored with their lives."

"I doubt I count as the average lady," she said. Then again, she doubted the lightskirts he consorted with spent their days embroidering proverbs in genteel drawing rooms.

"Angeline, I won't pry, but you mustn't let the actions of a dishonorable man dictate the rest of your life."

She gave him a wan smile. "It is kind of you, but there is no reason to worry." Of course, she would never admit how many times she had gone over the events in her mind. She'd pinned the exact moment when Brentmoor joined her group at Vauxhall, uninvited. The lanterns had added a little ambiance as they'd walked along. When he'd dared her to set foot on the dark walk, she'd refused and dismissed him from her thoughts. That had not deterred his single-minded courtship, but it marked their first encounter, one she wished she could expunge permanently from her brain.

As time went on, Brentmoor had uttered all the right words and persuaded her that he was a changed man because of her, and yet, somewhere deep inside there had always been a seed of doubt. She'd ignored it to her detriment.

"You seem pensive," Colin said.

She didn't want to waste the day thinking about Brentmoor. "I've had more time to ruminate than I ever wished. Today I'm going to make myself useful. Hopefully we will encounter a great deal of potential and very few problems." Belatedly, she realized she'd revealed too much and made herself seem pathetic. So she added, "Mind, I rarely waste time ruminating." *Liar*.

"I'm grateful for your assistance," he said. "It's been years since I've been inside. It feels strange," he said.

Twenty-five years had elapsed. She hadn't considered that he might feel apprehensive about entering the house, but it would be perfectly natural. He'd been only six years old when his mother had died, and his father had never returned here.

"Whatever we find, promise you won't be disappointed," Angeline said.

"To be honest, I expect the house will need numerous repairs. Whatever is wrong can be righted." He paused and added, "Hopefully."

Colin opened a door and led her inside the anteroom. There was a dusty marble fireplace and a large bookcase—floor to ceiling. After he set the hamper on the floor, he pulled back the covers over a large round mahogany table.

"It is in excellent condition," she said.

"The carpet beneath is faded," he said.

"That should have been rolled up and stored."

"I believe my father left in some haste after my mother's funeral."

She felt a pinch in her chest at his words. Despite the many years that had elapsed, he must feel the void. Even in her exile to Paris, she'd read the news in English scandal sheets where his barely concealed identity and exploits were so easily discerned and served up a few weeks old like warmed-over gossip.

Angeline motioned Agnes and set her to dusting the anteroom. "There's a sturdy ladder by the shelves. When you're done, find me."

"Yes, my lady."

She turned to Colin. "We'll need at least two footmen to lift the table and someone to move the carpet."

With a sigh, Colin pulled out his notebook and pencil. "I'll request the help of footmen or tenants."

"I could make the notations while you inspect," she said.

"Very well." He gave her the notebook and pencil. Then he looked about. "There are marks on the walls where paintings must have hung."

"Do you recall the paintings at all?" she said.

He shook his head. "It was long ago, and I was too young to pay attention. I imagine they're in the attic." He walked over to the fireplace. "There are no coals in the bin. Lord only knows what might be in that chimney." He opened a tinderbox. "It's empty. I'll have to bring one the next time and see about having coals delivered. That way I can test the chimneys for any issues."

She finished scribbling her notes and turned to the maid. Angeline noted the marks on the black-and-white checkerboard marble floor. It needed scrubbing. The carpets and the runners on the stairs were probably dusty and possibly faded as well, but for now, she would focus on the ground floor.

Colin looked up at the chandelier. "Cobwebs."

Angeline shuddered.

"What is it?" he asked.

"I hate spiders."

Devilment showed in his eyes as he walked his fingers along her arm.

She swatted his hand. "Stop that."

His deep chuckle called to a wicked place inside of her.

"Speaking of cobwebs, you'll need someone to clean the chandelier," she said, adding that to her list.

"This way," he said, indicating another room on the ground floor.

"Behold, the breakfast parlor," he said as they entered.

She removed the covers, and he set the hamper on the bare table.

He pulled a chair back. "The cushions are faded."

"I noticed the drapes are as well," she said. "Before refurbishing anything, we should check to see if there are external blinds. If not, you'll need to have them installed to protect furnishings and carpets from the sun."

"Won't that make it awfully dim?" he said.

"You'll want it primarily for summer, and the blinds can be withdrawn up a pelmet when not in use."

"There are shutters," he said, "but they need to be repaired." He sighed. "We've barely started, but it's clear the work is going to be far more involved than I'd expected."

"We don't know the condition of the drawing room," she said. "It's possible the furnishings and carpets there are in better shape."

"You're right," he said. "Once we've had a chance to inspect everything, we can decide which projects have the highest priority."

He'd used the word *we* three times.

"Sorry," he said. "I assumed you wished to continue to be involved, but you shouldn't feel obligated."

"I look forward to the challenge." She already felt purposeful, and as a result her spirits had risen.

"It's obvious the place has been neglected," he said. "I still can't figure out what prompted my father's sudden urge to sell."

"Someone expressed interest," she said.

"Yes, but I'd wager it wasn't the first time," Colin said. "I think my father is bent on marching me to the altar."

"The offer must have been attractive. The house hasn't been kept in good order and has stood empty for all these years. Has he ever returned here?"

"Not to my knowledge."

"He obviously cannot bear to return, and he has no surety that you will occupy it anytime soon."

"I always assumed it would be mine," he said.

"I know it is difficult," she said, "but he relented today. It is far from hopeless."

He shrugged. "It is the first time my father has ever let go of control."

"Forgive me for prying, but have you ever asked if you might be of assistance?"

"I gave up years ago," he said. "He used to take me with him when he visited the tenants, but he's the sort of man who feels only he can do something. One of the reasons I've stayed away from Deerfield is because I've felt useless. My father will speak of what has to be done, but he won't allow me to take over any of the responsibilities. It's provoking."

"He allowed it today," she said. "That's a start in the right direction."

"Yes, but now I find myself suspicious that he has yet another plan he intends to spring on me."

She frowned. "When did you become so pessimistic?"

"If I expect the worst, I'm never disappointed."

"But then you are never pleased, either," she said.

"Point taken."

Belatedly, she realized she was a hypocrite, but her

tempt me, then I won't miss it. Now, if you are about to tempt me, which will never work, I suggest we have a look at the principle drawing room—or is there more than one?"

He finished off the brandy. "I've no idea."

"Perhaps you will recall more about the house as we explore," she said.

inside.

d desk, a standing globe, and to discover a bay window. He watched as she excellent light in here. I should think you working here." his hips. "Yes, the light shows all covered side tables." asked.

I thought

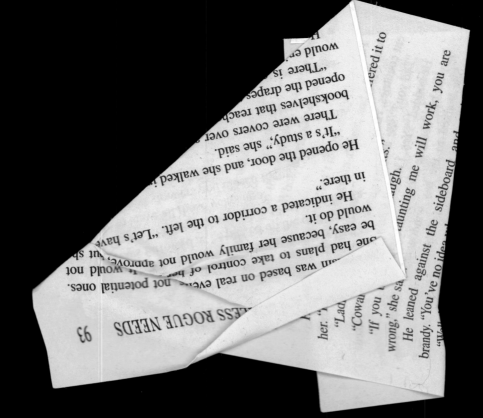

He scoffed. "Or find buried treasures."

"You are entirely too cynical," she said, marching out of the study. "It will spoil your appetite."

He watched her round little bottom and said, "My appetite is definitely whetted."

As they walked into the breakfast parlor, the aroma of fresh bread filled the air. Colin's stomach growled, making them both laugh. "We might as well eat now," she said. Then she opened the hamper and unwrapped the cloth keeping the bread warm.

Agnes appeared and bobbed a curtsy. "My lady, I await your instructions."

"You must be hungry."

"If it pleases your ladyship, I'll duck out to the barn and eat with John."

After she left, Angeline frowned. "It is a long walk to the barn."

"The alternative is to join us, and you know she would be uncomfortable. John will welcome her company."

"You're right, of course."

He opened up the hamper and retrieved a container of lemonade and two glasses. They sat next to each other where there was a patch of warm sun that made her want to curl up like a cat. They dined on cold chicken, ham, cheese, bread, and biscuits for dessert.

"Would you care for more chicken?" he asked.

She placed her hand over her stomach. "I'm full and fear I'll be lethargic all afternoon if I eat any more. May I serve the rest to you?"

"Lord, no. I'm stuffed."

She started packing the food, and he set the plates inside the basket. When she handed him the leftover bread wrapped in a cloth, their hands brushed. The accidental touch stirred something inside of her. She caught him looking at her with slightly parted lips. Then he took a deep breath and looked away.

Angeline told herself she was imagining the heightened awareness between them. At any rate, she could not afford to make a misstep. He was a family friend, and she was here only to assist him. Nothing else could or would ever transpire between them.

Unbidden, she recalled his strength as he'd swung that ax two days ago and the dark hair on his chest and forearms. He was the sort of man who made women forget to breathe, but she reminded herself that he was a rake, a man who pursued pleasure first and foremost. There were probably dozens of women he'd left in his wake. She'd made one bad mistake; she had no intention of making another.

When she closed the hamper, there was an awkward silence.

He cleared his throat. "Shall we investigate the drawing room now?"

"Yes, I'm curious to see what we'll find."

When he offered his arm, she took it and immediately discerned warmth from his body and the scent of him. She glanced at his profile. Although she was tall, he still towered over her. The cleft chin, straight nose, and strong jawline were familiar and yet somehow more pronounced. One dark curl fell just above his brow. She remembered that he'd despised his wavy hair, but his untamable curls were definitely part of his appeal.

After they reached the landing, he led her inside a

drawing room. She surveyed the overall space and thought it had potential. "The carpet escaped fading here," she said.

He opened shutters. "You can see the reason."

"It is unfortunate they weren't used in the other rooms."

He leaned his head back. "The ceiling appears to be in good shape."

She looked up as well. "Is that a portrayal of Hercules?"

"I'm unsure."

"Your sisters will be delighted if you tell them it is."

"Well, let's not tell them yet," he said. "Otherwise they'll hound me, if you'll forgive the pun, to let them see it."

He went to investigate the fireplace and squatted.

If she was a proper lady, she would not dare admire his bottom, but what he didn't know wouldn't hurt him.

"The hearth has a hob grate. You can heat a kettle," he said.

"You would ring for a maid."

He rose. "I didn't care about the basket grate in the anteroom, but I like to make tea on the hob."

She stared at him. "You do it?"

"I only have one manservant in my rooms at the Albany," he said. "On his half day, I have to do for myself."

"You're joking," she said.

He turned to her. "No, but tea is the limit of my domestic talents."

"Your resourcefulness will see you through the transformation of your house."

"It isn't mine, and may never be."

He'd sounded a bit testy. She ought to be more careful with her words.

"My guess was right," she said. "The furnishings are Georgian."

"How can you tell?" he asked.

"The oval cushions and the red damask fabric covering the chair and settee are distinctive of the period." She walked to the wall. "Mark the wainscoting. In the previous century, it was used to protect the walls from the chairs. These days no one uses such an arrangement."

"The furniture is entirely too feminine. I need something sturdier."

"Your future bride might like it."

He fisted his hands on his hips. "Why do I suspect you are purposely trying to needle me?"

She bit back a smile. "Since you have no immediate plans to occupy the house, I recommend you keep the present furnishings. You may find there are more pressing issues that need immediate attention."

"Let us go up to the bedchambers," he said.

He led her up the next flight of stairs. She couldn't help noting the lack of family portraits on the walls, though she could discern where they had once hung. She told herself they were only rooms, and she was here to assist him with the inspection. Yet she thought of how her father would react if he learned she'd gone into a bedchamber with Colin. Oh, for pity's sake, her father would never know, and Colin certainly wouldn't mention it when they returned to Deerfield.

She never used to be so skittish, but she'd disappointed her family. Her guilt was like the fog. It inevitably rolled in.

The first bedchamber was a well-appointed room with

tall mahogany bedposts and rose-colored bed hangings that matched the drapes. A chaise longue with rose-colored cushions was angled in the corner.

"Was this your mother's room?" she asked.

"I imagine so," he said. There was determination in his expression as he opened the drawer of a night table.

She didn't think much of it at first and walked to the window where she drew the draperies open. "I think you could have a wonderful flower garden in the spring."

Footsteps alerted her. Colin was opening and closing drawers in the dressing table.

"Are you looking for something?" she asked.

"Yes."

He strode to the wardrobe and opened the doors.

She thought it was odd that he'd not told her what he was seeking.

He released an exasperated sigh and checked the other night table.

"Perhaps I can help," she said.

"Everything is empty." He walked through the connecting door.

Angeline followed him, concerned about his strange mood.

"This must have been your father's room." The bedposts were enormous and the bed hangings were a dark crimson. In the corner was a mirrored mahogany shaving stand.

He began searching through the wardrobe and the chest of drawers.

"Colin?"

He said nothing at first. When he spoke, his voice was rough. "It's as if she never existed."

Her heart felt as if it had fallen to her feet. "If you tell me what you're looking for, I will help you find it."

"I don't know if you can."

"Perhaps if you describe it to me, I will have success."

"It's a miniature...of my mother."

Oh, dear God. She took a shaky breath, needing to compose herself for his sake. "When did you last see it?" she asked.

"It was on her dressing table, but I might be mistaken. It was long ago." He sighed. "I have nothing to remember her by."

She swallowed hard. "It's bound to be somewhere in the house. Was there anything special about the miniature?"

He frowned. "I'm imagining smooth stones for some reason."

"You were very young," she said.

He walked to the window and planted his hands against the wavy glass.

"Colin, what troubles you?"

He turned toward her. "I can't remember her features."

She bit her lip, because her tears wouldn't help him.

He blew out his breath. "It's been too long."

She inhaled slowly. "I imagine servants moved everything to the attic."

"Probably." He paced the room. "I should have stayed in London and let it be."

"No," she said. "Sommerall is important to you."

"I could have investigated the property years ago. I just assumed I would inherit. God only knows what has rotted or fallen apart."

"Colin, your father is still the owner, and as such, it was his responsibility."

"You miss the point. I ignored Sommerall until my father expressed his intention to sell."

"You mustn't criticize yourself," she said. "You could not have predicted that your father would decide to sell."

He huffed. "If my father hadn't sent that letter informing me that he meant to sell, I would have made excuses to avoid the house party. Make no mistake, Angeline. I'm a selfish man. I've done bad things, but I won't sully your ears. Believe me, I have earned my rakehell reputation."

Angeline recognized self-loathing, because she'd experienced it. How many times had she silently rebuked herself for falling for a man she'd known was trouble? Instead, she'd believed his claims that he was a new man because of her. "None of us can change the past, but we do not have to be slaves to it, either."

He huffed. "Here is something you ought to know. Rakes are irredeemable."

"I have no intention of trying to reform you. I have made mistakes, and so have you. That doesn't mean that you don't deserve to find your mother's miniature, and that doesn't mean that you don't deserve Sommerall."

"If you had any sense, you would demand I return you to Deerfield immediately."

"I'm not afraid of you, Colin."

"You should be," he said.

"Yes, you are a big, bad rake."

He narrowed his eyes. "Why do you want to help me? Do you imagine it is akin to taking hampers to the poor?"

He was proud and probably regretted admitting his mistakes. "There is an old saying: Do not look a gift horse in the mouth."

"You are bored with needlework and are only interested in renovating this house."

"I thought I had made that clear. I have no interest in renovating you."

A laugh escaped him. "That's just as well. You are likely to find nothing salvageable in me."

She had not told him the real reason. She'd tried to imagine how it would feel to lose her family and move away from her childhood home at such a young age. That year in Paris without Penny and Papa had been so hard, and she'd been an adult. At least she'd known she would see them when she returned home.

How would it feel to never see her mother again? How would it feel to never hear her voice ever again? How would it feel to have nothing concrete with which to remember someone you loved? She could not even contemplate the pain for a young child.

He'd been only six years old when he'd lost his mother. Now all he wanted was to find her miniature and preserve her resting place.

"Are you certain you want to do this? You might regret it," he said with a mocking smile.

You might regret it. Her neck prickled. The night she'd first agreed to dance with Brentmoor, he had uttered those very words and smiled as if he were sharing a good joke with her. He'd warned her, and she'd not taken him seriously.

Angeline met Colin's gaze and knew a moment of doubt. She couldn't make another mistake. Once was bad enough. But this time was different. Colin didn't want *her*; he only wanted her help with the house.

"There will be nothing to regret," she said. "If you

truly want to see the house restored to its former beauty, I will do all in my power to advise and help you. If you do not, tell me now."

"Well, then, it seems we have struck a bargain."

"We will find the miniature," she said. "I daresay it is in the attic."

"It will be like searching for the proverbial needle in a haystack," he said. "I can't afford to spend time looking for it when there is so much else to be done. I have to think about the most urgent business."

"I will help you," she said. "We will work long hours and take time every day to sort through the attic."

He shook his head. "I cannot ask it of you."

"We will find it," she said. "We will go through every trunk, every drawer, every nook and cranny."

"I have nothing to give you in return for all of your assistance."

"But you already have," she said. "I need occupation." She didn't tell him that the main reason was to keep the bad memories at bay.

He met her gaze. "I feel as if I'm taking advantage of you. It's not as if we're the best of friends."

"But we are not enemies," she said.

"Years ago, you most certainly considered me an enemy."

"Years ago, I was haughty and headstrong. I thought I was invincible."

"No one is invincible," he said, "but you are strong. You always have been."

She'd lost much of her confidence, but Colin's words helped her to see that she was still the woman she'd been before the scandal. There was much she could not change, but she could change the way she felt about herself.

Chapter Five

Angeline found a well with water and lye soap in the kitchen. She set Agnes to cleaning the marble floors. The maid advised against using sand, as it would scratch the marble.

"I hope you are able to clean the marks," Angeline said.

"I'll put my elbow into it, my lady."

Afterward, Angeline returned upstairs and saw Colin. "What are you doing?"

"I'm off to the attic to search for buried treasure," he said.

"Well, I hope you do not meet up with any pirates."

He arched his brows. "Ahoy, my pretty one. Would you like to walk the plank with me?"

She shook her finger. "No shirking your duties. Back to digging for you."

He made a ridiculous courtly bow and strode away.

Angeline inspected the other bedchambers. Most were

similar and varied only in the colors of the bed hangings. Fortunately, the carpets in the bedchambers were in good condition as the heavy draperies kept out the sun. They were dusty, however, and Angeline made a note to instruct Agnes to beat the rugs and the stairwell runner when she finished cleaning the marble floors.

The few paintings in the bedchambers were predominately pastoral scenes. Thus far, she'd seen no family portraits. There were no personal items in any of the rooms. Servants must have moved all of it into the attic.

At a minimum, the bedchambers needed new paint or wall hangings. The draperies kept out the sun, but they were dusty as well. She already knew the drawing room needed new shutters, carpet, and draperies. Fortunately, she'd found no evidence of water damage to the ceilings or near the windows. However, they had very little time to resolve any problems they were likely to uncover. The best she could do in such a short time was to advise him.

Angeline went downstairs to check on Agnes's progress. The maid was on her hands and knees scrubbing.

"Are you able to remove the marks, Agnes?"

"Yes, my lady. It just takes a bit of time."

"Alert me when the floors are dry."

Angeline returned to the drawing room and tried to imagine how the room would appear with paper hangings and new furnishings. The red walls seemed too dark for this small drawing room. Angeline envisioned a gold interior with bright yellow cushions for the furnishings. Gold festooned draperies across the south wall would give the room a dramatic appearance.

Angeline sat on a chair and took out the notebook and

pencil. She quickly sketched her ideas in the notebook. Later, she would show it to Colin. Of course, he did not own the property, but at least she could give him an idea of how the drawing room could be transformed. The current carpets must go, but the new ones would have to be purchased in London. All, however, was contingent upon Colin inheriting Sommerall, and that matter was far from resolved.

She ascended the next flight of stairs and opened the middle door. A rocking chair sat in front of the window. This must have been a nursery. In the corner, something was covered by a sheet. When she lifted it, she drew in a sharp, visceral breath.

It was a cradle.

His mother had died while giving birth to a stillborn infant.

Her heart hammered. No wonder the marquess had departed Sommerall in a hurry. The tragic reminders would have been too hard to bear.

Angeline backed away and quit the room immediately. She eased the door shut, but her heart was thumping hard as she pressed her back and hands against the door.

She didn't want Colin to see the cradle.

Agnes walked down the corridor. "My lady, do you want me to clean these rooms?"

"Not today, Agnes. Dust the drawing room, please. The sideboard and furnishings need attention."

After she left, Angeline released her breath. Colin would discover the nursery soon enough, but she didn't want him to see the grim reminder on this first visit. She couldn't imagine the heartache he'd experienced as a child. It struck her that it must have been terrifying for him.

She mustn't let him see her guarding the door. With a deep sigh, she went to the last bedchamber and hoped she would find the miniature.

Ten minutes later, she closed the last bedchamber door and walked down the long corridor. She'd not expected to find the miniature in one of the bedchambers, but she'd not counted on her own disappointment. If he had the miniature in his possession, he would find a measure of peace, because he would be able to see his mother's features.

Was it possible to heal a wound that had left scars after so many years? She needed to believe it was possible—or perhaps more important, he needed to believe it.

"Angeline, wait."

She halted and turned toward him. He'd shed his coat and carried it over his shoulder. His cravat was wrinkled and his shirtsleeves were rolled up, and somehow he managed to appear more devilishly handsome than any man ought.

"Did you make any progress?" she asked.

"I went through the contents of one trunk. Nothing is organized. It appears the servants stuffed whatever they found into the trunks as quickly as possible."

The servants must have found the task distressing. "What did you find?"

"Books with crumbling and missing pages, old letters, quills, handkerchiefs, vases, and skeins of yarn all tumbled together."

Evidently, the servants had been left to their own devices.

"It will be a tremendous chore to sort through," he said.

If the frame for his mother's miniature was made of gold or silver, there was a possibility of theft. She would not broach the distasteful subject to him. If it did not turn up, he would be better off believing it was simply lost.

"We should take time each day to go through the contents," she said. "Whatever you do not wish to keep, we will give away to the servants and tenants."

He put his hands on his hips. "This is a monumental undertaking. How am I to make any headway with the time constraints?"

"Divide and conquer?" she said.

"It's an overwhelming task," he said.

"We will accomplish as much as we are able. I'm confident you will manage it all very well, even after I've departed."

"If this is an attempt to cheer me up, it isn't working."

His cynical façade was no mask. He expected the worst, because he'd experienced a terrible loss at a young age.

"When did you become so optimistic?" he said.

"Since arriving here."

He arched his brows.

She'd meant it, but he looked taken aback. "It was a joke," she said. Truthfully, she'd become a cynic her first year out in society. She'd learned the art of studied ennui, but she'd grown truly bored with the fashion for self-proclaimed misanthropists. All during those years, she'd depended on her sarcastic wit and her father's title as a shield. But in the end, none of it had helped. Now she no longer felt like that woman who found everything and everyone boring. It had been nothing but an invisible mask. But her pretense had failed to protect her from wounds.

She did not want to remember any of it now, because it reminded her too much of her mistakes, and dwelling on the past would change nothing.

He regarded her with an unnerving expression that made her uncomfortable. She opened the notebook. "What is next on the agenda?" she said with her pencil poised.

"I need to have coal and a tinderbox delivered tomorrow so that I can check the chimneys."

Thank goodness, she'd diverted him. "Perhaps the cook at Deerfield can spare a bit of time to look over the kitchen. I'll speak to Margaret about it."

"Thank you," he said. "Once I determine for certain that the basic structure of the house is sound, I'll see about painting."

"You may wish to consult the architect who drew the plans and hired the workers when we made over the principle rooms at Worthington Abbey. Mr. Rotherby is highly praised for his designs and innovation."

"I suspect his services are beyond my financial means," Colin said.

"There's no harm in listening to his suggestions and getting an estimate for the work. You will not be obliged."

He ran his hand through his hair. "I fear this will be a waste of time."

Her mouth twitched.

He frowned. "What do you find so amusing?"

"Come with me," she said, opening the door to the bedchamber that she assumed had belonged to his father years ago.

"Angeline, what are you about?"

"There is no need to worry. I've no intention of seducing you."

He sighed theatrically. "What a pity."

"You will have to look elsewhere for sympathy." She took him over to the shaving stand. "Have a look in the glass."

"My hair is even more of a disheveled, curly mess than usual." He met her gaze in the mirror. "When I was a lad, I used to spit in my hands and try to wet down the curls."

She laughed. "Eww."

"I'm tempted now."

"For whose benefit? I do not care if your hair is standing on end." *Liar.*

He turned and clutched his hands to his heart. "Woe is me."

She would never tell him that his unruly curls only added to his masculine appeal.

A slow smile tugged at his mouth. It was a knee-weakening, toe-curling rake's smile meant to disarm a lady. She was, of course, impervious to him. Well, maybe not completely.

"You're a bit disheveled, too," he said.

"What?" She walked over to the shaving mirror.

"Got you," he said, laughing.

She spun around. "You're as horrid as a little boy."

"I may be horrid, but I'm no boy."

"You're in luck. I find you mildly tolerable today."

"Lucky me," he said, beginning to close the distance between them.

She tried to ignore the husky note in his voice, but the deep sound hummed inside her. Tension hung in the air, and unbidden, she recalled the way his muscles had strained while he'd wielded that ax. She dared not let him know how he'd affected her.

"I have a confession to make," he said.

Now she couldn't breathe, because he was too close and the scent of him swirled all around her.

"I find you charming today."

She took a step back and lifted her chin. "It will wear off quickly."

He took another step. There was a languorous expression in his eyes. She might have noticed the amber hues in them, but only because she was perceptive by nature. Drat it all. Why couldn't he have a long nose, pointed chin, and no muscles at all? And why after all these years did she find him irresistible?

He advanced again. Now his boots were inches away from the toes of her slippers.

She took two more steps back and bumped against the mattress.

He closed his big hand around the bedpost and his gaze flickered briefly to her décolletage. Her breasts felt heavier, and her nipples tightened. The sound of his breath was faster and a little rough. She was drawn to his full lower lip. Something inside of her gave way to desire. She wanted to be closer to him.

As if he could read her thoughts, he closed the scant distance between them. He angled his head and looked into her eyes. "Is this surrender?"

The sensual haze cleared, and she glared at him. Outrageous man. How dare he look at her bosom? Angeline straightened her spine. "Do you think I am intimidated by you?"

"Not at all." He wagged his brows. "Those two steps back were merely dance steps. Am I correct?"

She closed the distance between them in an effort to assert herself, but she realized the disadvantage immediately. While she was tall for a lady, he was easily half a head taller and much too close. He filled her senses and belatedly she realized she'd invited a rake into a bedchamber. Had she lost her wits?

"You are a shameless libertine."

His chest shook with laughter. "Not entirely shameless. I've had one or two guilt-ridden moments, but fortunately they dissipated quickly." His gaze slid over her body. "I suspect you've been told many times how very beautiful you are."

She knew it was a rake's trick to murmur sweet words and tempt a lady to loosen her morals, but he looked at her with intent. Without thinking, she wet her lips, and that drew his attention. She'd inadvertently signaled she wanted a kiss, but of course she would rather kiss a snake.

Tension vibrated between them. Now was the moment to step away, but she stood rooted to the spot as if her feet were mired in a bog.

He reached for her nape, just as the knocker downstairs rapped repeatedly.

She gasped, and they sprang apart.

Rake that he was, he winked and said, "Saved by the knocker."

Her face flamed. "Nothing happened," she said under her breath as he shut the bedchamber door.

"I'm sorry to disappoint you."

"You did not—"

He put his finger over her lips.

She pulled his hand away. "If Agnes were to walk by, she would conclude we are having an assignation," she said under her breath.

"I'm amenable if you are." His eyes were full of merriment. "When shall we begin?"

"When Satan ice skates in Hades," she muttered. Oh, God, she was so embarrassed. How could she fall under Colin's spell of all people? They had always despised each other. Her face was still hot with mortification.

The marquess's voice echoed in the great hall. "Where the devil are they?"

"That is your father," Angeline said under her breath. "We must hurry."

"Calm yourself first or they'll know something is afoot."

She fanned herself with her hand to cool her face. "Do not be ridiculous. Nothing happened." But what would have happened if not for the timely interruption? Nothing, absolutely nothing would have transpired. The last thing she needed was to let another rake sully what was left of her tattered reputation.

But he was not just another rake. He was a friend of her family. That definitely put a damper on matters. Cold water would do as well, but there was none at hand.

She inhaled and exhaled on a shaky breath.

"Ready?" he said, offering his arm.

She took it. "There will not be a repeat performance."

"Of what? Nothing happened."

"Exactly," she said, lifting her chin.

He led her down the stairs and spoke overly loud about the sorry state of the carpets and the need for more internal shutters. Clearly it was a performance. He was as cool as an ice at Gunthers.

"Father, Wycoff, this is a surprise," he said. "Are you here to give us advice about our renovation efforts?"

The marquess narrowed his eyes. "We came to ensure the pair of you haven't engaged in fisticuffs."

Angeline released Colin's arm and forced herself to smile. "Nothing of the kind," she said. "We are taking the divide-and-conquer approach."

Wycoff frowned. "What?"

Chadwick leaned toward him. "I think she means they're working in separate rooms. It's for the best. Less chance of blood being shed this way."

Colin clasped his hands behind his back. "We made progress today."

While Colin spoke to his father, Angeline approached her father with more than a little trepidation. "Did you enjoy shooting today, Papa?"

"I did, Daughter, but I am mortally humiliated. Chadwick shot a pheasant, and I bagged nothing."

"Did you enjoy tramping about the property? You always said it was the best part."

Her father's eyes softened. "You remembered."

I remember all the times we spent together, and I miss you. "I hope you shoot a bird tomorrow," she said.

"Maybe not tomorrow, but I intend to before the house party concludes."

"We mustn't speak of the bird I shot earlier today," the marquess said. "The twins will be overset."

Angeline turned to the marquess. "Oh, I suppose they are tenderhearted about all creatures."

The marquess snorted. "Nothing of the kind. They

wanted to come along with us today and insisted that ugly dog could fetch for us."

"Well, Wycoff, I suppose we should be off. Perhaps you wish your daughter to travel with you?" the marquess said.

"We're both covered in mud. I don't want to inadvertently muss your gown, Angeline," Wycoff said.

"It's only mud, Papa." *I love you and hope you have forgiven me.*

"Your mother would not be pleased if I dirtied your skirts."

"Well, we'll go on ahead," the marquess said. "Colin, you will take the maid up in the carriage, of course. Do not dally. Your stepmother will have a good dinner waiting."

Colin joined Angeline at the door. She bit her lip as the marquess's carriage rolled away, but her eyes welled.

"Angeline, I hope I did not discompose you earlier."

"Of course n-not." The catch in her voice troubled him.

He feared he was responsible, but he wasn't sure what he'd done wrong.

The sound of horse hooves alerted him. "There's John now," he said.

Agnes appeared from the direction of the servant's stairs and bobbed a curtsy. "I left the feather duster and broom in the kitchen, my lady."

"Thank you, Agnes," Angeline said. "We are ready to depart."

Colin locked the door and turned to her. "Is all well with you?" He knew something was amiss, but he'd never understood women.

"Yes, I'm gratified to see my father in such good spirits."

She'd implied that her father had been in poor spirits. Obviously the events surrounding Angeline's broken engagement had been difficult for the entire family. She probably felt guilty, but in his opinion, she'd made the right decision to call off the engagement.

The only thing he didn't understand was why her father had approved the engagement. Brentmoor was well known for his ruinous gambling and indiscreet liaisons. That begged the question as to how she'd ever gotten involved with the man in the first place.

Angeline had her faults, but she'd never been anybody's fool. Until, apparently, Brentmoor.

He escorted her to the carriage and helped her negotiate the steps. He sat across from her with his back to the horses and knocked his cane on the ceiling. Minutes later the carriage rolled off. He looked out the window and knew he'd made a mistake today. While he'd only intended to tease her, his blood had definitely heated more than a few degrees.

Nothing of import had happened. Granted, he'd felt a stirring of desire, but he'd not acted upon it.

He tried telling himself he was making too much of it, but she'd been through an ordeal with her former fiancé. The gossip had spread far and wide. Her mother had felt the need to take her abroad because of it. Her father must have taken it hard.

Hell. She'd offered her expertise, and he'd come very close to kissing her, but he had not. He'd teased her, but there was no harm in that. The trouble was he'd wanted more, but that would prove disastrous if he were ever foolish enough to act upon it.

He had no idea what had happened between her and

Brentmoor, but he knew the man had ruinous gaming debts and bragged about the numerous married ladies he'd bagged. Colin thought the man disgusting.

There had been countless women in his life, but they had all been fleeting encounters. None of them had meant anything more to him than a tumble between the sheets, but he'd never misled them. He'd never felt an ounce of remorse, because they had all been more than willing. Not once had he considered he might have wounded them. He'd never stayed long enough to know. He wouldn't even let himself think about the courtesans.

Angeline was a lady, and their families were close. The last thing he needed was to unintentionally set up expectations. He needn't worry. She'd made no secret of her low opinion of him. There was nothing to worry about. She'd agreed to assist him only because she was bored witless with needlework and apparently enjoyed making over rooms. He need not worry about taking advantage of her talent. She wanted to be involved.

All the same, he vowed to keep their encounters focused on the renovations and avoid flirting with her. She had enough troubles, and he couldn't afford the distraction.

That evening after dinner

After the desserts, the marchioness rose and all of the ladies followed her to the drawing room while the gentlemen drank their port. Angeline was anxious for their return and hoped to persuade her father to play chess with her. They had not played since her return from Paris. Today, her father had seemed his old self again. She'd worried so much and blamed herself for his melancholy.

While she'd not wanted to attend this house party, she was so grateful, because it had enlivened her father.

The twins sang while Penny played the pianoforte. Angeline was proud of her sister. Penny had a natural talent, but she blushed and lowered her eyes the entire time she played.

When she finished, Angeline's protective instincts rose up. She sat on the bench beside Penny. "I'll turn the pages while you play."

Penny smiled. "Thank you, Angie. I always feel braver when you sit beside me while I play."

"You will practice playing before others at the house party, and if you concentrate on the music, that will help. If you think too much about others watching, it will make you nervous.

"Remember that all the other girls are as nervous as you are. Keep your eyes on the music sheets and shut out everything else."

"I will remember," Penny said, and started to play again.

Penny had to overcome her fear of exhibiting before a crowd. It was important, because she would be called upon to play next spring at her debut. Angeline bit her lip and hoped that her scandal would not affect Penny's come-out. She'd discovered that she could withstand horrible gossip and humiliation, but she could not bear it if her mistakes prevented her little sister from making her debut.

Margaret stood. "Angeline, I must apologize. You received a letter today. How could I have forgotten?"

"Thank you, Margaret." Angeline whispered to her sister, "Keep playing."

She walked over to the window seat, broke the seal, and turned the paper. "It's from Charlotte." She'd not had a letter from her friend in all the time she'd been abroad. She'd missed her and thought she would never hear from her again. Her emotions rose up, but she had learned how to keep it all buried inside by imagining a steaming kettle. Take if off the fire just before the steam reaches the boiling point.

Out of the corner of her eye, Angeline saw her mother watching. In need of privacy, she rose, and as she walked to the window seat, she overheard Margaret say the letter seemed like a good omen. Angeline could not imagine it. With a deep breath, she started reading.

Dearest Angeline,

It is my greatest hope that this letter finds you well. Please forgive me for my lapse in correspondence. It was not of my choice, and now I must not tarry. My husband would be displeased if he knew. Please know that not a day has gone by that I haven't missed you.

In the interval since she'd returned home from Paris, she'd been isolated with her family. It was one thing to know her reputation was damaged in the abstract, but it was quite another when it was poor enough that a friend's husband forbade contact. She knew the reason and still felt guilty because Charlotte's husband had been furious.

I confess I was torn whether to inform you or not, and I had no one I felt comfortable asking for ad-

*vice. After a great deal of contemplation, I realized
if it were me, I would prefer to hear the news from
a trusted friend. It pains me to inform you that
Brentmoor has returned to England.*

She felt as if a broadsword had pierced her heart.

Oh, God, he'd returned.

Her fingers trembled, and she had to smooth the letter
on her lap so that no one would see her vexation. At all
costs she mustn't let on, because she didn't want Penny
to ever know what had happened. She took a deep breath
and continued reading.

*As I write this letter, I know it is bound to wound you.
The events have incited renewed gossip. Others have
unfairly painted you as a jilt and intimated worse.*

Deep down, she'd always held out a thread of hope that
she could recover from the scandal, but Brentmoor's return was a staggering blow.

Her stomach felt a bit queasy. An engaged couple was
allowed to be alone, once consent was given and the contracts were signed. She'd cried off a fortnight after the
contracts had been drawn up, and Brentmoor had made
matters far worse by spreading filthy lies about her.

Her spirits sagged. She'd held on to the hope that he
would never return and that the gossip would subside.
She'd hoped to repair her reputation with time. Now that
Brentmoor had returned, there was no hope.

*You will likely wonder how he ever managed such
a feat, given his timely escape from his creditors,*

but he is married to a woman with thirty thousand pounds, and she is the same shameless woman you discovered with Brentmoor that awful night at the ball. After less than a year, Lady Cunningham has left off her mourning and married Brentmoor, fool that she is, for he will surely spend her entire fortune. They now have an estate at Woodham Hall.

That was the property Mrs. Quimby had mentioned. Clearly the reverend's wife had not known his name or his circumstances. But the ton would know.

A fog enveloped her, but she caught her mother's eye and managed to fold the letter perfunctorily.

"Angeline, what news do you have from Charlotte?" the duchess said.

She had to recover quickly, because she did not want Penny to hear the truth. All she could do was fabricate a story. "Charlotte is well and happy. She sent her regards and apologized for her lack of correspondence, but she was only just made aware of our return."

"How lovely to hear news from your friend," Margaret said.

Her mother's expression lit up. "This is wonderful news. I know how much you've missed Charlotte."

She would not be able to hide the truth for long. Her mother's remaining friends would send letters. Soon, everyone in the ton would know about Brentmoor's return.

Two years ago, she'd sealed her fate, but her worries were for her innocent sister. Angeline's chest ached. Because of her, Penny might never have a debut.

* * *

Colin rose from the table after an excellent port. He'd only half listened to his father and Wycoff discuss politics. Instead, he'd made a mental list of items he wanted to deal with at Sommerall tomorrow.

"I suppose we should join the ladies," Wycoff said.

"Go on ahead," Chadwick said. "I wish to have a word with Colin."

Colin faced his father. "I suppose you want a report of what I accomplished today."

The marquess sighed. "You can give me a report next week. I have a concern."

"About what?"

"I was taken aback by your appearance in the hall today."

Colin frowned. "I heard the knocker and escorted Angeline downstairs."

"You held your coat over your shoulder, your sleeves were rolled up, and your hair was disheveled." He knew it was forbidden to appear before a lady in such a casual manner, but he'd decided to be sensible while working.

"I was sorting items in the attic," he said. "It's dusty and crowded with all manner of items. What did you expect?" Of course he wouldn't mention the highly charged tension between him and Angeline. Why be concerned when nothing had happened?

"At the very least, you ought to have put on your coat in the presence of a lady."

"For God's sake, we were working."

"You ought to have donned it before coming downstairs. It is a mark of respect for Lady Angeline and for Wycoff."

Colin stiffened. "He took it as an insult?"

"No, he would not have mentioned it, but Wycoff is eaten alive with guilt over his daughter's misbegotten engagement. When I saw your cavalier manner with her, I grew concerned that he might misinterpret your familiarity."

Colin rubbed his temple. Damn it all. He had been familiar with her, and there had been that moment in which he'd felt the insistent tug of sensual awareness. "You approved of the two of us working together. If I did not treat her in an amiable manner, I believe *she* would take it as an insult."

"Son, I agree, but you are missing the point. The cloud of scandal hangs over Wycoff's entire family. It is very likely that Margaret will have to sponsor Penelope this spring. Lady Angeline's future is...uncertain. You never even questioned why I brought Wycoff to Sommerall."

He gritted his teeth. "If Wycoff was concerned, he should have spoken up beforehand."

"He did not express concern, but I brought him there to reassure him that all was well. As a father, I can only imagine how I would feel if it was one of your sisters."

Colin inhaled sharply. The very thought of a scoundrel even breathing near one of his sisters made his blood boil.

"I see you understand now."

He gripped the back of the chair. "I would kill any man who dared to trifle with one of my sisters."

"I sincerely hope not, since dueling is officially illegal and you are my heir. However, feel free to beat any man to a pulp who expresses even the slightest interest in the twins."

"Father, I do not want to treat Angeline differently because of what happened to her. I imagine she's faced too much of that already."

The marquess clapped his hand on Colin's shoulder. "You reaffirmed my belief in you. However, this does not mean you are off the hook."

He frowned. "What?"

"If you want Sommerall, you must find a bride. I tire of hearing about your many lightskirts and drunken escapades. A wife will cure that. You might want to consult Margaret. She has some distant cousins."

"After the house is in decent shape, I will make every effort to find a wife." *In a year or two.*

"I've managed to put off the buyer, but he won't wait forever. You will make an effort."

Colin figured his father was bluffing. He would manage to put it off as long as possible.

"There you are," Margaret said. "I was beginning to worry."

"It is my fault," Colin said. "I insisted upon discussing the renovations and delayed our return."

The marquess shrugged. "He is determined."

"You missed the news," the duchess said. "Angeline received a letter from her friend Charlotte. She did not realize Angeline had returned home. Soon my daughter will be able to renew her acquaintances after a long absence."

Angeline's smile looked frozen.

"We are making plans for the spring season," Margaret said. "I believe a Venetian breakfast would be just the thing."

He saw the duke pouring a drink at the sideboard and joined him. Wycoff downed the brandy and poured another. His grim expression looked foreboding. Colin poured a finger and swirled the liquor. "Thank you for allowing Angeline to assist me. She's quite knowledgeable."

"They are making too much of that letter," he said under his breath.

Colin was at a loss to reply. He sipped his brandy and grew increasingly uncomfortable when Wycoff poured an exceeding amount of brandy. If he kept this up, he'd be foxed in no time.

Angeline approached. "Papa, will you play chess with me? It has been ages since you last trounced me."

"Not tonight," he said gruffly.

She winced.

"Excuse me." He set his glass down and quit the drawing room.

The devil. The man might feel guilty, but he ought to be kinder to her. Colin set his own glass aside. "Come, play backgammon with me."

She looked a bit shaken. "I fear I will have trouble concentrating."

"We will make it appear we are playing. It will give us a chance to talk."

"I can't," she said.

"You would do me a great favor. Otherwise, I will be called upon to turn the pages at the pianoforte, and you will have to listen to their plans."

She nodded. "Very well."

He seated her at the game table and sat across from her. "I will set the pieces out, and we will throw the dice and make our moves while we talk. Now, tell me what is awry."

"Everything, but that is hardly new."

"Angeline, your father said the ladies were making too much of the letter." He paused and handed her the dice. "Throw them to make it appear we're really playing."

She threw the dice and moved one of the backgammon stones. "I lied about Charlotte's letter."

He threw the dice and moved a stone. "Why?"

She picked up the dice and dropped them. "I didn't want Penny to hear. She knows nothing about the scandal."

"She knows something is wrong."

Angeline made her move. "I mean to keep it from her as long as possible."

He suspected Penny knew more than she let on, but he said nothing of that to Angeline. "Did your friend mention Brentmoor in her letter?"

She met his gaze. "He has returned and is married to the widowed Lady Cunningham."

"I see. She will regret it when he spends her entire fortune. Is she a friend?"

She listlessly dropped the dice. "No, a distant acquaintance."

"It's understandable that the news would discompose you, but you are well rid of him."

She met his gaze. "She is the one I found in bed with Brentmoor."

He winced. "I'd no idea."

"Adultery is hardly news in the ton."

She rolled and moved the stones. "Foolishly, I assumed he would never return because of his creditors. I did not count on him marrying an heiress."

Colin scooped up the dice and rolled, but her pale complexion worried him. "He is likely to spend himself into debt again. Men like him are their own worst enemies."

"You don't understand."

"Help me understand."

She rolled the dice. "I thought if he was gone forever, that others would forget. I foolishly held out hope that with time, I could repair my reputation. Now that he has returned, I must face the truth. I will always be a pariah."

"You may not believe me, but you did the right thing by crying off."

She moved a stone. "I knew something was wrong, and I ignored my instincts." She paused and said, "To my detriment."

The clock chimed.

"It is very late," Angeline said. "Shall we retire for the evening?"

He assisted her out of the chair and put away the game. As she quit the room, he wondered anew why she'd ever gotten involved with Brentmoor. The back of his neck prickled. Something had gone terribly wrong. Why else would the duchess have taken her to Paris? Multiple possibilities occurred to him. One made him pause. He'd heard stories about increasing women who fled to the continent to bear a secret child. More often he'd heard of elopements. But all of this was nothing more than conjecture. He hoped for her sake that it was merely betrayal.

The next day, Colin and Angeline traveled early in the morning to Sommerall. Colin wanted to ensure they arrived in a timely manner. The marquess had made arrangements for men to bring a wagon with coal, lanterns, fuel, and tinderboxes to the property along with footmen to move the heavier furnishings and remove the faded carpets.

Angeline put on an apron in preparation for working in the attic. She'd worn sturdy half boots and pulled a mob-cap out of her apron pocket. When she stood before the foyer mirror, she slipped on the cap. Colin walked up behind her and snatched it off.

Agnes tied her apron and couldn't quite hide her smile as she took the hamper and walked toward the breakfast parlor.

"Give the cap to me," Angeline said, reaching for it.

He stepped back and put the cap behind him.

She ran behind him and tried to grasp the cap, but he held it over his head.

"Give it to me," she said.

"You must ask politely."

She scowled. "Please return my cap," she muttered.

"Muttering is hardly polite."

She inhaled. "You... you are horrid."

"Take off that apron," he said.

She gaped at him. "I beg your pardon? You will not order me about."

"You will not dress like a maid."

"Be practical. The attic is bound to be dusty."

"I forbid it," he said. "You are a duke's daughter and a lady."

"You are ridiculous." She poked around in her other apron pocket and pulled out her old gardening gloves.

"You will not need them. You may supervise Agnes."

"I am not a wilting flower, and I most certainly am not afraid of a little dust in the attic. The gloves will protect my hands. I do mean to work. In case you've had a memory lapse in the last hour, let me remind you that we have very little time available to us."

When the clatter of hooves sounded, Colin opened the door and stuffed her ugly cap in his inner coat pocket. "The coal has arrived."

"I'll set Agnes to cleaning out the ashes in the hearth." She hurried up the stairs.

He turned around and admired her bottom as she ascended the steps. What red-blooded man wouldn't have a look?

The footmen brought in the coals along with lanterns and two tinderboxes. He led them to the drawing room where Agnes finished sweeping and stepped back.

Two other footmen moved the heavy tables and took the carpets to the wagon. The marquess's steward would ensure the carpets found good homes.

"Agnes, help me put the covers over the furniture," Angeline said.

Colin shrugged out of his coat and strode over to her. "Take my coat please." He rolled up his sleeves and noticed Angeline watching him.

He tossed the covers over the furniture, smiled, and took her arm. "Step out into the corridor in the event the flue isn't working and smoke billows out."

"You had better come along," she said. "You don't want to get your shirt and cravat dirty."

He leaned down and said under his breath, "I'm a man. We like dirty things."

She narrowed her eyes and marched out into the corridor. His shoulders shook, and he figured she'd give him a tongue-lashing after the footmen left.

A few minutes later, a weak fire started. Colin held his breath, hoping smoke wouldn't fill the room. He didn't even want to consider the damage to the painted ceiling.

With the application of the bellows, a fire crackled and no smoke billowed out into the drawing room. He exhaled. "Success."

When the footmen stepped back, Angeline instructed Agnes to dust the interior shutters.

Colin made sure she wasn't paying attention and tossed her ugly cap into the fire. Then he directed the footmen to dump the coal ashes.

Angeline faced him. "I am coming with you to the attic. There is much to be done there, and we will not waste time arguing over the matter."

Her brows knitted. "Where is my cap?"

He shrugged. "Did you lose it?"

Her eyes narrowed and she held out her palm. "Give it to me."

"I can't. It's gone."

"What do you mean it's gone?"

He shrugged.

"You will pay for this."

He grinned. "I look forward to your punishment."

She regarded him suspiciously, as well she should. "No doubt it has something to do with dirt."

Her saucy reply tickled him, but he'd better focus on the work. He lit one of the lanterns and escorted her up two flights of steps to the attic. The dormer window was grimy, but he set the lantern on a scarred table. He put his hands on his hips and looked around. Then he made his way past several trunks. "Ah, just what we need."

When he returned to her, he held carpet pieces. "We can kneel on these."

"Very handy," she said.

He pointed at one trunk in the corner. "That is the one

I went through yesterday. The strap is broken, and there's nothing of value to me."

"I imagine the servants or tenants would appreciate the yarn, quills, and handkerchiefs."

"Then it's a good thing you're here, because I was ready to toss it all in the rubbish bin."

He pushed a heavy trunk forward. The muscles in his upper arms strained. She placed one of the carpets before a trunk and knelt, but her eyes kept returning to his bulging biceps. She fumbled with the straps, mostly because she couldn't take her gaze off him.

He interrupted her ogling and strode over to her. "Let me unbuckle them."

She stood just as he took a step, and she bumped into him. He caught her shoulders, and there could not have been more than a few inches between them. The moment suspended as their gazes met. His big hands were warm and strong. Her toes curled in her slippers.

"Pardon me," he said, stepping aside.

She released her pent-up breath. Dear God, did he rub a secret bait salve on himself to lure unsuspecting females? While she continued to recover from their physical encounter, he worked on the straps of a trunk as if he were completely oblivious to her.

When he tried to open the trunk, he muttered something under his breath, likely a curse. "It's locked." He straightened his tall frame. "I'll go down to the kitchen and see if there is anything I can use as a lever."

He left the attic door open as he strode down the corridor. She released a ragged breath. Sanity returned slowly. She was not attracted to him. Not at all. *Liar*. Granted, she would have to be dead not to notice the bulging muscles in his arms and his incredibly muscular thighs. But she could not, would not allow her attraction to him to bloom. It would be madness. She'd fallen under one rake's spell, and she wouldn't make that mistake again.

God help her. Angeline thought a few prayers might be in order for her salvation.

She needed distraction from thoughts of Colin's all-too-enticing athletic body. Angeline walked through the crowded attic to force her thoughts elsewhere. There was an old bookcase with scratches in the wood—a tenant might find that useful. She located a pair of scales, a flask, and a sword propped up against the far wall. There was a bust, too. She removed her gloves and fingered the smooth marble. Was it his grandfather?

When she turned, she happened upon a tall wig in a box. It reminded her of her late great-grandmother. Why in the world did the ladies back then wear those horrendous wigs? They were truly hideous and probably hot as well. What a lark it would be to don the wig and surprise Colin. She would no doubt startle a laugh out of him when she pranced around in a ridiculously high wig.

She started to reach inside the box to extract the wig. Then something moved. A mouse poked its beady nose out. She jumped back and screamed.

Colin walked up the stairs with a big mallet. He figured he could break the lock with it. He reached the second landing, and a scream sent him running. His heart stampeded as he ran. The devil. What if Angeline had fallen and gotten hurt?

She turned the corner and ran toward him. Relief

flooded his veins. He dropped the mallet and caught her in his arms. "Are you hurt?"

She was shaking uncontrollably. "N-no. The-there w-was a m-mouse in the w-wig."

"Oh, Lord." He held her tightly, relieved to find her unharmed. "You scared me."

She clutched him. "Stupid m-mouse."

"Hush now. You've had a fright." She shivered again, and without thought, he caressed her spine. Eventually her trembling subsided, and he was all too aware of her soft, feminine body pressed against him. When his groin tightened, he knew he'd better put distance between them, and he reluctantly released her.

"I'm so mortified," she said, looking up at him.

"You needn't be."

She looked at the mallet. "What in heaven's name were you planning to do with that?"

"Break the lock on the trunk."

"Oh." She frowned and worried her hands. "I suppose we should return to the attic."

He laughed and picked up the mallet. "Angeline, I'm fairly certain the attic is the last place you wish to go. Tomorrow I'll bring a mousetrap or two."

"There's so much to do," she said. "I feel badly for slowing our progress."

"One day will not make that much difference," he said. "By the way, did you find anything of value in the bedchambers yesterday?"

She hesitated. "I went through all the rooms."

"Why are you hedging?"

"There's a nursery," she said.

His neck prickled. "Where is it?"

"Colin, don't go in there."

He set the mallet down and started opening doors. She followed him. "I'm sorry. I should have told you yesterday."

When he opened the door to the nursery, he strode inside and immediately tore the covers off the rocker. He went over to a shelf where a tin box sat. When he opened it, a look of wonder crossed his face. "My tin soldiers. I always wondered what became of them."

"I didn't notice them yesterday."

He frowned at her. "It is in plain view. Something is amiss. You might as well tell me."

She sighed. "There is a cradle underneath the cover."

He whipped it off. Inside was padded bedding. He felt no shock or melancholy. Only numbness.

She slipped her hand through his arm. "I hope you will forgive me. I thought to spare you."

He patted her hand. "I understand, but I prefer to confront things."

"Yes, I think it is for the best. Shall we return to the attic? If the mouse decides to make another appearance, I'll let you confront it."

He smiled a little. "Very well."

By late afternoon, they had sorted items from five trunks. He'd found an old bagwig he was certain had belonged to his grandfather and a pair of men's buckled shoes with heels. He thought the bust probably was his grandfather.

They put all of the items he didn't want in crates. He planned to make them available to the tenants and servants. The mouse had evidently disappeared.

They had not discussed the miniature, but it had yet to turn up.

After he carried a crate downstairs, she looked through some correspondence she'd found. One set was tied with a blue ribbon. She pulled a letter out and saw the address to Lady Elizabeth Montleigh. She wanted very much to read it, but she ought not pry. She folded the letter, set it aside, and retrieved another from the others tied with the blue ribbon. This one was also addressed to the same woman. When she started to fold it, she saw the last line.

My darling Elizabeth, you are my heart and my love forever more.

She yearned to be loved, truly loved, but it seemed that was not to be her destiny.

Colin returned. His shirtsleeves were wrinkled and his cravat looked a bit wilted. Somehow he managed to look every bit the handsome rogue.

"You found correspondence?"

"A letter from your father to Lady Elizabeth Montleigh."

"My mother," he said.

She lifted her eyes to him. "I read only the last line."

He took it and walked over to the table where the lantern burned. "I would never have guessed my father was so sentimental."

"The letter indicates he loved her deeply," she said. "Do you think he would want the letter?"

Colin frowned. "I've no idea. All I know for certain is that he left Sommerall after her funeral. I don't remember anything except leaving here for Deerfield." He folded the letter and set it on the table. "Two years later, he made a marriage of convenience with Margaret."

"It may have started out that way, but I believe he loves her now."

"He is fond of her, but I'm sure he wanted a spare heir."

His blunt words stunned her. "Perhaps he was lonely and wanted a second chance at love."

He considered her with a patronizing expression. "There are practicalities, including the contracts, as you are fully aware. I assure you my father's primary concerns dealt with the marriage contracts. She brought a considerable fortune into the marriage."

She bristled. "So do many women."

"I'm only stating the facts, Angeline. You know the realities of aristocratic marriages, and to be frank, her father was a merchant and saw an opportunity to better his family."

"Margaret was educated as a lady."

"Yes, I know, but you cannot be unaware that your mother's influence paved the way for Margaret in society."

Angeline was breathing hard. "Do you think I give a damn?"

His eyes widened at her words.

"Margaret was one of the few ladies who came to support my mother and me during one of the worst times of our lives. Everyone else stayed away from fear of contamination from my scandal." Angeline wiped tears from her face. "She is one of the kindest ladies I have ever had the pleasure to call friend. And she deserves far more credit than you give her. She wants only to please others and believes herself undeserving because her father was in trade. She is your father's wife and the mother of your sisters. You should respect her."

"I do not disrespect her," he said testily. "I only stated the truth."

"You just did."

"Angeline, you are unreasonable."

"Well, we cannot all be as perfect as you," she said.

"The sarcasm is unwarranted."

Her face heated. She marched out of the attic. How dare he speak so coldly about Margaret? He was a rake and yet he thought himself above everyone. She thought him a hypocrite and wouldn't be surprised if he had notches on his bedpost. Horrid man.

His rapid footsteps echoed behind her. She hurried her step, but he caught her arm. "Stop," he said.

She glared at him. "I agreed to help you because I thought you deserved the opportunity to prove yourself, but I will not aid and abet you when you have so little respect for your family."

He opened a bedchamber door. "Come inside. Agnes is cleaning the banister, and I don't want her to hear us."

She followed him inside and turned to him. "You are judgmental."

His nostrils flared. "*I* am judgmental? You judge me unfairly, my lady. All I did was state the facts, but you presume to know my feelings about my own family."

"What was I to think when you spoke in such a cold manner about Margaret? The circumstances of your father's second marriage do not matter. Your father adores her, as well he should. She brought happiness and light into your father's life after your mother's death. But for reasons I do not understand, you hold yourself aloof from your own family."

"You know nothing about it."

He'd said he was selfish, and she certainly believed it now. "You have not been home since last Easter. Your sisters are growing up without even knowing their brother, and I suspect you resent Margaret."

"I don't resent her, but we are not close and never have been."

How could he be so unfeeling? "Whose fault is that? You make no effort."

"Did it ever occur to you that maybe she was the one who didn't make the effort?"

She shook her head. "That's ridiculous."

"I think it is ridiculous to expect it of an eight-year-old."

"What?" He'd shocked her.

"My father started a second family while I was away at school. I did not even know about it until he brought me home from Eton for Christmas holidays. He told me I had a new mother, but I was eight years old and didn't even know how to address her. Was I to call her Stepmama or Margaret? No one ever thought to tell me for days."

"I cannot believe it of her or your father."

"I have no reason to lie about it. I lived it—you didn't."

"How could it be possible? Margaret is too kind to ignore a child."

"She didn't ignore me, but she was not my mother, and I wasn't her son."

"I don't understand," she said.

"It happened long ago, but it is clear to me now why it was so awkward. She was educated as a lady, but there is a big difference between that education and learning the distinctions of society. I can imagine how difficult it was for her to assimilate. She had to have been terrified. Have you never stopped to think about why she relies so much on your mother?"

"They are friends."

"Yes, but that friendship likely came about because your mother saw the need to help her. In those early days, she was much younger and probably overwhelmed and intimidated."

"You were a child. How could you know?" she asked.

"I remember when several ladies called when we were in London. I was probably eight or nine years old. After they left, I saw Margaret sitting in the drawing room weeping."

Angeline smoothed her skirt. "I had no idea."

"We were born into this world, but she had to learn. On top of it all, she had to deal with an unhappy stepson."

Angeline winced, realizing she'd made assumptions without knowing all the particulars. "Please forgive me."

"There is nothing to forgive. It was just circumstances. I spent most of my time at school and half my summers with Harry at his uncle's pig farm," he said. "I was happy there and for the most part at school as well, but over time, my relationship with my family grew increasingly distant. I adore my sisters, but they are half my age. I'm glad my father found happiness with Margaret, but their lives went on and so did mine. No one is to blame. It was just the situation."

Angeline felt awful. "I'm sorry for misjudging you."

He scuffed his boot on the carpet. "You weren't wrong. I was resentful for many years. I felt as if I did not belong. Undoubtedly it was an erroneous perception on my part."

"I think it would be difficult for all involved when there are such drastic changes to a family," she said.

"When I arrived at Deerfield, I was shocked at how much my sisters had grown." He paused and said, "I should make more of an effort."

"I am sorry. I have no right to judge anyone when I've made grievous mistakes."

"Regardless, you didn't deserve to be treated so ill."

"I am responsible."

"You mustn't blame yourself," he said.

She deserved no sympathy. From the beginning, she'd been suspicious of Brentmoor, as any sane and virtuous woman would be, but she'd let vanity and pride overcome her judgment. All because she knew others were whispering about her single status at the ripe age of thirty. She'd not heeded her mother's warnings about waiting too long to marry, and she'd paid dearly for it.

"It's not your fault," he said.

If she'd married sooner, she could have avoided her mistakes. "I take responsibility, but it is not enough," she said. "There is nothing I can do to change it."

"No, but you can go forward. Don't let him ruin your life."

He didn't understand. She could never reconcile what she'd done to her family.

Chapter Six

Breakfast the next morning

Colin finished his baked eggs, sausages, and roll. He drank his tea and smiled at Angeline. "I'm anxious to get started for the day."

"I look forward to it as well," she said. "I plan to take an apron so that I can help you in the attic again."

"In the attic?" Margaret said. "I had no idea you were working in the attic."

Wycoff frowned. "Angeline, such a task is beneath you. Let the maid do the work."

"She will not know what is valuable and what is not. There is much to do, and I'm determined to be useful."

Colin was glad to see her in much better spirits this morning, but after his conversation with his father yesterday, he wanted to make sure Wycoff knew they would preserve the proprieties. "The maid will be there at all times and will perform tasks as directed."

Ames entered the breakfast parlor before his father

could reply. "My lord, Mr. Faraday has arrived. I've installed him in the anteroom."

The marquess set his cup aside. "I'm ready, Ames. Send him to my study in ten minutes."

"Yes, my lord."

"Colin, I will send for you after I conclude my meeting," the marquess said.

He'd wanted to leave as soon as breakfast ended. What the devil did his father want now? There was nothing for it. He would have to cool his heels and hope that his father's first meeting did not take too long.

"Angeline, you will join us in the drawing room until Colin is ready to depart," the duchess said.

While everyone else filed out, Colin and Angeline lingered for a few moments.

"I'd hoped to leave sooner," he said.

"I will count the minutes until I can put my needle aside," she said. "Patience is not one of my virtues."

"At least my father knows I'm serious about the property."

"Perhaps by the end of the week, we will have something to show for our efforts. Your father will have no doubt you intend to transform Sommerall."

He appreciated her belief in him, but there was something in her attitude that troubled him. Colin wondered how much her father's neglect had wounded her. Whatever had happened to her, he didn't believe it was hopeless. She'd been engaged to a rotten man and ought to be applauded for having the good sense to end it. Good God, her father was a duke. Surely his influence could have turned matters around, but he did not know the particulars.

Obviously, she'd not known the man's bad character.

But Wycoff must have known. Why had he given his blessing?

Chances were he would never know. Perhaps that was for the best.

Forty minutes later, after a footman summoned Colin, he strode to his father's study and knocked on the door.

"Come in and shut the door, please," the marquess said.

He took a chair in front of his father's desk.

"I will get to the point," the marquess said. "Mr. Faraday is very interested in the property, even though he understands it needs a great deal of work."

His father's words stunned him.

"I daresay you thought I had invented the offer in an attempt to force you to find a wife. Am I correct?"

He briefly considered prevaricating and then decided to be honest. "It crossed my mind."

"Mr. Faraday is aware of your concerns about your mother's mausoleum, and as such, he is willing to make a higher offer as recompense, but there is another property that interests him."

He gripped the arms of the chair hard. "There isn't enough money in the world to compensate."

"I am not insensible to your feelings on the matter, but there is something important I wish to ask you. You need to be honest with me."

"Very well."

"Sommerall was always intended for you, but I could not bring myself to step inside the house. At one point, I considered selling because I knew it needed attention. Yesterday was the first time I've been in the house since your mother's death. I loved her dearly, God rest her soul, but life went on. It was Margaret who convinced me to keep the property for you. She has always blamed herself for your estrangement from our family."

He swallowed hard, remembering his conversation with Angeline about his family. Yet, his stepmother was the one who had convinced his father not to sell. "It was not her fault."

"Of course it wasn't," he said. "Are you planning to occupy the property? That means marriage, because I know you won't do it when you're single." He folded his hands on his desk. "I don't want to hear excuses or promises that you will wed in a few years. I have an offer, and I need you to tell me the truth. Are you willing to find a wife soon and reside at Sommerall?"

"You gave me six weeks to find a bride," he said. "Will you rescind that decision?"

"No, I made it in good faith. Faraday understands that it will not be available until then, but again, it is not the only one he is considering," the marquess said.

His temples ached. "You asked for honesty. I don't want to rush the decision and find out too late that I've made a mistake. It is for life. I need more time."

"Time is the one thing I cannot grant you. I previously told Faraday the property would be available in six weeks. That is what we agreed upon."

Bloody hell. "I will occupy the house, but I need five months to find a bride. The season will open, and I will begin a serious search for a wife. I believe it is a reasonable compromise."

"No doubt you mean to do as you say, but I know what will happen when you return to London. You will fall back into your old ways with your reckless friends. You will drink to excess, gamble, and chase lightskirts. You may even consider settling down—someday in the future. Like every bachelor in the world, you are convinced that your life will end as you know it. And it will—for the better."

He had to bite back a sarcastic remark.

"If you're not serious about wedding and occupying the property, tell me now."

He flexed his hands. "I'm not inclined to make spur-of-the-moment decisions."

"Why wait? You either know you will decline or accept."

"This is a lifetime decision and I wish to think it over carefully."

"You're stalling," the marquess said.

He gripped the arms of the chair in an effort to control his reactions. "Call it what you will, but I want the entire six weeks."

The marquess rose. "Very well. Our meeting is concluded."

Colin stood. *Damn you, I will not give up without a fight.*

Colin's expression was as grim as the overcast sky.

Angeline kept silent as he escorted her to the carriage. Clearly his meeting with his father had not gone well.

"My father instructed me to take Agnes up in the carriage, but she's sitting beside John."

"She will feel more comfortable keeping John company." More important, Angeline knew Colin was angry, and he needed to air his grievances.

After they boarded the carriage, he sat with his back to

the horses and knocked his cane on the ceiling. Minutes later, it rolled off. She was tempted to ask him what had transpired, but he turned his attention to the window.

When the carriage turned onto the main road, he sighed. "I beg your pardon. I ought to have called off the journey to Sommerall, but I could not bring myself to stay at Deerfield for the remainder of the day. I should have informed you that I must call off all further efforts, but I knew that would cause a stir."

"Sit with me so that I don't have to raise my voice," she said.

He moved over to her bench.

"Do you wish to tell me what happened? If not, I will understand."

"My father met with the man who is very interested in the purchase of Sommerall. The marquess will honor the six-week agreement we made. At the end of that time, he will sell to Faraday if the man chooses it over the other one he is considering."

"Surely he's not serious."

"Yes, he is very serious. We agreed I would give him my decision, one way or the other, in six weeks." He blew out his breath and laughed without mirth. "I actually considered going to London and choosing the first lady who crossed my path, but I can't do it. I should have told my father no immediately. His demands are impossible. Now I must reconcile myself to losing Sommerall."

"He ought to trust you. You are his only son."

"Isn't trust earned?" he said.

His cynical expression stunned her. "What do you mean?"

"There are reasons my father doesn't trust me. Make

no mistake. I had no intention of attending the house party, and he knows it. The only reason I made the journey was because my father informed me in a letter that he meant to sell Sommerall." He met her gaze. "I would never have traveled here otherwise."

"Not even to see your family?"

A hard look came into his eyes. "Do you want the truth or do you want the fairy-tale version?"

She laced her gloved fingers and stared at her hands. "You wish to persuade me you care nothing for your family." She met his gaze. "But I have seen your affection for your sisters. I do not deny you have a bad reputation, but I do not believe you are quite as wicked as you wish me to think."

"I'll not argue degrees of wickedness," he said, "but you know to be wary of a man like me."

She wondered if his words about himself were meant to push her away. "The marquess is a wealthy man," she said. "He has no urgent reason to sell."

"Of course he does," Colin said. "Look around you. It's a miracle the place is as sound as it is, but eventually neglect will take a toll."

"I understand, but what difference will five months make to him? None. But for you, it is crucial. Marriage cannot be undone, at least not without scandal. He should give you a chance."

He leaned his elbows on his knees. "I've given him reason to mistrust me." He sighed. "I am sorry to have misled you today. If you wish, I can stop the driver and turn back."

He looked defeated. "We will continue on," she said. "Because there is something we can do with the time allotted to us. The house party will not conclude for another three weeks. We will search through every trunk and every box until we find your mother's miniature."

"It may not turn up."

She set her hand on his sleeve. "No matter what happens, we will make every effort." At least he would know that he'd tried, although there was little comfort in it.

He nodded. "It's bound to be in one of those infernal trunks. I have little time to find it."

She prayed that it was in one of the trunks. He would take it hard if they never located it.

They worked tirelessly in the attic. Colin set the paintings of his grandparents aside, along with one of his father. Angeline found one of him holding a puppy. "I love this one of you."

"Ah, Spotty," he said. "He was a good dog."

"How old were you in this portrait?"

"I don't know."

"I can tell it is you."

"No, you cannot," he said.

"Of course I can. I would know those curls anywhere."

He laughed. "I used to go along for the shooting with my father and grandfather. Spotty would fetch any birds they hit, which wasn't very often. Our fathers are truly the worst shots in England."

She laughed. "Was there a portrait of your parents?"

"These are the only ones I've found. The others are probably stored at Deerfield."

He'd saved only a few items in one trunk, including the correspondence they'd forgotten to take yesterday after their heated exchange.

He opened another trunk and said little as he piled crates high with pewter dishes, clocks, bottles, candles, sheets, brushes, shaving accoutrements, soap, and old clothing. There was more, but it all seemed like a blur to her. The detritus of another lifetime filled the room.

When Agnes entered the attic much later, Angeline stood and realized her arms were a bit sore from the work. She removed her gloves and addressed Agnes. "Have you finished cleaning the furnishings in the bed-chambers?"

"Yes, my lady."

"You might as well take your meal with John."

"I took the liberty earlier. Didn't want to disturb you, my lady."

"That's very thoughtful of you, Agnes."

"If it pleases you, I'd be glad to test the range in the fireplace. I found sand for the floor."

Angeline blinked. "Sand?"

"Yes, my lady. It's for catching any sparks and preventing fires."

She was a scullery maid and would know such things. Angeline looked at Colin. "Do you have any reservations?"

He opened another trunk. "Agnes, I presume you have experience?"

"Yes, my lord. It's my job to start the fire in the kitchen and fireplaces at Deerfield."

Colin dusted his hands. "Ring the bell if there's a problem, even a minor one. Safety first."

"Yes, my lord." She bobbed a curtsy and left.

"That will save us the bother of bringing Cook here," Angeline said.

Colin took out his watch. "It's after two o'clock. You must be starving."

She smiled. "Are you hungry?"

"Yes, this is hard work," he said. "I fear this is a fool's errand."

"I disagree," she said. "You found portraits, and the items in the crates will find good homes. We will find the miniature. It's bound to be here somewhere."

His smile faded. "There are only two trunks left."

She must keep positive for his sake. "Well, we just haven't rummaged in the right trunk yet."

He sighed. "Let's repair to the breakfast parlor. I don't want you to swoon from hunger."

She scoffed. "I've never swooned in my life, and I do not plan to start now."

He put his hands on his hips. "And deprive me of rescuing you?"

"No doubt it has escaped your notice, but I'm not one of those dainty, petite ladies. You're likely to put your back out."

A devilish gleam entered his eyes as he advanced on her. "You think I'm too weak to pick you up?"

"Do not be ridiculous."

"You say that frequently," he said, cornering her.

"Stop that nonsense. I'm hungry."

He caught her by the waist. She squeaked when he put her over his shoulder. "Put me down."

"Say *please*."

"I'm going to kick you. One…two…"

Her feet hit the floor. She adjusted her bodice and shook her finger. "You will not do that again."

"By now you should know better than to challenge me."

"You had better keep an eye over your shoulder. I intend to get even."

He laughed and led her downstairs to the breakfast parlor. She realized he'd managed to charm her, and she thought how easily she could develop tender feelings for him. In the process, she would look very much the pathetic spinster. No matter what had happened to her, she still had her pride, and she refused to be the object of anyone's pity.

After they finished their meal, she realized his earlier good mood had disappeared.

"Colin, don't worry. We will find the miniature."

"Even if we do, it won't change anything. Sommerall will pass out of my family."

"Do you want to visit your mother's resting place now?"

"No."

"Perhaps tomorrow?" she said.

"Tomorrow I will give my father notice to sell."

"You can't give up," she said. "You negotiated for six more weeks."

He sighed. "It won't change anything," he said.

His shoulders were slumped and his expression was dispirited. Part of her wanted to encourage him to do everything in his power to retain Sommerall, but he clearly wanted to be done with it forever. She feared he would regret giving up, but it was his decision, not hers.

"Let us go upstairs. I want to finish quickly."

He opened the last two trunks. They knelt side by side. She prayed for a miracle as she set the folded sheets, blankets, and candleholders aside. There was nothing else inside.

"No luck here." Colin stood and extended his hand to her. She took it and felt his loss as if it were her own.

"I'm sorry," she said.

"I expected it."

She had no words of comfort and knew they wouldn't help anyway.

"Will you come with me to the drawing room? I don't want to depart just yet," he said.

"Yes, of course."

He led her down the stairs and into the drawing room. She perched on a sofa, and he sat beside her.

"Thank you for your faith in me and for your assistance," Colin said. "While our efforts were for naught, I am grateful to you."

"I wish you would reconsider approaching your father. You deserve at least six months."

He shook his head. "He is adamant. Once he makes a decision, he rarely changes his mind. In this case, he won't. We will have little opportunity to talk with so many others about, but thanks to you, I will make more of an effort with my family."

At least she'd managed to help him in that regard. "You will never regret it."

"There is something else, and you are under no obligation to answer. I'm greatly disturbed by what happened to you and about your father's state of mind. The day he came here, his spirits seemed good, but when he heard our mothers discussing plans for you, he was extremely discomposed. He was also drinking copious amounts of brandy. I don't want to judge him, as I've been guilty of overindulging, but I had the impression that he is over-wrought."

She looked at her clasped hands. "It's my fault."

"You're not responsible for his reactions."

She met his eyes briefly. "I was taken in by a cad."

"Angeline, it occurs to me that you have no one to talk to about what happened. I know whatever occurred is painful for you. You've likely had to hold it all inside. I think that must make matters far worse. If you prefer privacy, I understand, but I will listen without judgment."

He'd honed in on one of the most difficult aspects. She'd had no one to confide in and had never felt comfortable discussing the events with her mother. In truth, she'd hidden much from her mother in Paris to spare her additional pain.

She took a deep breath. "You are perceptive. There has been no one I could trust, and by the time everything fell apart, I had no friends to confide in. Everyone had shunned me. I don't blame them at all. We both know the rules of the ton. Almost anything is tolerated except indiscretion, but I am beforehand in my tale."

"Start from the beginning," he said.

"Not once did it ever occur to me that I might ever be in danger from a rake. Who would dare meddle with a duke's daughter? So I flirted, danced, and traded quips with gentlemen. I ignored my mother's dire warnings that I'd gained the label of flirt and was courting trouble. Then one day, I awoke to the realization that I was thirty years old and in serious danger of becoming a spinster."

"How did you get involved with Brentmoor?"

"Charlotte invited me to join her and her husband, Viscount Portsworth, at Vauxhall. There was a large party in the box, and I felt safe with my friends. Brentmoor joined the group, but he was not one of the invited guests. Portsworth did not ask him to leave, probably because he didn't want to create a stir."

Colin nodded. "Yes, it's usually best to ignore the interlopers, but I suspect Brentmoor made a habit of it."

"I knew Brentmoor had a bad reputation, but I didn't give him a second thought. I figured he would not dare trifle with me in the presence of esteemed friends. After a while, someone suggested the group walk along the lighted avenues. Brentmoor made it a point to walk beside me. When he tried to flirt, I told him he was wasting his breath. I might as well have waved a red flag in front of a bull. The evening concluded without incident, and I promptly dismissed him from my thoughts.

"Thereafter, he seemed to be at every entertainment I attended. He tried to charm me, but I refused his requests to dance. One night I left a crowded ballroom to get some air on the landing. I fanned my hot face and paid scant attention to the group of gentlemen nearby. Then I overheard one of them say that I was headed for ape territory."

Colin gritted his teeth. It was a derogatory term for spinsters. "Who was he?"

"I've no idea. As you can imagine, I did not want to face them. In hindsight, I should have stared them down with my head held high, but I was humiliated. My mother had warned me about the perils of waiting too long to marry, but I didn't think it applied to me. I thought my father's rank would protect me. I was desperate to keep my composure, but I was shaking. Then Brentmoor was at my side. He'd heard it all and damned the cads who had dared to speak of me in such an insulting manner.

"He insisted on escorting me into the ballroom to my father, where I would be safer. Then he apologized and said he knew he wasn't worthy of me. Of course, I negated that statement, and my father was grateful. After all, he was kind to me and admitted his character was imperfect. The next day he called upon me and spoke to my father. Once again, he admitted he was unworthy, but he had wanted to ensure I had recovered from that heinous insult. He stated that he would not presume to call again, because he was unfit.

"My mother was suspicious, but my father thought Brentmoor's honesty about his faults showed his character wasn't all bad. Thereafter, he would seek out my father at entertainments."

"He was scheming," Colin said.

"Oh, yes, but we did not know it then. He discovered my father loved to play chess, and my father invited him to call. Afterward, he regularly came to our town house to play with my father."

"He is an opportunist," Colin said.

"My first inkling of doubt came from Penny's reaction. She left the drawing room every time Brentmoor called. She is especially sensitive. When I asked her about it, she said his eyes lied. I thought it strange and let it go. I should have paid attention.

"Then one night after we'd danced, he told me that he was in danger of falling in love with me, but of course he was undeserving. Deep down, I knew that something wasn't quite right, but I persuaded myself that I was in love, because I feared being a spinster. He admitted to my father that he was in debt. His father was a known drunkard, and he said that he gambled because his father was

almost bankrupt. I did not know it then, but my father
loaned him money."

"The devil," Colin said.

"My friend Charlotte tried to counsel me to be wary of
him. She was very worried, because her husband had told
her that I was making a bad mistake. I was a little angry
at her presumption. At every point, I ignored the warning
signs, because I feared that I would end up a spinster. Oh,
God, if I had only known."

"He duped your father. Do not blame yourself."

"How can I not blame myself? I had doubts. I knew
something wasn't right."

"There are men who are experts at deceiving others. They
sense other's vulnerabilities and take advantage. When
doubts come to the forefront, they manage to ease them."

"You describe his character well. I feel like a fool."

"You should not."

"He proposed, and I accepted. By then, he'd said all
the right things to my father, who approved. My parents
had a row over it. Like Penny, my mother saw through
him. I pleaded with her. Brentmoor was trying to turn
his life around, and he'd not had a good father to guide
him. My own father agreed, and the contracts were duly
signed. It was at that point his true character emerged."

"What happened?"

"One night at a ball, Brentmoor took me aside and
complained he was frustrated. He said he feared I was a
prude and wanted me to prove myself, but I refused to allow him liberties until we were married."

"Good for you," Colin said. Privately, he was relieved.
It would have been a nightmare if the scoundrel had gotten her with child.

"He was determined. At another ball, he pointed out the lanterns in a garden and the other guests walking about. He assured me there was no impropriety. At first, all was well, but then he took me away from the lanterns. When I chided him, he managed to make me feel guilty for denying him. We were engaged, so I let him kiss me. I believed he would behave like a gentleman, but when a group of men came near, he gave me a lascivious kiss and plastered himself against me. I could tell it excited him for others to see us, but I was mortified."

"You ought to have slapped him."

"In front of others? I dared not create a scene."

"I never thought about how a woman might be entrapped that way."

"Of course you would not, because you would never do such a thing. I knew in my heart that the way he was treating me was wrong. I should have called off the engagement at that moment."

"Why did you not?" Colin asked.

"Because I knew if I broke the engagement that it would hurt my reputation." She shook her head. "I should have consulted my parents, but they were in disagreement over my engagement, and that alone should have decided me."

"Angeline, I suspect that he twisted matters and caused you to question your judgment."

"He did," she said. "He was very persuasive—he had to be or my father would never have let him step over the threshold. He concentrated all of his charm on my father and me. But he ignored Penny and Mama. They saw through him."

"When your father thanked Brentmoor for rescuing

you at that ball, he'd given Brentmoor the opening he
needed. He concentrated on you and your father because
you were the decision-makers. In order to get what he
wanted—your fortune—he needed to make you believe
he was a gentleman who had experienced undeserved
misfortune at the hands of his father. Similarly, he needed
to persuade your father that he was seeking parental guidance. He gulled you and your father. When your father
spoke well of him, you believed Brentmoor was a gentleman. Similarly, when you mentioned Brentmoor's wish to
improve his character, your father believed him worthy of
consideration, particularly because he was so humble. In
essence he played the two of you simultaneously. What
finally prompted you to end the engagement?"

"One evening, Brentmoor made plans to meet a friend
at White's. I was glad for the reprieve. To be honest, I felt
I needed to think carefully about the step I was about to
make. I was starting to feel a little panicked. If he really
loved me, he would have respected my decision to wait
for marriage and not press me constantly. I had so many
doubts and wish now that I had listened to my own heart.

"That very night, my friend Charlotte invited me to accompany her to a ball, because her husband was out of
town. I welcomed the invitation, and her younger brother
escorted us. I never thought anything could possibly go
wrong at a respectable entertainment.

"I distinctly recall seeing Lady Cunningham, whom
I'd met once. She was the widow of a much older man.
She had the strangest expression when I saw her staring
at me from a distance. The word that came to mind was
gloating. I ignored it.

"The ballroom was hot and crowded. I do not know

how much time passed when I went to get a cup of punch. A footman approached and asked if I was Lady Angeline, and when I said yes, he handed me a folded note. I did not recognize the handwriting. I sought out Charlotte and showed her the strange note with instructions to go up two flights of stairs and knock on the fourth door on the right. Charlotte advised me not to follow the instructions, as it might be a trick. Curiosity got the better of me, and Charlotte reluctantly accompanied me."

"What happened?" Colin asked.

"When we reached the door, Charlotte begged me not to knock. I told her that I wanted to confront whoever had sent that note. When I knocked, Brentmoor's voice rang out. I will never forget his words. It was ugly."

"What did he say?"

"Go away, I'm...well, you can supply the filthy word he used. A feminine laugh rang out. The squeaking of bed ropes told me more than I wanted to know."

"He is beyond disgusting," Colin said.

"Charlotte pleaded with me to leave immediately, but I was enraged and knocked repeatedly. The bed ropes squeaked again. I heard the rustling of skirts. When he opened the door, his trousers were only half buttoned. Lady Cunningham smirked at me as she shook out her skirts. Fury raced through me like a wildfire. I was enraged and slapped him. Of course the commotion led others to race up the stairs. I had done the unpardonable by creating a scene. You know the ton will tolerate many things, but not indiscretion."

"What happened?" he said.

"Charlotte's brother ushered us downstairs, but by then the gossip was flying. My face was as hot as fire, but

I walked down those stairs and through the foyer with my head held high, even though I saw others staring. I thought they would support me, because he had been unfaithful. I was naïve to believe it.

"My heart hammered, and I kept telling Charlotte I was sorry for ever involving her. After her brother took me home, I was still shaking as I walked into the house. My parents had not returned from the opera. I decided to wait until morning to confess the sorry story, but I did not sleep at all that night.

"You can imagine my parents' horrified reaction upon hearing what had occurred. My father's face grew mottled and my mother was pale. When I told them I would cry off, my mother rushed out of the drawing room. I was worried and followed her. She'd gotten sick. The consequences had not yet dawned on me. I was not thinking clearly or I would have realized that breaking an engagement would result in gossip, but I didn't realize it would get far worse."

"You were still in shock," Colin said.

"My father sent round a message to Brentmoor, demanding he present himself posthaste. When Brentmoor arrived, he said it was all a misunderstanding and that he sought relief elsewhere to protect my feminine sensibilities before the marriage."

"The devil," Colin said.

"An apt description of him. At that point, my shock had worn off. When I told him that we were no longer affianced, his face paled. No doubt he'd counted on my fortune. After he departed, I was relieved, but it did not last. Charlotte called on me three days later. After my mother left the room, Charlotte reluctantly divulged the horrible news her brother had revealed. Brentmoor claimed he'd..."

"What did he claim?"

"He said he had l-lain with me many times."

"He should be shot," Colin said. "Why did I never hear a word about it?"

"Most likely no one would have repeated it to you because of our family connections. I never told my parents about the slur. Mama was a ball of nerves, and Papa wouldn't even leave his study."

"Why would anyone believe Brentmoor?"

"We had been affianced for a fortnight, and others had seen him plastered against me in the unlit portion of the gardens."

Colin scowled. "He planned it."

"Probably. I will never know for certain. The repercussions were awful. My father refused to see anyone."

"He blamed himself," Colin said.

"My mother's two closest friends called four days later to warn her about the gossip. It was bad. My mother's friends advised taking me to the Continent. It did no good. My reputation followed me to Paris, though my mother still has no idea."

Colin frowned. "What do you mean?"

"A number of Frenchmen made me scandalous offers."

He bounded off the sofa and fisted his hands. She could hear him breathing like a racehorse. "Colin, it is in the past. Nothing can be changed."

"I will call him out."

"If you did, it would only make matters worse because it would renew the scandal."

"He deserves to be horse whipped."

"The part that keeps me awake at night is what I've done to my family."

"You are innocent," he said.

"You don't understand. The scandal will follow Penny. She is the innocent in all of this, and she will suffer by association." Her face crumpled. "My sweet little sister m-may never have a come-out because of me."

He strode back to her and pulled out a handkerchief. "You did nothing wrong."

She blotted her eyes. "My quick temper landed me in trouble. Had I maintained my composure that night, had I walked away as a lady ought, had I listened to Charlotte, I would have escaped the scandal. I could have survived a broken engagement. My mother's friends would have championed me. Others might have questioned my virtue, but I could have overcome it if I had not played into Lady Cunningham's scheme. I am sure she was behind it."

"Angeline, I cannot believe there is no way to resolve this."

She huffed. "There is. Marriage to a very wealthy and titled gentleman, but no man with sense wants a woman with a ruined past. He would have to be desperate."

Colin stared at her.

The backs of her hands prickled at his intense expression. "What are you thinking?" she asked.

"As it happens, I am desperate."

Chapter Seven

*S*he leaped off the sofa and nearly bumped into him. "Have you lost your wits?"

"Hush and listen. It's the perfect solution."

"No, it is insane." She'd thought he had better sense, but apparently she'd been mistaken.

"Angeline, we would both benefit."

He was outrageous. "I'm not marrying you so you can claim Sommerall."

"You said if you married a wealthy and titled gentleman, all of your troubles would disappear. I am the Earl of Ravenshire. Granted it's a courtesy title, but it's hardly objectionable."

"Are you feverish?"

He grinned. "No, but come a bit closer. I'm sure my temperature will rise."

She wasn't taking the bait. "You are proposing that we marry so that you can keep the property and I can repair my tattered reputation. That is the most bizarre reason I have ever heard for marrying."

"Is it? My father made a marriage of convenience with Margaret, and they seem to rub along well enough."

Damn him. How could she object to that? "We are incompatible," she said.

"We've done fairly well working at Sommerall, which, by the way, you could renovate to your heart's content. Although we might want to temporarily move into Deerfield to avoid paint fumes. It's a big house, so we wouldn't be in anybody's way."

She sank onto the sofa and massaged her temples. The marquess and Margaret had found love after marrying for convenience, but it did not mean that it would happen for Colin and her. In truth, it felt very much like a business matter.

But as he'd pointed out, all aristocratic marriages were based at least partly on practical monetary considerations. Marrying for love had become popular, but it did not negate the necessary contracts.

He joined her on the sofa. "I forgot to mention I have money from investments in shipping, so that should reassure you. No need to fear we'll be beggared anytime soon."

"I cannot decide if you're practical or a lunatic. Possibly both."

"I am serious about the marriage. Maybe this happened because it was meant to be."

No, it happened because we're both desperate.

"You may take your time to make a decision. I have six weeks to find a bride, but you will be here for only three more weeks. I understand that it is a momentous decision."

She thought about what she'd done to her family and her fears that Penny would never have a come-out. She thought about her father's melancholy and the day her mother had gotten violently ill upon learning Angeline meant to cry off. Most of all, she thought about Penny's tears that day she and Mama had left for their journey to Paris.

She remembered thinking that she would do anything to make the scandal go away.

"I can practically see the cogs and wheels churning in your brain. What is on your mind?" he said.

I owe it to my family to accept your proposal.

She turned to him. "If we are to wed, we should discuss our expectations of marriage."

"What specifically do you mean?"

"Is it to be a true marriage or one in name only? I know you need an heir, but..."

"But what?"

He sounded angry. "I was affianced to a rake, and he hurt me."

Colin stood and walked over to the window. Then he spun around. "You compare me to that scoundrel?"

"I am not comparing you to him, but I have a right to know what to expect and so do you. It may be common for spouses in the ton to enter into liaisons, but I do not think I could bear another betrayal."

"You assume that I will be unfaithful."

"No, I assume nothing. I want to know if you will honor the marriage vows."

"I'm not planning to betray you," he said.

"An interesting answer," she said.

"I will honor the vows, but that begs the question, Will

you be my wife in truth or will you shut the boudoir door to me?"

She realized he was angry, because he'd felt she was accusing him. "Colin, I would never do such a thing. It would only push you to take lovers. While we are on the subject, I know there are women in the ton who betray their husbands, but I would never do that to you. I could never be so cruel."

He put his hands on his hips. "How did something so simple become so complicated?"

"If it were easy, all marriages would be made up of hearts and flowers every day," she said.

"I really hope you don't expect flowers daily."

She laughed. "No, but you might find yourself rewarded for a posy now and then."

He clutched his chest. "My kingdom for a flower."

"Do not be ridiculous."

"There you go again." He paused and said, "Why am I standing across the room when there is a beautiful woman waiting for me on the sofa?"

When he sat next to her, he took her hand. "Do you find the idea of marriage to me abhorrent?"

"Not on principle." She was terrified of making another mistake. Part of her wanted to believe that underneath his rakehell exterior lay a man of honor. From all she'd heard, he'd earned his notorious reputation. She wanted to believe that he would give up his raking and settle down. What she needed was a surety and knew it was impossible. "It occurs to me that while we have known one another all our lives, we don't really *know* each other," she said.

"I believe that is probably common," he said. "Especially with arranged marriages."

"When you first brought up the subject of marriage, I felt obliged to say yes immediately. I know my parents would be grateful and relieved. Penny would most likely be able to have her come-out, and I could attend. She wants me to be there with all of her heart, and I yearn to watch my little sister dance at a ball for the first time. It is true the starchiest ladies of the ton will never forget. I do not care a snap for them, but I am concerned about the consequences for you."

"You need not worry about me."

"Gentlemen gossip," she said.

He shrugged. "You are trying to make a point, are you not?"

"If others know a man has been cuckolded, is he the object of derision?"

"Yes, if it's blatant. What does that have to do with us?"

"It is quite possible that others will speak disdainfully of your marriage to me."

"If any man dared, I'd slap a glove in his face," he gritted out.

"How many times will you have to defend me?" she said.

"Are you trying to persuade me *not* to marry you? It seems you are looking for reasons to discourage me. Believe me, no man will ever question your honor or mine if he expects to live."

"Colin, I worry because I have a notorious reputation. Others will gossip about me."

"They would never dare insult my wife," he said vehemently.

"Not in your presence," she said.

"Damn it, Angeline. You are pushing me away."

She didn't want to say it, but she knew it was necessary. "Colin, men said things to me when I was in Paris. Awful things. I am not exaggerating about my reputation. If we do not discuss it now, it may come between us." She feared it would anyway.

"No man will come between us unless he has a death wish. Now, will you allow me to make a proper proposal of marriage to you?"

Panic set in and her lungs constricted. She'd made a bad decision once before. "There is no rush. We have three weeks remaining until the house party ends. I think we should use that time to learn more about each other. Meanwhile, we can contact the architect I mentioned to you earlier. I'm sure he would make the journey in a prompt manner." It was so much easier to focus on practical matters.

"There is a problem," he said. "I can't very well hire a man and keep the engagement a secret. My father would question why I was spending money but making no effort whatsoever to hunt for a wife."

She sighed. "I so had my heart set on it."

"I'd rather hoped it would be me that made your heart thump, but perhaps I'd better use the three weeks to woo you." He set his arm around her shoulders.

She inhaled his scent and everything inside of her wanted to be closer to him, but she wasn't ready to go farther. "Did I give you leave to be familiar?"

"Not in so many words, but your dreamy sighs as you looked upon my fair countenance encouraged me."

She laughed. "You are being ridiculous again."

"I'm only trying to be romantic, but it seems my almost-fiancée is not."

She wondered if his witty remarks hid his own misgivings about the marriage. When she turned to him, he cupped her cheek. "So soft."

He had the sort of face that made women stop and stare. His chiseled square jaw, cleft chin, and straight nose were both beautiful and masculine at the same time. There was perfect symmetry to his face, but it was his eyes that drew her.

He angled his head and kissed her so gently, she sighed afterward. Whatever fears she might have had seemed to float away.

Then he kissed her again, and this time, he kissed her like a starved man. He licked her lips and when she opened for him, he slid his tongue inside and pulled her closer. She was powerless to deny him; no, she didn't want to deny him. She wrapped her arms around his shoulders and wanted to be closer to him. The scent of him wrapped around her, a seductive potion that made her forget all of her misgivings.

His breathing was harsh and labored as he nuzzled her neck. When he cupped her breast, she drew in a ragged breath at the pleasurable sensations. Her nipples ached as he palmed her through the thin muslin of her bodice.

He fumbled at the back of her gown, and she felt cool air on her back. When he pushed her sleeves down her arms, she thought of denying him. He circled his thumbs around her nipples, and she bit her lip to keep from begging him not to stop. She was neither afraid nor disgusted the way she'd been when Brentmoor tried to fondle her. She'd always pushed him away, and now she was glad that she'd never let him, because he'd never cared about her.

Thoughts of her former fiancé fled as Colin lowered his head and circled his tongue around her nipple. She clutched the back of his head, her fingers threading through his thick, curly hair. When he suckled her, her head fell back, and she wanted more of him.

"I knew you would be beautiful, but you have surpassed my every expectation."

She felt as if she'd drunk too much champagne. The desire still lingered, making her a bit lethargic, but he pulled her sleeves up and hooked the back of her gown. She was aware of dampness between her thighs and a yearning for more of the pleasurable sensations he'd excited in her.

He smiled a little as he gazed at her. "I find myself amazed and humbled by your response. Whatever else may come, I think in this, we will be very compatible."

His words sounded too good to be true. Yet she was torn between wanting to believe him and her knowledge that he desperately needed a wife in order to keep Sommerall. Worse, she knew that she would never have even considered marrying him if she weren't so worried about her sister's come-out.

God in heaven, how could she marry a man simply to ensure her sister got her heart's desire? But how could she not do everything in her power to restore her honor and that of her family? She had brought scandal upon them, and she owed it to them to do whatever she could to restore her family's honor.

But she was afraid, more afraid than of being an independent spinster. At least that way she would never have to worry about exposing herself to society or finding herself awake in a cold, deserted bed while her husband found comfort elsewhere after having secured the property he wanted. There was no question that if she accepted, this would be a marriage of convenience, and Angeline knew it would be foolhardy to hope that love and affection would follow the way it had for Lord Chadwick and Margaret. Their marriage may have started as a convenience, but they were one of the rare, lucky couples who had fallen in love.

Angeline couldn't allow herself to even consider the possibility that tender feelings might develop in this marriage. She had to be pragmatic, and that meant accepting an offer of marriage that she was far from confident about, but it wasn't as if she had better choices. That thought alone made her feel horrible, because every instinct inside of her shouted that she was selling herself for a season in London for her sister.

God help her, she would do anything, even marry, to make sure her sister had a fairy-tale come-out ball.

When footsteps sounded, Angeline straightened her neckline and squared her shoulders. Agnes appeared at the door. "My lady, the kitchen hearth is sound. I took the liberty of scouring the pots and pans with sand." The scullery maid lowered her eyes. "John awaits on the drive."

"Thank you, Agnes," Colin said. "Tell John we will be only a few minutes."

"Yes, your lordship." She bobbed a curtsy and disappeared.

"Angeline, is all well with you?"

She thought he must be worried about what had transpired. "Yes, I'm well and ready to depart." The heady sensations of his kisses and touches had worn off quickly as her worries had taken over. He'd offered marriage, the one thing she'd known could reverse all of the bad things that had happened. At first, it had seemed like a dream, but it was not. Quite possibly, it could end in a nightmare for her.

He'd agreed to grant her more time to give her answer when the house party ended. She wondered if he was as reluctant as she was about this marriage. At least there was no question about their motives for marrying. They both knew exactly why they were doing this. But could they build a lifetime on a sham marriage?

She would reconcile herself to the marriage, make the best of it, and be grateful. Because Providence had provided her with a chance to redeem herself—a gift to her family.

They would marry, and she would be able to attend her sister's debut. There would still be whispers, but once she was married to Colin, no one would dare openly cut her. The combined strength of both their families would help as well.

Could it really be that easy? She hoped with all of her heart that it would, but only time would tell.

Yet her thoughts were of her family, not of him. She worried that he'd made a decision based on hearing her sad tale, but he would benefit as well. God willing, he would not regret his decision. There were three weeks left for both of them to figure out if they could forge a life together, one that could bring them happiness for a lifetime.

But would three weeks be enough?

It was a daunting prospect. She wanted to believe, more than anything, that they would fall in love like his father and Margaret had. But she must not count on it. She'd been disappointed and humiliated once before. The scars inside her had yet to heal, but she didn't have the luxury of waiting. There would be no other opportunities.

A voice deep inside warned her that a marriage based on winning a property and salvaging her reputation was insufficient for a lifetime, but it was more than she'd thought possible. From the moment she'd broken her engagement to Brentmoor, she'd shut off her dreams of love and forever-after happiness. Now all she hoped for was contentment.

But would there be? No matter how kind he had been to her, she could not forget that he was a notorious rake. She'd heard ladies whispering immoderately about him in the retiring rooms at balls, and she had seen him walking out into dark gardens with scandalously dressed ladies at balls.

Her instincts told her he was different. He'd shown sympathy for her and made her feel better about herself for refusing Brentmoor's insistence on intimacies. But she couldn't forget Brentmoor's attentive concerns when she'd first met him. Colin was different. He was.

Yet she'd had to persuade herself the same way she'd done with Brentmoor.

After dinner that evening, the ladies had repaired to the drawing room while the men drank their port. Angeline was aghast to learn her mother and Margaret were making lists for the party they were planning to ease her back into society. She had to stop them somehow, because it might well end up in disaster.

"Mama, Margaret, I beg you to forget this party for

now. I am not ready to face society. I am simply unable to entertain the thought. Perhaps the time will come, but I am too uncomfortable with the idea right now."

"Angeline, by spring, you will be ready," the duchess said.

"Please do not move forward yet. I'm not ready for this step. I hope you understand and will abide by my wishes. It would be a mistake at this time."

"Of course, dear," the marchioness said. "We've no intention of forcing you, but Charlotte's letter sounded so positive."

"Charlotte has been a good friend to me for many years, but I believe she would counsel me to wait. I think it is for the best."

Margaret turned her attention to the duchess. "Perhaps we should wait. Angeline is sure to receive many invitations. It would make for an easier entry back into society."

They still did not understand, but she had no intention of elaborating. Her mother and Margaret were grasping at straws, and Angeline found it unbearable. Then it occurred to her that she could divert them. "Perhaps we could discuss the girls' debuts."

When Penny heard mention of a debut, she and the twins left the pianoforte to join them.

"Angeline, tell us about your debut," Penny said.

A lump formed in her throat. As an elder sister, she ought to have brought it up earlier, but that was before she had been afraid to encourage Penny.

"Oh, yes, please do," Bianca said. "I wish to hear about every moment."

Angeline recollected standing still in the receiving line, waiting for the first guests to arrive. Silly thoughts had flitted through her mind, and she'd had to stifle a giggle. Had she really ever been so young and naïve?

"Tell us about your gown," Bernadette said.

"At first I thought it a bit plain. It was white with a high waist and made of beautiful lace. In the candlelight it was gorgeous," she said. "The best part was that Mama relented and allowed me to have white slippers with scarlet stripes."

"Do you still have them?" Bianca asked.

"They're packed away in a trunk for safekeeping at Deerfield."

"Mama, will we go to London and have gowns made up by a modiste?" Bernadette said.

Margaret smiled. "Yes, you shall have new gowns, slippers, bonnets, and stockings."

"We shall have to pour through all the fashion books," Bianca said.

"Girls, you must practice at the pianoforte, as you will be called upon to exhibit after you debut," the duchess said. "You must attend to your dancing lessons as well."

"I shall probably make a cake of myself," Bianca said.

"We always do," Bernadette said, laughing. "We had better pay attention to Mama's lessons in deportment."

Penny hunched her shoulders. "I fear I'll make no impression at all."

"We won't let you be a wallflower," Bernadette said.

"Exactly," Bianca said. "We will not let you out of our sight, unless a handsome swain asks you to dance."

"My palms are damp just thinking about dancing with a boy," Penny said. "Angeline, you will be there? I cannot do this without my wonderful sister."

"You will do very well." She met her mother's eyes

briefly and looked away. If she were a better daughter, she would confess today's events to her mother. But she could not do it, because she didn't want to raise her mother's hopes, and if in the next three weeks, she or Colin determined that they would not suit, it would be best if their families never knew.

The marquess finished his port and regarded his son. "You were at Sommerall today?"

"Yes. I wish to complete my inventory of the items in the attic. I covered the few paintings I discovered and set aside those items you might find useful. If you are amenable to sending a wagon, I've put items in crates that the tenants and servants might find useful."

The marquess arched his brows. "Well, I did not expect you to labor in the attic. Servants could have accomplished the task."

"They would not have known what was valuable and what was not. I found correspondence that I left on your desk. You were out shooting."

Wycoff narrowed his eyes. "My daughter was with you?"

"Yes, she helped. The scullery maid attended us again." Although Agnes had not shadowed them, he did not divulge that information. He wanted to reassure Wycoff, especially after hearing what had transpired with Brentmoor.

Colin had intended only to give her a relatively chaste kiss, but the moment their lips met, he felt as if his blood were on fire. He imagined taking her on walks and sharing heated kisses, but he should not take advantage of her. If at the end of three weeks she changed her mind, it would prove dashed awkward when they parted ways because of the long-standing friendship of their parents.

He turned his attention to his father. "Agnes is a resourceful servant. She doesn't wait for orders; she makes suggestions. You might mention it to Margaret."

"I will," the marquess said. "Have you decided that marriage is too high a price for Sommerall?"

Wycoff rose. "I'll give you privacy."

Colin noted Wycoff's wan expression and slumped shoulders as he trudged out of the dining room.

The marquess sighed. "Wycoff's spirits plunged again after hearing Margaret and the duchess exclaiming over that letter. I mentioned to Margaret that it might be best to leave off the plans for his sake, but she was adamant that the letter proved there was hope for Angeline."

Colin circled the rim of his glass with his finger. He figured silence was for the best.

"I've thought of telling Wycoff to make an effort to rouse himself from this melancholia."

"He blames himself."

The marquess narrowed his eyes. "How do you know? Even I am not privy to the details of Angeline's problems."

He'd better be careful what he said, because Angeline had spoken to him in confidence. "I assume that he does based upon his actions and his reaction to that letter Angeline received in particular."

"I suppose you're correct," the marquess said. "Now, you have not given me an answer about your intentions for Sommerall."

"I'll give you my answer when the house party ends."

His father scoffed. "I'll grant you the remaining three

weeks to give me an answer, even though I'm fairly certain you would rather give up the property than marry."

"If I did not want to take possession of Sommerall, I would have told you so immediately."

When the duke entered the drawing room, Angeline was determined to persuade him to play chess with her. She hurried to intercept him, but her father walked past her and offered his arm to Penelope. Her father set up the board and seated her sister. Angeline trudged over to the window seat and considered quitting the drawing room, but someone would likely inquire why she was leaving, and the last thing she wanted was to attract attention.

There was no doubt that her father had withdrawn his affection. It hurt so much. She had once been her father's favorite, and now he ignored her. Worse, Angeline found herself jealous of her little sister. They had always had a special bond, and of course, she shouldn't begrudge her. But her father's rejection cut like a knife in her heart.

A deep voice cut through her thoughts. "You look a hundred miles away."

She lifted her gaze to find Colin. "I suppose I am." She didn't want to tell him about her father. The pain was unimaginable, but how could she blame her father for being disappointed in her? No, *disappointment* was too weak of a word to describe what she'd done to her family.

"You seem dispirited," he said.

"It will pass." She knew it would be a long time before the aching guilt left her.

"I wish there was something I could do to cheer you," he said.

"I appreciate your concern."

His gaze turned away from her. "Is it your father who troubles you?"

She stiffened. "Why do you ask?"

"He is not himself at all," Colin said. "Have you noticed?"

She nodded, but she didn't want to discuss the issue now. The wounds were still too raw.

Colin reached between them and squeezed her hand. "I know it is difficult now, but trust that everything will come about."

She felt his gaze upon her and looked up at him.

"Everything will be well, Angeline."

She wasn't sure if his words were a promise or simply encouragement, but tonight, she needed someone to help her believe that everything would work out for her—for both of them.

"Are you afraid of me?" he said under his breath.

"No, I'm not afraid of you, but I fear that at the end of the house party you will feel obliged to marry me," she said quietly. "I beg you to be honest. I could not bear it if you felt trapped."

"You worry too much," he whispered. "You look careworn."

"I'm a little done up tonight." She didn't tell him it was because she was heartbroken that her father had snubbed her once again.

"Get some rest," he said. "You will feel better tomorrow because of it."

"Thank you, Colin." Perhaps they would be able to find happiness together, but if they were to do so, she knew it was crucial that she not compare him to Brentmoor. Colin had been honest with her about what he wanted. They both would benefit as long as they were truthful with each other.

There had been that moment when she'd questioned his reasons for asking her to marry him, but he had been completely honest and so had she. As she wearily climbed the steps, she told herself that she must do it, despite her doubts. They would manage, and while it would never be the fairy-tale love match, it was preferable to a lonely life as a spinster.

Chapter Eight

The next morning after breakfast, the marquess cleared his throat. "Bianca, Bernadette, your mother reported to me that the maid found bones in your room. Clearly that ugly dog has taken up residence with you. I made it clear that Hercules must stay in the kitchen until such time as a servant walks him. You have disobeyed me."

Colin noted his sisters' sorrowful expressions.

"Oh, Papa," Bianca said. "Hercules is scared of the banging pots. He made a puddle in the kitchen."

"Better the kitchen than the water closet," the marquess said.

Colin thought his sisters were talented enough to tread the boards onstage, but of course, ladies did not flaunt themselves. Nevertheless the twins were experts at manipulating their father. Colin ought to take lessons from his wily sisters.

"I am not finished," the marquess said. "I have noticed bite marks on the legs of the furniture. That dog is teething on chairs that cost a fortune. Either you teach that dog not to chew the furniture or he goes out in the rubbish bin."

"Your father is jesting," the marchioness said. Her attention turned to Bernadette. "Do not feed scraps to Hercules from the table. You are teaching him to be an unmannerly dog."

"That begs the question as to what constitutes a mannerly dog," the marquess said.

"One that can shake hands like Hercules," Bernadette said. "Shake, Hercules."

On command the dog put his paw in her hand, and the marquess rolled his eyes.

Everyone laughed, with the exception of Wycoff.

Cook brought out a hamper and set it on the sideboard.

The marquess frowned. "Colin, is it really necessary to spend every single day at Sommerall? I'm sure Angeline would prefer entertainment to working every day like a servant."

Colin regarded her. "I do apologize. Of course you wish to enjoy walks and drawing."

"No, I want to help at Sommerall," she said. "Today I will begin a series of sketches of how I envision the drawing room."

"Lady Angeline," the marquess said, "I'm sure you are only being polite, but it is unnecessary."

"I am committed," she said, "and it is something I enjoy. I insist."

"Angeline," the duchess said in shocked tones.

"It is quite all right," Margaret said. "I've seen some of her sketches. Angeline is very talented."

"I must admit the architect who came to Worthington Abbey was very impressed," the duchess said.

"Mama, I'm sure he was only being polite," Angeline said.

"I'm sure he was being honest," Colin said. "You are talented."

Her face grew warm. "I enjoy it very much, and I'm looking forward to sketching my visions of the drawing room at Sommerall."

The marquess turned to his son. "While Lady Angeline is slaving away with her sketches, what will you do? Nap on the sofa?"

Everyone laughed.

"John brought a ladder from the barn," Colin said. "I plan to check the outside blinds. If I'm not mistaken, some of them are tangled or broken."

Margaret rose. "The hamper is ready and Agnes is waiting. We will have our walk, and Chadwick and Wycoff will take their mud baths."

"Very funny, Margaret," the marquess said. "By the by, could you manage to lose that ugly dog during your walk?"

"Papa, no," Bianca cried.

"Your father is only teasing," Margaret said. "Chadwick, that is enough."

The marquess laughed. "We will discuss this in more detail later, Margaret."

"Wycoff, it's about time you bagged a bird. I can't kill them all by myself," the marquess said.

"I'm not up for it."

The duchess laid her hand on his. "Go along, dear. It will do you good."

An uncomfortable moment passed. Finally, Wycoff assented. "Very well."

Colin met Angeline's gaze. Her father was in a very bad way. He hoped another day out shooting would help. Perhaps his father would press Wycoff to make more of an effort after all. Whether it would do any good was questionable.

After they boarded the carriage and it rolled off, Colin moved over to Angeline's bench. "Give me a kiss."

"I beg your pardon?"

"We're affianced now. Well, secretly." He plucked her sketchbook out of her hand and set it aside.

"It is only a trial engagement to see if we suit," she said.

Devilment showed in his eyes. "Well, since it is a trial, we should practice so that we can perfect our kisses."

"You need no practice. You are clearly an expert."

His smile stretched across his face. "Like my kisses, do you?"

"They are...tolerable."

He pulled her onto his lap and she shrieked.

"Good thing it's so noisy on the road. Otherwise, John and Agnes might suspect I'm having my wicked way with you."

"I might point out that there is plenty of room on the seat," she said. "So I'll avail myself of the space."

He clamped his arms around her. "Please, can I have a kiss? Just one?"

"Very well." She pecked him on the mouth, thinking to escape, but she'd underestimated him. He plucked at her lips and she opened for him without a thought in her head.

The sweep of his tongue mesmerized her. She grew a little bolder and experimented touching her tongue to his, and when he groaned, she knew he liked it. She wanted so much more from him, but their wraps and gloves prevented them from going farther. It was probably for the best. Then his hands burrowed inside her cape. "We must not," she said.

"I know, but I yearn to touch you and for you to touch me."

Beneath her bottom, she could feel the evidence of his desire.

"I beg your pardon. Have I shocked you?" he said.

Her face grew hot. "A little."

He wrapped his arms around her again. "I am undone."

When he captured her lips again, she opened for him as if it were the most natural thing in the world, but in truth, she could not deny that his erotic kisses and strong arms made her feel wanted and wonderful.

Their combined breaths frosted in the carriage. "Are you too cold?" he asked.

"Only a little."

He rubbed his nose against hers. When he kissed her again, she opened her mouth for him, and he slid his tongue inside. She suspected he was imitating what he really wanted. He was so hard against her, and she understood his need, but they weren't really engaged. "Colin? We had better stop."

He tore his mouth away. "God almighty, I want you badly."

"We can't. Not here."

"I know. I would not," he said. "I am a gentleman, and it is cold."

"I am a lady—well not so much in the carriage."

"How do you feel about a trip to Gretna Green?"

She laughed. "I think you have lost what few wits you have," she said. "I know you are jesting, but we agreed to three weeks. It's so little time for us to learn more about each other. We should not waste it."

"I know." He paused. "If we marry, we will probably set the house on fire."

She laughed. "I like that you make me laugh."

"Kiss me instead."

She opened her mouth for him, and she was lost in the sensation of his lips and tongue and the sweep of his hand over her breast.

"We have to stop," she said. "We should talk about things that matter."

His breathing was as labored as hers. "Can we get married now? I don't want to wait."

"You just want to bed me," she said.

"So do you," he said. "Angeline, this part is important."

"That is why we have to stop," she said, "because I've never wanted a man more."

He set his forehead against hers. "You have no idea what I want to do to you."

"Tell me," she said. Her breathing sounded labored to her own ears.

He captured her hand and guided it to his chest. "I want your hands all over me."

Had she just stopped breathing? "Do not tempt me."

"I have too many layers of clothes, and so do you," he said.

"That may be for the best; otherwise, we're liable to do bad things in the carriage."

"We could do that," he said, "but you're a virgin."

"How do you know?"

"You aren't?"

She pushed him. "Of course I am."

He laughed and hugged her tightly. "It is too cold anyway."

She leaned her forehead against his shoulder.

"Is it always like this?" she said.

"Like how?" he said, his voice rough.

"Like a craving, one that is forbidden and so hard to resist."

"No, it isn't always this strong." He cupped her cheek. "This is special."

"Are you just saying that so I will touch you again?"

He looked into her eyes and his expression was solemn. "No."

Eventually, their breathing slowed.

When the carriage rolled around the drive, she adjusted her bodice and closed her cape over her gown. "Now we must behave."

"Drat," he said.

She gave him an exasperated look. "Go find the ladder. I'll have Agnes clean kitchen utensils. "I'll be in the drawing room making sketches. When you get hungry, come find me and we'll have luncheon."

She watched him move the ladder along the house. John stayed with him. Angeline walked upstairs with her sketchbook and sat on the sofa. She envisioned a gold-framed mirror above the sideboard. Then she walked to the windows where Colin was hammering something. She smiled. He was no dandy, and clearly not afraid to get his hands dirty. Standing there, she realized that a long balcony just below the French windows would make the perfect place for flowers and maybe chairs for guests to look at the stars in summertime. She sat cross-legged on the floor and drew her design quickly so that she wouldn't lose the idea. Then she rose and walked to the stairwell and ascended it to the highest point. She imagined a three-tiered chandelier suspended before a series of Palladian windows. It would look very dramatic at night. She thought guests arriving for a dinner party would be impressed. When she made a quick sketch, she drew figures of gentlemen and ladies looking upward.

Her heartbeat quickened as she hurried down the stairs to the dining table. Fortunately, it was well covered and the chairs had no cushions. The chairs and table were mahogany and elegant. They would not need to replace them, but the walls did nothing for the space. She had a daring idea. Rather than walls, she could set off the dining room with four ionic columns and a beautiful Axminster carpet for color. Mind, she would need to consult and review samples in design books. She ascended the stairs, sat on the sofa, and started drawing her idea for the dining room.

Angeline had no idea how much time had passed when she heard footsteps on the stairs. Her excitement mounted, and she met Colin at the door. "Come, I wish to show you my sketches."

"Very well." He sat beside her on the sofa.

"This is my favorite. Do you see how dramatic the Palladian windows will be at night with the light of a chandelier?"

"I imagine so," he said.

"I have so many ideas, but this one is my favorite."

"There are no walls."

"Exactly. Is it not daring and yet elegant? I know without color it is probably difficult to envision. Oh, and I thought of something else I'm sure you will like. It is a balcony built all along the south façade. Guests could sit in chairs with small tables to watch the stars. What do you think?"

"I think it is fantastic and fanciful," he said. "I would never be able to imagine something like this."

"I've no idea of the cost, but I could write to the architect, Mr. Rotherby, or perhaps you..." She trailed off, realizing her mistake. "I am sorry. Obviously, you cannot move forward, but I do believe you will inherit."

He cleared his throat. "Angeline, you are very talented." He met her gaze and she could see the discomfort in his eyes. "It is still my father's house, and I'm in danger of losing the property."

"Do forgive me," she said, closing the sketchbook. "I always get carried away with my sketches and ideas. I just wanted to show them to you." She rose and shook out her skirts, and naturally he stood as well.

She pasted on her society smile. "Shall we eat luncheon in the breakfast parlor?"

"Yes, I'm hungry, thank you."

He offered his arm and escorted her downstairs. Her arms were chilled. Their easy camaraderie had disappeared, because she had all but spoken on the assumption that the marriage would take place. She had not made a conscious decision and certainly had not thought it through before speaking. Instead, she'd allowed her enthusiasm to bubble up, and now she worried he would feel obliged to propose.

She felt foolish and realized the difficulty of their decision to have a trial engagement. At the time, it had seemed like the perfect solution. The problem was that they were in a constant state of uncertainty. Yet, they had succumbed to desire. She had willingly sat on his lap, let him touch her, and touched him in return just as if they were married or truly affianced. But nothing was decided. Everything was contingent on something else. His father might sell the property when the house party ended. All of their clearing and sorting in the attic would help the servants and tenants, but there was a chance neither of them would ever benefit from the work they had done.

By the end of the house party, either one of them might decide they would not suit. They had both agreed they could easily part without rancor or wounded feelings. Now she realized they must have been daft to think such a plan would work.

There was nothing for it except to brazen it out and pretend that nothing was awry. She served their usual luncheon on the plates while Colin opened a bottle of claret. He sat beside her, and it struck her how quickly they had already formed habits here. But like their trial engagement, it was nothing more than an illusion.

When he handed her a glass of wine, she sipped, but she only nibbled at the chicken, because she felt anxious. Because of her incautious words, their comfortable friendship had suddenly become awkward. She hated that it had because she was beginning to have feelings for him, and he surely had no strong attachment to her. It was her responsibility to say something to break this chilled atmosphere.

"I do apologize for my foolish enthusiasm. I'm generally a very practical person, but when it comes to my designs, my imagination runs away with me, and I start to prattle. I'm sure you were amused by it."

"I was impressed with your ideas. They are unique. You should not feel badly about your enthusiasm."

"It is so impractical," she said. "I can't very well make over the drawing room at Deerfield every year." *Please do not think I meant to urge you to propose.*

He set his glass aside. "If you enjoy it, your designs need not be practical or have a specific purpose."

She released a relieved breath and changed the subject. "Are the blinds outside in bad shape?"

He nodded. "They all need to be replaced. John said it shouldn't cost a fortune and advised me to be wary of anyone trying to charge me more because I'm a 'nob.'"

She laughed a little and started putting the food away. "I haven't even checked on Agnes."

"It probably isn't necessary. She's not the type who needs constant instruction."

Angeline nodded. "She sees what needs to be done and makes recommendations. I'll go check on her progress just in case."

"If she is finished, we can return to Deerfield," he said.

"Yes, of course," she said. "Excuse me."

Colin rubbed his temples. She'd taken him by surprise. Clearly she'd been inspired and thrilled with her ideas. She was very talented, but when she'd mentioned writing to the architect, he'd been shocked. It was as if she'd completely forgotten he didn't own Sommerall.

Perhaps she'd expected him to propose today, but

she'd said that she wanted to use the time left to them to learn more about each other before making a final decision. It occurred to him that he ought to make the offer regardless, but if he did it today, she would think he felt obliged, and then everything would get bloody complicated. He didn't want that to happen.

He rose and walked to the kitchen. When he pushed the door open, Agnes gasped, immediately lowered her eyes, and bobbed a curtsy. "Beggin' your pardon, my lord."

"It's not necessary, Agnes, and I'm sorry for startling you. Angeline, if you are finished here, would you please accompany me to the drawing room?"

She lifted her chin. "Yes, of course."

He noted her resolute expression and figured she was embarrassed. While he'd known her all of his life, he'd not *really* known her until they had begun work at Sommerall. He'd discovered she was proud and very sensitive, something she hid beneath a haughty mien.

Angeline said nothing as he led her up the stairs to the drawing room. When she started to sit in a chair, he shook his head. "Please, sit with me."

"Very well."

He took her hand in his. "I feel awful for dampening your enthusiasm."

She did not look at him. "There is no reason for you to feel awful."

"It's embarrassing. I've asked you for a trial engagement, and yet all I have to offer is a house in need of repair that isn't in my possession and may never be."

She was silent for a long space of time. "I've wanted to be positive for your sake all this time, but I became so enthused and sure that you would inherit." She looked at him. "I beg your pardon for making matters uncomfortable, but I think we are making a mistake."

"What do you mean?"

"We're doing this for all the wrong reasons."

"It wasn't so very long ago that you defended my father's and stepmother's marriage of convenience. Will you abandon our agreement to a trial engagement before it barely starts?"

"How can a marriage based on a property and restoring my reputation work?"

"Angeline, most marriages are based on convenience. You know it to be true, but you are looking for reasons to halt it. Perhaps I'm wrong, but I think you're afraid. After what you've been through, it is perfectly understandable.

"I don't want to rush into this, even though we are clearly compatible in at least one respect," he said, smiling a little. "We've known each other all of our lives, but there is much we don't know. I want you to be honest with me, and I'll be honest with you. If at any point you decide that you do not want to move forward, you must tell me. This should not be about obligation, because it is a lifetime decision. Do you agree?"

"Yes," she said.

"If Agnes has completed her chores and you are ready, we should probably return to Deerfield."

Her silence on the drive back exasperated him. "Angeline, I would much rather you tell me what is troubling you than have you refuse to speak to me. It is frustrating. If I have offended you, then tell me."

"You haven't offended me."

"Then tell me what troubles you," he said.

"I know the reality of my situation, and still I find myself wishing I could change what happened."

He gathered her in his arms. She tried to push him away, but he hushed her. "Angeline, I won't deny that your circumstances were difficult, but the worst is over. All will be well."

"How can you say that to me? You asked for honesty, well, so do I. Don't tell me things will be fine when they clearly are not. My mother is deluded enough to think a party will restore my poor reputation, my father won't speak to me, and my little sister may not have a come-out ball because of me. Do not tell me that all will be well when you know what I face. At least respect me enough to do that."

"I do respect you," he said. "I respect you for refusing that bastard who tried to coerce you into intimacies. I respect you for holding your head up high at that ball where that bastard betrayed you, and I respect you for being a clever and caring woman. Every word is my honest opinion of you. If I think so highly of you, and I know Margaret does as well, then believe that you deserve happiness."

"Be honest. Do you feel obliged to make our temporary engagement a real one?" she asked. "Please don't lie to me."

"No, I do not feel obliged, and I hope you do not, either," he said. "To be honest, I think all of this is about your embarrassment, but there is no reason for it. We agreed to a three-week courtship, one that is known only to us," he said. "It will be awkward if one or both of us decides at the end of three weeks that we don't suit, but that is the chance we take. You are free at any time to end it, and so am I. If that isn't acceptable, we should end it now. I am willing to go forward, but are you?"

"Yes, I am." Even though it worried her. What would happen after they married? They would not even be considering marriage if not for his father's decree and her need to restore her good reputation.

Angeline was afraid of what the future held in such a marriage, but she knew it would be the right thing to do for her family. She had only two choices: spinsterhood or a marriage of convenience. At least the latter afforded her a measure of respectability.

There were still three weeks for them to make this decision. She could not imagine that she would change her mind, because she owed it to her family and she wasn't likely to get another chance.

But it wasn't her decision alone. How would she feel if he told her that he had reconsidered and could not marry her? Dear God, what had they gotten themselves into?

Chapter Nine

Wycoff was in better spirits after having bagged a bird. At dinner earlier, Colin had noted that Angeline had focused her attention on her father. When her father proposed a game of chess after his port, Angeline's face lit up like a dozen candles. He was glad to see her happiness and hoped it would last.

When the ladies withdrew, Wycoff and the marquess talked endlessly about the shooting today. Colin said nothing, as his thoughts were elsewhere. He wondered why so many had believed Brentmoor's ugly words about Angeline. Then he realized her mother's friends had given her bad advice. When the duchess had taken her daughter to the Continent, she'd inadvertently signaled that her daughter had been guilty of Brentmoor's coarse accusations. However, Colin realized that Brentmoor's return could well be advantageous. If enough high-ranking friends spread the word that she'd been falsely accused of something that had never happened, her good name could be restored. He could not be sure that others would champion her, but it was worth the effort.

He would say nothing for now, but it was important. The first time they had spoken about a marriage of convenience, she'd said that she felt obliged to accept his offer for the sake of her family, but she ought to have a choice. If she declined his offer of marriage, however, he would probably lose Sommerall. He wanted the property badly, but he was in danger of losing it. He remembered her words: *We're doing this for all the wrong reasons.* It was too easy to imagine the marriage souring, because it was based on his motivation to keep the property and her wish to help her family. But he could not let Sommerall fall into a stranger's hands. Damn it all, he had to figure out a way to ensure he gained possession.

"You are uncharacteristically silent," the marquess said to him.

"Just thinking."

"How to outwit me for Sommerall?"

Wycoff laughed. "Doesn't every bachelor have cold feet?"

"Right." Colin finished his port.

"You are in the doldrums," the marquess said. "By the by, how did you find things at Sommerall?"

Wycoff rose. "Finish your port, Chadwick. I promised Angeline a game of chess. She will no doubt trounce me."

"Tell my wife we'll be along shortly."

After Wycoff departed, the marquess poured both of them another port. "He is a shell of the man he used to be."

"Has he ever told you what happened?"

"He told me very little, but I suspect you know."

"Angeline told me in confidence." He sighed. "I figured she had no one to confide in, so I listened."

"How bad is it?"

"Did Margaret ever speak to the duchess?" he asked.

"When it happened, she told Margaret how the vile man deceived them all, but the duchess was understandably vexed at the time. I think their journey to Paris was a mistake. It only made it appear that Angeline was guilty of something."

"I agree." Colin sipped his port and set it aside. "It was very bad. She told me in confidence, but I will say this much. She's innocent of the disgusting claims that Brentmoor made."

"Son, what did he claim? I only ask because I've been racking my brains how to help her, but I can't if I don't know what I'm up against."

He told his father how Brentmoor had pressed her for intimacies and how they'd been seen kissing out of doors in a dark area. "He probably wanted to make sure she felt guilty enough to marry him. She admitted that she'd had doubts. After she cried off, he must have been bent on revenge. Her friend's brother revealed that Brentmoor claimed he'd lain with her multiple times."

"Hell," the marquess said.

"Others believed it because she'd been spotted in a compromising embrace with him in the unlit area of a garden. I might add he pressed her constantly. Of course she was seen, something he probably planned, to ensure she would feel too guilty not to marry him. She's innocent of everything."

"When the house party ends, I will contact friends," the marquess said. "We need supporters."

"I'll write to Harry. His mother is famous for her at-homes."

"I'm not sure that's a good idea. I've heard it's nothing but tittle-tattle," the marquess said.

"Harry would do anything for me," he said. "As I recall, his mother is fond of Angeline. I'll see if I can pull in Bellingham. He's got more influence than anyone, except for you."

"Hah. But I agree. Bellingham is a brilliant politician. Ruthless son of a bitch, but he's loyal to those he respects. I've half a mind to start straightaway, but that would only raise questions."

"Agreed," Colin said. "After the house party, we can get support from friends. By the time the season begins, we will hopefully clear her name. Then we'll see the bastard drummed out of every club and blacken his name."

The marquess narrowed his eyes. "No offense, but why are you so hell bent on this mission? The two of you have never been on the best of terms."

"It's a point of honor," he said. "And Brentmoor has none."

Colin and his father returned to the drawing room. When Colin saw Angeline putting away the chess pieces, he poured himself a brandy and waited for her to finish before approaching her. He needed to speak to her about Sommerall and ensure she knew what to expect. It had become a daily journey for them, but he had to be realistic about the time they were spending there. As much as he enjoyed her company and the privacy Sommerall afforded them, he had to think about her first and foremost. She'd been through hell, and the last thing they both needed was for their families to discover that they were spending time at Sommerall when there was nothing more they could do until and unless the marquess granted the property to Colin.

After she put the game away, he made himself wait for a moment so that he wouldn't appear so anxious. That was a very real issue for them. They had to be careful and make sure that they were not inadvertently creating expectations with their families.

He caught her eye, and then he walked over to the window seat that the twins and Penny had recently vacated. He swirled his brandy and stretched out his legs. A few minutes later, Angeline stopped to look at Margaret's needlework. Obviously she was commenting about it. He took a slow drink of brandy and waited. Not long after, she joined him on the window seat. "I assume you wish to speak to me," she said.

"Clever of you, but I'm not surprised."

"Do you wish to play backgammon?"

"No, I wish to talk without distractions."

She frowned. "This sounds ominous."

"It isn't, but we have no more business at Sommerall."

"What do you mean? There is much work to be done. It needs new carpets, new shutters, updated furnishings, painting, paper hangings, and a new runner for the stairs."

"I've no doubt that all you've mentioned needs attention," he said, "but I cannot spend a farthing on a property that I do not own and may never own. We have reached the limits of what can be done."

She looked at her clasped hands in her lap. "Well, I am disappointed, but I ought to have seen this coming. I've known all along about your father's decree. I still think he ought to cede the property to you, but I know it is none of my affair."

"I appreciate all that you've done so far, Angeline. I enjoyed your company there, but we will simply have to find other ways to talk about our engagement."

"We will have almost no privacy," she said. "If we go for a walk, the others will join us. If we decide to ride, everyone else will decide to come along. If we play a game indoors, others will stop to watch and comment. Even now we must speak under our breath so that no one hears us."

"We are fortunate to have had time alone. Now we must become inventive without appearing furtive."

"How are we to do that?"

"We have to rise very early. I'm no lark, but we will arrange to meet at six o'clock in the morning. It is the only time we can ensure privacy."

"It is better than nothing," she said. "I am disappointed about Sommerall. There is so much I wanted to accomplish there."

"Do you want to meet tomorrow?" he asked.

"Yes, but where?" she said. "Never mind. I forgot Penny asked to stay with me tonight."

"Why does she want to sleep with you?"

"She likes to be near me. It started after we returned from Paris. She has begun to relax, now that she knows we will not leave England again, but when she grows anxious, she wants to sleep near me."

"Day after tomorrow, then, at six o'clock. No one will stir at that hour. I'll meet you at the back door. Then we'll walk out together."

"It feels as if we're sneaking off," she said.

"Don't think of it that way," he said. "We are just seeking privacy to talk."

After breakfast the next morning, the marquess turned to Colin. "You are not planning to journey to Sommerall today, are you?"

"No, I believe we have gone as far as we can at this point."

"I have a business issue I wish to discuss with you. Meet me in my study in a quarter of an hour," the marquess said.

"I will," Colin said. He wasn't sure what his father wanted, but he'd find out soon enough.

"We have yet to see your sketches, Angeline," Margaret said. "You must show us your plans."

"They are not really plans. The sketches are rather whimsical and impractical." She bit her lip.

Colin remembered her excitement and felt a bit badly about it.

Everyone rose and started filing out, but Colin held back with Angeline. "I wish we could spend time alone, but I have a duty."

"I'll take the girls and Hercules for a walk. We might as well enjoy the sunshine while it lasts," Angeline said.

Colin briefly touched her hand. "Perhaps we can ride this afternoon if you wish."

"I would be delighted," she said.

He hoped that they would not be shadowed by everyone else, but he resigned himself to the fact that their ride would likely be a group activity. They couldn't even go off by themselves without raising suspicion about their relationship. He wanted to keep it as private as possible, but it was far more difficult now that they no longer had Sommerall as their refuge.

Fifteen minutes later, Colin walked into his father's study and closed the door.

"Be seated," the marquess said.

"I expect you wish to discuss who we should contact to gain support for Angeline."

"Not at this time," he said. "Faraday wishes to see Sommerall again. He has another prospect in mind, but he wants to look over Sommerall once more. I plan to meet him there in one hour, and I want you to attend."

Colin gripped the arms of the chair. "I don't see the point in my presence. I have nothing to add. My wishes haven't changed, and I know yours have not changed, either."

"I want you to see it from his perspective."

"Why?"

"I have my reasons. I requested Ames to have the carriage ready. We will depart now."

He almost refused, but his father had something up his sleeve. Colin nodded and followed his father to the carriage.

The marquess walked about the ground floor and headed into the anteroom. "It's immaculate, but the carpet is faded badly."

"The shutters were left open," Colin said. "The ones in the breakfast parlor are also faded."

"Otherwise, the room is immaculate."

"Angeline directed Agnes to clean all the rooms."

"I mentioned to Margaret that the scullery maid ought to be promoted." He tramped into the breakfast parlor. "I see what you mean about the rugs."

"I imagine the tenants might want them," Colin said. "There are also crates of items that are of no use to us. They are stored properly in the attic. I imagine the servants and the tenants might make use of them."

"I'm surprised you thought of it," the marquess said.

"It was Angeline's suggestion."

The marquess wandered into the study. "Another faded rug." He walked to the desk. "I forgot all about this inkstand. Clever design."

"You should take it," Colin said.

The marquess shook his head. "I think not."

Colin supposed his father associated it with his first marriage.

"Do you want to survey the kitchen? It's in good working order according to the maid, Agnes."

"God, no. Why would I care about it?"

"Faraday might."

"Hopefully he won't think of it. Let's have a look upstairs."

Colin took him into the drawing room. "Angeline said it needs something. I think she called it paperings or some such."

"Don't look to me for help," the marquess said. "The ceiling is in good order. The carpet is in decent shape here."

"That's because the shutters were closed in here," Colin said.

"Let's see the bedchambers," the marquess said.

He walked into the second one. "My old shaving mirror. I used to put a dab of soap on your cheek when you watched the valet shave me. You would use your finger like a razor."

Colin huffed. "I remember."

.The marquess sighed. "It was long ago." He gazed about the room and walked to the connecting door. Then he paused. "Is it in good order?"

"Yes." His father evidently did not want to walk into his mother's room. "There is nothing of a personal nature in there—or in any of the other chambers."

The marquess walked out into the corridor, and then he paused at the closed door of the nursery. He started to reach for the door and dropped his hand. "Did you go inside?"

He clenched his jaw. "Yes, but I do not advise it."

The marquess inhaled. Then he opened the door, strode inside, and halted abruptly.

Colin swallowed hard. They'd forgotten to cover the cradle.

"Ah, hell." His father took out a handkerchief and blotted his eyes.

Colin set his hand on his father's shoulder. He could feel his father shaking.

The marquess blew his nose and exhaled. "After all these years, I didn't expect it would still have the power to wound me."

"I understand," Colin said.

"I've seen enough. Faraday can explore on his own when he arrives."

They went downstairs and waited more than an hour in the study.

"I expect he isn't interested enough," the marquess said. "We might as well depart."

Colin pulled the drapes closed over the window. They walked out into the great hall just as the clatter of wheels and horse hooves sounded.

"Seems he saw fit to make an appearance." The marquess folded his handkerchief and put it away.

The knocker rapped. "I'll see him in," Colin said.

He expected a vulgar bumped up chit, but the man before him was young and well dressed. Faraday was clearly a gentleman.

"Please come in," he said. "I'm Ravenshire."

The marquess met him. "Faraday."

"I beg your pardon," Faraday said. "I was delayed by the unexpected arrival of the doctor. My wife is in expectation of a happy event, and I grew concerned when she complained of pains, but the doctor said it wasn't unusual. It is too early... Well, that's probably more than you wanted to know, but I do apologize for the delay. First-time father jitters."

"I understand," the marquess said, walking through the hall again. "I'll leave you to have a look over the house again. The study is just off that corridor," he said, pointing. "Meet my son and me there when you're done."

Faraday bowed and went off to explore.

Colin sat in a chair before the desk. His father took the chair beside him. "Faraday is having trouble making up his mind. I suggested he bring his wife this time. Women always know what they want, but obviously she wasn't well enough to attend him."

"The second visit probably means he will choose this one over the other," Colin said.

"We shall see," the marquess said. "Of course, you still have time to choose a bride and make the property yours."

Colin said nothing, but he was dispirited. In a short time, he'd become attached to Sommerall. He would probably always associate the time he'd spent here with

Angeline. He wished that they could spend one more day here, but they couldn't. It had ended all too soon.

Feeling restless, he rose and walked over to the tall bookshelves, but he wasn't in the mood to read.

"You are welcome to any that interest you," the marquess said.

"I'll look them over before Faraday takes possession."

"It's not an inevitable conclusion," the marquess said.

Colin figured the man had already decided to make the purchase and was only having one more look before making his decision. Then he would have to either persuade Angeline to marry him or his father would sell the property when the six weeks were up.

Fifteen minutes later, he rose again, walked to the window, and nudged the drapes open. It was a clear day, but he couldn't see the mausoleum from this vantage point.

Footsteps alerted him. He turned as Faraday stepped inside and bowed.

The marquess rose. "Well, have you decided?"

Colin's heart raced, knowing what was to come, but he held his breath anyway.

"I'll have one more look at the other property," Faraday said. "You will have my decision soon." He paused and said, "I understand that it will not be available for six weeks."

The marquess cleared his throat. "Very well, Faraday. I hope this is the last delay."

"Yes, my lord. I just want to make sure." He paused and said, "There's a cradle in the nursery."

"I would like to take it and the rocker," Colin said.

His father arched his brows.

Colin had surprised even himself. He'd made the request without a thought, but the rocker and the cradle now made sense. It was a tangible link to his mother, and the only one he would ever have.

"I'll see myself out," Faraday said. "Thank you for your patience."

After he left, the marquess frowned. "What the devil are you going to do with a rocker and cradle?"

"I want to keep them for the day I start a family," he said.

"When might that illustrious day be?"

"I don't know." But it would not be long. Otherwise, he stood to lose all.

"It appears no one can make decisions today," the marquess said. "However, I can. Come with me to your mother's resting place. I haven't been in some time."

The fallen autumn leaves crunched beneath their boots. The wind was up, and his father's thinning hair blew about after they both removed their hats. "Your mother was a beautiful lady inside and out," he said. "I fell madly in love with Elizabeth, and I was terrified because I had a competitor for her hand."

Colin regarded his father curiously. "What happened?"

"I tried flowers, sweetmeats, and poetry. She remained unimpressed until one day I found a kitten. When I called on her, I feared the cat had stolen her affections from me. She laughed when I admitted it. She loved that kitten."

"How did you win her?" Colin said.

"I told her the truth," he said. "That I couldn't sleep or eat, and I thought about her all the time. Then I told her that I didn't have any pretty words, but I loved her so much it hurt to think of l-losing her." His father's voice broke. "I did anyway."

Colin put his arm around his father's shoulder. "I imagine you were very happy when you married."

"Oh, yes. One day the kitten got out somehow, and I thought I'd never be able to console her. Not long after, she discovered that she was expecting—you. We were overjoyed. I thought I'd go mad while she labored to bring you into the world. Your grandfather, rest his soul, plied me with entirely too much brandy."

He smiled a little. "I remember Grandfather well."

"All I got for it was the devil of a head, but when I finally got to see her, I was so relieved. There you were, a wrinkled, red, squalling infant. I was afraid to hold you, but she insisted.

"It was a happy time. You were a healthy boy. She used to sit in that rocker in the nursery in a patch of sun and sing to you. I was so proud of you. I used to show you off to the tenants, the vicar, and all the parishioners. Elizabeth said I embarrassed her."

Colin looked at his father wonderingly. This was a side of him that he'd never imagined.

"Elizabeth had two miscarriages afterward, and her health declined. She wanted another babe, but I was afraid and took care not to let it happen. She was determined, and we laughed afterward that she'd seduced me. Six months later, she passed away while giving birth to a little girl so tiny she could not have thrived. The babe was...buried with her."

Colin briefly closed his eyes. "You must have been wild with grief."

"Your grandmother had passed the year before, but your grandfather came to collect us both. I remember you cried and cried for your mother. It broke my heart."

"I used to pray for a miracle that she would come home," Colin said.

He sighed. "Life goes on, son. You were healthy and inquisitive. We spent a great deal of time together. You would sit on my lap while I read to you."

"I remember," Colin said. "*The History of Little Goody Two-Shoes.*"

"You made me read it over and over again. I was tempted to burn it, but I saved it for the day you have brats. I hope they make you read that book repeatedly."

Colin laughed.

"When it was time to send you to school, I didn't want to leave you at Eton, but I knew I had to do it. Two years later, I met Margaret's father. He was in trade of all sorts and had pots of money. One day, the wily man let me see his daughter. I was smitten immediately." He sighed. "I felt guilty for having feelings for Margaret. It felt as if I were betraying your mother, but you were at school, and I was lost until I met her."

Colin could hear the melancholy in his father's voice.

"It was an arranged marriage and hard for Margaret. Her father knew he was ill, and he wanted her to be safe and secure. Back then, she was shy and terrified of living in our world. I vowed then that I would earn her affections, but as it turned out, she earned mine."

The marquess bowed his head. "I will love you until the end of time, Elizabeth."

Colin's eyes burned. He turned away and took out his handkerchief.

The marquess clapped his shoulder. "It's time to return."

Colin regarded his father. "Thank you for sharing memories of my mother. It helps."

That afternoon, Colin managed to evade a group outing and took Angeline to the stables where he chose a mare for her. "We'll only trot," he said. "Those side saddles are dangerous. On second thought, I'll take you up in front of me on Aries."

"You know I have a good seat," she said.

"Humor me. Your father will kill me if you fall."

"Colin, no."

"Yes, do as I say. Aries is waiting."

Aries snorted as if he agreed.

The groom helped her up even as she continued to protest.

"Hush," Colin said. "You'll enjoy this."

"I rather doubt it," she said.

He walked the horse along the path.

"Colin, why even ride if we're going along at a grandmother's pace?"

He kissed her neck.

"Keep your eyes on the path," she said, "or we'll both fall off."

"I'll not let that happen. Hence the slow pace." He didn't mention the enticing feel of her bottom against his groin. "You can enjoy the scenery much better at a walk."

"If I wanted to walk, I would use my legs," she said.

He laughed. "Relax."

"What else can I do?"

"That's better," he said. Lord, her soft bottom felt too damned good.

"Do you have a destination in mind?" she asked.

"Nothing in particular."

"I don't believe you," she said.

"Just a few more minutes," he said. Ahead, he saw a spot beneath one of the barren oaks. He halted the horse and slid off the saddle. Then he reached for her and let her slide down his torso.

"You did that on purpose," she said.

"Did what?" he said, pulling off the rolled blanket.

"If you're thinking of rubbing down Aries, you are wasting your time. He's probably put out that you forced him to a sedate walk."

Aries snorted again and cropped the grass.

Colin took her hand. "Come along."

"Where?" she said in a snippy tone.

He liked it when she got feisty. "Trust me."

"Hah!"

He spread the blanket and pulled her down onto it with him.

"Why do I suspect you are scheming?"

"Because you're smart."

"If I were smart, I would walk back to the house."

"Don't be a spoilsport." He lay on his side and propped himself up with his hand. "Relax."

She sat on the blanket and wrapped her arms around her shins. "I know what you're thinking," she said, "but it will not happen."

"What do you think will happen?"

"You want to kiss me."

"Will you let me?"

When she didn't answer immediately, his hopes leaped in his chest. "Do you want to kiss me?"

"What I want and what I should do are two different things." She looked at him. "What happened with Faraday?"

"He's trying to decide between Sommerall and another property."

"What is he like, this Faraday?" she asked.

"He's a gentleman. Arrived rather late." He told her about Faraday's wife.

"Has she seen the house?"

"Apparently not. My father thinks she would make up her mind quickly one way or the other, but she obviously wasn't feeling well enough to join him."

"So it ended up to be a waste of time," she said.

"No. My father asked me to accompany him to my mother's mausoleum. He told me quite a bit about her." When he told her the rest, she sighed.

"What?" he said.

"It must be wonderful to be so in love."

She sounded wistful. Angeline wanted hearts and flowers, after all. He supposed most women did hope for love and happily-ever-after. It would be so much easier if she only wanted to repair her reputation and see her sister make her debut in the spring.

"I'm glad your father told you about his relationship with your mother. You were so young, but now you know more about her. I'm glad you found out they were happy."

"It helps." He told her about how his father had met Margaret.

"She has been good for him. He would be lonely without her and the girls." Angeline took off her jaunty little hat and lay on her side to face him. "What will you do if Mr. Faraday makes the offer in six weeks?"

Her words felt like a kick in the gut. "There is nothing I can do unless you decide to make an honest man out of me before then." He'd spoken in a joking manner, but his nerves were on edge.

"We have three weeks to make that decision—well, two and one-half weeks, I suppose."

He didn't have much time. After meeting Faraday, the threat of losing Sommerall had become all too real. What could he do to persuade her? Desperation caught hold of him like talons. He took a deep breath and forced himself to ask the question. "Are you having doubts?"

She shrugged one shoulder, the way she'd done the first night he'd seen her at Deerfield. "I suppose it is only natural for us to have doubts under the circumstances."

Given her skittishness, he feared she would decide that she couldn't marry him, even to ensure her sister's debut. If that happened, he would lose Sommerall.

"Do you like living in London?" she asked.

"I suppose. Harry is always up for a lark." He remembered his friend's reaction to the actress upon seeing her in his rooms and grinned.

Angeline huffed. "He's like a little boy, always wanting to pour spirits in the punch bowl."

"Do not let Harry fool you. He may like a lark now and then, but no man crosses him and walks away unscathed."

"I've never seen that side of him," she said.

"Few do." Colin grinned. "Did I tell you he almost drowned last year?"

"That's horrible. Why are you smiling about it?"

"We were foxed from one too many bottles at Vauxhall, and Harry was supposed to pay the waterman to take us across. My purse was empty from paying for all the bottles, but Harry discovered he had pockets to let. Somehow or another, he fell into the Thames. I jumped in to save him, and then another fellow dived in to help. That's how I met Bellingham."

She laughed. "That's awful."

"Good memories," he said, smiling.

"Men," she said, rolling her eyes.

He smiled. "I had a feeling you wouldn't appreciate it."

She regarded him with an intense expression. "Was there a reason you brought me here?"

"Yes." He leaned over and kissed her lightly on the lips, and then with more intention. When she opened for his tongue, he grew aroused and thought at least in this they would be more than compatible. He cupped her face, and for a rash moment, he considered lying and telling her he loved her. With a deep breath, he started to form the words, but she spoke first.

"I'm reluctant to leave, but we had better return." She sat up and pinned her silly hat to her hair. He helped her up. *Say the words. Lie to her. Make her believe you.* His breathing was too fast and he couldn't force the words out.

"Colin, what is it?"

He met her gaze and the guilt got hold of him again. "It's nothing." He rolled the blanket. Then he mounted Aries and gave her a hand up in front of him. He kept his eyes on the path, but the entire time he was aware of her scent, her sweet bottom, and her trust in him. She deserved better, and he wasn't sure how he could convince her to marry him. He needed to prepare himself mentally first. Now was not the right time, but he didn't have much time left.

After leaving Aries in the care of a groom, Colin offered his arm to Angeline and escorted her along the path. He knew what he had to do, but his chest tightened. The devil. Surely there was another way to ensure she would marry him, but he'd racked his brain and could not think of an honorable way.

When they walked inside Deerfield, Wycoff and his father were standing in the hall in muddy boots as usual. The marquess was scowling at Bianca and Bernadette.

Colin noticed tear tracks on his sisters' faces and the dog sitting there lolling his tongue. "I take it something is amiss."

Bernadette sniffed. "Papa means to give Hercules away to one of the tenants."

"Hercules didn't mean to have an accident in the water closet." Bianca dabbed a handkerchief at her eyes. "H-he is still a puppy."

"Thus far, he has ruined a pair of boots, several legs on the tables, and to top it all off, he breaks wind," the marquess said gruffly.

Colin burst out laughing.

Angeline clapped her hand over her mouth, but her shoulders were shaking.

Margaret hurried down the stairs. "What is all this commotion about?"

"Papa is making Hercules an orphan," Bianca said.

"Oh, for pity's sake," the marquess said. "I rue the day that dog set foot in our house. Enough is enough. Margaret, I know you side with the girls about the dog, but he is damaging our home and is uncouth."

"Lord Chadwick," Angeline said. "Hercules is a smart dog. The girls have already taught him how to shake hands. He only needs to be trained properly. I will gladly help the girls with his training."

"You know how to train dogs?" Colin said.

She nodded. "I had a dog, but he died before we left for Paris."

Colin met his father's gaze and then looked at his sisters. "If you want to keep Hercules, you should demonstrate to our father that you will teach him how to behave."

"You must be consistent," Angeline said. "When he does well, reward him. That is how he will learn."

"Papa, will you give us another chance with Hercules?" Bianca said. "We promise to train him."

"I don't know," the marquess said.

Margaret walked over to her husband and patted his arm. "Perhaps we could train you to remove your muddy boots before you walk in the house."

Colin shared a smile with Angeline and then he turned to his sisters. "You might thank Angeline," he said.

They put their arms around her. "Thank you," they said in unison.

The marquess sat on a bench in the great hall and removed his muddy boots. The marble floor was a mess.

Margaret held her hands up as if beseeching a higher power. "I give up."

Late that night in bed, the marquess sighed. "You have never failed to make me a happy man, Margaret."

"You are a lusty man," she said, laughing.

He kissed his wife gently. "I do love you, my dear."

"And I you." She sighed. "What do you make of Colin and Angeline?"

"What do you mean? They haven't killed each other. We're safe from violence." He chuckled.

"Chadwick, you know very well what I mean. He took her up on the horse to keep her safe. I find that very chivalrous."

"For a married woman, you are remarkably naïve, my dear."

"What do you mean?" she said.

"Chivalry had nothing to do with his decision. No doubt my son was enjoying the close proximity of the lovely Angeline."

"I've seen the way he looks at her when he thinks no one is noticing," Margaret said.

"He's a man, Margaret. Put a curvaceous beauty in front of a male, he will look."

"Chadwick, you had better not look at any other woman or you will sleep in one of the guest rooms."

"But I have no reason to look elsewhere when I have my own beautiful, curvaceous wife close at hand."

"Good answer." Margaret sighed again. "The girls are so excited about their debut next spring. It is all they talk about. Even sweet Penny is enthused."

"I fear society is not prepared for our twins. No doubt they will create mayhem wherever they go as they're wont to do."

"Be serious, dear. I worry that our efforts to champion Angeline will not succeed."

"You have not said anything to the duchess, have you?"

"No, dear, I would never presume to do so. If it does not work, it would be very hard on our girls as well as Penny. I know Angeline is worried on her sister's behalf."

"Margaret, we must leave this to Angeline and my son. If it is meant to be, it will be."

She snorted inelegantly. "I should have known better than to consult you. Do you think I will leave this up to Providence?"

"My dear, you are determined to play matchmaker, but I suspect Lady Angeline is far too practical to fall for our roguish son. Any woman with half a brain would avoid him."

"Chadwick, he is our son. You ought to be ashamed."

"I am, Margaret. Ashamed that I didn't curb him years ago. You know I could have done it by withholding his funds, but I didn't. Something must be done. I am taking care of it."

"Chadwick, please be kind to him. He is our only son."

He cupped his wife's cheek. "That is what I love about you, Margaret. You champion everyone, including our rakehell son."

"Underneath his rakish exterior, he is a good man. He only needs a good woman to help him see it."

"You are remarkably naïve, Margaret, but I love you for it, and now will you let me love you again?"

She opened her arms to him, the way she'd done the first night of their marriage, and he knew that he was twice blessed.

Chapter Ten

At breakfast the next morning, Angeline and the twins joined everyone else at breakfast.

"We plan to teach Hercules to sit," Bianca said to the marquess.

"One would think that would be a natural thing to do," the marquess said.

Angeline smiled at Colin and then addressed the marquess. "Hercules is learning to sit after getting a verbal command. He has done very well."

"He likes the treats he gets for obeying," Bernadette said.

"That is progress," Margaret said. "Thank you, Angeline. I know the girls are grateful as well."

The marquess snorted behind his paper.

Ames brought a sealed letter on a silver dish to the marquess. "It is marked urgent," Ames said.

Colin finished his meal and accepted another cup of tea.

The marquess opened the letter and scowled. "What in blazes is wrong with that man?" he demanded.

"Chadwick," Margaret said. "We do not shout at the table."

"I'll shout all I want. That fool Faraday probably takes all day to decide it's time to take a sh—"

The duchess gasped.

"Father," Colin said. "Ladies are present, including my very impressionable sisters." From the gleaming expressions in the twins' eyes, Colin figured they had added some very colorful words to their vocabulary, probably from the stable boys when they had their riding lessons.

"I can't believe it," the marquess said. "Now he wants to bring his wife to have a look at the house. How many times must he see it? I tire of his foolishness. Colin, go meet the man. I'm liable to say something exceedingly impolite or throw him out on his ar—"

"Chadwick," Margaret said in shocked tones. "You forget yourself."

"I beg your pardon," he grumbled.

"If Mrs. Faraday sees the house and approves of it, she may be more likely to make a decision quickly," Margaret said. "Lady Angeline, you have a great deal of knowledge about design and architecture, perhaps you could speak to Mrs. Faraday."

Colin set his cup aside slowly. He hesitated a moment, knowing what he meant to do was dishonorable, but he couldn't let the opportunity pass or he would surely lose Sommerall.

"Wycoff," Colin said, "if you are amenable, I think it might help if Angeline attended. She could answer any questions Mrs. Faraday might have."

The marquess addressed his friend. "The other couple will be there, so there's no question about propriety. I'd be obliged if you will allow it. Your daughter probably knows more about the house than any of us."

"I can verify that," Colin said.

"I'll allow it," Wycoff said, "provided you return as soon as the business is concluded. I don't want there to be even a hint of impropriety."

Colin made himself meet Wycoff's eyes. He told himself that he could persuade Angeline to agree to the marriage through honorable means. She had certainly given serious thought to a marriage of convenience, but she had not given him a definitive answer. If she said no, he stood to lose Sommerall. Perhaps today, he could persuade her to make the engagement official.

Margaret rose and rang the bell. "I'll have cook prepare a hamper in the event the house inspection takes longer than expected. It occurs to me that Mr. and Mrs. Faraday may wish to see the grounds as well."

"Thank you, Margaret," Angeline said. "That is very thoughtful of you."

"You had better dress warmly and take an umbrella," Margaret said. "The clouds are rather gray, and the wind is blowing. You do not want to catch a chill."

"I don't think we're in any danger of that," Angeline said. "At any rate, a bit of rain won't hurt us."

"Can we come with you?" Bianca asked.

"Absolutely not," Colin said.

"Colin, please," Bianca said.

"The answer is no," Colin said. "You will only be in the way."

"Margaret," the marquess said, "do you know the going price for unmannerly fifteen-year-old girls? We might get a bit of extra coin if we sell the twins to Faraday along with the house. Their value has increased somewhat since they started speaking the King's English instead of twin gibberish."

"There's the hamper," Margaret said to Angeline. "I hope your journey isn't too soggy."

"We should be off," Colin said. "I don't want to be late."

The marquess lifted his gaze from the newspaper. "I wouldn't be in any rush if I were you. Faraday is liable to keep you waiting for some time."

The carriage had just turned off the drive when the rain started in earnest. Angeline sat beside Colin and looked out the window. "I hope the rain doesn't keep Mr. and Mrs. Faraday away," she said.

"I have high hopes they won't show," Colin said.

"Oh, I'm sorry, Colin. I spoke heedlessly."

Don't feel sorry for me. "He's probably afraid to take her out in the rain."

"Well, it is damp and chilly," Angeline said. "You indicated she is in a delicate condition."

"We shall see what happens." If she balked at the idea of marrying him, he would have no choice but to take drastic measures. He would have to make it seem as if they'd gotten lost in passion. God, he'd never done anything like this in his life. He'd never even contemplated it.

"I was surprised you agreed to meet Faraday," she said. "You have nothing to gain and everything to lose in this sale."

"You think so?" *I'm praying Mrs. Faraday hates the*

house, because the thought of seducing you is killing me.

"What are you planning?" she said. "I can see something is on your mind."

"I was thinking I might point out all the work that must be done for the house to be in a proper state of order."

She stared at him. "You cannot be serious."

He removed his hat and set it beside him. "The thought might have crossed my mind." *It is preferable to what I intend for you.*

"Faraday has doubts enough that he's returning for the third time," she said. "I think his doubts are in your favor."

"He must be very interested or he would not bother to bring his wife," he said. "Frankly, I'm trying to think of ways to discourage him."

"You know I support your claim to the property, but you should not discourage him," she said.

"Even if it means I lose Sommerall and strangers tramp across my mother's resting place?"

"I understand your feelings," she said, "but you would not feel right about doing it."

You have no idea what I would do to keep Sommerall. "The truth is the house needs work—a great deal of work as you well know."

She set her gloved hand over his. "Colin, you surprise me. Honesty is always the best policy."

He narrowed his eyes. "Are you saying you would never use your wiles to get something you want very badly?"

"Not at someone else's expense."

His blood heated. He'd grown angry with her. She knew he was a rake. Why was she foolish enough to trust him? "Can you imagine using your wiles for someone else? Your sister, perhaps?"

Her face turned red at his words. "How dare you say such a thing? You know how much I worry about my sister."

"So the rules are different for you than for me?"

"Stop the carriage this instant," she said.

"Angeline, I apologize—"

"Stop the carriage. Take me back to Deerfield."

He'd muddled things up now. "Angeline, calm yourself."

"No, I will not. How can you be so cruel?"

She has no idea how cruel I mean to be.

"You know how much I worry about Penny."

He caught her hands. "Listen. It slipped out and was badly done on my part. All I have is a sorry excuse."

"You're worried about losing Sommerall," she said. "It must be the vexation."

She took off her bonnet and laid her head against his shoulder. "I understand." She drew in a shuddered breath. "I should have been more understanding and sympathetic."

"Please forgive me." He was miserable with his dishonesty and so tempted to confess, but if he did, he would set events in motion that would hurt her and the friendships of both their families.

"I know how much Sommerall means to you."

I'm a selfish bastard, but I swear I'll make it up to you.

"It is not wrong for you to want to keep the house to preserve your mother's grave. The house does need work. There are marks on the walls, the carpets have to be replaced, and the furnishings are out of date. You do not have to exaggerate the problems, but you do not have to point out the virtues, either."

He clenched his teeth. *I don't deserve you.* "My guess is our row has been all for naught," Colin said. "Most likely, Mr. and Mrs. Faraday will not show."

As the carriage rumbled along, Angeline found herself hoping that Colin was right about the Faradays, because she was having doubts about their trial engagement. She wanted to grasp his offer of a marriage of convenience, because it was a chance to redeem herself. Most of all, it was a gift she wanted to give to her sweet little sister, and for that, she would use her wiles and even marry to make sure Penny could make her debut in London next spring. But it wasn't fair to Colin. None of her reasons involved him, and that wasn't honorable at all.

Thunder rumbled. Colin held the umbrella as they ran to the door. The wet made it a bit chilly, and Angeline was glad for her warm cape. He unlocked the door and ushered her inside. They hung their damp wraps and set their gloves on the marble hall table.

"I'll set the hamper in the breakfast parlor," Colin said.

"Thank you," she said. The gold mirror in the foyer, the marble floors, and the banisters gleamed. She realized she'd made a mistake by instructing Agnes to clean and shine everything so well that it fairly sparkled.

Angeline removed her bonnet and guilt left a bruised place in her chest. It had been foolish of her to argue about Sommerall when she hated the thought of him losing the property. It really was all he had left of his mother, other than the cradle and the rocker.

Colin strode through the great hall. "We might as well go to the drawing room. I imagine we shall have a long wait," he said.

"How long do you think they will be?" she asked as Colin escorted her upstairs.

"He was an hour late the last time, although to be fair he was concerned about his wife."

They had just cleared the landing when the knocker rapped.

She met his gaze. "They are on time. Do you suppose Mrs. Faraday insists upon punctuality?"

"Probably," he said.

"Shall we greet them?"

"Yes, of course. We will also get our exercise going up and down the stairs." He leaned down. "Thank you for coming with me, and I'm sorry for cutting up at you."

"So am I," she whispered. Her vexation had increased each day that went by. She could no longer lie to herself. She had developed feelings for Colin, very strong ones. She knew he deserved a wife who didn't have a sullied reputation, and it worried her. It was one thing to plan a marriage of convenience, but it was quite another when tender feelings were involved. She was at a crossroads, and she did not know what to do. But she must think of Colin's feelings now, rather than her own.

Even though it was not Mr. Faraday's first visit, Angeline figured it could not be easy for Colin to watch strangers walking about his house—or rather his father's house. Yet he was bearing up to it better than she would have done.

When Colin opened the door, he bowed and welcomed

the couple. The lady was much shorter than her husband and very pregnant. She rested her hand on her belly as she gazed upon the foyer. "How lovely," she said.

"Lady Angeline, may I present Mr. and Mrs. Faraday," Colin said.

Mrs. Faraday smiled as she followed Angeline to the great hall. "How long have you and your husband lived here?"

"He is not my husband," Angeline said.

Mrs. Faraday's eyes widened. "I see." She pinched her lips and regarded Angeline with raised brows. "Well, you are certainly forthright about your situation."

Colin frowned and held his hands up from his place behind Mr. Faraday as if asking what was wrong.

Angeline bit her lip to keep from laughing. Apparently Mrs. Faraday assumed Angeline was living in sin with Colin.

"Lord Ravenshire is an old family friend," Angeline explained. "I have been making recommendations to him about Sommerall."

Mrs. Faraday's brows almost shot to her hairline. "Doubtless he is, er, appreciative." She shook out her fan, caught her husband's arm, and whispered something to him. When he started to look back at Angeline, Mrs. Faraday swatted him with her fan.

The woman must have thought Angeline was lying about her title.

"If you wish, you and your husband may go upstairs and look over the rooms," Angeline said. "Meet us in the drawing room when you are finished."

Mrs. Faraday practically dragged her husband up the stairs.

Colin escorted Angeline to the drawing room. "What was that all about?" he muttered.

"Mrs. Faraday apparently believes I'm your mistress posing as Lady Angeline."

"No," he said, laughing.

She nodded. "As soon as I explained you were not my husband, I could see she was both shocked and titillated."

His shoulders shook with laughter. Then he walked to the window and opened the drapes. "No wonder it's dim in here. The clouds are even darker now."

Rolling thunder rumbled. Angeline joined him at the window, transfixed by the lightning brightening up the sky. "Oh," she said. "The lightning is awful."

"I hope we're not in for a storm."

When she shivered, he cupped her elbow. "Let's return to the sofa. It will pass soon."

The clock struck the half hour and voices sounded outside the drawing room.

Colin and Angeline rose.

"Mrs. Faraday would like a look at the drawing room," Mr. Faraday said.

"You are welcome to examine the room. If you have any questions, we will be glad to answer to the best of our knowledge," Colin said.

As it turned out, Mrs. Faraday had a number of questions regarding the drawing room. She seemed a bit put off by the marks on the walls where paintings had once been. "It would have been better to leave the paintings to cover the marks."

"The family portraits were removed to a different property," Colin said.

"I see," she said, walking about. "The furnishings and chair rails are very old fashioned."

"The house has not been occupied for some time," Colin said.

"To be sure, there is much work to be done." Mrs. Faraday placed her hand on her rounded belly again. "How am I to find the time? I'll have my hands full soon enough."

"That is something to consider," Angeline said. Privately, she thought the woman terribly persnickety. Mrs. Faraday's numerous complaints about minor issues grated on her nerves, but she maintained her poise.

When Mrs. Faraday examined the ceiling, she said, "Is this a reproduction?"

Angeline exchanged a smile with Colin.

"It is original," Colin said.

"You're sure?" Mrs. Faraday said.

"It has been in my family for many years," Colin said.

"Where are the carpets?" Mrs. Faraday said.

"They faded," Angeline said.

"I suppose they can be replaced, but that's additional expense, Mr. Faraday," his lady said.

"To be sure it is, Mrs. Faraday," her husband said.

She took her husband's arm. "I adore the nursery, but I understand you wish to keep the cradle and rocker, Lord Ravenshire."

"Yes, I do," Colin said.

"There is much to like, Mr. Faraday," his wife said, "but I feel I must look at the other one again. This property is priced on the higher side compared to the other. There are some drawbacks, but we will take all into consideration."

Angeline bit her lip. Really, the woman's blatant attempts to lower the price were too obvious.

"It is such a difficult decision," Mrs. Faraday said. "Nothing ever quite suits me."

Colin cleared his throat. "Mr. Faraday, do you have any questions?"

"No, my lord. I will contact your esteemed father in a week or so. We should have a decision by then, provided we don't decide to have one more peek at the house, that is." Mr. Faraday chuckled.

"Come along, Mr. Faraday," his lady said. "I've a mind to see the other place one more time." She paused and said, "We are serious about the property. The location is especially convenient, as we have family in the area."

"I understand," Colin said, his tone neutral.

Colin and Angeline led the way downstairs.

When Colin opened the door, it was raining harder. "Mind your step," he said as Mr. and Mrs. Faraday hurried to their carriage.

A crack of thunder made Angeline gasp. Colin shut the door and looked at her. "No wonder my father is exasperated."

"I cannot believe Mrs. Faraday asked if you were certain the painted ceiling was an original."

They both laughed.

"Your father should not indulge Faraday again. The man has no spine, and his wife is a bit vulgar. Can you imagine how often Mr. and Mrs. Faraday would call at Deerfield?"

"That would certainly be a deterrent to sell to them," he said.

"Perhaps your father will grant you the property

now," she said. "I'm sure he would enjoy having you close."

"Are you hungry? We might as well eat luncheon since we have the hamper," he said. "We can depart afterward."

She noticed he'd not responded to her statement about him living at Sommerall. Evidently, he did not wish to discuss the matter.

When they reached the breakfast parlor, Colin lit a branch of candles because it was dim.

Angeline served the chicken, ham, fresh bread, cheese, and biscuits. He found a bottle of claret and they drank wine with their meal. Afterward, Angeline sighed. "We didn't eat even a quarter of the food."

"It will keep until we return," he said.

"It is a cozy breakfast parlor. Do you have any memories of this room at all?"

"No, I only have vague recollections of being in the nursery," he said.

Another loud crack of thunder startled Angeline. Colin opened the shutters. Lightning lit up the sky, and he squinted through the wavy glass. "There's the carriage. John is taking it to the old barn."

"Oh, dear," Angeline said, standing beside him. "I'm glad there's a safe place for John and the horses."

Thunder clapped again and lightning snaked through the sky. She rubbed her arms. "Lightning has always frightened me a little," she said.

"It is dangerous to be out of doors in a lightning storm," he said.

The wind gusted, and the slanted rain sheeted.

Within minutes something was pounding the roof. He used a napkin to clear the fog on the window. "It's hail."

"What an awful storm," she said.

"We'll just have to wait it out," Colin said. "Shall we go to the drawing room? I'll light a fire, and we can have another glass of wine while we wait."

She was still rubbing her cold arms. "I wish I'd brought a shawl."

"I'll pull a blanket off one of the beds and bring it to you, and then I'll make a toasty fire."

"Very well." It seemed they would not be able to leave until the rain and hail abated. Hopefully, the storm would blow over soon.

He brought the wine bottle and she carried their glasses. He set the bottle on the sideboard. "I'll be only a moment," he said.

Thunder kept rolling and the rain and hail pounded the roof. She walked to the window and pulled back the drapes. It was raining so hard that she could make out very little through the wavy glass except sheeting rain. Footsteps thudded and she was relieved to see Colin. "I looked out the window. The rain is drumming the roof."

"It's the hail you hear." He stood behind her and wrapped a blanket around her shoulders. He was so close she caught the scent of sandalwood on him. "Better?" he said, his breath tickling her neck.

"Yes, thank you."

His hands lingered a moment, and she was all too aware of him. She felt cherished for a moment as if he were her husband and she were his wife. It made her a little sad to think that she might never know such a simple, comforting gesture ever again.

"I looked out from the master chamber," Colin said, his mind clearly on the storm. "Water is already standing on the grounds. I walked through the bedchambers and didn't see any leaks from the windows."

"That is good news. I'm glad we arrived before the storm hit."

"I'm glad Mr. and Mrs. Faraday left before the storm got worse. Otherwise, we'd be stuck with their company."

"Perish the thought," she said, laughing. "I wonder how long the storm will last."

"Eventually, the rain will relent. We may have to wait a few hours until the roads dry a bit, but we'll survive."

"Indeed we will." She crossed the room, kicked off her slippers, and curled her legs on the sofa.

His hands were on his hips. "You look quite comfortable."

"It is unladylike, but I doubt you care."

"I'm shocked," he said, clutching his chest.

"Drink another glass of wine. That should cure you."

"But nothing ever suits me," he said.

They both laughed.

"Oh, my stars," Angeline said. "You absolutely cannot let them purchase Sommerall."

He sobered. "I've no say in it."

He seemed to have forgotten he could marry her to prevent his father from selling. Perhaps he regretted having ever broached the subject of marriage but didn't have the heart to tell her.

"I'll cross that bridge soon enough," he said.

"Are you worried?" she asked.

"Everything will come about, one way or the other."

It was one of those statements meant to reassure someone but seldom ever did. She wasn't encouraged at all.

She suspected he was having second thoughts about marrying a woman with a past. While she'd spoken very plainly to him about what he might endure if he married her, he was a gentleman and unlikely to tell her if he was troubled. Now was the perfect opportunity to discuss the issues, but she put it off. Their last row had left her drained like a bloodletting.

He set the candle branch on the hearth where a tinderbox and spunks for transferring the fire were stored. "I promised you a fire."

After he managed a spark, he removed his coat, squatted before the hearth, and applied the bellows. As the fire caught, the flames crackled.

His linen shirt stretched across his back as he worked. When he stood and applied a poker, she allowed herself to survey his long muscular legs. She recollected the sparse dark hair beneath his shirt and on his arms the day he'd wielded that ax. From what she knew of his reputation, she'd not expected to find him so fit, but evidently, he enjoyed fencing.

He set the poker aside and topped up their wineglasses.

When he joined her on the sofa, he sat close and handed her one.

She sipped it, and he smiled. "Your lips are red from the wine."

"So are yours," she said.

"Are you warm enough?" His voice was low and a little rough.

She nodded and found herself breathless as she looked at his full lower lip.

He laid his arm along the back of the sofa, and his hand was only inches from her shoulder. The tension inside of her wound up like a clock. She realized she was a tiny bit foxed and set the glass aside.

She walked to the window again and pushed the drapes aside, but the wavy glass combined with the relentless rain made it impossible to see anything.

"Angeline, you are restless."

She regarded him over her shoulder. "I'm worried. It's bad out there."

"We're safe here. We have food and drink. There's a caddy of tea in the basket and a jug of water. I imagine there's a kettle in the kitchen we can use. It may be several hours before the rain stops, but eventually the roads will dry enough for us to travel."

"I'll go to the kitchen and find a kettle." She hurried downstairs and walked into the kitchen. After a few minutes, she located the kettle and a teapot. After a long search, she found a tray and placed the kettle, teapot, a strainer for the tea, and two cups on it. Pleased with her discoveries, Angeline walked back to the drawing room.

He met her halfway down the steps. "That tray is too heavy for you."

"Thank you for the help," she said, and followed him back to the drawing room.

She poured water from the jug into the kettle, and Colin set it on the hob in the fireplace. Afterward, she added tea leaves to the pot. Thunder boomed again, startling her. She pressed her hand to her heart. "That was fearsome."

He smiled. A few minutes later, the kettle shrieked. He rescued it and poured the hot water in the pot. After he set the kettle back on the hob, he said, "Now all we need to do is wait for the tea to get dark."

"A hot cup of tea is always welcome when it's chilly."

He shook the blanket out and laid it over her. "Warm now?"

"Yes, thank you." His simple gesture made her yearn to have someone love and care for her. Someone who would take a heavy tray or bring a blanket to her. Someone who would laugh with her and hold her close and reassure her when the weather was bad. With all of her heart she yearned to have someone to lean on, someone to depend on, someone who would love her even though she had made mistakes. But unless something changed, it seemed the poor choices she'd made would dictate the few choices available to her.

The rain grew fiercer.

He looked up at the painted ceiling. "So far it's holding."

"The house is sound," she said. It was a fine house for a family. Of course it was small compared to Worthington Abbey and Deerfield, but it would make a good house for a young couple. Little wonder the Faradays kept coming back.

She wished that she and Colin would live here, but it was a foolish thought, one she shouldn't entertain because it would only make her sad when he inevitably told her he did not think they would suit.

It would happen. No sane man wanted a wife with a wanton reputation, no matter how undeserving.

"If it doesn't let up soon, we may not be able to leave," he said.

"Oh, no," she said. "We have to return before nightfall."

"We may not have a choice, but there's no need to fret.

It won't last forever. As soon as the roads are passable, we'll depart."

"Our families will worry."

"The rain isn't our fault. It's every bit as bad at Deerfield as it is here."

"You're right," she said. "No doubt we'll be able to leave in the next hour or two."

He sighed. "It won't be in the next hour or two."

"Perhaps we should try to travel now before it gets dark," she said.

"With this much rain, the roads are bound to be muddy and potentially dangerous. In case you haven't noticed, the hail is still pounding the roof and the water is standing outside."

She poured tea over the sieve into the cups. "Come, I made you a cup of tea."

When he returned, he leaned down and kissed her cheek. "Thank you."

Oh, dear, he seemed a bit amorous, but perhaps he just forgot himself. She reminded herself not to interpret the gesture as a tender one.

He sat right next to her and sipped the tea. "It's good."

Who am I trying to fool? Myself? She inched over next to the rolled arm of the sofa. "Yes, the tea is just the thing. I'm glad we have supplies. It would be miserable if we had no food or drink." *I am prattling like that silly Mrs. Quimby.*

He eyed her over his cup with an amused expression.

"What is it?"

"Nothing."

"I wish there were cards or a game to play," she said.

"We never found either," he said, setting his cup on

the tray. "Someone or some persons probably took them along with my mother's miniature."

"I'm sorry. I'd hoped to find it."

He set her cup aside for her and cupped her cheek. "So sweet," he said, his voice low and full of sensual promise.

"Are you ready to give up your life in London for Sommerall?" she asked in a voice just barely above a whisper.

Before departing London, he recalled waking up to the devil of a head, bottles on the night table, and an actress whose name he'd forgotten again. "I've not put a time table on it. When the time is right, I'll know."

Meaning it wasn't the right time now. He was studiously avoiding the subject of marriage. On the other hand, they had agreed to use the three weeks to get to know one another better. Yet it troubled her. When the three weeks ended, their conversation was bound to be uncomfortable, but she would take the lead and assure him that she did not expect him to sacrifice for her. For now, she would take advantage of the opportunity to be alone with him and learn more about him.

"Tell me something about you I don't know," she said.

"I like hot baths and stay in until the water grows cold and my toes and fingers wrinkle. Now tell me something about you I don't already know," he said.

"I love scents," she said. "They mesmerize me. I stop sometimes to inhale the smell of beeswax candles."

He regarded her with fascination. "What other scents do you like?"

"Rose soap and warm sugar biscuits." She paused. "I love the scent of freshly washed and ironed linens; they smell of sunshine. Sometimes I hold them and keep breathing in the warmth and the sun. What scents do you like?" she murmured.

He nuzzled her neck. "I like the scent of your skin and the feel of your soft cheeks." He met her gaze. "I like your slender fingers and the pearl earrings that dangle from your ears." He flicked one with his finger. Then he smiled a little. "I like when you're feisty and want to spar with me."

"Surely you jest," she said, laughing.

"No, I like that you're spirited and clever." He considered her with a mischievous expression. "There are other things about you I like very well, but I'll keep them to myself."

She sniffed. "Doubtless they are wicked."

He laughed. "I'm not telling."

"Good," she said.

"Am I forgiven?" he asked.

She frowned. "For what?"

"This." He leaned down and captured her lips.

Chapter Eleven

When he drew his tongue over the seam of her mouth, she opened for him, welcomed him, and hoped she would never forget the taste of this man she'd known since before she could remember. Despite everything that loomed between them—her past and his raking—she craved him. But it was more, much more than a craving. It was need, soul deep, for him, just him.

Little by little, he'd captured pieces of her heart. She remembered the sweat running down his face in the woods, despite the bitter cold wind, and his guttural shout as he'd swung that ax. She recalled the day at the folly when he'd thought no one cared about his mother's grave, and though he'd clenched his jaw, she'd known it had hurt him. Most of all, she remembered his bleak expression when they had failed to turn up his mother's miniature. She'd wanted to take him in her arms to let him know that she'd felt his loss as if it were her own.

She'd been in denial, because she was terrified of making another horrible mistake, but she recalled him saying he would make the engagement official that very moment if she wished it. There was so much more to him that others never saw. He'd hidden his wounds behind his sharp wit and rakehell reputation.

She could no longer deny what was in her heart. She was madly, deeply in love with him.

Unlike her bitter experience with Brentmoor, she did not have to persuade herself that she was on the verge of falling in love or nearly in love. There was no comparison. This time, she did not doubt her feelings. She felt giddy and anxious at the same time. No matter what happened—or did not happen—she swore she would never regret loving him.

The faint fragrance of sandalwood soap clung to him, and the warm scent emanating from his skin intoxicated her. Unable to resist, she kissed him back, and he grew more ardent. She was lost in the taste of his lips and threaded her fingers through his hair. When she dared to return his kiss, he answered with the sweep of his tongue. Rivers of desire coursed through her. She focused on the feel of his hard chest, his ragged breathing, and the heat emanating from his body. It wasn't enough. She loosened the knot of his cravat, flipped up the shirt points, and tossed the long length of cloth aside.

He pulled her onto his lap, and she unbuttoned his waistcoat and ran her hands over his linen-clad chest. She somehow managed to get his waistcoat off. When he stood, he let her slide down his hard body, and she caressed him through the linen shirt, but it wasn't enough. She yanked down the braces, pulled his voluminous shirt out of his trousers, and slid her hands underneath his shirt.

"God have mercy. What have I unleashed?" he said.

She withdrew her hands, pulled his head down, and captured his lips. Then she slid both hands over his rock-hard chest and down his flat belly. She feasted her eyes on the bulge in his trousers.

"I never thought it possible to ignite from a woman's gaze, but you have seared me." He kissed her again, a long, wet tangling of tongues. Then he reached for her bottom and pulled her up to her toes. She could feel his erection against her belly and planted kisses over his chest.

Then he lifted her in his arms.

"Colin, what are you doing?"

"I plan to let you have your wicked way with me."

"Then set me down and let me."

Angeline looked at his confident expression and decided to take matters into her own hands. She might have limited experience, but having seen his reaction to their previous kisses, she figured she could wrest control quickly enough. When he let her slide down his body, she reached out to him. "Your wrists, please."

He grinned as he held out his arms.

She knew he was as strong as an ox, but she could distract him long enough to have her wicked way with him, as he'd put it so boldly.

When she tied his cravat around his wrists, he laughed. "What do you plan to do with me?"

"You will see," she said, leading him upstairs by the cravat. "Mind the steps," she said.

He clearly thought he had the upper hand, but she had something in mind.

"I'm anxious to see what you have in store for me," he said.

"Behave," she said.

"Oh? Will you punish me?"

She looked back at him. "Only if you beg."

He was grinning from ear to ear as if he thought he would be the victor in this game, but she intended to have more than a little fun with him.

Once inside the lady's bedchamber, she pushed him onto the edge of the mattress.

"What now, my captor?" he said.

She rose, cupped his face with both hands, and gave him a lascivious kiss.

He tried to reach up, but his hands were still tied. "Release my bonds."

"Only if you behave."

"Yes, mistress," he said, laughing.

A moment later, he was naked to the waist. She caressed his chest and ran one finger down the center of his torso. She noted the line of dark hair below his navel and feathered her finger along the arrow.

He sucked in air. She noted the bulge in his trousers and smiled. "What do you want?"

"Touch me."

She cupped him through his trousers. "Like this?"

He caught her hand, rose, and circled his finger. "Turn round so I can undo your fastenings and loosen the corset."

"I didn't give you leave to do it," she said.

"You'll be uncomfortable if I don't." He leaned down and kissed her cheek. "Let me, so you can sleep."

"I'm sleeping at Deerfield."

"Angeline, listen to the pounding on the roof. We will not be able to leave tonight."

"We have to leave."

"Hush. Turn round, and I'll unhook and untie you."

"I cannot believe this," she said, turning her back to him.

"Do not fret," he said. "It can't be helped."

Her face grew hot anyway. She'd wanted to be worldly, but her limited experience showed.

He went to work on the fastenings, and then he helped her step out of her petticoat and skirts. The laces on her stays were trickier, but he managed to loosen them. Her head bowed as he pulled the stays over her head. She stood there a moment in her shift and stockings. He took her hand and walked with her to the bed. Then he pulled the pins from her hair.

"Colin, I can do it," she said as her hair fell in waves over her breasts and shoulders.

He sifted his fingers through her locks. "You are even more beautiful with your hair down."

She refused to let his compliment go to her head— well, maybe just a tiny bit.

"You're quite skilled with lady's clothing."

"It's cold," he said, and assisted her into the bed.

He pulled the covers over her and kissed her lightly on the lips. Then he slipped his shirt on again. "I'm going to bank the fire in the drawing room, and then I'll start one in here afterward."

She thought about the way he'd stayed her hand earlier, but she'd loved touching him. Now she suspected that he would sleep in another room. Of course, that would be the virtuous choice for both of them, but she was worrying over something that would not happen. She released a frustrated sigh. Why did he have to be noble now?

* * *

It had to happen tonight.

Colin ascended the stairs and walked down the corridor to the slightly ajar door where she lay abed. There was no doubt about his reasons or his intentions. He would do anything to keep from losing Sommerall. He would take advantage of this one last opportunity for them to be alone. He leaned his forehead against the door. Damn it all to hell. She deserved better. He didn't want to do this, but he had no choice. He feared this would be his only opportunity, and he couldn't be certain she would agree to marry him.

The truth would only hurt her, and he wanted to avoid causing her unnecessary pain.

He meant to compromise her thoroughly, and then she would have no choice but to marry him. It was true that they were unofficially engaged, but they'd agreed that either one of them could end the secret engagement. It was clear to him that Faraday meant to purchase Sommerall, and he could not let it happen.

She would never know he'd planned it as long as he played the game with all of his considerable experience. The trick, of course, was to make it seem as if it were the result of unbridled passion. He had the sensual skills to seduce her, but his damned conscience plagued him.

He told himself she needed a husband in order to restore her reputation and help her family. It would not be a fairy-tale romance, but he could provide her with a home, security, and the chance to redeem her reputation. No one but him would ever know.

He didn't want to hurt her, but if he didn't do something, he would lose the property. He had just cause, but his damned conscience bothered him. She'd been through a terrible ordeal with her first engagement, but he had no intention of wounding her. He would make sure she never discovered the truth. She would benefit as much as he did. There was no reason for guilt, but his stomach clenched anyway.

He thrust away the remorse. She would be happier once she had the protection of his name. Seeing Faraday today, it had all become too real. Colin knew the man would make the purchase. He couldn't let it happen. Sommerall was his birthright and his mother's resting place.

Damn it all to hell. She deserved better. He didn't want to do this, but he had no choice. God willing she would never know the truth.

She clutched the covers and waited for Colin. It continued to rain, though not as hard as before. Angeline slid off the bed and walked to the window, but it was too dark to see anything. Foolishly, she'd wished he would kiss her again, but of course, she would rather melt in the rain than let him know she yearned for him.

A draft chilled her. She shut the drapes and returned to the bed. Even though she'd explored all the bedchambers at Sommerall, she felt restless all alone here. The blasted rain continued to pelt the windows and roof. She looked up at the dark canopy and wished Colin would hurry. It was too dark and silent, reminding her of all the nights she'd lain awake these two years past, despising herself for what she'd done to her family.

He'd expected her to be fast asleep when he entered the chamber, but she sat up and hugged her knees.

"You must be cold." He poured the coals and managed to start a fledgling fire.

He applied the bellows and paused to look back at her. "Why aren't you sleeping?" He'd rather hoped she'd fallen asleep, because he was having second and third thoughts about his wicked intentions.

She didn't answer right away.

"Were you anxiously awaiting me?"

She huffed. "Your head is swelling again."

"What is keeping you awake, Angeline?"

"You."

"You can tell me," he said.

"I've already said too much."

Apparently, she regretted telling him about Brentmoor. "Whatever you told me in confidence will go no further," he said.

"I know."

Her confession apparently bothered her nonetheless. He dusted his hands, picked up the candle branch, and set it on the bedside table. Then he walked to the bed. "Lie back now," he said, pressing her shoulders gently. He leaned over her, his hands bracketing her face on either side of the pillow. He kissed her softly on the lips. Then he sat on the edge of the bed and pulled off his boots.

"Are you taking off your clothes?" she said.

"My boots." *Shout at me to leave.*

He drew his shirt over his head and laid it on the chair. *Tell me to go to hell. Tell me you despise me. Tell me I'm the worst scoundrel you've ever met.*

She sat up. "Come to me."

"Aren't you afraid? I'm naked to the waist." *Tell me to go away.*

"I want to see you," she said.

He did her bidding. "What do you want?" he said in a harsh tone.

She caressed his chest and abdomen. "You're so hard everywhere and beautiful."

"Men aren't beautiful."

She planted a kiss where his heart beat hard. He clenched his jaw. *You should hate me.*

He reached for the falls of his trousers, but she brushed his hand away. "Let me."

A harsh exhalation escaped him. *Do not make this easy for me.*

She slipped the first button free and let her fingers slide over the fabric. His cock stirred. As he watched her, heat and desire collided. He got harder and harder as she took her time with the buttons. When his cock sprang free, she kissed the tip, and he realized she'd become the seducer. "Angeline, you are an innocent."

She smiled up at him. "Do you like it?"

His harsh breathing ought to tell her. "Yes, but I cannot let you."

She pulled the covers down. "It's cold. Get in the bed."

"Tell me to leave. Now."

"I don't want you to leave," she said.

"You know what will happen if I get in that bed. I can't do it." He'd thought he could seduce her, but he couldn't. He should have known better. "I'll sleep on the sofa."

"You banked the fire. It will be cold, and you are too big. Your feet will hang off the sofa."

Lord help him. He hadn't expected any of this. "I'll leave my trousers on."

"For pity's sake. You'll be uncomfortable."

"If I didn't know better, I'd suspect you want me naked."

She bit her lip. "Perhaps you should keep the drawers on—just to be safe."

He laid his trousers over the chair and removed his stockings. Then he pressed a curl back from her forehead. "You are too good for me."

"I'm glad you recognize it," she said, grinning.

Hell, so much for his big, bad rake reputation. "Angeline, you keep me on my toes. No other woman can match your clever retorts."

"Colin, you must be cold. Get in the bed."

"Yes, mistress," he said in a faux weak voice. He got under the covers and lay on his side to face her. "Brrrr. We'll keep each other warm."

"Colin, I may be a virgin, but I'm not stupid."

He laughed and leaned over her. "You are adorable."

"If I allow you to stay, you have to promise to be a gentleman."

"I'm always a gentleman in bed. Ladies first."

"You make no sense; you must have a touch of fever."

He placed his finger over her lips. "I won't lie to you. I want to kiss and touch you, but you can say no at any point, and I will stop." He nuzzled her neck. "Mmmm." Of course he knew exactly how to ignite the fire within her. Soon she would be so far gone, she would only realize her mistake when it was all over.

"If I said to stop now, would you?" she said.

He lifted his head. "Yes. It must be your decision." He would never force any woman. "Do you want me to stop?"

She bit her lip.

He sighed. "I'll go."

"No, stay."

"Angeline, I shouldn't."

She thought about all the lonely nights that might be ahead of her. She thought about his wicked sense of humor. Most of all, she thought about how he desperately wanted to possess Sommerall, because he could not bear for strangers to occupy the land where his mother was buried. He'd earned his rakish reputation, of that she had no doubt. But he'd sworn to stop at any point, and she knew instinctively he would honor that promise.

Tonight he'd enchanted her, teased her, and made her laugh. There were far worse things to fear, such as never knowing a man's ardent kiss in bed or the way it felt to have strong arms hold her. She loved him and knew that no matter what the future held, she would always cherish this night with him.

"Angeline, if the answer is no, you must tell me now."

She kissed him gently and then with more intent. He leaned over and returned it. "Do you want me to stop?"

"No." She opened for him and suspected the way he plunged his tongue inside her mouth was an imitation of lovemaking. He made her feel shivery and hot at the same time. When he looked into her eyes, he pulled the covers down to her waist, and then he lowered his head and dipped his tongue between the hollow of her breasts.

She drew in a ragged breath, but before she could even think to stop him, he ran his tongue all along the inside seam of her shift. He was very wicked, and very hard to resist. "Oh, my."

"Do you want me to stop?"

"Not yet."

He cupped her breasts and circled his thumbs lightly over the fabric covering her nipples. She drew in a shuddering breath.

"Do you like it?" he whispered.

"You devil; you know I do," she said. "Oh."

"You'll like this even better." He slipped the straps of her chemise down her arms, exposing her breasts. He circled his tongue around one nipple and then the other. When he suckled her, she arched up to him. "Oh, my God, I had no idea."

He cupped her face and looked into her eyes. "I will say this only once, but I'm glad."

I love you.

He pulled her shift up to her waist.

She caught his hand.

"Do you want me to stop?"

She swallowed. "No, not yet."

"I'm going to do something that may shock you."

"What is it?"

"I'll show you."

He put his knee between her thighs, and she grew very still. Could she let him?

He set her feet on the bed and slid down a bit. When he touched the folds of her sex, she jerked.

"Shhhh," he said. "It's very wicked, but you will like it."

"I'm not so sure," she said.

He slowly stroked his tongue along the soft folds to pleasure her.

A feminine sound came out of her throat.

"You like it?"

"Oh, dear heaven. Oh, oh."

He repeated the long, slow stroke. Her back arched and she threaded her fingers in his hair.

"Do you want me to stop?"

"Do not dare stop."

He chuckled and did it again and again and again.

She bit her lip. He could feel the tension in her legs. He carefully inserted his finger. The erotic sound of moisture nearly made him mad with lust. "You're tight inside and soaking wet."

When she looked at him, he said, "The wetness is preparation for coitus, but you can say no at any time."

"Oh."

He gave her three more long strokes of his tongue. Then he slipped his hands under her bottom and focused quick strokes on her sweet spot. She arched up until her head fell back. Then she came apart with a little cry and collapsed.

Her chest still rose and fell quickly. He smiled because he was rather proud of himself.

She opened her eyes. "Good Lord. No wonder virgins are kept in the dark. They would all be lifting their skirts for any man willing to . . . do that."

He burst out laughing. "That might depend on the man's skill."

"Yes, you clearly would earn high marks in the school of pleasure." She looked down at his tented drawers. "You are aroused."

He hesitated, knowing what he had to do, but when he looked at her sweet face, he realized how difficult it would be to rob her of something that ought to take place after the marriage vows.

"I'll take care of it privately." He got off the bed and pulled her shift down to cover her legs.

"Colin?"

"Go to sleep," he said. He should have done it. He was giving up everything, but he couldn't. Damn it.

"Don't leave," she whispered.

He drew in a long breath. "My restraint is limited."

She touched him through the fabric of his drawers.

"Oh, God."

"Is there no way for me to pleasure you?" she whispered.

"It's messy."

She held out her arms to him, and devil that he was, he couldn't resist. He told himself he would only show her how to pleasure him with her hand. Nothing else would happen. He mustn't let it.

He removed his drawers and joined her in the bed. When she put her knee between his legs, he smiled. She planted kisses all along his torso until she reached his erect cock. When she licked the length of him, his head fell back. He could not believe she had done it. He was ready to propose now, but he couldn't speak.

She continued the long strokes and cupped the sacs. He gritted his teeth as he got harder and harder. If she kept this up, he would explode any minute.

She took his hand and guided him to her folds. "I want you." She swallowed. "Inside."

"I'm trying very hard to be honorable for your sake."

"I don't want you to be honorable. I want you to make love to me."

She'd made it all too easy for him, but it was no longer

selfish thoughts that gripped him. He hovered over her on his elbows. "Tell me no."

"Yes," she said. When she stroked him with her hand, he was wild to be inside of her. Then he showed her how to guide him.

He felt the barrier give way, and she gasped. He stayed very still until the tension inside her eased. Then he withdrew part of the way and entered again slowly. He kept his gaze on her as he rocked in and out in a slow rhythm. Soon he realized it would be more pleasurable for her if she rode him. "Hold on tight," he said. Then he flipped them.

She blinked. Then he showed her the rhythm. She started slowly but eventually she rode him faster. He pulled her forward and suckled her while she rocked against him. When he switched to her other breast, she cried out and her inner muscles contracted all around him.

He pressed her back to the mattress and entered her again. His heart was thudding fast in his chest, and his skin tingled. In some dim place in his brain, he knew he needed to withdraw at just the right moment. When she wrapped her long, soft thighs around him and squeezed, he strained and exploded inside her.

As his breathing slowed, he pulled the covers over them and gazed into her eyes. "Sleep," he whispered.

Chapter Twelve

Colin awoke to find her watching him. "You are awake," he said in a sleep-roughened voice.

Her face grew hot.

"Is something wrong?"

She shook her head.

Clearly, she must be remembering the things they'd done in bed. "I'll announce our engagement when we return to Deerfield tomorrow."

She drew the sheet over her luscious breasts. "I beg your pardon?"

He plumped the pillow behind him. "Angeline, do not kick up a fuss. I had every intention of making a timely exit, but I lost control, and now it is quite possible we have created our firstborn."

She snorted. "It only happened one time. My friend Charlotte did not conceive for nearly six months."

"You're not Charlotte, and I'm not Portsworth. It only

takes once, and I'd rather not have to face your father after your belly expands."

"You speak as if it is a foregone conclusion," she said. "Furthermore, if we announce an engagement tomorrow, our families will know what we've been doing."

He released a loud sigh. Damnation, he was still in danger of losing Sommerall. Of course she was right. He imagined Wycoff pointing a rifle at him. Granted the man was a terrible shot, but Colin knew he'd make an easier target than a flying bird.

"When will you know if there are consequences?" he asked.

"Oh, my stars."

"Angeline, after the things we did in this bed, I'm astounded by your sudden bashfulness."

"A week," she muttered.

"Ah, well it matters not one way or the other."

"How can you be so cavalier about it?" she said.

"Because, darling, I want to announce our engagement."

"You do not have my permission," she said.

"Angeline, it is true that we both will benefit from the marriage, but it is equally true that I took your virginity."

"Well, you can't put it back."

He laughed. "In all seriousness, my honor demands that we marry."

"What nonsense."

"You know the rules as well as I do. Why are you being so difficult?"

"I need time to think," she said. *I'm scared that you will never love me.*

"Let us be officially engaged," he said. "That way we

will have freedom, and we can talk about our expectations."

"Suppose we find we do not suit. I cannot break another engagement, Colin." Panic set in.

She might be engaged to him in a week. Why did that frighten her? He wasn't Brentmoor. Yes, he had a rakish reputation, but he had never lied to her or tried to manipulate her. They had already agreed to a trial engagement. The only reason they had waited was to learn more about each other so that they could see if they would suit. She ought to be rejoicing, knowing that the marriage would resolve all of her problems and his as well.

"I know you, Angeline. You are worried. Tell me what troubles you."

You don't love me. "It is nothing, really."

His eyes softened. "Are you feeling guilty about what we did?"

"No." *I probably should, but I cannot when I love you.*

"You will tell me one way or the other when you know if there are consequences," he said.

She knew he was only being practical, but she yearned for a declaration of love that would not be forthcoming.

"You should not worry. I will not abandon you," he said.

Of all the foolish things to say. "Hah! I might abandon you."

"Where are my smelling salts?" he said, his chest shaking with laughter.

"In all seriousness, we should not rush into an engagement just because we made love."

"Angeline, we already discussed the possibility of marriage. We agreed to spend time together to discover if we are compatible. We are."

"You mean in bed," she said.

He kissed her cheek. "You surpassed my greatest hopes."

"You think I'm wanton."

"No, I think we're both passionate and compatible. Granted, we like to spar, but that is part of the passion. You must admit we have worked well together at Sommerall."

"Searching through trunks and making notes of the work that is needed is not the same thing as a marriage," she said.

He folded his hands behind his head. "Isn't marriage made up of everyday things? Breakfast, lovemaking, dinner, lovemaking, tea, lovemaking."

"You are incorrigible."

He turned on his side and propped his head up. "No, I'm delighted—with you. I think we'll rub along, pardon the pun, very well."

He was still under the influence of passion. "I think we need to continue our original plan to learn more about each other. We only have two and one-half weeks left."

He lifted her hand for a kiss. "Perhaps we can find a reason to return to Sommerall."

"I think we had better use caution. If we were caught, it could cause hard feelings," she said. "My father suffers enough guilt for what happened and so does my mother. You do not want to disappoint your father, either."

"Trust me. He is disappointed in me and has been for some time."

"I do not believe that he is disappointed in you. You find his ultimatums ridiculous. He can be difficult, but you manage to work around it."

"I tire of it." He rubbed his nose against hers. "But not of you."

He was flirtatious, but they needed to talk about the things that really mattered if they were to make the engagement official. "We are facing the possibility of bringing a child into the world. Yet, we need to discuss if we want a large family or not."

He shrugged. "I never thought much about it. I figure babies will come along when they will."

Yet, his mother had died in childbirth. Many women succumbed, particularly when there were multiple pregnancies. "It can be prevented?" she said.

"Tonight, I proved it can be a tricky business to prevent. I am sorry. Usually I...never mind."

"Finish what you meant to say."

"You are more delectable than...I expected."

That was not what he'd almost said. "You are speaking very carefully," she said. "To preserve my feminine sensibilities, perhaps?"

"Neither of us can change the past," he said. "You are a lady and my secret fiancée. I rather like the idea; it sounds mysterious. If all goes well, you will be my wife, provided we are both in accord now or when the house party ends. Now, wasn't that easy?"

"I know you've had mistresses."

"That is what bachelors do before they marry. This should be no surprise to you."

She summoned up the courage to ask what she really wanted to know. "Have you ever been in love?"

He remained silent for a long moment. "I thought so once."

"What happened?" she asked.

"Why do you want to know? It happened ten years ago."

"Then why do you hesitate to tell me?"

"Because it ended very badly. Leave it be."

"Did she break your heart?"

His eyes blazed. "I was mad for her, but her husband took exception to the affair de coeur."

Angeline inhaled sharply. "Who was she?"

He shook his head. "My father bought my way out of a duel. He has reasons for being disappointed in me."

"She was older, wasn't she?"

"I knew this would happen. I shouldn't have told you."

"You do realize how hypocritical you are," she said. "I told you every detail about Brentmoor. There were no other serious relationships. I think the reason you do not tell me is because you do not trust me enough to confide in me."

"I did not want you to hear the sordid truth, and I don't want to remember it, either. I'm not proud of it, Angeline, but I was young and stupid."

"You loved her," she said.

He was silent for a long moment. "Her husband banished her to Scotland. I thought I would lose my mind."

She squeezed her eyes shut. He had loved her.

"Turn on your side," he said. "You must be tired." When she did, he curled up behind her and cupped her breast.

She'd insisted that he tell her. Now she knew. Another woman had once won his love. It shouldn't matter, but it hurt. All along, they had agreed to a marriage of convenience, but she'd hoped he would develop tender feelings for her. He liked her, but he didn't love her. She wondered if he ever would.

Something tickled her neck and something hard pressed against her back.

Colin pressed her shoulder to the mattress. "Good morning."

Memories of the night before flooded her brain. Her face heated as she realized she was naked. Her shift was half dangling off the foot of the bed.

He nudged her thighs apart and suckled her breasts.

She inhaled.

He kissed her neck again.

She wanted to succumb to pleasure, but she was worried. What would happen when he tired of her? "I think we need to talk," she said.

He groaned and rolled onto his back. "Something is troubling you," he said.

"I'm a little concerned about what will happen."

"You worry too much."

"How can I not worry? You know my past. I've no idea what will transpire between us. Yes, I worry."

"It will do no good to worry about what might happen or what happened in the past," he said. "Think about the present."

How could she not think about the past? Brentmoor had betrayed her, and she'd had trouble trusting anyone afterward.

"I can see the worry on your face," he said. "Tell me what it is and I will do my best to reassure you."

"We will both make every effort to treat each other with kindness and respect."

He looked very serious. "I rather thought that was a given."

"Of course," she said, "but even the happiest of couples have disagreements."

He lifted his palms. "You are worrying about something that has not even occurred. Do you not see that anticipating trouble at every turn will frustrate me and make you unhappy? Promise me that you will make every effort to curb this tendency. No good will come from it, Angeline."

She nodded and knew he was right, but she also knew it would not be easy to put her faith completely in him all at once.

"Allow yourself to be happy," he said. "You deserve it. We both do."

"The rain stopped," she said. "We had better dress."

He donned his drawers and walked to the window and pulled the drapes back. It was still dim out, but the sun would rise shortly.

She managed to pin her hair in a simple twist. "Colin, I need your assistance with the stays, please."

He captured her gaze and tossed the stays aside.

"What are you doing?"

"I can't get last night out of my head."

"You are wicked," she whispered. Evidently she was, too.

"You are as irresistible as sweet cream." He was breathing faster. "I want to taste you again."

Her breasts felt heavier, and she realized his words had made her slick between her thighs.

He took her hands and regarded her with concern. "Be honest. Are you...well this morning?"

Her heart melted. "I am well...and a little undone."

He took her in his arms. "Are you sorry about last night?"

"No, quite the opposite." She was happy and carefree for the moment. There hadn't been many carefree moments for her in the last year.

"I'm glad," he said.

She wanted to confess what was in her heart, but then he would feel an obligation to her, and she wished for him to want her for his wife. She could not bear it if he felt forced. Yet, she knew if she discovered she was with child, they would have no choice.

Angeline realized she was borrowing trouble again. She gazed into his eyes and told him as much of the truth as she dared. "About last night," she said. "I failed to tell you something."

His expression grew wary.

"I failed to tell you that it was wonderful, and I feel a little bemused this morning."

His smile was as dazzling as the sun spearing through the crack in the drapes. He caught her hands and pulled her up to his chest. When he gave her a lush kiss, she found herself tingling all over. His hands slid down to her bottom. He lifted her up to her toes and pressed her against him. "Do you know what you do to me?"

His breath was as labored as hers. "I suspect the same thing you do to me."

"This may be our last chance for some time. Will you let me make love to you once more?"

"Yes." She wanted him again.

He kissed her like a starving man. She tangled her tongue with his and threaded her fingers in his hair. When he lowered his head, he suckled her through her shift, and she cried out. He pressed the straps of her shift down her arms until it pooled on the carpet. She loosened the ribbon on his drawers and shoved them off. He held her, and he was hard against her stomach. She reached between them and caressed him.

He drew in a ragged breath and touched her intimately. She was lost in the sensations, lost in the heat of his body, and God help her, lost in love with him. She kissed his chest where his heart beat rapidly, because she dared not speak the words that were in her heart. It would hurt too much to listen to his silence.

He took her hand, walked to the chaise, and sat in the middle. Then he pulled her onto his lap and entered her. He suckled her breasts as she found the rhythm and the pleasurable sensations crested quickly until she cried out.

He stood, carried her to the bed, and entered her again. As he pressed inside, she whimpered a little because he felt so good. She loved the feeling of sharing her body with him. He moved slowly and never let his gaze slip away from hers, and she loved him all the more for it. But eventually he seemed to lose himself in the pleasure and he thrust inside her faster and faster. She wrapped her legs around him and felt him throbbing inside of her. Afterward, he rolled to his side and smiled at her. "I hope this was not too much for you."

Her face grew warm. "I think you know I liked it."

He slid on his trousers. "You have enslaved me."

She grinned. "Will you do my bidding?"

"I am yours, mistress, but you must let me recover."

"I have high hopes you will rise to the occasion."

He burst out laughing and hugged her. "You are wonderful."

She loved being so close to him. "I will miss this when we return to Deerfield."

"We will have to leave soon," he said.

"I wish we could stay."

"You will think me greedy," he said, "but I want to make love to you once more."

"I want you again," she said.

A sly expression entered his eyes. "Will you be my mistress?"

"What are you about?" she said.

He led her back to the chaise. "On your knees."

"What game do you play?" she whispered.

"You can say no, but will you do my bidding?"

She wet her lips. "Why should I?"

"Because I will reward you," he said in a rough tone.

She knelt on the carpet between his spread legs. The bulge in his trousers gave evidence to his excitement.

"What do you bid me to do?" she whispered.

"Release the buttons on my falls."

She let her fingers brush over him as she slowly released the buttons one by one. The game made her breathless. Her breasts felt heavy, and she wanted him inside her.

When he sprang out, she looked up into his eyes. "May I touch you?"

"Yes." His voice sounded harsh.

She ran her finger in circles around him. There was a drop of moisture on top.

"Have I pleased you?" She liked pretending she was a libidinous courtesan.

He pulled her forward and lifted the skirts to her waist. "Touch yourself."

She looked at the carpet. "I am too shy."

"Straddle my leg."

When she did, he took her hand and guided it to her sex. "Do you like it?"

"I like your touch better."

He caressed her intimately until her legs felt like jelly. Then he inserted first one and then another finger. "You are slick and wet. I like the sound of moisture as I pleasure you."

She was breathing fast, and so was he. His words encouraged her to be brazen. "You please me," she said, "but I am wanton and greedy."

"What are you greedy for?" he said.

She wrapped her hand around his aroused cock.

"You want to ride astride me?"

"Yes."

"You are new at this," he said, "but you are eager."

"I am eager for you."

"You may straddle me now," he said.

She did his bidding. "Will you pleasure me?"

"Yes." Her breathing grew labored with the caress of his fingers.

"Do you want me?" he said, his voice low.

"Yes, I am lascivious and live for pleasure."

"I want to watch you."

She rose up on her knees and guided him. He went slowly, but God almighty he'd never been this lust-crazed in his life.

When she rocked into him, he almost spent his seed immediately, but he was as hungry as she to continue their role-play. He splayed his hands over her bottom as he lifted up to meet her. Then as he sensed she was as close to the edge as he was, he locked his mouth to hers and mimicked his tongue play with his thrusts inside her. She was panting and cried out. He could feel the contractions of her release all around him, and he spilled his seed again.

She clutched his shoulders. Their bodies were still joined.

"You have to marry me," he said.

"No, I'm a famous courtesan. I refuse to keep only one man."

He laughed a little. "Darling girl, you may pretend to be anyone you wish, but you will never escape me now. I've had more than a taste of you, and it will never be enough."

He dressed in yesterday's clothes and helped her into the stays, petticoats, and gown afterward.

"Angeline, I've been thinking. Let's announce the engagement."

"No, we need to use the time to talk."

"There is nothing to be proved by letting this drag on. You know we will have no privacy at Deerfield."

"I need time, Colin."

"For what? We will figure things out as we go, like any other couple."

"I know what you stand to lose at Sommerall," she said, "but you know what I've been through, and I cannot be rushed."

"Do you trust me or not?"

"Of course I do," she said.

"Then let me make our engagement public."

"If we announce it now, they will suspect what we've been doing."

The clatter of hooves sounded. He looked out the window. "There's John."

"I wish we could stay," she said.

"So do I." He wrapped his arms around her and kissed her deeply. Her head was spinning, and her heart was full of love for him.

"One week, Angeline, and I will announce our engagement."

When she hesitated, he said, "I know you're afraid, but you need to trust me, starting today. One week."

"Very well," she said.

He hugged her hard. "We must go before your father decides to send out a search party."

They arrived at Deerfield to discover Wycoff and the marquess about to board a carriage.

"I began to think you might have drowned last night," the marquess said to Colin.

"Angeline was frightened and wanted to leave, but of course we could not. It wasn't safe to travel."

"Daughter, are you well?" the duke demanded.

"Yes, I'm fine, Papa. Just a little rumpled in yesterday's clothing."

"I'm sorry for the miserable night," Colin said, meeting her eyes. "I'm sure you will wish to rest once you are in your room."

"I am fatigued. It was a long night, but I'm glad the storm passed."

It was one of the best nights he'd had in years, but he kept that between his teeth.

"Well, we might as well go indoors," the marquess said. "Colin, after you make yourself presentable, please attend me in my study."

He nodded.

An hour later, he knocked on his father's door and sat before the desk.

"That was quite a storm last night," Colin said. "Is everything fine here at Deerfield?"

"Lightning struck a tree limb. I've got men chopping it now. Your sisters scared Penelope by telling ghost stories last night."

He laughed. "I'm not surprised."

"That ugly dog howled most of the night. I threatened to turn it out in the storm, but Margaret accused me of cruelty. Then your sisters started crying, and I thought we'd never get everybody in bed and asleep. What a night." He paused and said, "What happened with Mr. and Mrs. Faraday? Did they show?"

"Oh, yes," Colin said. When he finished the story, he said, "You probably would regret having them as neighbors. You would likely find them calling a little too often."

"Something needs to be done," the marquess said. "I can't let the place go to rack and ruin, and it most certainly will if I do nothing. It's a miracle the place has withstood the years as well as it has."

"Last night, I feared the heavy rain would expose leaks, but everything appeared to be in good order."

The marquess sighed. "I expect you know that Wycoff is concerned about you staying in the same house alone with his daughter."

"We had no choice," Colin said. "Would he have preferred I risk her life, that of the driver, and the horses?"

"Of course not," the marquess said, "but it wouldn't hurt if you reassured Wycoff that his daughter suffered no harm."

Colin looked out the window and then he turned to his father. "I have no intention of reassuring Wycoff. I know she is his daughter, but it is disrespectful on his part to question either of us. Moreover, we are not sniveling adolescents."

Of course their nocturnal and morning activities had not been innocent, but they were thirty-one years old and more than mature enough to deal with any consequences. Mind, he hoped there weren't any, but if so, they would marry in a hurry.

But that only brought to mind this ridiculous secret engagement. Thank goodness he'd persuaded her to make the announcement in one week. He'd grown weary of it and did not see how they would prove anything by allowing the situation to drag on for another two and one-half weeks.

"Colin, you know what their family has been through," the marquess said.

"Yes, a roué treated her badly, but Wycoff should take a portion of the blame. He has plenty of connections, and he let a known libertine hoodwink him."

"I came to the same conclusion. He is a good friend, but in the case of Brentmoor, his judgment became clouded."

Colin nodded. "Men like Brentmoor train their sights on the unwary. They recognize others' vulnerabilities and take advantage." He felt like a hypocrite. He'd taken advantage of Angeline last night. Of course, he would never admit it.

"Wycoff needs to own up to his mistakes, and he needs to be kind to his daughter," Colin said.

The marquess frowned. "What do mean?"

"Wycoff is wrapped up in his own guilt. He keeps away from Angeline, and my understanding is that they were close before this all happened. He is wounding her as badly as Brentmoor."

The marquess clasped his hands over his slight paunch. "I hesitate to get involved."

"Who better than his oldest friend?" Colin said. "You will tell him what he needs to hear, not what he wants to hear."

The marquess sighed. "It may well end in the ruin of a lifelong friendship."

"He won't like it," Colin said. "What man would? But when he becomes defensive, you will tell him that he must stop wallowing in his guilt and be a husband and father to his family."

"Where the devil did you acquire this wisdom?"

Colin huffed. "From you."

His father burst out laughing.

Chapter Thirteen

Two days later

The grounds were too soggy and muddy for walking, so everyone was forced to spend their days indoors, except for the marquess and the duke, who didn't think a little mud would hurt anyone. Margaret disagreed, but she'd long ago thrown up her hands when her husband tracked mud or dirt indoors.

Colin invited Angeline to play backgammon with him. He knew it would be a challenging game, because she was more clever than most, but he recalled their conversation the last time they had pretended to play. Since Margaret, the duchess, and the girls were involved in needlework, he figured the others would leave them to concentrate.

As they set up the stones for the game, he glanced at her. "You are well?"

"Yes."

"Were there questions?" he asked.

"My mother was appalled that you unlaced me, but I

told her to be sensible. You were the only one available."

"How did she react?"

Angeline moved a stone. "She fears you took a disgust of me. I explained that it was only circumstances, and she blamed herself for allowing me to attend you."

"That's foolish. I hope you did not take it to heart."

"I told her I could not be a martyr to my stays."

He grinned.

"Did you take a disgust of me after my wanton behavior?" she whispered.

He met her gaze. "I started the game. Were you disgusted? Be truthful."

"No, I found it . . . exciting." She rolled the dice.

"Now you are remorseful?"

"No, but . . ."

"But what?"

"I want to do it again," she whispered.

His breath whooshed out of him, and his groin tightened. "Me too."

She moved a stone. "I'm shameless."

His shoulders shook with laughter.

"Do not laugh. They are liable to ask what is so funny," she whispered.

He rolled the dice. "I am eager for another visit."

She blinked. "I beg your pardon?"

He leaned forward and whispered, "From the famous courtesan."

"She is entertaining other gentlemen," she said under her breath.

"I forbid it. She is mine and mine alone."

"Exclusive visits will cost you. She demands rubies and sapphires."

He looked into her eyes. "She is beautiful and very desirable."

"I can hardly believe I was capable of the things I said and did. I don't know what is wrong with me."

"Nothing is wrong with you. It's only fantasy."

"It is not ladylike."

He leaned forward and said under his breath, "Angeline, I've never wanted a woman more in my life."

"You are only trying to be polite and spare my feelings," she whispered, "even though I acted like Satan's mistress."

He laughed, but his imagination soared. He pictured her walking in a room in nothing but one of those enormous shawls women favored. Then he imagined tearing it off of her luscious body and having his wicked way with her on the carpet.

"Colin, why do you have that gleam in your eyes?" Bianca said.

Uh-oh. "I am about to trounce Angeline."

"You are not," Angeline said.

He looked at the board. "What happened?"

"I beared off all fifteen stones," she said. "I won."

While he'd been entertaining fantasies of her naked, she'd been strategizing.

"I am a gentleman and naturally let you win."

"Keep telling yourself lies," she said, "but I know better."

When everyone gathered for breakfast, the marquess folded his hands. "I have it on the best of authority from one of the groomsmen that at long last the grounds are dry in most of the areas. I imagine everyone is anxious to be out of doors for a change."

A round of applause went up. Colin smiled at Angeline. They would probably have to spend the first hour or so walking with everyone else, but he hoped that he and Angeline would be able to take a different path so that they could discuss whether they could build a life together.

"Mama, can we ride?" Bianca asked.

"Not today," the marchioness said. "We will all enjoy a very long walk about the grounds, and then afterward, we will have luncheon, as everyone will be hungry from the exercise."

"Mama, may we take Hercules?" Bernadette asked.

"Yes, but bring his leash in the event he manages to find a puddle or mud." Margaret rose. "Chadwick, do try not to step in every mud puddle."

"Wycoff and I are not afraid of mud," the marquess said.

"I know, dear, but given the amount of mud you have managed to find, I would be grateful if you might condescend to avoid some of the puddles."

"We shall see," the marquess said. "Ah, here are the guns."

Margaret shook her head. "Let us all put on our warmest wraps, gloves, and hats. We will meet in the hall in fifteen minutes."

Colin knew it was important that he treat Angeline as a friend only in front of their mothers and sisters. It was not an easy task when she favored him with one of her brilliant smiles and walked beside him. But he thought better of being familiar with her. Wycoff had been displeased about the night they had spent at Sommerall. Fortunately, the marquess had told Wycoff to let him know the day he could predict the weather, as he would sell tickets for miles around.

Hercules forged ahead and the leash slipped from Bianca's gloved hand. "Hercules, come back!"

The dog ignored her and ran farther and farther away.

"He'll be lost," Bianca cried.

Colin whistled as he chased after the dog. Naturally Hercules ignored him. "Come back here!" he yelled. Hercules spied a red squirrel and chased it yards ahead until the squirrel ran up a tree. The foolish dog pawed the tree and barked continuously. Colin scooped the dog up, and of course, he got dirty paw prints all over his coat. "No wonder my father threatens to put you in the dustbin," he muttered.

The girls surrounded him and clapped their hands.

"Bianca, put the leash on him. I saw some mud puddles," Colin said. "Father is liable to make good on his promise to get rid of Hercules if you don't take care of him."

"Thank you for catching him," Bianca said.

"I thought you meant to teach him some commands," Colin said.

"Such as?" Bernadette said.

"Command him to sit."

"Sit, Hercules," Bernadette said.

The dog lolled his tongue.

"Push his bottom to the ground."

Colin looked up at the sound of Angeline's voice. "Good idea."

"Sit, Hercules," Colin said, pushing the dog's hind end to the grass.

Hercules promptly stood up and lolled his tongue.

"You'll have to do it repeatedly for him to learn," Angeline said.

"You've trained a dog before?" he asked.

"Yes, but I gave him a small treat as a reward when he obeyed."

He met her gaze and remembered the command he'd given her that morning at Sommerall. He still couldn't believe she'd played along.

Her lips parted and she shaded the brim of her bonnet as she looked away. Ah, she might well be remembering.

Colin handed the leash to Bianca. "Today let's not let him loose since there are mud puddles, and it would be just your luck he would find them."

"After we return to the house, ask Cook for some bits of meat that you can use to reward him," Angeline said. "Teach him one command at a time."

"Thank you, Angeline," Bianca said. "Papa makes fun of Hercules, but he really is a smart dog."

"You must take care of him and teach him manners," Colin said.

Hercules broke wind.

"Pew," Colin said, waving his hand.

"He does some very unmannerly things," Bernadette said.

Angeline and his sisters laughed.

Colin groaned. "You had better train him not to do that in our father's presence. That might be the last straw for Papa."

Colin stood. "Margaret is waving from the folly. Shall we catch up to them?"

This time Colin let the girls walk ahead and lagged behind with Angeline. "It seems a long time since we last had a conversation."

"I think we are all grateful to be out of doors."

"I don't suppose you have any news," he said.

"Not yet." She paused. "Colin, are you sure about the engagement? There are only three days left. We do not have to rush."

He couldn't tell her that he dared not wait any longer for fear of losing Sommerall.

Unlike him, Angeline would do anything for her family. She would marry to make her parents and her sister happy. When he thought about the way he'd ignored his own family, he was ashamed. He'd been a selfish man.

He couldn't change all the years he'd sullenly come home for Christmas. Without fail, he'd resented attending the annual house party and often left early to rake, drink, and gamble in London. He'd preferred the company of acquaintances he didn't care about over the members of his own family. But he could change for the better and start afresh. He could make amends and be there for his father, stepmother, and sisters. But there was someone else who needed him, someone he'd mistreated.

Since the day Angeline had told him what Brentmoor had done to her and her family, he'd seen himself as the good man, the one who would never hurt her. But he'd been a cad. He'd actually told her he wouldn't abandon her if she found herself with child. Now he felt the shame bone-deep. She was the daughter of his father's best friend, and he'd bedded her, without offering a single tender word. She deserved better.

Guilt would not help either of them, but he could help her reclaim her life and her rightful place in society. It would not be a simple matter, but for once in his life he would give to someone he cared about without expecting something in return.

Three days later

It had rained twice more, and now the grounds were saturated, and the paths were muddy. The roads were as well. The marquess and duke continued to trudge through mud, and Colin was so wild to get out of doors that he accompanied them one day. He attempted to shoot a pheasant and ended up shooting into mud that splattered in his hair and all over his clothes. He returned to the house, preferring confinement in a two-hundred-room mansion to mud.

This particular morning, he played billiards, though it wasn't much fun with no competition. His mood perked up when Angeline darted inside, until she closed the door.

"You had better open the door," he said.

"Colin, I dare not open the door."

His heart thudded in his chest. "You have news?" Was he going to be a father? Was he ready for such a step?

"There were no consequences," she whispered.

He almost sagged with relief. "That is good news."

She nodded, but she didn't look happy about it.

He took her hands. "Were you hoping for a baby?"

She shrugged. "We are fortunate to escape the consequences."

"It would be better to get such news after marriage." He paused. "Tonight, in the drawing room, I will make the announcement."

She wet her lips. "Yes."

"Are you afraid?"

"I suppose everyone is a bit anxious before a life-changing event."

"I'm glad about the engagement, Angeline. Our parents will be as well."

"I had better return to the drawing room before someone discovers me here."

"You are miserable doing needlework?"

"I'm going mad," she said, leaning against the door.

"Angeline, no one is forcing you. If you don't wish to do needlework, read a book."

"I will feel guilty, because everyone else is mending or embroidering handkerchiefs or darning stockings. The mending does need to be taken care of."

"Perhaps you could read to everyone else while they mend or embroider," he said.

"You're brilliant. Margaret has a copy of *Sense and Sensibility*. I could read it to them."

"Well, it's hardly a brilliant suggestion, but if it pleases you, it pleases me."

She stepped closer to him. "I miss you."

As much as he would love to kiss her, he didn't want someone to catch them alone behind a closed door. It might create problems between their families, and he wanted the announcement to be void of any possible scandal. "You had better return, Angeline. It would not do if we were caught alone in here."

She nodded. "I promised to tell you."

Someone knocked on the door. He winced.

I'm sorry, she mouthed.

He opened the door. Penelope stood there.

"I beg your pardon," Penny said. "Angeline, will you come with me to the drawing room?"

"Yes, of course," Angeline said. "I just needed to tell Colin something I remembered about Sommerall."

Penny regarded him with a slight frown. "Come, Sister. Mama will worry if you are gone too long."

"Angeline," Penny said as they walked through the great hall. "Mama sent me to find you when you did not immediately return to the drawing room."

"Mama is overly finicky." She wished her mother would not hover.

"You were expected to attend. Everyone noticed you were gone."

"I had every intention of returning to the drawing room." Where else could she go when the grounds were soaked and muddy?

"You will be cautious, will you not?"

Penny's question made her heart race. "About what, dearest?"

"You should not have gone to the billiard room."

Relief filled her. "Oh, you worry for nothing."

"You are spending a great deal of time with him."

"I have been helping him at Sommerall," Angeline said. "There's nothing to be concerned about. It is only Colin."

Penny halted. "Why did you close the door?"

The question caught her unaware. "I only meant to tell him something, and I was on the verge of leaving when you came." It was all true, but not nearly as innocent as she'd made it sound.

"Please be careful," Penny said.

"Yes, I do not wish to inadvertently give the wrong impression," she said. Her stomach felt a little queasy. She'd had to tell him there were no consequences. It would have been cruel to make him wait.

"I do not want you to ever have to leave again," Penny said.

Her sweet sister's words stung her heart. "I didn't want to leave you, but Mama insisted I must be presented in Paris."

"I know something bad happened," Penny whispered. "Papa shut himself in his study. Mama's friends no longer called. Lord Brentmoor went away."

Chill bumps erupted on Angeline's arms. Penny knew. "It is all over."

"You must be careful," Penny said. "Ladies must always guard their reputations."

Angeline inhaled on a shaky breath. "That is wise advice, Penny, but Colin is a friend of our family. You need not be concerned." She had only wanted to reassure him. It never would have been necessary if she had not abandoned herself to him. Tonight, however, they would announce their engagement. It was beyond anything she had ever imagined.

Of course, she'd wanted a kiss from Colin and words of reassurance. He'd been obviously relieved. She ought to be as well, but at the moment, she was tired and out of sorts.

"Penny, my head is aching. Will you please make my excuses to Mama and Margaret?"

"I hope you are not ill," Penny said.

"No, it is only a headache. All I need is to lie down for a bit."

She slept for two hours. When she awoke, she realized that she was fatigued from the anxiety. She'd managed to catch him alone, but Penny had come along, and Angeline realized how close Penny had come to hearing their conversation.

She'd sworn she would never regret that night with Colin, and she did not. She would never have made love to him if she did not love him dearly. They had been trapped by the violent weather at Sommerall, and she had wanted to share her body with him. She loved that he wanted to champion her, and she loved that he thought her smart. She loved his teasing, and she even loved him when he pointed out that she worried over the past and the future rather than focusing on the present. She had not even realized it until he'd told her.

But now it occurred to her that she'd done the very thing she'd been accused of doing with Brentmoor. She'd had an assignation with Colin.

She told herself that it was different because she loved him, and he wanted to make their engagement official tonight. But it was eerily similar to Brentmoor, who had entreated her to agree to their engagement.

The situations were not comparable. Colin had never lied to her. He had never tried to press her into intimacies. She had given herself freely to him, and he had not betrayed her. He had never expressed tender feelings for her in so many words, but he'd showed how much he cared about her.

It was true he would gain Sommerall, probably immediately. For a moment doubts plagued her. The Faradays had made the third visit, and soon after, Colin had persuaded her to announce their engagement. There was nothing nefarious about it, but she could not quite push away her misgivings.

Once before, she had ignored the silent warnings and paid a high price for it.

"No," she said. Colin was not a cruel, heartless man. Furthermore, he wasn't the only one who would benefit from their engagement and marriage. Once she married him, she would be respectable again, and she would be able to attend Penny's come-out in the spring. There might be a few high sticklers who cut her acquaintance, but she had weathered far worse things.

From the very beginning, she and Colin had both been honest with each other that they were seeking a marriage of convenience, one that benefitted both of them. With all of her heart, she hoped that he would fall in love with her. If that day never came, she knew it would make her sad, but she would make the best of things. She would have children, and she would not have to live in seclusion as a spinster with a companion.

It surprised her how quickly her feelings had grown for Colin, but it should not. He'd changed. She suspected that the possibility of losing Sommerall had made him realize what he stood to lose. It was not just about the property, however. It was also very much about his family. He meant to spend more time with them. Colin would embrace his family. They were as imperfect as her family, but Angeline thought that only made families more interesting. Really, wasn't love the only thing any family needed?

Doubts crept in again, but she pushed them away and did her best to focus on the present. Tonight, she would be happy. He was a good man, a changed man. They would find happiness together. It would not be the love match she'd always dreamed of, but she would find contentment in their marriage. Starting tonight, she would focus on him rather than herself. She would do everything in her power to see to his happiness and comfort.

He felt like a wretch.

Colin sat at his desk with his forehead in his hand. In so many ways, that last night had been one of the most wonderful nights of his life, but there was no denying that he'd purposely set out to bed her. She'd been a virgin for God's sake, and he of all people knew how vulnerable she was because of what had happened to her. But he had not known what else to do. So he'd pressed her into agreeing to announce the engagement tonight, because he feared that if he waited, she might change her mind. The sooner they were engaged, the better. This was pure hell, knowing that he'd betrayed her trust. While she would never know, he swore he would spend the rest of his days making it up to her. She deserved a better man, but he'd made her his that last night, and now he must take responsibility.

They were more than suited to each other in bed, but marriage was forever. It could not be undone. He knew too many men who abandoned their wives for their clubs and mistresses. That would make Angeline miserable, and what would be the point of marrying if he only returned to his bachelor life.

The devil. Soon he would be married. He could hardly countenance it.

Not long ago, he'd awakened with his boots on to find three bottles, two glasses, and an actress in his rooms at the Albany. His freewheeling bachelor days were numbered in hours now.

He hoped he could make her happy. She deserved it. Lord, they would likely have a brat by this time next year if not sooner. The realization shook him. He questioned whether he could be a good husband and father to the children that would inevitably come along.

He did something he couldn't remember doing in a very long time. He bowed his head and asked for forgiveness. He'd been selfish most of his life, but he remembered what his father had said. *When a man has a wife and children, he leaves behind his selfishness because his family means more to him than dissipation.*

He knew it to be true. She would soon be his wife and his responsibility. He rose and felt like a different man already. God willing they would find happiness together. He would do his best to think of her needs first and keep her safe. Tonight, he would take that first step.

That afternoon, he was attempting to compose a few lines for his proposal to Angeline. Unfortunately, he was having trouble concentrating. Damnation. She would expect something romantic, but his stomach was performing somersaults. This was beyond ridiculous. He probably would have to settle for the age-old "make me the happiest man." He sighed and set his pen aside. Lord only knew how her father would respond when he approached Wycoff. If the man asked if he'd touched his daughter, Colin would admit to kissing her. Anything else was none of Wycoff's business.

Someone tapped on the door. "Come in," Colin said.

A footman entered. "My lord, you have a caller." He handed over the silver dish with the card. At first, he frowned at the card. *Harry Norcliffe, Duke of Granfield.*

Colin's skin prickled. Good God, Harry's uncle must have died. "Where is he?"

"The main drawing room, my lord."

Colin shrugged into his coat and ran down the stairs. Margaret sat next to Harry. The duchess and Angeline were there as well. "Harry, old boy." He clapped his friend's shoulder.

Harry looked as if he'd not slept in a week. "I decided to make a brief call on my way back to London. My uncle passed quietly and unexpectedly."

"I am sorry."

"Would you like another cup of tea?" Margaret asked.

"I'll get you a brandy," Colin said.

"Perhaps we should give you both some privacy," Angeline said. "I am sorry for your loss."

Colin looked at her gratefully.

"If you need anything, please ring the bell," Margaret said.

After the ladies left, Colin poured a brandy for Harry and himself. "What can I do?"

"Nothing, really. I've got meetings with solicitors, bankers, and estate managers in London. I just wanted to see a familiar face."

"You're welcome to stay as long as you wish."

"My mother and female cousins are taking his death very hard. They're depending on me. All of them. I find myself wishing I'd paid more attention to my uncle's lectures about the estate. Instead, I just laughed about the pigs."

"You'll manage," Colin said. "Your uncle had good people working for him. If you need recommendations, Bell will know the right people."

"I thought you would have returned to London by now, but I checked before leaving the city, and the landlord said you weren't there."

It seemed like a lifetime ago since he'd left the Albany. "You look done up, friend. Stay the night and rest."

He sipped his brandy. "I must return soon. There is a mountain of paperwork and much to learn. My carefree days are over."

Harry looked bad. "I insist you stay," Colin said. "The paperwork will keep, but you need to rest."

Angeline returned to the drawing room and directed Agnes to set the tea tray out. "There are cold meats, cheese, fruit, and a bottle of claret."

"I've persuaded Harry to stay the night," Colin said, looking at her meaningfully.

"Of course, he must stay," she said.

The marquess entered the drawing room. "I just heard the news. What can I do?"

Harry shrugged. "Nothing at this time. I'll manage."

"I've persuaded him to say the night at least," Colin said.

"Yes, you need a good night's rest," the marquess said. "I am sorry to hear the news. Granfield was a good man."

"I'll leave you all now," Angeline said.

Harry regarded her through red-rimmed eyes. "Thank you for your kindness, Lady Angeline."

Four hours later, Angeline walked into the drawing room. Colin stood at the window and turned in her direction.

"Where is Harry?"

"Poor fellow. He was so exhausted. I convinced him to rest. I checked on him ten minutes ago. He's sleeping."

Colin pinched the bridge of his nose. "I'm sorry for the delay in our announcement."

She shook her head. "Your friend comes first."

"I am reminded not to take family for granted," he said.

"So am I," she said.

He squeezed her hands and gazed into her eyes. Something in his chest turned over. He lifted her hand and kissed it. "You are a special lady," he said.

"Make sure he breaks his fast in the morning," Angeline said. "He is overwrought and likely to forget."

"I will, Angeline. He means to leave very early."

"You will tell him Godspeed for me," she said.

He kissed her cheek. *My God, I think I'm falling in love with you.*

Two days later

Colin clasped his hands behind his back and paced in the great hall. He'd awoken early, hoping he might be able to have a private word with Angeline. He'd tossed and turned last night trying to think of exactly the right things to tell her. In the end, exhaustion had claimed him. He would simply have to rely on instinct and honesty.

Running footsteps sounded on the stairs. Bianca and Bernadette hurried down the steps while Angeline followed behind, carrying Hercules. Evidently, the twins were still hiding the dog in their bedchamber.

A ray of sunshine from the high windows promised a clear day. When he caught Angeline's gaze, something turned over inside his chest. He'd never felt anything quite like it before.

After his sisters ran down the stairs, they were a little out of breath.

"Penny is still sleeping," Bernadette said, "but Angeline offered to help us train Hercules in the kitchen this morning."

"Ah." He smiled at her as she joined them. "It is very generous of you to help my sisters train Hercules."

"I figured it was best to work with him early in the day before other activities. It's important that his training be as consistent as possible. He's a clever dog and will respond well if given the chance."

Angeline attached his leash and set him down. Naturally Hercules tried to run off and his toenails slipped a bit on the marble. Angeline gently pulled back the leash and said, "Halt."

The dog tried to run again.

Colin picked him up.

Angeline ruffled the dog's short fur. "I think we need to focus on sitting and work on the leash later."

Angeline handed Hercules to Bianca. "We had better head to the kitchen now so we won't be late for breakfast."

"May I join you?" Colin asked.

"If you wish," Angeline said.

Her voice had sounded guarded. What was wrong?

The twins hurried ahead.

Colin turned to Angeline. "Is something the matter?"

"We will talk later," she said.

"There are things I wish to discuss with you. I don't know when we might have a chance. Perhaps we could meet very early in the morning tomorrow."

"I promised to train Hercules every morning," she said.

"Perhaps after the training tomorrow?"

"What do you wish to discuss?" she asked.

"Things I neglected before," he said. "Things I should have said."

She sighed. "Are you suffering from a guilty conscience?"

"It's more than that," he said. "I was cavalier with you, and it troubles me greatly. I had no right to touch you. You are a virtuous lady, and I took advantage of you."

"I am not a twenty-year-old single lady, Colin," she said under her breath. "You did not take advantage of me. I'm a grown woman. That night, I decided to make love to you with the full knowledge of what I was doing."

"I took your virginity, for God's sake," he said.

Her expression showed disappointment. "You took nothing, Colin. I freely gave myself to you. Clearly you are having delayed remorse over what happened, but it is entirely unnecessary. What happened cannot be undone. There were no consequences, and I'm quite certain you were relieved when I informed you."

"Angeline, I was only relieved because I had been irresponsible."

"Your guilt is misplaced. There was no seduction. I agreed to all of it. If you are seeking absolution, I don't have any to give you, because there is no fault on either side. We both knew exactly what we were doing. Now I recommend you let it go, because there is nothing else to be done about it."

"You know there is," he said. "I have a responsibility to you."

"No, you do not. Now, if you will excuse me, the girls are waiting."

"I will come with you. They are expecting me."

"I'll make your excuses," she said.

"Why are you being so cold to me?" he whispered.

"This is neither the time nor the place for this discussion. I will meet you in the library at two o'clock in the morning when servants aren't about, and we can talk without listening ears.

"Now, I must go," she said.

His jaw clenched as she hurried away. How the hell had his good intentions gone so wrong?

Angeline sat in her customary place at the table next to Colin. She'd cut up at him because she'd thought his words demeaning, but she knew he'd not meant them to be. He was a little late to be worrying about his careless behavior, but as she'd told him, she was a grown woman and there had been no seduction.

She didn't want his good intentions or his guilt or his pity. She deserved nothing less than his respect. What had really troubled her was his remorse, because that night had been special to her, and he'd turned it into something that implied wrongdoing. Based on his words, she knew he didn't understand, but late tonight, she would tell him how it had made her feel.

There was the other issue—the dangling proposal. Granted, Harry's appearance had halted everything. But Colin probably was having second thoughts and felt he couldn't honorably back out. So tonight she would tell him that he had no obligation to marry her. No, she would tell him late tonight that she felt it would not be in either of their best interests to marry.

"You are very quiet, Angeline," Margaret said.

"Forgive me. My mind was elsewhere."

She glanced at Colin. He'd barely touched his customary baked eggs. Now she felt badly, but she'd been honest with him.

She also felt guilty because she could turn everything around for her family if she married him. The trouble was she loved him, loved him more than he would ever know, and it would not be fair to him if she accepted his proposal. She and her family had much to gain from it, and when he'd first spoken of it, she'd had no qualms and believed that she would accept. But it was not based on those elements that she thought were important for a happy marriage.

She could not count on love developing for them the way it had for the marquess and Margaret. Colin might not know it, but he deserved to find love and happiness with a woman who did not come to the marriage with baggage.

As for Sommerall, she had a plan. It might not work, but she would ask on his behalf, though making the request might prove difficult to arrange. If she succeeded, she would ask that he never know about her interference. She would make this request for him, because she loved him and wanted his happiness more than her own.

Angeline read to the ladies while they applied their needles. When she'd made the request, everyone had agreed it was a splendid idea and made their sewing efforts far less tedious. She had Colin to thank for the suggestion, but she kept silent on that point.

"Ah, here is the place I marked where we left off," Angeline said. "If everyone is ready, I will continue the story."

"Please begin," Margaret said.

Angeline read, "'Marianne's abilities were, in many respects, quite equal to Elinor's.'"

"If Elinor and Marianne were twins, they would be equal," Bernadette said.

Angeline continued on, and the girls questioned her about Marianne's behavior. "The author tells us that Marianne is everything but prudent," Angeline said. "So it is possible that she still has much to learn about life."

Margaret's eyes brightened. "Goodness, I wonder who might resemble Marianne."

"The youngest sister's name is Margaret," Bernadette said.

Margaret continued stitching. "Yes, but the fictional Margaret is only thirteen years old, younger than my girls and Penny."

"Is it a love story?" Penny asked.

"Oh, yes, very much," Angeline said, "but like all good novels, there are difficulties and sometimes it will seem all is lost."

"Is there a handsome gentleman?" Bianca asked.

"Yes, but he is not what he seems," Angeline said.

"If he is cruel and wicked, I will not like him," Penny said.

"Girls," Margaret said, "do be silent so that Angeline can continue the story."

"Oh, do read more," Penny said. "I'm anxious to find out what happens."

A footman entered with a tray of mail. Angeline had not responded to Charlotte's letter because she feared creating havoc for her friend, but she found herself hoping for a letter nonetheless.

Margaret sorted through the letters and handed one to the duchess. "This one is addressed to you."

The duchess broke the seal and gasped. "It is from my son," she said, standing. "Lady Landale has been delivered of a healthy boy. Both mother and child are well."

Everyone exclaimed.

Margaret rose to hug the duchess. "I am so happy for you. Your first grandchild."

Angeline clasped Penny's hand and smiled. "What do you think, Penny? We are aunts now."

"Oh, I can hardly believe it," Penny said. "Mama, have they named him yet?"

"He will be christened John. Oh, I cannot wait for Wycoff to return." The duchess brought out a handkerchief. "It has been a long time since we've had happy news."

Angeline forced herself to smile. Her mother had not meant to wound her. Angeline was simply a little sensitive today after her difficult conversation with Colin. Perhaps she was also a little out of sorts because she'd foolishly hoped for another letter from Charlotte. She ought to have known better. Charlotte had written the one letter in secret, because her husband had forbidden her to write to Angeline.

"Oh, Mama, when can we go see our new nephew?" Penny said.

"Very soon, I hope," the duchess said. "I will have to consult with Wycoff, but this news will surely be all that he ever needed. A boy. I am so overjoyed." She pressed the letter to her heart.

Angeline closed the novel and set it aside. She rose and leaned down to kiss her mother's cheek. "Mama, I am so

glad for all of our family. I am especially happy for you."
It was true, but it was also true that the news was a stark
reminder that she might never be a bride or a mother.

"Thank you, dear," the duchess said.

"I wish to compose a letter to my brother straightaway," Angeline said. "Mama, Margaret, will you excuse me?"

"Of course, dear," the duchess said. "I'm sure you're
bubbling over and wish to express it to your brother."

"We will continue the novel tomorrow," Angeline said.
When she quit the drawing room, she squared her shoulders and walked up the stairs. Under no circumstances
would she allow herself a drop of pity. She would not do
anything to spoil this wonderful day for her family.

She bit her lip, walked quietly into the bedchamber,
and sat at the corner desk. She removed a sheet of paper
and found the ink and the quill. When she attempted to
dip the quill in the ink, her hand shook. She set it in the
holder and told herself that she only needed a few moments to gain her composure.

She drew in air and released it. She did it again. Once
more, she retrieved the quill, but her fingers still trembled. She set it aside, stood, and crossed to the bed.
She sat on the edge of the mattress, and the bed ropes
squeaked, reminding her of that horrible night she'd
caught Brentmoor betraying her. Her hand shook as she
covered her mouth. Then she pulled out the drawer and
rummaged for a handkerchief. She blotted her eyes,
blew her nose, and took another deep breath. Then she
walked to the washstand, poured cold water into the
bowl, and bathed her hot face.

It was foolish to feel sorry for herself, but she feared

that she would never have a husband and family because of what had happened with Brentmoor. With a shaky sigh, she supposed she wasn't the only woman in the world to indulge in a little self-pity. Of course she did not begrudge her brother and his wife. She was happy for them, and she was elated that the news had made her mother so happy. It was just that some days like today were made up of happiness for some and gray clouds for others. Sometimes it just seemed like a thunderstorm, and too overwhelming.

She had released the pent-up sorrow and felt a little abashed at her emotional reaction. But now she was done with it.

Angeline returned to the desk and managed to write a short letter expressing her heartfelt joy to her brother and his wife for the safe delivery of their son. She wrote that she was thrilled to be an aunt and could not wait until she could visit and hold little John. She wrote a few lines about the house party and the weather. Then she promised to write again soon.

She felt a little embarrassed that she'd shed tears when she was happy for her brother, his wife, and all of her family.

One hour later

Angeline sat in the chair applying her fan and looking out the window. A knock sounded at the door. Angeline thought it might be Penny, but when she answered, she found Margaret there.

"May I come in?" Margaret said.

"Yes, of course," Angeline said. She was glad that

she'd bathed her face earlier, so no one would see the telling sign of a red nose.

"Let us sit on the bed like young girls and talk," Margaret said.

They both kicked off their slippers and crossed their legs on the mattress. Margaret eyed the handkerchief.

She'd failed to cover up well enough. "I expect you know that I became a bit of a watering pot after hearing my brother's news."

"I anticipated this would be difficult for you," Margaret said. Her gaze flew to the desk. "Yet, you wrote the letter."

"After I shed a few tears," she said.

Margaret took her hands. "I knew you would manage to write that letter."

"I actually felt better afterward."

"When you allow yourself to be happy for someone else's good fortune, it will someday be returned to you. Maybe not the way you imagined, but it will come."

"I have been angry for so long," she said.

"You are stronger than you know, but I also suspect that you put up a wall to protect yourself. It would be a natural reaction after what you have been through."

She had not thought of it that way. Had she tried to push Colin away? "You are very wise," Angeline said.

"It is only life experience," Margaret said. "When I first married Chadwick, I was terrified. You are aware that it was a marriage of convenience. I was scared and furious with my father. I did not want to wed an aristocrat, much less a man who was twelve years my senior. Frankly, I thought Chadwick only wanted my fortune. I expected misery. That first night of our married life, he told me that because of me his heart had come back to life. I didn't understand until he told me that his first wife had died. I fell in love on my wedding night."

Angeline sighed. "I told Colin that you brought happiness and light into Chadwick's life."

Margaret smoothed the covers. "My biggest regret is Colin. I had very little confidence in those days, and I was young. I was also afraid of making a mistake, so of course I made even more. I didn't know how to approach Colin. I feared that he would think I was trying to supplant his mother, and so I was too careful with him. He needed a mother's love, but it was awkward. I think he resented me."

"You had just married into an instant family. It would be difficult for anyone. But he does wish to spend more time with his family. I think that will bring all of you closer."

Margaret smiled. "I feel certain that we have you to thank for it."

"He would have come to that conclusion eventually," Angeline said. "It just takes men longer."

Margaret sighed. "Angeline, you have sustained an emotional wound. It is natural to want to protect your heart in such circumstances. If you keep the gates closed, you will manage to avoid pain and sorrow, but you will miss the best of what life has to offer. Love is what brings us joy. There is no other experience on this earth to equal it. If you love Colin, let him into your heart." She rose. "It would give me great happiness to call you my daughter-in-law one day."

"I fear we will have to settle for friends."

Margaret smiled. "I'll tell you a secret."

"I'm all ears."

"I have a wager with Chadwick."

"Do you? How intriguing," Angeline said.

"You would not believe the fun you can have as a married woman. I very much want to win this wager, as I have my heart set on a ruby necklace." Margaret wiggled her brows.

Angeline smiled. "What is the wager?"

"I'll give you a hint. It has to do with love and family, and I might add I'm counting on you, Angeline."

"You leave me in the dark," she said.

"I think you will find the light."

After Margaret left, Angeline sighed. Tonight she was meeting Colin in the library. She could have suggested an outdoor walk this afternoon, but those always ended up being a group affair, and there was no question that they needed to resolve matters. It seemed rather furtive, but given the lack of privacy, they had little choice. Even an early morning walk might draw others.

She was, however, feeling more than a little isolated and decided to go to the kitchen and try to train Hercules again. Angeline meant to invite the twins to join her, but she heard the sounds of the pianoforte and didn't want to distract them from practicing. She figured the pug would enjoy some attention. They had not spent much time with Hercules this morning because of her confrontation with Colin.

When she reached the kitchen, the pug looked rather forlorn in his basket. Agnes brought some bits of meat on a paper, and Hercules wiggled his funny tail.

Angeline sat on the floor with him. At first she had to push his rump to the floor with each command, but when she added the treat, he started responding to the verbal commands. She would not be at Deerfield much longer, but she would show the twins how to teach him to stop and lie down. She ruffled his short fur. "You're a clever dog, Hercules."

She stood and shook out her skirts. Then she returned to the great hall at the same time the marquess walked out from his study. Her opportunity to make a difference in Colin's life stood before her.

The marquess frowned a bit. "Lady Angeline, is something amiss?"

His thinning hair looked a bit damp. He'd probably bathed after stomping around in the mud. "May I speak to you in your study?"

"Yes, of course, follow me."

He ushered her inside and shut the door. "Please, have a seat."

She expected him to sit behind his desk, but he sat in the cross-framed armchair next to her. "How may I help you?"

"It is about Colin," she said.

"Ah."

"My lord, I must be frank and tell you that I have been privy to all of your recent decisions about Sommerall. I think it is important that you know."

"Very well. Perhaps you could elaborate, as I'm unsure what your interest is in the property other than the work you've done up to now."

"My lord, I am more concerned about your relationship with your son."

The marquess's brows lifted. "What precisely concerns you?"

"First, I know he has a rakehell reputation, but there is more to him than that."

"I see. You have evidence of this?"

Angeline noted the marquess's slight smile. "I know he has not always been responsible."

The marquess nodded. "Yes, I distinctly recall him showing up late and foxed at your come-out ball. Has he recently insulted you? You may tell me, and I will have a long discussion with him."

"No, he did not," she said. The marquess didn't need to know every word of her conversations with Colin.

"Lord Chadwick, do you love your son?"

Her question clearly startled him. "Yes, of course I do."

"I know he cares about you, even though you frustrate him."

The marquess looked as if he were trying to hide a smile.

"He really does want the property, but it is not for financial gain. He recently told me he has a tidy little fortune."

"Ah, yes, the shipping investments. Odd that he told you about them."

"He had good reason at the time. Even if Colin doesn't occupy Sommerall immediately, I know that he intends to reside there and probably sooner than even he expects."

"How do you know this, Lady Angeline?"

"I suppose he just changed right before my eyes."

"That is interesting. I have noticed the differences, and so has Margaret. She believes you are responsible for his burgeoning transformation."

"When people change, it is because they want to change."

"I will share this confidence with you," the marquess said. "I forced him to make choices that were perhaps a little unfair but necessary. Sometimes a person needs a nudge. My son needed a swift kick in the— Never mind. I knew it had to be a threat of some sort. Prior to this house party, he took for granted that he would inherit Sommerall." The marquess sighed. "Not once did he ever inquire about the property. One day, Bianca asked me why Colin never came home, and I felt that it was past time to remind my son what he was missing.

"As it happened, Faraday came along to ask about the property. You know the rest. My son is as stubborn as I am, and while I've had my doubts, I am seeing positive changes in him."

"Do you mean you were not serious about selling Sommerall?"

"I was serious about a number of things. To be honest, I knew the only reason he made the journey here is because his mother is buried at Sommerall. I felt it was important to give him a chance to demonstrate he was worthy of the legacy.

"And I had my doubts. I will not sully your ears with some of his infamous exploits in London, but I grew increasingly concerned. Then he walked into the drawing room that first night of the house party. I thought steam would come out of his ears. That is when I knew he did care, but I didn't know whether it would sustain or not. So I presented him with one challenge after another. I needed to know whether he truly cared about Sommerall. By the by, my own father used a similar tactic to lure me away from my dissolute pursuits."

"I will never understand men," Angeline said.

He patted her hand. "That is probably for the best. Do you have any other observations?"

"Colin has shown his willingness to see that the house is properly taken care of and kept in good order. I know it would mean a great deal to him if you saw fit to grant him the property."

Lord Chadwick let out a loud sigh. "There is a complication."

"What is it?" she said.

"I think it is something that I must tell him."

She swallowed hard. "What do you mean?"

"Lady Angeline, you look very anxious. May I ask why you are so concerned about the property?"

"Colin can no longer remember his mother's features. We searched for her miniature, but we never found it."

The marquess frowned. "I see."

"I think he wishes to hold on to the few objects that are a link to her, such as the cradle and the rocker. I know it helped when you told him about her."

"It seems that you and my son have grown close."

"I believe that is not unusual when people work together. I hope the complication doesn't mean the Faradays are leaning toward the purchase of Sommerall. You would not like having them as neighbors."

"That is certainly something to consider," the marquess said, his mouth twitching a bit.

"Now I have taken enough of your valuable time," Angeline said. "Thank you for hearing me out."

"I appreciate your observations, Lady Angeline."

When she quit the room, the marquess shut the door and thought his son would be a damn fool if he let her get away.

Chapter Fourteen

Of all nights, this was the one that Penny chose to stay with Angeline.

"Penny, I have been restless in my sleep and fear I will keep you awake," Angeline said.

"Let us ask Marie to bring a hot brick and warm milk," Penny said.

Angeline eyed the clock. It was half past eleven. Two and one-half hours remained before her meeting with Colin. She'd not anticipated her sister's request and idly wondered if Penny could somehow sense when something was brewing. But remembering how much she'd missed her little sister while she was in Paris, Angeline could not deny Penny's request.

"I will ring for Marie," Angeline said, "but once we finish the milk, you must rest."

"Thank you, Angie."

After dinner tonight, she'd played backgammon with Colin, but it was difficult to concentrate. All of the talk had been about her brother's new son. She was happy that her father and mother were ecstatic. They had been worn down by her scandal, though none of them ever spoke about it. There had been times when the silence was just too much, and that was when she'd started walking every clear day. The freedom of walking had helped tremendously.

Now she was anxious about meeting Colin and wasn't sure what to tell Penny.

After Marie appeared, Angeline bade the maid to bring the brick and warm milk. She removed her pearl earrings as she walked to the dressing table, and as she set them in her jewelry box, she was reminded of Colin flicking one of them at Sommerall. She pressed her thighs together as thoughts of his touches and kisses chased through her head, but she could not allow it to happen again. They had been lucky there were no consequences.

Marie brought in the wrapped hot brick. When Penny finished her milk, Angeline braided her sister's hair.

"Thank you, Angie," Penny said. "I wish I had your hair."

"Whatever for? You have beautiful thick locks, Penny."

"Is it my imagination or is my hair getting redder?"

"Stay there," Angeline said. She retrieved the hand mirror and returned to bed. "The light is not the best, but look how your hair shines like cinnamon and gold. It is very unique. You will stand out in a crowd at your come-out ball."

Penny turned to her. "Angie, if I ask you a question, will you tell me the truth?"

The backs of her hands prickled. "What is the question?"

"I have been thinking about how Mama receives very few letters and you have had only one since returning to England. I know something went very wrong with your betrothal. I also realized that each time I asked if you would be at my debut, you never said yes."

It was one of those indelible moments when everything slows and the ordinary things stand out for no reason at all: the heat from the brick at the foot of the bed, the red-gold wisp of hair at the nape of her sister's neck, and the scent of the flickering beeswax candle that was reflected in the oval mirror above the dressing table. Such commonplace things for uncommon circumstances.

"Why do you hesitate, Angie?"

She would not soon forget her sister's question or her own inability to answer.

"I will not be welcome at balls, will I?" Penny said.

Was it really possible for someone to steal your breath?

"It is true, isn't it?" Penny said.

She must recover for her sister's sake. "No, it is not true, but I doubt I can attend."

"You are vexed," Penny said. "You worried about telling me, did you not?"

For months, she'd dreaded having to tell her sister, and tonight she wasn't prepared. "I kept hoping that something could be done, and I will continue to hope. I want so badly to see you make your debut, but all is not lost."

Penny hugged her. "I'm sorry, Angie. I know you worried about me, but you must not. I'm sure I would have sat on the wallflower row, wishing I were home."

Angeline's throat felt as if it were closing, but she was the elder sister, and it was her responsibility to take charge and put matters in as positive a light as possible. She took her sister's hands. "I wanted to wait to tell you what I believe will happen. Most likely Lady Chadwick will sponsor you. This is only my assumption, but you will probably make your debut with Bianca and Bernadette."

"Mama will not be there?"

"I am unsure. We will ask her later. For now, I think we should let her be happy about our new nephew. Do you agree?"

"Yes, I think that is for the best."

"Your come-out may not be exactly how we envisioned, but it will be wonderful. You will have pretty new gowns, bonnets, slippers, and gloves. You will enjoy shopping with the marchioness and the twins. You know how much fun they are." She would not be there to share this exciting experience with her sister, and she knew it would hurt. It already did.

"I know you didn't do anything wrong, Angie. Brentmoor was a bad man. I could tell by his eyes. There was meanness in them."

Angeline drew in a long breath and let it out slowly. "Always rely on your instincts about people. I ignored mine and kept thinking that I was imagining things. Promise me, Penny."

"I promise," Penny said.

Angeline hugged her sister. She'd always thought she would be by her sister's side to protect her from the cynics and the rakes in the ton. She'd always imagined helping her sister step into her first ball gown. She'd always dreamed of watching Penny dancing with a young man for the first time, but it was unlikely she would see any of it.

She could withstand the disdainful stares, the whispers, and yes, even the suggestive invitations from so-called gentlemen, but missing her sister's debut ball would be very hard.

Penny wrapped her arms around her shins. "Colin has nice eyes."

"I think he's too old for you, Penny."

Penny laughed. "No, silly, I said it all wrong. I meant he has *kind* eyes."

"I think he has laughing eyes much of the time," Angeline said.

"It is kind laughter," Penny said. "The twins said he is a genuine rake, but I believe he is honorable."

"You approve of Colin?" she said.

"Yes, anyone who likes animals is usually a good person," Penny said.

"Next spring, you will send me a letter every day describing the dances, the gowns, and the music. Will you promise to do that, Penny?"

When her sister nodded, Angeline hugged her and wished for a miracle, but Penny would have a magical season and that was all that mattered. It was easy to say, but when the time came, Angeline knew it would leave an ache in her chest. It already had, but she knew what she must do.

Tonight she must put an end to the engagement with Colin. It would probably be far too easy to end, but she told herself that it was for the best. She would not hold his feet to the fire, especially for an engagement born of desperation on both their parts.

She loved him dearly, and the thought of leaving him behind hurt far more than she'd expected. In a fairy-tale world, he would sweep her off her feet and carry her over the threshold at Sommerall House. But she had decided that she wanted more than a marriage of convenience.

She wanted what she deserved—a husband who loved her and couldn't live without her. Tonight, she would tell him the truth. Then she would request the help of her mother, Margaret, and Charlotte to help her turn the tide and refute the ugly claims Brentmoor had made. She did not know if it was possible, but she figured she had nothing to lose. She was the daughter of a duke, and as long as she had breath, she would never let anyone besmirch her good name or that of her family ever again. After all, she was an elder sister, and it was her duty to set a good example for Penny.

At one forty-five in the morning, Angeline slid off the bed. She'd left a candle burning on the side table near her. Then she donned her wrapper and claimed the candle. When she reached the door, Penny's voice sounded. "Angie, where are you going?"

She winced and debated whether to just leave Colin waiting or tell Penny the truth. The one thing she did not want to do was lie to her sister. "Penny, I want you to listen carefully and trust me. I am meeting Colin in the library."

Penny sat up. "No, Angie. You know that is forbidden."

"There are important matters we have to discuss, and we need privacy. The problem is there are always people around us, and we cannot talk in front of them."

"You should not be speaking of things to him that you wouldn't say around others."

Angeline wet her lips. "Penny, you said he is honorable, and he is."

"Angie, this is not honorable, not at all."

She sighed and sat on the edge of the mattress. "He offered to marry me."

Penny gasped.

"Listen. I cannot accept him. We were both ready to make a marriage of convenience to solve our mutual problems."

Penny gaped at her. "Have you gone mad?"

When I'm with him, yes. "Shhh. If I married him, I could be respectable again—at least to some extent. I'm unsure how much to be honest."

Penny frowned. "You meant to marry him so that you could come to my debut?"

"Partly, yes. But you see, he has a problem, too."

"I think you both fell down and cracked your heads," Penny said.

"I decided I cannot marry him, and I must tell him tonight, because, well, we had a secret engagement, but please do not tell anyone."

Penny frowned. "Angie, that sounds like one of the twins' witless ideas."

"I suppose it does, but I really do need to talk to him privately. We had a row, and before I leave here, I want to reconcile with him. He deserves that much. Now go back to sleep. I'll not be gone long."

"You will not go at all. I will ring the bell if you try to leave," Penny said.

"Penny, please. Nothing bad will happen. I just need to speak to him."

"Do not stay long, Angie. Say what you must and return as fast as possible or I will worry."

"I will." Angeline marched to the door and heard Penny's voice again.

"Angie?"

"Yes, dearest."

"Did he kiss you?"

"Close your eyes, Penny. I'll return shortly."

He was sitting on a sofa in the library. A branch of candles on the table provided limited light. When he stood, she saw that he was dressed in trousers and a banyan. In the dark, she couldn't see his expression.

He strode over to the door and shut it. His hands bracketed her on either side of the door and his big muscular body acted as a shield as if he meant to trap her. "I never intended to demean you," he said. "If anything, it was the exact opposite."

There had been no prelude whatsoever.

"I'm sure you meant well," she said, "but I have thought this through and I'm sure you will agree."

"Agree to what?" he said.

"We need to end this engagement."

"I knew you would say that, because you are scared."

"I am not scared, Colin, but I want more than a marriage of convenience. Come sit beside me."

He sighed and followed her. "I am sorry for making those assumptions."

"I realized that wasn't what really troubled me, Colin. What troubled me is that I believed I didn't deserve to find happiness because of what happened with Brentmoor. I felt so guilty about the scandal that I lost myself for a time, but I am no longer lost. I am very sorry if this means you will lose Sommerall, but I advise you to discuss this with your father once more."

"Angeline," he said, reaching for her.

"No, Colin, I cannot allow you to touch me."

"Why?" he said.

"Because you are irresistible and I apparently have no self-restraint."

His deep chuckle called to her—a wicked sound.

"I must leave now," she said.

"Stay," he said. "Tell me what I can do to reassure you."

"Reassurance isn't what I need," she said.

"Tell me what you need."

He truly had no idea.

The clock chimed the quarter hour. "I must go."

"Tell me," he said his voice harsh.

"I want the fairy tale." She rose and took a step.

Colin stood and caught her hand. "Angeline, will you run away before you kiss me?"

She found she could not resist one last kiss. When his lips met hers, the kiss was butterfly gentle.

"I must go," she said. "Penny will worry."

He frowned. "She knows you are here?"

"Don't worry, she thinks we're as witless as the twins."

"Somehow I am not reassured."

"Good-bye, Colin."

"You make it sound so final," he said.

"Our families will always be close, and I hope that we will remain friends," she said.

"Don't leave."

"I must." She hurried to the door, because it hurt more than she'd expected.

Angeline closed the door behind her and dashed her fingers under her eyes. She loved him, but one-sided love wasn't enough for a lifetime. With a deep breath, she tiptoed into the room and set the candle on the night table. Penny stirred when Angeline got under the covers.

"Angie, you were gone a long time. Did he kiss you?"

Her sister was apparently fixated on kissing. "Go to sleep, Penny."

"You didn't answer me. He kissed you, didn't he?"

"We talked."

"Angie, you should not lie."

"About what?"

"You went to see Colin because you wanted to kiss him," Penny said. "You mustn't do that anymore, Angie. It would create a lot of hard feelings if our father found out."

"I won't kiss Colin again," she said. The words pinched her chest as she said them.

"Angie, what is it like to kiss a boy?"

"I think it depends on the gentleman, but wait for someone who has kind eyes and always treats you with respect and dignity," she said. "Now we must go to sleep. It's late and Mama will scold if she finds out I kept you awake until the middle of the night."

"I would never tell," Penny said.

"No, but your sleepy eyes would."

* * *

Angeline lay awake, thinking about Colin and all that had happened. Having spoken to the marquess previously, she was certain Colin would inherit Sommerall—and probably soon. She had put in more than one good word for him and managed to gently remind the marquess of his son's many virtues. Perhaps it didn't cancel all of his vices, but no one was perfect. Granted, he'd certainly sowed wild oats and kept mistresses, but that was surely behind him now. He would probably miss her sultry performances as a famous courtesan. She'd rather enjoyed her short-lived pretend career as a lightskirt.

Most important of all, she was glad that she'd spoken to the marquess. He would surely agree that it would be much better to have his son as a neighbor than Mr. and Mrs. Faraday. Who wanted to be neighbors with people who could never be pleased and couldn't make up their minds? Angeline understood the marquess had felt the need to test his son and make sure he truly wanted the property and meant to take care of it.

She loved Colin with all of her heart. A year from now, they would likely meet up again at the annual house party. He might be married by then. She might be as well, but there was no point in dwelling on the future.

Chapter Fifteen

The next morning before breakfast

Colin donned his coat and allowed Horace to fiddle with his cravat and shine his boots. He'd hoped to feel better after their meeting last night, but she'd ended their engagement. He couldn't let that happen. As he buttoned his coat, it struck him that he could have ended this farce and proposed to her the day after the storm, but in retrospect their trial engagement had not been such a great idea. They had both been so hesitant, with good reason. A marriage based on property and a come-out ball sounded pretty flimsy in hindsight. He supposed it said much about their mutual desperation.

But now he was feeling desperate again, because he was in danger of losing her, and he didn't want to lose her. Why did he always realize what he stood to lose only when matters were at their worst? He had to believe that he still had a chance. Once they were properly wed, he would request her services as a famous pretend courtesan. He would object, however, to her keeping other pretend men and knew that would tickle her fancy. Most of all he would make her laugh every day, because he knew there hadn't been much laughter after that fiend tried to destroy her and her family.

She didn't know it, and he had no intention of telling her, but he meant to avenge her. Brentmoor was something of a pretty boy, but he wouldn't be after Colin used his handy fists to rearrange Brentmoor's nose and blacken his bloodshot eyes. But first Colin had to gather all the supporters he could find, because he meant to give her the one thing that would make her happy. She was a duke's daughter and a beautiful, clever woman who loved her sister and her parents.

More than anything, he wanted to give her a gift, her heart's desire. She didn't want anything for herself. She just wanted it for her sister. He didn't know if he could manage it, but he would do everything in his power to make it happen.

When Colin took his usual chair next to Angeline at breakfast, he saw how tired she looked and felt badly. Mostly, he was worried because she'd ended the engagement, and he feared she wouldn't give him a second chance. He figured he'd probably better get on his knees this time and beg her, because she'd sounded serious last night. He didn't want to lose her.

Penny looked a little sleepy, too, and the duchess eyed her daughters suspiciously. "I understand that Penny stayed in your room last night, Angeline. Why do you both look so fatigued?"

"I was restless last night," Angeline said. "I kept Penny awake."

"The next time you are restless and wide awake, come to our room," Bernadette said. "We'll tell ghost stories."

Colin decided to scare his sisters. "Muahahaha."

Naturally the twins squealed.

The marquess rolled his eyes. "Colin, do not encourage your sisters in ghoulish nonsense. Margaret has enough trouble with the usual nonsense."

Colin finished his breakfast and cup of tea. "The sun is out. I imagine Hercules would enjoy being outdoors, if that is acceptable, Margaret."

"I think we should take advantage of the sunshine," she said.

Colin turned to Angeline. "How is Hercules's training progressing?"

"He is doing well. The girls have already taught him how to shake hands as you've seen. As long as his training is consistent, he will do very well. He is smart."

The marquess snorted.

"Chadwick," Margaret said, "you know how much Hercules means to the girls."

"I would hope not more than their papa."

"Are you jealous of Hercules, Papa?" Bianca asked.

"Mortally," he said, folding his paper.

"Are you shooting today, Papa?" Angeline asked the duke.

Wycoff cleared his throat. "Not today, Daughter. Chadwick and I have a business matter to discuss."

The marquess set his cup on the dish. "Speaking of business, Colin, if you have finished your breakfast, please come to my study in fifteen minutes."

Colin wondered what surprise his father meant to spring on him now, but he would find out soon enough.

His chest felt tight again, and he had a feeling this would not be good news.

Angeline looked at Colin. "Should we wait for you?"

"I beg your pardon," the marquess said. "The business matter will probably take some time. I suggest the ladies go on ahead with your planned outing."

Everyone rose and went to collect their warm wraps. Angeline stayed back with Colin. When everyone else had left, she turned to him. "I have a feeling this is good news for you."

Colin's heart beat a little faster. "Do you know something?"

She smiled. "I might know a little."

Perhaps his father meant to grant him Sommerall. After all, Faraday had shown insufficient interest, and as far as Colin knew, there were no other interested buyers.

"I shouldn't get my hopes up. They're likely to be dashed."

"I do not know for certain, but I'm sure it will all turn out well."

He searched her eyes and thought he was lucky to have someone believe in him that much.

She really was special and beautiful and unbelievably seductive. Now Sommerall meant more to him than it had when he'd first arrived, because if he could persuade her to marry him, it would be their home. He'd better grovel this time.

He should make up for it with a waltz at her sister's debut. That would please her immensely. Now all he needed to figure out was the best place and time to propose. He also needed to work on the words he meant to say, because he didn't want to make a mess of it.

If a soothsayer had predicted this, he would have scoffed, but it mattered not. He would claim Sommerall—and soon Angeline—for his own. All he had to do was get her to agree. Hell, he'd beg if necessary, because he refused to lose her.

Fifteen minutes later, Colin tapped his knuckle on his father's slightly open study door.

"Come in and close the door, please," the marquess said. He sealed a letter and set it in the tray. Then he rose and walked around the desk. "Please be seated."

To Colin's surprise, his father sat in the chair next to him rather than behind the desk. The fine hairs on the back of his neck prickled. He suspected this was not what he'd anticipated. "Is something wrong?" Colin asked.

The marquess sighed. "I understand from Angeline that Sommerall has significant sentimental value to you."

"What?" The words took a moment to soak into his brain.

"I figured you had no idea that she spoke to me on your behalf."

The room temperature grew chilly. "No." But she had hinted that she knew something.

The marquess folded his arms over his chest. "She made quite a case on your behalf and said there was more to you than just your rakehell reputation."

He got up and walked to the window. "What else?"

"I was amused and absolutely charmed."

Colin turned around and gaped at his father.

"If you let her slip away, you're a damn fool," the marquess said, "although it escapes me why she'd have anything to do with the likes of you. Then again, Lady

Angeline enjoys fixing and renovating things. I imagine she considers you a challenging project."

It took a moment to sink in and then Colin guffawed.

"Be seated, son. We need to talk."

He claimed the chair next to his father. "Something is in the wind."

The marquess sighed. "I have received a definite offer from Faraday."

He couldn't breathe for a moment. Then he shook his head. "But you gave me six weeks to find a bride."

"I know you have made no efforts in that regard. You'll not find a bride before the time is up."

Hell. He should have proposed, but she'd called off their trial engagement.

"You cannot sell to the Faradays. It's a family legacy," Colin said.

"Yes, and your mother is buried there."

Colin leaned forward. "Tell me what the offer is and I will beg, barter, or steal to match it."

"The thing is I led him to believe it was available. I take responsibility. I mistakenly assumed he wasn't serious about the property."

"Tell him it's no longer available."

"I would, but he was under the impression that it was still available, and he turned down the seller of the other property."

"He can find another," Colin said.

"Son, his wife will be delivered of their firstborn within the month. They have spent considerable time searching for a property that suits their needs. I might mention that they're supporting her elderly grandmother as well. If I were to take it off the market, what would they do? Mrs. Faraday is in no condition to travel to several properties, and they want to live in the general area because they have family nearby. The only other property available is not within their means. I know Sommerall has special significance to you, but it would be dishonorable for me to refuse them now."

Colin's nostrils flared. "I should have known something would go wrong."

"I am disappointed in myself," the marquess said.

Colin shook his head. "None of us thought they were serious. You can't blame yourself for an unfortunate turn of events."

The marquess rose, walked around his desk, and opened a drawer. "I have something for you."

Colin stood when his father approached. "Angeline mentioned that you were searching for it."

The marquess opened the box and revealed the miniature of his mother in a pearl-encrusted frame.

"I put it away in my desk to keep and took it out from time to time just to remember her. I didn't want Margaret to see it. I think she's always felt like second best, though God knows I've always thought her an angel."

Colin swallowed. "I don't want to take it from you."

"No, it's better this way. You should have it. I'll have one made of Margaret. I should have done it years ago. I think it is past time."

"Thank you, Father."

"I'm sorry to disappoint you about the property," the marquess said. "It was always intended for you."

Colin nodded. His thumb smoothed over the pearl frame. "Thank you, Father. If you don't mind, I'd like to ride over to Sommerall one last time."

"Of course, take your time. I can send men later to collect the cradle and rocker."

He nodded. "I appreciate it."

Angeline led the group indoors. "I don't know about everyone else, but I'm ready to warm my hands in front of the fire."

"It is brisk outside," Margaret said. "Girls, do not leave your wraps on the banister. Take them upstairs."

Penny and the twins ran upstairs with their wraps. Not long after, the three giggling girls ran back down.

Angeline crossed her arms. "Is this your idea of deportment, girls?"

"We'll try it with books on our heads after luncheon," Bianca said.

Margaret held her palms up as if beseeching a higher power for help.

"I'm starving," Penny said.

"You're in luck," Margaret said. "Luncheon is being served now."

The marquess and Wycoff joined them.

"Papa, I'm surprised you and Lord Chadwick did not go shooting today," Angeline said.

Wycoff exchanged a look with the marquess as everyone took a seat at the table.

Angeline looked at the marquess. "Where is Colin?"

"At Sommerall," the marquess said. "You might as well hear it now since we're all gathered. Mr. and Mrs. Faraday wish to purchase the property."

Angeline gasped.

"Angeline," the duchess said in a reproving tone.

"It's perfectly understandable," the duke said. "Our

daughter recognizes what the property means to Ravenshire."

When the marquess finished explaining the circumstances, Angeline rose. "Lord Chadwick, may I have the use of a carriage?"

"You should stay here," the duchess said.

"Actually, Duchess, if you and Wycoff approve, I think Colin would welcome Angeline's company," the marquess said. "She was instrumental in assisting him, though I understand there is far more to be done—or would have been done."

"I will approve," Wycoff said. "They are adults, after all."

"Thank you, my lord," Angeline said. "Thank you, Papa."

"I'll make the arrangements for the carriage," the marquess said.

Margaret rose. "I'll have a hamper put together. He probably did not eat before he left. This is such a disappointment. I so hoped he would take possession and be near us at long last."

Thirty minutes later, Angeline boarded the carriage with the hamper. She figured it would feel like the longest carriage drive she'd ever taken, even though it wasn't all that far to Sommerall. She was glad that no one had complained about her journeying to him without a maid. This had to have been a low blow for him, and she wanted to console him.

When the carriage rolled into the drive at last, John stepped down and offered to carry the heavy hamper. Angeline hurried up the walk. The wind was blowing papery autumn leaves, and the gray sky looked forbidding.

The noise of the carriage must have alerted Colin because he opened the door. She ran straight into his arms. "I came as soon I heard," she cried.

"Hush," Colin said. "Come inside out of the cold."

John set the hamper on the foyer table. "My lord, I await your instructions."

"Drive the carriage back to Deerfield. Lewis took the other to the barn. Inform him that we'll depart at four o'clock."

"Yes, my lord."

After John left, Colin wrapped his arms around Angeline again. "Thank you for coming."

"How could I not?" She wiped a stray tear.

He offered his handkerchief. "You're not weeping over an old house, are you?"

"I was so sure it would be yours." *I wanted it to be ours.*

"It's not the end of the world," he said. "There are far worse things."

He hugged her. "Come to the drawing room with me. I have something to show you."

Why did everything have to fall apart? She knew it was ridiculous to think that way, but they had worked so hard, and she had wanted him to possess the property so that he could have his own home and be near his mother's grave.

When they stepped inside, he walked to the hearth. "I'll make a fire. It's a bit chilly in here."

"I could prepare a tea tray," she said. "Margaret sent a hamper."

"That would be nice," he said. "Let me help. It's a bit heavy for you."

Not long after, he got a decent fire going, and the kettle

whistled. He removed it while Angeline added tea leaves to the pot. He poured the hot water and sat beside her.

"While we wait for the tea to get dark, I thought you might like to see my mother's miniature."

He took out the box and showed her the pearl-encrusted frame.

"She was beautiful," Angeline said. "Where did you find it?"

"My father had it stowed away in his desk. I suppose he felt a bit guilty keeping the miniature because of Margaret. He gave it to me. So you see all is not lost."

Angeline bit her lip and nodded, because she was an adult and it was silly to cry on his behalf, but she felt his disappointment in her own heart. "I imagine Mr. and Mrs. Faraday will be kind enough to allow you to pay your respects to your mother periodically."

"Yes, I'll speak to them. It shouldn't be too much of an imposition, I hope."

She poured the tea. "I confess I'm a little sad. I'd looked forward to replacing the furniture and draperies. We never did get around to discussing a laundry and a spring vegetable garden, but that's no longer your concern."

They drank their tea in silence.

She set her cup aside. "Will you be staying through the Christmas holidays?"

"I have business in London. I'll journey home a few days beforehand."

She felt as if a clock were winding backward to the first night she'd seen him outside the drawing room at Deerfield. Everything had changed and then settled back to where they started the journey to the house party.

"Would you like to walk to your mother's mausoleum?" she asked. "I would be glad to accompany you."

"Thank you. I would like that very much."

The wind was blowing autumn leaves everywhere. A red squirrel scampered past, reminding her of Hercules. When they reached the mausoleum, he took out the miniature and kissed it. "You will not be forgotten," he said.

Tears poured down her cheeks.

He took out a handkerchief and blotted them. "I think she would have liked you." He put his arm around her shoulder and led her back to the house.

"Do you want to walk through once more?" she asked.

"Yes, I think so." He lit a lantern and led her up the stairs. "Let's start at the attic, shall we?"

She gave him a weak smile. "We did spend a great deal of time there."

They stepped inside. "Everything is in order," he said. "But I don't see our mouse."

She laughed.

"I expect my father will send servants for the rest of the items."

Colin took her hand, and they walked through the nursery. He retrieved the box of tin soldiers. "I think I'll take this for sentimental reasons."

They walked into his father's old room where the shaving stand stood. Then he led her through the connecting door to his late mother's room.

"Well, the bed didn't catch fire, but it was a near thing."

He startled a laugh out of her. "Oh, I cannot believe the things I said and did."

"You may scoff, but truly it was one of the best nights I've ever had." He looked at her from the corner of his eye. "I hope you have no regrets."

"I don't," she said. *I will never regret loving you.*

He sat on the edge of the bed and patted the mattress. "Sit with me. There is something I wish to tell you."

She took a deep breath and joined him.

"I have sent letters to my friends. I gave them no particulars, but, and this hopefully will not unsettle you, they are very aware that Brentmoor mistreated you. Harry and Bellingham are willing and more than able to bring in supporters for you. With your permission, I would like to do everything in my power to restore your good name."

She stood and walked to the window. When she pulled back the drapes, brown and orange leaves swirled in the wind. "I intended to ask my mother, Margaret, and Charlotte to help."

"I believe Mrs. Norcliffe will help as well, but I want justice for what he did to you and your family."

"I don't know if it is even possible," she said. "I could refute certain things, but more than one man saw me in the gardens with Brentmoor."

"He tricked you, and I'm certain it would not surprise anyone, given his bad reputation. I'll leave the choice to you, Angeline. You don't have to decide now."

She thought about the way Brentmoor had manipulated her father. She thought about the way he'd tricked and humiliated her in those gardens, and she thought about all the lies he'd told. All those things welled up inside her.

"I'm tired of worrying about how this is affecting my

family. I am furious with that man for what he did to me, and undoubtedly what he has probably done to other women."

"You're shaking," he said.

"I'm shaking with fury. How dare he hurt my family and me? I want him brought down to his knees."

"Consider it done, Angeline. I promise you, I'll see him literally brought to his knees."

Two days later

Everyone had gathered for a walk. Bianca attached a leash to Hercules. Angeline bent down to the dog and said, "Sit."

Hercules licked her hand.

The marquess strolled by and scoffed.

Colin laughed and then a knock sounded. He walked toward the foyer and saw Ames handing over coin to a man bringing the post. When the butler shut the door, he looked at the addresses and held them out to Colin. "My lord, you have two urgent letters from London."

He suspected who had written them, but he would say nothing in front of the others. Colin exchanged a long look with his father. Then he said, "Please go on ahead with the walk, everyone. I will join you after I have dealt with a business matter." He bowed and hurried up the stairs.

Colin gritted his teeth. He had to be strong for Angeline, even though he might have to read disgusting and false rumors about her. Better him than her. But he also had to gather as many supporters as possible to attest to her good character. It was a daunting prospect, but he'd sworn to clear her name, if at all possible.

Dear Colin,

You will never believe the lies that Brentmoor is now spreading. I've kept silent at the club until I am able to consult further with you. Of course, I wish to abide by the lady's wishes first and foremost. I also want to prevent fanning the flames higher, but Brentmoor's return has added fresh fuel to the firestorm. He is spreading coin everywhere now that he has inherited property. In addition, he is drowning himself in strong drink and claiming that Lady Angeline has spread lies about him! He claims that she had already cried off when he and Lady Cunningham were discovered at that ball. Furthermore, he is reportedly telling everyone that it was Lady A's idea to go out into the dark gardens. Can you believe it? The man is all but suggesting that she seduced him!

"Good Lord," Colin muttered. "I'll kill the bastard." He took a deep breath and continued reading Harry's letter.

It would be laughable, but he paints her as shameless and without moral restraint.
The two main problems aside from the fiend himself are that the stories are spreading like wildfire in the scandal sheets and clubs, because they are of a salacious nature and because other men saw Brentmoor with his hands on her in a poorly lit gar-

*den. Forgive me for being blunt, but I do not want it
to come as a surprise at a bad time.*

Colin had to pause a moment. He knew the fiend had
tricked her and purposely exposed her, but it was still difficult to read. He gritted his teeth and continued on.

*Doubtless he planned it that way and probably has
a disgusting perversion for exposing himself with
any unfortunate female he tricks. There are many
who have taken a disgust of Brentmoor, but they
hesitate to publicly denounce him because they do
not wish to be involved.*

*However, as my mother said, anyone with a con-
science will lend support to a cause when someone,
particularly a mistreated lady, is maligned. In order
to clear Lady A's name, it will be necessary to
gather as many gentlemen and ladies who are willing to support her and her family. I cannot assure
you that the plan to restore her reputation will
work, but I do believe it is worth the effort.
Bellingham is standing at the ready. His influence
will make an enormous difference. Send word when
you intend to travel to London.*

*P.S. For what it is worth, my mother suggests
marriage to a wealthy and titled gentleman would
do the trick, but you know females always think
marriage is the answer to all of life's problems.*

Colin blew out his breath. Now he knew it was worse
than he'd expected, but he was determined to vindicate
her honor and see Brentmoor brought to his knees.

He opened the next letter, which was considerably shorter and to the point. Colin would have recognized Bellingham's style anywhere.

Colin,

To put it bluntly, Brentmoor is no better than a sewer rat. It infuriates me to know that an innocent lady has been vilified by those who ought to know better. For now, it is necessary to concentrate on turning the tide for Lady A.

I wish to be there the day you blacken Brentmoor's eyes and break his nose. Harry has given me the particulars about how this happened. I am startled that Wycoff should fall for Brentmoor's lies, but I understand the fiend is like a charismatic snake and has fleeced more than one man out of his money with tales of his underserved misfortune at the hands of his sire. He has also demanded money from the fathers of ladies he's meddled with, and most have paid to keep him from ruining their daughter's reputations. I've investigated the man's activities and discovered he has more than a few victims. Clearly it is for the good of all society to expose this man for his evil schemes. You may count on my support. I assure you I have more than a few friends and acquaintances who will stand behind Lady A.

P.S. Laura suggests you marry the lady posthaste and says you will be much happier once you are a married man. Do forgive me for including her opinions, but she insisted. Laura is with child again and frankly not always rational. I have found it best just to agree.

Colin counted himself a lucky man to have loyal friends. He huffed remembering Angeline's horrified reaction to the story of how he and Harry met Bellingham. They'd had some amusing times at White's last spring.

A tap sounded at the door. Colin answered and was more than a little surprised to see his father. "Come in."

"Thank you. I see you've been reading your letters."

"Did you need something, Father?"

"No, but I'm fairly certain your friends wrote to you with news about Brentmoor and advice about Lady Angeline."

He sighed. "Have a seat."

"Your expression leads me to believe it's even worse than you thought."

"Read the letters. You'll see the details. I warn you, it's bad."

His father removed his spectacles from his inner coat pocket and read both letters without comment. "It comes as no surprise that there have been other victims. Obviously, Brentmoor is adept at winning over the sympathies of others and then taking advantage at just the right moment."

"He has to be stopped," Colin said. "No lady should be treated in such a revolting manner."

"I agree," the marquess said. "When will you travel to London?"

"I'll stay until Wycoff and his family members depart."

The marquess's brows rose. "That is surprising. I thought this would be the perfect excuse for you to speed away and kick up your heels in London again. I was sure the lures of actresses, lightskirts, and gaming hells would tempt you."

He smiled a little. "I have my reasons for staying."

"Angeline?" the marquess said.

"She lent her expertise and was supportive of my claim to Sommerall."

"I see," the marquess said. "If you need anything, do not hesitate to ask. Oh, and by the by, I could not help noticing the ladies advised you to marry Lady Angeline. I found it rather amusing, given that the pair of you have been at odds forever."

He said nothing. If he married her, she would be able to attend some society entertainments, but it wasn't enough. Worse, she'd made it clear she didn't want to marry him. He meant to change her mind, but first she must take her rightful place as Lady Angeline and then God willing, she would consent to marry him and become Lady Ravenshire. If he was really lucky, she would make frequent private appearances as a famous courtesan in the boudoir. The idea of marriage was becoming more enticing by the day.

"I'm sorry about Sommerall," the marquess said. "I've wracked my brains trying to figure out a way to refuse to sell it to Faraday, but I've yet to come up with an honorable solution."

"Thank you for trying," he said. "I take the blame. I took Sommerall for granted. It might have been mine years ago if I'd made efforts to show I deserved it, but I didn't. It's a lesson I won't soon forget."

The marquess opened the door and then looked back at him. "Son, I'm proud of you."

"Thank you, Father."

"Carry on," the marquess said, and closed the door.

Colin sighed. He would never be able to take possession of Sommerall now. In the light of day, the secret engagement seemed a rather cold business. At the time he'd suggested it, they had both been desperate enough to seize upon that witless plan. But he'd grown attached to Sommerall and was sorry his quest to possess the property hadn't worked out. He'd lost it forever, but he would carry the memory of making love to Angeline that stormy night for the rest of his life. She was an incredible woman, and he certainly wasn't going to let her get away. She had a big heart and a saucy retort always at the ready.

He wanted to clear her name completely and freely, but it seemed rather daunting. He had no illusions about the difficulties she faced, but he knew how much it would mean to her to attend her sister's debut. Perhaps at the very least, she could attend quietly with support from a handful of true friends.

She should be able to choose her spouse rather than have to settle for an arranged marriage, but it was complicated. He did not want to lose her, but he feared he might be too late. He might have to do something drastic, although he wasn't sure what that might be. Angeline deserved a proper wedding, and God knew he would be ready to settle down after he used his fists on Brentmoor.

Sunday morning

Colin tugged on his cravat and ducked his head in his father's study. "Oh, good, you're *not* working."

"Is this another special occasion?" the marquess said. "It's seven o'clock in the morning. I expected you to be in bed after a nightlong debauch."

"Alas there is a dearth of debauches in the country, so I'll have to settle for church."

"God save us."

"May I come in?"

The marquess regarded him over his spectacles. "Yes, of course. Be seated."

Colin slouched in the cross-framed armchair. "Is Margaret really that strict about the Sabbath?"

"Oh, yes. Now, I'll give you a tip about women since it appears your friends' mothers and wives are urging you to leap into matrimony. Never lie to a woman. They can sniff it at fifty paces."

"So, did Margaret catch you *not* working?"

"I always knew you were clever. What is on your mind, son?"

He cleared his throat. "Well, two things."

"Start with one," the marquess said.

"I was thinking of looking for a property in the neighborhood."

The marquess put his hand behind his ear. "Repeat that please before I fall off my chair."

"You heard me. I wondered if you have any recommendations."

The marquess set his pen aside and crossed his arms on the desk. "Are you unwell?"

Colin laughed. "No."

The marquess drew out a quizzing glass from his pocket and peered at his son. "Hmmm. I don't see any spots or fevered cheeks. But something tells me you are suffering from a malady known to many young men. Could it be you are in love?"

Colin's ears got a little warm. "I haven't asked—not properly."

The marquess dropped the quizzing glass. "Do I want to hear this story?"

Colin shook his head. "Definitely not."

"Do you plan to make a proper proposal to Lady Angeline?"

"Yes, but she turned me down."

"Botched it, I suppose."

He nodded. "How amenable do you think Wycoff would be?"

"Well, he might try to shoot you, but he's a worse shot than I am. The odds are in your favor."

"Ah, that is reassuring," Colin said.

The marquess sighed. "I think the most significant question is whether Lady Angeline is receptive to your proposal. I know the two of you have been in one another's pockets, but we both know she has endured a rough time. I've no doubt she will come about and be the toast of the ton once again. But marrying and participating in the London season may be too much for her all at once. I don't know. Margaret and the duchess would have you rush to the altar. However, you know Lady Angeline better than anybody, and I think the two of you are especially fortunate that you have had the opportunity to really know one another before the marriage."

"It was purposeful," he said. "She suggested it."

"Do you love her?"

He swallowed. "Very much."

"And?"

"We've had a spat or two, but to our credit we reconcile well enough."

"Ah, yes, reconciliation." The marquess rose, walked around his desk, and clapped Colin's shoulder. "I can't think of a better wife for you, son. No doubt the two of you will have many spats, reconcile frequently, and present me with my first grandchild within nine months."

Colin laughed. "Thank you, Father."

"Do you plan to journey to London next week?"

"Yes."

"Your friends are prepared and the plan is solid?"

"Yes, everything is in order."

"Son, I'm rather fond of you, though I'm not certain why."

Colin laughed.

"I will give you a bit of advice. Beat the bloody hell out of the bastard, but don't kill him. His foul blood isn't worth having on your hands. When it's over, have him hauled off to a press-gang. He'll wish he were dead and that's punishment enough."

Colin nodded. "Thank you, Father."

"Take every precaution, son. You have a beautiful young woman who will be waiting anxiously for your return and so will I. Finish this nasty business once and for all. Then we will celebrate upon your return. While you're in London, you might consider purchasing a special license."

Colin nodded. "I appreciate all of your advice, particularly the reminder for the special license. I would very much like to wed her upon my return."

"You might propose first," the marquess said.

"Yes, on bended knee this time."

"Do I want to hear about the other time?"

Colin shook his head. "Probably not."

"I love you, son. Go defend her honor, and then come home in one piece. I'll see what I can do about finding you a property."

That evening

The marquess did his neighborly duty and invited Reverend Quimby and his wife to dinner. Mrs. Quimby once again regaled everyone with minute descriptions of Harwell, Baron Overton's property. Angeline politely conversed with the reverend, but she was anxious. Her father had announced they would stay an additional week at Deerfield and gave no other explanation. Earlier this afternoon, her father, the marquess, and Colin had gone into the study. They had remained there for several hours. Angeline was very concerned. She feared that Colin would challenge Brentmoor to a duel. All afternoon, she had waited for an opportunity to speak to Colin, but she'd ended up reading to the ladies while they stitched this afternoon, and there had been no chance to have a private conversation with Colin. She was anxious and hoped that they would be able to talk in the drawing room, because she needed reassurance that he would not duel.

When dinner ended, the ladies withdrew to the drawing room for tea and stitching. Penny played "Robin Adair" and the twins sang. For once, Angeline focused on stitching, hoping to evade a "coze" with Mrs. Quimby.

"Lady Angeline, you have been especially quiet this evening," Mrs. Quimby said.

"My thoughts have been elsewhere, Mrs. Quimby. Do forgive me. How are you and all of your family?"

"We are all happy and well. Reverend Quimby received a letter from Baron Overton a few days ago."

"Ah, letters are always welcome." Angeline exchanged a smile with Margaret. Clearly Mrs. Quimby was ready to launch into her favorite topic.

"Of course, all is prospering at Harwell House," Mrs. Quimby said. "I am only sorry that the reverend and I missed Baron Overton's dinner party. But I have the letter here. It will only take a moment to find it in my reticule."

Angeline met her mother's resigned gaze. She hoped there was only one letter.

"Ah, here it is," Mrs. Quimby said, smoothing out the paper. "Yes, Baron Overton writes that he was gratified to invite the most illustrious guests who are new to the neighborhood, Lord and Lady Brentmoor." She paused. "Are you acquainted with the family, Lady Angeline?"

Angeline hesitated for a moment, and then she pulled the embroidery thread. Mrs. Quimby could not have known that the mention in the letter would cause great consternation.

Margaret had a gift for maneuvering guests who overstepped the bounds. "Mrs. Quimby, do you have friends or relations near Baron Overton?"

"Unfortunately, no. If I did, I assure you, I would be in raptures. The thought of Mr. Quimby and me in the same neighborhood as Baron Overton is one I sometimes entertain."

"How delightful," Margaret said.

Now that Margaret had distracted Mrs. Quimby, Angeline released a sigh of relief.

"We will journey there at the end of the month. I do hope to make the acquaintance of Lord and Lady Brentmoor. I have heard she is a great beauty," Mrs. Quimby said. "Is that true, Duchess?"

"I do not consider beauty a recommendation for making acquaintances," the duchess said. "Character is the important factor."

Angeline thought that Mrs. Quimby could not fail to notice the duchess's chilly reply.

"Oh, to be sure," Mrs. Quimby said, "but one cannot help noticing great beauty. I wondered if you had an opinion of her looks."

The duchess lowered her embroidery. "I do not."

Angeline was certain her mother's curt reply would quell the woman.

"It is a shame that Lord Brentmoor lost his esteemed father, and of course, his grief must have been large," Mrs. Quimby continued, "but a fortune will always be welcome, to be sure." She laughed.

Angeline thought the woman exceedingly vulgar.

Margaret turned her attention to Mrs. Quimby. "Allow me to pour you another dish of tea."

"That is so kind of you, but I'm not thirsty. Lady Angeline, you did not say whether or not you had met Lord and Lady Brentmoor?"

Unfortunately, the reverend's wife was not the sort of woman who sensed undercurrents in conversations. Again, Angeline chose to ignore the question.

Margaret rose. "Duchess, let me bring you another cup of tea."

Angeline noticed her mother's lips were drawn tightly. *Poor Mama to have to suffer Mrs. Quimby's prattle about Brentmoor.*

Mrs. Quimby continued, undeterred. "Lady Angeline, I believe you did not hear my question about Lord and Lady Brentmoor."

Angeline smoothed out her embroidery. "Mrs. Quimby, the persons you mentioned are not friends of mine."

"Oh, well, I'm sure Baron Overton would be glad to make the introductions—"

Margaret approached Mrs. Quimby. "Unfortunately, Baron Overton is not here to perform the introductions. May I get you a second cup of tea?"

"Oh, no, I'm perfectly satisfied, though I do thank you. Well, I hope you will have a chance to meet Lord and Lady Brentmoor during the spring season in London, Lady Angeline," Mrs. Quimby said.

Margaret leaned forward and touched Mrs. Quimby's arm. "I do beg your pardon, Mrs. Quimby. Would you be willing to play for us? I'm sure we would all enjoy it."

Margaret spoke to the girls briefly. They left the drawing room, and their voices receded.

Mrs. Quimby prattled on about what an honor it was to be asked to play. Margaret managed to urge her across the room and onto the bench. After setting up the music sheets, Margaret walked away as quickly as possible. She smiled at Mrs. Quimby and turned to Angeline. "I am sorry."

Angeline sighed. "She has no idea her words are unwelcome, Margaret."

"My head aches from listening to her," the duchess said. "Her manners are deplorable."

"Your headache will be the perfect excuse," Margaret said. "I will be concerned about contagion when the gentlemen arrive and will ask Chadwick to order the carriage immediately to take them home."

"Thank you, Margaret," Angeline said under her breath. "I do not want Mama to suffer any more talk of that fiend and his wife."

"My concerns are for you, Angeline," the duchess said.

"I hope the gentlemen are prompt," Margaret said.

When Mrs. Quimby finished, she turned. "Would one of you like to exhibit? I do not wish to be greedy." She laughed.

"Please, continue," Margaret said. "We are all enjoying your performance."

"She is blind to the feelings of others," the duchess said. "Margaret, you will have to take her in hand. She will cause problems, because her husband is the vicar, meaning one cannot simply ignore her, which is impossible anyway."

"I have tried repeatedly to deter her," Margaret said.

"You are too gentle," the duchess said. "A woman with her nature only understands the stark truth. You see the way she ignores suggestions, other than to show off at the pianoforte."

When the gentlemen returned to the drawing room, Angeline caught Colin's eye. He escorted her over to the window seat. "You look a bit distressed," he said under his breath.

"Mrs. Quimby is oblivious. I will tell you soon. Margaret is speaking to your father now."

"Oh, dear," the duchess said. "I am not at all well."

Mrs. Quimby halted. "Oh, my. Perhaps another cup of tea would work."

Margaret hurried to the duchess. "Oh, dear, you are looking pale. I hope there is no contagion. Chadwick, please have the carriage brought round."

He looked a bit taken aback, until Margaret said, "Chadwick, please do not delay. I could not be easy if Mrs. Quimby and Reverend Quimby remain when there is a possible contagion."

"Ah," the marquess said, lifting his chin. "I agree. We cannot expose Reverend and Mrs. Quimby. Let me ring for Ames to arrange matters."

"I'm sure it is nothing," Mrs. Quimby said, turning to her husband. "Do you not agree?"

Margaret took Mrs. Quimby's arm. "I would never forgive myself if either you or Mr. Quimby fell ill. In fact, it is quite cold out this evening, but there are woolen rugs in the carriage, and you will be comfortable on your journey."

Nearly half an hour elapsed before Margaret and the marquess returned to the drawing room.

"That woman does not know when to stop talking," the marquess said. "I can't very well ignore the reverend, but I cannot abide his wife."

"Subtlety is lost on her," Margaret said. "Be glad you were not here, Chadwick. It was a most distressing performance on the part of Mrs. Quimby."

After Margaret described the events, the marquess groaned. "The woman is completely unaware of others' feelings."

"Chadwick, something must be done," Margaret said.

"Oh, no," the marquess said. "I'm not stepping in that mud puddle."

Angeline sagged against the sofa. "She is unbearable. One hates to wound her, but apparently no one has ever curbed her prattling."

"I very much doubt she will change at this late date," Colin said. "Father, I suggest that you invite them only for tea."

"We've set a precedent," the marquess said. "It can't be avoided now."

"Lord Chadwick," Angeline said, "perhaps you could suggest to the reverend that he include some examples in his sermon of how we learn more from listening than speaking. Then when Reverend and Mrs. Quimby call, you can always bring up what a wonderful sermon it was and how he and Mrs. Quimby are such wonderful examples. Every time Mrs. Quimby prattles, bring up the subject of your favorite sermon."

"Excellent idea, Angeline," Margaret said.

The marquess's eyes gleamed. "Clever, Lady Angeline."

"Well, I'm for bed," the marquess said. "It has been a long day."

Everyone else agreed. Soon, Angeline and Colin found themselves alone.

"If I didn't know better, I would think they planned this," Angeline said.

He cupped her face. "I'm sorry for the disturbing evening."

"We weathered it," she said.

He kissed her gently. "I have business in London, and I leave tomorrow."

Angeline laid her head on his shoulder. "You're planning to call him out."

"Something must be done," Colin said.

She was so afraid of losing him. "He may not even be there," she said.

"Bellingham sent word. He is luring him."

"Oh, God," she said.

He wrapped his arms around her. "You've nothing to worry about," he said. "All the plans are in place."

"What if something goes wrong?" she said.

"It won't," he said.

"No, Colin. It's not worth risking your life. Do you know what it would do to me if something happened to you?"

"I know this is hard, Angeline, but I promise that all will be well very soon. I won't risk my life. I am my father's only heir, after all, and I do want to live. There is so much I wish to share with you. When I return, I will be expecting your kisses."

"Please be careful. I could not bear losing you."

"All will be well," he said. "I promise."

She looked up at him. "I wish you would not go."

"I know, but I will not rest until he is made to pay for what he did. When it is all over, I will return to you and demand kisses."

The day after Colin left, the duke requested a meeting with Angeline after breakfast in the marquess's study. Angeline's stomach clenched. She'd missed her father so much and did not know what to expect from him. He had only spoken warmly to her that one time at Sommerall, and he'd ignored her for the most part afterward. She took a deep breath, lifted her chin, and walked inside the study.

Her father stood and made her a very formal bow.

"Angeline, my closest friend in all the world gave me a dressing-down. I am doubly ashamed of having failed you."

"Papa?" His red-rimmed eyes alarmed her. "Are you ill?"

"No, but I despise myself for letting you down. I should have booted that bastard out of our house immediately. I let him take me in, and I could not even look you in the eyes because I failed you. If I had been a better father, he would not have hurt my little girl."

She ran into his arms. "Papa, he played us both off each other. We didn't know until it was t-too late."

"I cannot change my mistakes, but I beg you to forgive me."

"I love you, Papa," she said. Oh, she had missed him so much.

"I also am ashamed because I made it seem that I favored Penny over you. I didn't mean to do it. I just felt a responsibility to her. She was so lonely after you and your mother went to Paris. If not for your little sister, I think I might have gone mad. I missed you and your mother so very much."

"We will be a whole family again, Papa."

"I have much to mend," he said, "but I would very much enjoy playing chess with you again."

"Thank you, Papa. I would appreciate the distraction. I am very worried about Colin."

"He will come home safe and sound," the duke said. "I have it on the best of authority that he has someone he wishes to see as soon as this business is over."

She hugged her father hard. "You have made me very happy."

"Now, shall we play?"

She took his arm. "I do plan to trounce you."

"I will give you no quarter, Daughter, but you may try."

Chapter Sixteen

London

At precisely midnight, Colin strode into White's Club. He knew who awaited him and where, for it was all set up in advance. His heart beat a little harder than usual, but he greeted acquaintances as he strode through the club. Many were watching, having been recruited into the inner circle. Someone with pretensions to honor was polluting the venerable club. That man would be publicly exposed and severely punished for crimes against the fairer sex.

Brentmoor took a pinch of snuff, rather delicately, and offered it to Bellingham, who waved it off. Brentmoor was unaware that thirty men had waiting hacks outside and were planning a journey for him.

Brentmoor drank three bottles of Madeira, something Colin figured the cur would regret at dawn. Unbeknownst to Brentmoor, the men sitting with him had set him up. Two hours passed when Colin invited Brentmoor to join them at a private party. The bastard accepted and hesitated only when he stepped out and saw the line of hacks at the curb.

Brentmoor spun around and scrambled, but Bellingham caught his arms and roughly tied them behind his back while Harry gagged the villain. Colin stepped forward, stripped off his glove, and slapped it in Brentmoor's face. "Before this day ends, you will beg for mercy and you will get none."

Colin pitched a heavy purse to the driver, a bribe to keep his mouth shut. Harry and Bell ducked inside the carriage and Colin shoved Brentmoor onto the floor of the hack. Colin boarded, knocked on the roof, and the hack rolled off. He looked behind the vehicle and saw the other hacks rolling off one by one. The destination was Wimbledon Common, a dueling place.

Brentmoor struggled and groaned when the hack hit a bump.

"That's only a taste of what I have in store for you," Colin said.

When they arrived at the field, the servants stood by with lanterns. Colin dumped Brentmoor on the ground, where he writhed like a mangy dog. The other carriages arrived, and the gentlemen descended the hacks. They formed a queue, and one by one they spit on his face.

Colin stood a foot away and saw the murderous expression in Brentmoor's eyes. Then he pitched his voice so that all could hear. "Brentmoor, you are undeserving of the title gentleman. You have polluted the clubs and the ballrooms. Worst of all, you have preyed on innocent women. Today, you are judged by your peers as unfit to be a man."

Colin stripped off his coat and cravat and handed them

to a servant. "You have meddled with at least half a dozen innocent women, two of whom you got with child and abandoned. You are a snake, but on this day, you will receive your punishment and your sentence awaits you, but first, I have a personal score to settle. Untie and ungag him," Colin shouted.

He marched toward the center of the field, and Brentmoor strode from the opposite side. "Damn you," Brentmoor said. "I've no issue with you, Ravenshire."

"I beg to differ," Colin called out in a clear voice. "You are a coward, a liar, and a bully."

"Your accusations have no merit," Brentmoor called out, striding forward.

"You are not a man," Colin shouted. "You are a filthy swine who preys upon the fairer sex."

"Name the woman, Ravenshire. No doubt you've swived her already."

Rage pumped through his blood as he met Brentmoor on the field. The first punch resounded with a crack and blood streamed out of Brentmoor's nose. The cur rose up and landed a blow to Colin's ear. It rang afterward, but he refused to let it stop him. He punched Brentmoor in the mouth, blackened both eyes, and when the coward fell to his knees, Colin kicked him in the groin. Brentmoor groaned and rolled onto the grass.

Colin stood over him. "Tie him up and gag him."

Harry tied Brentmoor's hands and feet and Bell gagged him. Then Colin yanked Brentmoor to his feet and shoved him onto the floor of the hack. "Gentlemen, meet us at the docks."

Colin approached the driver with a second purse.

"Where to, guvner?" the driver said.

"The docks," Colin said, and entered the carriage. He knocked on the roof of the carriage and smirked. "Ah, we have one more destination, Brentmoor, your final one with us." Brentmoor stared at him with murder in his eyes, but Colin knew his bravado would soon turn to watery bowels.

The other carriages arrived, and the gentlemen stepped out to witness. Colin stood Brentmoor outside the carriage, untied the gag, and lifted his voice again. "Brentmoor, you are judged before your peers as unfit to be a man."

Brentmoor fell on his knees. "I beg for mercy."

"You do not deserve it," Colin said. "You have been judged and now you will receive your sentence. The press-gang a few yards beyond awaits you with open arms. I imagine they will have a little fun with a pretty boy like you."

Brentmoor's eyes filled with terror. "No, please God, no."

When the press-gang came to claim Brentmoor, Colin doffed his hat and said, "Compliments of Lady Angeline Brenham."

Deerfield Park

Angeline sat in the drawing room reading while her mother, Margaret, Penny, and the twins embroidered. *Sense and Sensibility* proved to be the perfect antidote for a misty, gray day. For Angeline, it was a temporary escape from all her worst fears. She would not rest easy until Colin came home.

Penny edged forward on her chair. "Angeline, I can

hardly contain my eagerness to find out what happened between Willoughby and Marianne."

Angeline smiled. "When last we left off, Colonel Brandon was inquiring about Marianne. The colonel reveals what he knows about Willoughby. 'He had left the girl whose youth and innocence he had seduced—'"

Bianca gasped. "Oh, what a devil."

"It is shocking," Bernadette said.

"Girls, allow Angeline to continue," Margaret said.

Angeline smiled. "'He had left her, promising to return; he neither returned, nor wrote, nor relieved her.'"

"He is a very bad man," Penny said. "Marianne is fortunate to have escaped him."

A deep masculine voice said, "Indeed, she is."

Everyone rose. Angeline wanted to run straight into Colin's arms, but she must be a good example to the girls. "You are well?" she said.

"Very," he said, "and glad to be home."

"Girls, let us repair to the music room," Margaret said. "The duchess and I wish to hear how you are progressing at the pianoforte."

"Indeed, you will be called upon to exhibit," the duchess said. "Regular practice will help ease any anxieties you may feel in a crowd, and others will remark upon your accomplishments."

When they left, he crossed the room and clasped her hands. "I'm sorry for the delay, but I had one last item of business."

Her eyes welled.

"Why are you crying?" he said, taking out his handkerchief and blotting her eyes.

"I'm so relieved you are unharmed."

He wrapped his arms around her. "I did not like being parted from you."

"I missed you."

"My ear still smarts a bit," he said.

She touched it lightly "What happened?"

"He got one punch in, but you will be pleased to know that he is gone forever. He will not come back. Even if he managed such a feat, his name is blackened. He was much worse than you know. He seduced and abandoned more than one lady."

She gasped.

"You escaped the worst, because you were too strong to fall into his trap."

"Oh, how awful for those poor women."

"There are probably others we know nothing about, but I thought you would like to know that thirty men stood witness against him for his disgusting treatment of you and other ladies and their families."

"I was scared, but you did the right thing."

"Now he can't hurt other ladies," Colin said. "Also, you might be interested to know that the former Lady Cunningham, now known as Lady Brentmoor, has fled the country."

"I suppose they both got what they deserved."

"He most certainly did," Colin said. "Now, enough of villains. I am here to collect a debt."

She smiled. "I promised you kisses."

He kissed her gently on the lips. "Now, there is one more business matter, before we return to the pleasurable part. While I was in London, Harry and I called upon his mother, Mrs. Norcliffe. She bade me to deliver this to you."

Angeline broke the seal on the letter. Her arms tingled. "She wishes to . . . give a ball in my honor, the first of the season."

"My understanding is that if you have the support of Mrs. Norcliffe, you are set for life," he said.

"I must write and thank her."

"Before I left, I realized I wanted to give you a gift, your heart's desire, and while there is nothing tangible, your name is clear, and Mrs. Norcliffe assured me that you will be able to attend your sister's debut ball."

Her face crumpled.

"Oh, no, please don't cry."

"I'm a watering pot today," she said, "but they are happy tears."

He blotted her face again.

She lifted on her toes and hugged him hard.

"I know it means the world to you."

"You mean the world to me," she said.

He raised her hands and kissed the backs of them. Then he knelt on one knee. "It isn't my first proposal, but this one will hopefully be a little more romantic."

She blinked back the moisture in her eyes.

"Angeline, I love you dearly. You are unique, funny, and a very talented pretend courtesan."

She laughed.

"But I cannot allow any other pretend men to enjoy your charms, because I want them all for myself."

She smiled. "I think you're man enough for me."

"Whew," he said, pretending to wipe a sheen of moisture off his forehead. "Now, I didn't prepare, but I know what I want to say. I will promise to smite any mice in the attic, and make wild, passionate love to you. Most of all, I promise to love and cherish you always. I beg you to spend a lifetime with me laughing and loving. Will you marry me?"

"Yes, I will marry you."

"Oh, thank God."

She laughed again. "Stand up, silly. I promised you kisses upon your return."

He stood and kissed her gently on the lips, and then the kiss caught fire. He opened her mouth and tasted her. She felt at last that she had welcomed him with no reserve and no fears. "I love you, Colin."

He rubbed noses with her. "I know. Who else would defend me to my father?"

"Do you think our families will be surprised?"

"No," he said. "Oh, one reason I'm late is I paid a visit to the archbishop. We will marry by special license."

"Oh, that should impress Mrs. Quimby."

His chest shook with laughter. "I had better ask your father's permission. My father assured me that Wycoff would probably want to kill me, but he's a bad shot so the odds are with me."

The duke stopped outside the door. "Ravenshire, you're home. Take your hands off my daughter."

"Papa, your timing is excellent," she said.

"Wycoff, I wish to marry your daughter. Will you give your blessing?"

"Hmmm." Wycoff looked at his daughter. "Are you sure you want him? He's not like a fish; you can't throw him back."

"Yes, Papa, I'm sure I want him."

He cleared his throat. "Well, then, you have my blessing."

"Excellent." Colin shook Wycoff's hand and then he picked up Angeline, and she shrieked.

Naturally footsteps followed. They turned to find their families invading the drawing room. Everyone exchanged hugs and congratulations. The marquess requested a bottle of champagne and said the girls could have a tiny bit. Margaret took Angeline aside and showed her the ruby bracelet and confessed she'd won the wager with Chadwick, who apparently had doubts about Colin and Angeline getting married.

In the midst of the celebration, the twins set Hercules down in the drawing room. He had a sealed letter in his mouth.

The marquess picked up the dog and set him at Colin's feet. "Drop it, Hercules," he said.

Colin bent down. The dog sank his teeth into the letter and growled.

"Drop it, Hercules," the marquess said.

The dog whined and the letter fell with a slight clink.

Colin grasped the letter, broke the seal, and a key fell out. He picked it up and looked at the letter.

Son,

I finally figured out a way. When all else fails, bribery usually works. May you and Angeline be happy always at Sommerall.

I'm proud of you.

Colin swallowed hard and showed it to Angeline. When her eyes welled, he put his arm around her. "You're not crying over an old house, are you?"

"No, I'm crying sentimental tears, because today is magical."

He leaned down and said, "No, you are." Colin squared his shoulders. "Father, I've been wondering about the Faradays."

"Oh, what about them?" the marquess said.

"They took your bribe so willingly."

"I made them an offer they could not refuse."

"Father, who the devil are they, really?"

"Traveling actors," he said.

Angeline gasped. "No!"

The marquess shrugged. "I was desperate and had to do something. By the way, Lady Angeline, Mrs. Faraday, the actress, bid me to apologize to you. Apparently, she thought you were living in sin with my son."

"I'll be damned," Colin said.

"Colin, we do not use that sort of language," Margaret said.

"Pardon me," Colin said. He noted that Bianca and Bernadette lit up like the lanterns at Vauxhall. He figured he'd just added to the twin's colorful vocabularies.

A fortnight later

"Are you nervous, Angie?" Penny asked.

"No, not really, but I am so happy that you agreed to attend me."

"I'm honored," Penny said, "but I will miss you, Angie."

"You know that you can always visit us. The twins are nearby. Best of all, this spring you will make your debut, and everyone will be there." *Including me, all because of Colin.*

Marie finished styling her hair. "You look beautiful, my lady."

"Thank you, Marie."

Her mother came inside the room. "You are not dressed yet."

"Mama, Angie insisted I must dress first," Penny said.

"You have always loved your sister, Angeline."

"Who would not love Penelope?"

"My lady, shall we dress you?" Marie said.

A tap sounded at the door. Margaret peeked inside. "May we come in?"

"Of course," Angeline said.

The twins sat on the bed and watched as Marie tightened the strings of the stays and smoothed them out over the petticoat. Then she stepped inside the beautiful white gown with yards of lace and rosettes on the hem. Her mother clasped her own pearl necklace on Angeline. Then she donned her slippers. "Well?"

Her mother carefully hugged her. "I am so very happy for you. No one deserves it more."

"Thank you, Mama."

Another knock sounded. Margaret opened the door. The duke stood there. "It is time, Daughter."

She took her father's arm. He escorted her down the stairs and into the waiting carriage. Her mother and Penny followed inside. The carriage rolled off, and Angeline inhaled. "Oh, goodness, I have butterflies in my stomach."

"That is normal," her mother said.

The duke looked at Angeline. "You have always been beautiful, but you are even more so today."

The carriage arrived quickly. Her arms were a little

shaky as her father escorted her down the aisle. Colin's friend Harry nudged him. Colin turned to watch her, and she knew she would never forget the look of love in his eyes.

At last Angeline stood beside him. Her little sister held her posy, and Harry winked at him.

The familiar words of the ceremony washed over Colin. Not long ago, his life had seemed so aimless, but standing in this church beside the woman who would be his wife from this day forward, he knew that there was a purpose to all things. Even before he took the marriage vows, he had sworn that he would never take her for granted, and he would tell her that he loved her every single day of their lives together.

Then it was time to repeat the vows. He slid the ring over her slender finger and looked into her eyes. "With this ring I thee wed, with my body I thee worship, and with all my worldly goods I thee endow."

Reverend Quimby said, "For as much as Angeline and Colin have consented together in holy wedlock, and have witnessed the same before God and this company, and thereto have given and pledged their troth either to the other, and have declared the same by giving and receiving of a ring, and by joining of hands: I pronounce that they be man and wife together, in the name of the Father, and of the Son, and of the Holy Ghost. Amen."

Deerfield

There was much rejoicing at the wedding breakfast. Angeline ate very little because she still had butterflies in her stomach. Colin made up for it by eating two slices of cake. Bellingham and his wife attended. Three times Bell had to grab his son, who tried to pull Hercules's curly tail.

The footmen circulated with glasses of champagne. Bianca and Bernadette got scolded after Margaret found them draining two glasses of champagne. The marquess was worried that they held their liquor like a man. He confessed to Colin that it didn't bode well. Colin advised him to have locks installed on the sideboard.

Penny took a slice of cake to Harry. When Angeline remembered Penny asking about kissing boys, she steered her sister away from Harry and took her aside. "He's too old for you, and he's a rake."

"He's ever so witty," Penny said. "I know he's too old, but a girl can look."

Someone dropped cake on the floor, and Hercules gobbled it up. Mrs. Quimby asked every single guest if they had made the acquaintance of Baron Overton. Mr. and Mrs. Faraday congratulated Colin and Angeline and said they had never had a finer time as actors.

The celebration lasted for hours, but as the autumn sun started to set, Colin took Angeline's hands, and she thought she might melt on the spot from the way he looked at her. They said good-bye to all their friends and family, and then they took the carriage six miles to their home, Sommerall House.

There was a chilly breeze as they hurried to the door. Colin unlocked the door, picked her up, and carried her over the threshold. Then he slid her down his body. "Welcome home, my wife."

She cupped his face. "My husband."

They removed their wraps and walked up the familiar

stairs. A fire was burning in the bedchamber where they had made love that rainy night. Someone, probably Margaret, had put the servants to work. The covers were turned down, and there was a bottle of wine.

He removed her stunning gown and all the rest of her clothing. Then he laid her on the sheets gently as if she were made of the finest crystal. After he shed his own clothes, he joined her in the bed and turned on his side. "Tonight is our first night as a married couple. I don't want to think what my life might have turned out like if not for you. Now I have my family and yours and ours together. All because of you, my beautiful Angeline."

She rose over him, "Lay back, Husband."

"Why?"

"I want to take advantage of you."

"Help," he said in a mocking meek voice.

In the next moment, he gasped for real as she used her tongue on him. "Have mercy, Wife."

Her only response was a wicked laugh.

Epilogue

London, spring 1822

At Angeline's request, Mrs. Norcliffe delayed the ball for Angeline's return to society in deference of the debuts for Penelope, Bianca, and Bernadette. Colin looked into his wife's shining eyes and thought she was even more beautiful. She did look as if she were glowing within. Now and then she placed her hand over her slightly rounded belly.

Colin leaned down. "Is *she* kicking?"

"*He* is stretching and pushing as if he thinks he can get out."

"*She* is anxious to make her debut, but it is too soon," he said.

Angeline shook her head. "Every other man in the world wants a boy, except you."

"I really don't care, love. I just want you and the babe to be healthy."

"We are," she said. Then she grabbed his forearm. "Look, a boy asked Penelope to dance."

He frowned. "Do her slippers have red stripes?"

"Yes, they were mine, but they fit her."

"Aren't those a bit . . . fast?"

"This from a reformed rake?"

He laughed. "By the by, are you planning to take all the walls down at Sommerall?"

She snorted. "Be careful or I will."

"There they go, queuing up for the dance," he said. "Shall we walk closer?"

"Yes, please," she said.

He escorted her, setting his hand protectively over her belly whenever they moved through a particularly dense part of the crowd. Angeline saw a number of matrons smiling at him. They sat in chairs on the sideline because her back tended to ache if she stood too long. He held her hand and gave her his handkerchief when her eyes grew misty.

"This is the best gift you could ever give me," she said.

"Most women want jewels and furs."

"Those women don't understand that the best gift in life is love."

His heart turned over once again, and he figured he was the luckiest man in the ballroom tonight.

With the recent loss of his beloved uncle, Harry Norcliffe, the Duke of Granfield, has no desire to participate in a dancing competition. But one look at his beautiful partner causes the nobleman to change his tune...

Please turn the page for a preview of

What a Devilish Duke Desires.

Chapter One

White's, London 1822

Three months after his uncle's death, Harry Norcliffe, the Duke of Granfield, needed to find his way back to his old life, which had disappeared under a mountain of grief. His uncle Hugh had been his father figure for as long as he could remember, and life at the farm in Wiltshire would never be the same without him.

Harry reached the door at the club, took a deep breath, and stepped inside the familiar hall. A servant appeared and bowed. "Welcome back, Your Grace."

"Thank you." He'd yet to adjust to his new title and felt oddly like an imposter. As he divested himself of his hat, greatcoat, and gloves, he remembered thinking there would be changes, but he'd not been prepared for so many. Tonight, however, he looked forward to meeting up with his old friends.

Harry strolled over to have a look at the betting book as he'd always done upon entering the club. Apparently Aubery had wagered Rollins a crown that it would rain on Tuesday. The frivolous bet reassured Harry that the world in London had gone on and so would he, despite the crushing loss of his uncle.

He strolled through the ground floor, looking for his friends. The clink of glasses and silverware echoed from the upstairs dining room, and the fragrant aroma of beefsteak teased his senses. Now he wanted nothing more than to quaff down one too many brandies and have a few laughs with his old friends.

He didn't get far before Lords Fitzhugh and Castelle hailed him.

"Congratulations, on the dukedom," Castelle said, pumping his hand.

"Congratulations, *Granfield*," Fitzhugh said with emphasis.

Several other acquaintances approached as well. Harry acknowledged their greetings with a nod, but he neither wanted nor appreciated their congratulations. He knew they meant well, but no title or fortune would ever make up for losing his uncle.

Someone clapped him on the shoulder and said, "It's the Devil himself."

Harry's spirits lifted immediately upon seeing his friend Bellingham. "I suppose it takes one to know one," he said, grinning.

"Come, our old table is waiting, and there is someone I want you to see," Bell said.

The world seemed right again as he followed his friend upstairs to the dining room. When they reached the table, Colin stood and pounded him on the back. "Harry, it's good to see you."

"And you. How is married life?"

"Well, Angeline hasn't thrown me out on my arse yet," Colin said.

"Oh, ho!" Harry said, laughing.

Bell motioned to Harry. "Do you remember this fellow?"

Harry frowned. When recognition dawned, he was astounded. "Is that Justin?"

Justin Davenport, the Earl of Chesfield, grinned as he extended his hand. "Pleased to see you, Harry."

"Good Lord." Harry turned his attention to Bell. "He was a skinny cub the last time I saw him."

"He's twenty-one now," Bell said, "and six feet three inches tall."

"What are you feeding him?" Harry said.

Bell laughed. "A great deal of beef."

Harry signaled the waiter to bring brandies. When they arrived, he looked at Bell. "I can't believe you're letting the sprig drink brandy."

"He's of age and knows his limits. I wouldn't have met his mother if not for that flask of brandy Justin hid very poorly," Bell said.

Justin laughed. "It wasn't my brightest idea, Father."

"Fortunately, you're past sowing wild oats." Bell narrowed his eyes. "Correct?"

Justin's smile slanted to one side. "Am I supposed to answer that?"

Everyone laughed.

Three years ago, Bellingham had sworn to be a lifelong bachelor, but he'd fallen hard for Laura Davenport. All of them had been fond of the recalcitrant lad, but he was a grown man now. The devil, how had time flown by so quickly?

After the waiter brought the brandies, Harry sipped his

and regarded Colin over his glass. "What news do you have?"

Colin's expression turned a bit abashed. "I will be a father by late summer."

"Congratulations," Harry said. Damn, his friends had become domesticated. He'd never thought he'd see the day. When he signaled the waiter again, Harry ordered beefsteak, potatoes, and cheesecake for his friends.

"Harry, do you still keep rooms at the Albany?" Colin asked.

"Yes, I still have my old rooms." He'd found them rather comforting. After all of the events that had sent his world spinning, he appreciated the familiarity, including the shabby furnishings.

"What have I missed while I was gone?" Harry asked.

Bell shrugged. "Pembroke lost more hair. Old Lord Leighton is in love with the widowed Lady Atherton, but she swears she prefers her sherry to him." He paused. "I almost forgot. Justin's former friend George wrecked the second curricle his father unwisely purchased for him."

Harry laughed and shook his head. "Some things never change, I suppose."

"My family is growing," Bell said. "Stephen is three now, and we have an infant daughter, Sarah."

Bell had changed a great deal. When they had first met, he'd been rather guarded. Over the course of one season, he'd become an indispensable friend to both Harry and Colin. Bellingham was definitely the sort of fellow one could count on.

When the waiters brought the food, Harry's stomach growled at the scent of the sizzling beefsteak. He'd not even realized he was famished, but then, he hadn't eaten well lately. Now that he was relaxing with friends, he wolfed down the beef, potatoes, and cheesecake.

After the waiter brought the coffee, Justin rose. "Please excuse me. Paul just arrived, and I'm planning to trounce him at the billiards table."

"Go on, then," Bell said. "Hail a hackney and don't make a lot of racket when you come home. You do not want to face your mother's wrath."

When Justin retreated, Harry said, "You've certainly tamed his rebelliousness. Well done."

Bell set his coffee aside. "He only needed guidance. I suppose we'll keep him after all."

"What about your family, Harry?" Bell asked.

He shrugged. "My girl cousins haven't changed much, but my mother threatens daily to introduce me to the latest beauty on the marriage mart."

Bell and Colin exchanged amused glances.

"What?" Harry said suspiciously.

"If you decide to get a lag shackle, we could form the old married men's club," Bell said.

"Ha-ha," Harry said, setting his cup aside.

"That reminds me," Bell said. "Laura invited you to dinner in a sennight."

Harry narrowed his eyes. "Let me guess. I will be seated next to a lovely lady that your countess has chosen just for me."

Bell's shoulders shook with laughter. "Laura will be heartbroken if you do not attend, but don't feel the least bit obligated."

Harry snorted. "I just remembered a pressing engagement."

"How are you holding up?" Colin said.

He'd known Colin since they were boys at Eton. "Well enough, I suppose."

"Your uncle was an exceptional man," Colin said. "I have fond memories of spending summers with you at his farm."

"After his funeral, I kept expecting him to walk into the room," Harry said. "He was like a father to me."

"The good principles he taught you will live on inside you," Bell said, touching his fist to his chest.

It helped to talk about his uncle with his friends.

After they finished their coffee, Bell turned to Harry. "When I came home from the Continent all those years ago, I found the estate business rather overwhelming. Your uncle's steward and secretary are competent?"

"They are, but I'm not."

"You'll manage, but if you need advice or assistance, do not hesitate to contact me," Bell said. "All the same, I have the greatest confidence in you."

"I appreciate the offer," Harry said.

Bell retrieved his watch. "Ah, damn, it's getting late. I promised Laura I would return before midnight."

"I must go as well," Colin said. "My wife and I have an early appointment with an architect. Pity me. Angeline is determined to tear down half the town house I just bought."

Harry laughed, but truthfully, he was a bit disappointed. In the old days, they would smoke cheroots and drink well past midnight. The differences between himself and his married friends weighed heavily on his mind. He enjoyed their company, but his friends' priorities had shifted to their families. Nothing would ever be quite the same again.

Harry followed his friends downstairs, where they all

donned their outerwear and walked out of the club. His breath frosted and the cold air chafed his cheeks as he shook hands with his friends.

"Can I give you a lift?" Bell said.

"No, it's only a few blocks," Harry said. "The street-lamps are lighted and a walk will clear my head."

The misty fog swirled around him, but it wasn't too dense tonight. Soon he must buy a carriage. He'd need one for inclement weather, and now that he was a bloody duke, he supposed he ought to have a decent vehicle for traveling. God knew he'd inherited an enormous fortune and could afford whatever caught his fancy. He'd always thought money would bring him happiness, but it hadn't. Perhaps in time he would feel differently.

He was only a block away from the Albany when he saw a thief tugging on a woman's basket. When she screamed, Harry ran as fast as he could and shouted, "Stop, thief!" The ragged man took one look at him and ducked down an alley.

"Are you hurt?" Harry said as he reached the woman. Lord, his heart was hammering in his chest.

"No, but I thank you, kind sir," she said, picking up the half loaf of bread and dusting it off.

He couldn't help noticing her shabby glove as she set the bread beneath a cloth in her basket. Yet she spoke in a crisp, educated manner. The hood of her threadbare cloak fell back as she straightened her small frame. The lighted oil lamp nearby revealed thick, red curls by her ears. She had the kind of hair that made a man want to take it down, but that only reminded him of her peril. "You ought not to be on the streets alone at night," he said. "It's dangerous for a woman."

She pulled her hood up and scoffed. "Sir, I assure you, I would not set foot on these mean streets if I had any other choice."

The woman's plump lips and bright emerald eyes drew his attention. She was a rare beauty. "If you will allow it, I will escort you for your safety," he said, smiling. "Surely you will not object to protection."

Her eyes narrowed. "You've done your good deed for the evening, Sir Galahad." She reached in her basket and brandished a wicked-looking knife. "My trusty blade is protection enough."

Holy hell. The fine hairs on his neck stiffened and every muscle in his body tightened.

She looked him over and shook her head. "Perhaps I should escort you for your safety."

He laughed. "That's rich."

"Evidently, so are you."

She'd obviously taken stock of his clothing and deduced he was wealthy. "Come now, I'm a man and far stronger than you. I can defend myself."

She angled her head. "Have a care, sir. I quickly deduced you have a full purse inside your inner breast pocket. And if I can surmise that this quickly, you can be sure ruffians can, too."

"You heard the coins jingling while I ran."

She looked him over. "I wager those boots were made at Hoby's. They're worth a fortune. So is all of your clothing. At the very least, you ought to carry one of those canes with a hidden blade. Not everyone is as merciful as I am."

"You believe *I* am in danger?" How the devil had this conversation taken such a bizarre turn?

She regarded him with a world of knowledge in her eyes. "Tonight, Sir Galahad, you are far more vulnerable than I am."

Stunned into silence, he watched her disappear into the wispy fog. Then he reached inside another inner pocket and took out the penknife. A second, longer blade, far more wicked, folded out at the opposite end. He'd kept it hidden because he hadn't wanted to frighten her. So much for gallantry, he thought wryly. He pulled up the collar of his coat to ward off the chill and continued on his way home, her impertinent green eyes haunting him the entire walk. And damned if they didn't coax a smile out of him.

The next afternoon

Lucy Longmore found the address of Lady Blenborough, who lived in an elegant house situated near Green Park and not far from White's Club. At least she would feel relatively safe in this neighborhood. Well, from everyone except her disgusting employer, Mr. Buckley, the dancing master. As much as she despised him, she needed the employment. Lucy was Buckley's assistant, although she often did all of the teaching while Buckley tried to charm his lady clients. At least she had found a job using her dancing skills. It provided her with some income, though not nearly enough. She'd taken to sweeping floors at a dressmaker's shop in the evenings, and that was the reason she'd been walking late last night. Of course, she was taking risks, but as she'd told the handsome stranger, she wouldn't do it if she had another choice.

Last night, however, she'd had trouble sleeping after her encounter with the handsome gentleman. She felt a twinge of guilt for having brandished her knife after he'd helped her, but he was a stranger, and she had to protect herself. There was no one else to look after her grandmama.

If only she could get a letter of character, she knew she could find a better situation at one of the schools for girls or perhaps even a position as a companion to an elderly lady. Unfortunately, even if she could procure the necessary character letter, she feared it would be difficult to persuade someone to allow her blind grandmother to come along with her. But she'd made it this far using her wits, and she refused to give up hope. She always kept her eyes open for any new opportunities, and she had more than a little talent as a dance instructor.

Lucy went round to the servant's entrance, and the kindly cook gave her a cup of tea and a roll. Lucy ate half the roll and stored the rest in her apron pocket for later. When Buckley peered inside the kitchen, he scowled. "I'll dock your pay for fraternizing with the servants."

She had learned the art of making her expression as blank as possible. It was her only defense against her horrid employer. When she followed Buckley to the drawing room, Lucy saw a plump girl who looked to be about twelve. A lady wearing a fine morning gown sat in a chair with a bored expression.

"Lucy, show Prudence the steps," Buckley said. "Lady Blenborough, do not despair. Soon Lady Prudence will be performing the dance steps with elegance and lightness."

Lucy noted Lady Blenborough roll her eyes and unfurl her fan. "Please get on with the lesson," she said curtly.

"Lucy," Buckley said, clapping his hands. "Do not dally."

She turned her attention to Prudence. "Watch me the first time," Lucy said. "This is the chassé step. Right foot forward takes the weight; the following foot closes behind." Lucy regarded the girl. "Now you may try."

Prudence just stood there and chewed on her thumbnail, until her mother, Lady Blenborough, spoke sharply. "Prudence, attend."

The sharp command startled Prudence. She tried, but when she closed the back foot, she landed heavily with a thump on the floor.

Lucy knew how important it was for Prudence to learn the steps. One simply could not get on well in society without learning to dance gracefully. Years ago, when her mother was still alive and life was easier, Lucy had danced at many a country assembly. Moving her limbs lightly through the steps made her feel temporarily carefree. Most of all, dancing brought back happy memories of her mother teaching her and other children in the neighborhood how to dance.

"Once more," Lucy said. "I know you can do it, Prudence. Watch and imitate."

Twice Prudence landed heavily and looked at her feet with a miserable expression.

"Imagine you are as light as a bird," Lucy whispered to her. "Chassé close."

Prudence hopped onto her right foot, wobbled, and fell on her bottom.

Lucy hurried to help the girl rise. The stains on Prudence's cheeks bespoke humiliation.

"Mr. Buckley, I fear my daughter is hopeless," Lady Blenborough said in a disgusted tone she didn't bother to hide.

"Not at all, Lady Blenborough," Buckley said, his voice oily in his attempts to soothe. "Here, allow me to demonstrate with my assistant. "Lucy," he said, snapping his fingers.

She knew what was coming and braced herself. He stood behind her and his foul breath on her neck made her want to shiver. When he attempted to move closer, she knew he would try to touch her. She pretended to mis-understand and performed the steps. Chassé close, chassé close, chassé close. Lucy ended with a graceful plié.

"Prudence," Lady Blenborough said, "try again."

The girl had wandered over to the sideboard and her mother's voice startled her again. Guilt was written all over her face as she held her hands behind her back.

Lady Blenborough rose. Her eyes narrowed as she yanked her daughter's hand forward. Sweetmeats scattered all over the floor.

"If you wish to make a pig of yourself, Prudence, then do so. I wash my hands of you," Lady Blenborough said.

Lucy winced as tears spilled down Prudence's face.

"My lady," Buckley said. "Do not despair. I am sure we will make a dancer of Prudence yet."

"I'm done with her dance lessons," Lady Blenborough said. "She is nothing but an embarrassment to me."

Lucy bit her lip. She wished she could help Prudence. With patience, the girl could learn to execute the steps, but her mother obviously had taken a disgust of her daughter. With a sigh, Lucy could not help thinking of her own sweet mother's patience with all of her dance students and wished she were still alive.

The dancing lesson ended, and Lucy looked past Buckley's shoulder when he took her by the upper arm.

"I'm docking your pay. See that you do not consort with the servants again," he hissed. Then he handed over half the coins that were due her. Lucy held in the anger threatening to boil over and bobbed a curtsy. Then she hurried out of the servant's entrance. It wasn't the first time he'd found an excuse to reduce her pay, but it still infuriated her.

She must find other employment. Starting today, she would find a better job. There was much she didn't have, but she was smart and educated. All she needed was one person to give her a chance. Lucy was determined to make a better life for herself and her grandmama. If there was a way, she would find it.

She walked quickly until she came to King Street, where a boy was handing out notices in front of assembly rooms. "Servers needed for Almack's. Wednesday nights," the boy called out. "Must be clean and polite."

Lucy snatched one of the papers. An older gentleman dressed in elegant clothing opened the doors. Lucy ran to him and bobbed a curtsy. "Sir, I understand servers are needed. I'd be obliged if you would consider me."

"I'm Mr. Woodward, master of ceremonies," he said. "Come inside."

She followed him and curtsied again. "I'm a hard worker, sir."

"You have a refined accent, young lady."

"I'm educated, sir, but my family has fallen on hard times." She swallowed. "If it pleases you, Mr. Woodward, I would be much obliged if you would consider me."

"Come to the back door on Wednesday in a sennight at seven sharp in the evening," Mr. Woodward said. "You mustn't be late. The Lady Patronesses are unforgiving."

"I won't be late. Thank you, sir."

Elated at the opportunity, she started to turn away when Mr. Woodward cleared his throat. "Miss, what is your name?"

She turned back to him. "Lucy Longmore, sir."

He took her hand and set coins in her palm. Then he closed her fingers over them.

"Bless you, sir."

"Wait a few minutes," he said. "I wish to help you."

Lucy put the precious coins in a small purse she hid in her apron. When Mr. Woodward returned, he gave her a letter. "This should help you to procure employment."

Oh, dear God. It was a letter of character. She could escape Buckley. "You've been so kind, sir."

"Godspeed, dear. We will see you at Almack's next week."

Her spirits rose as she walked out and crossed the street, dodging the mud and horse droppings. She realized she was near the place where she'd threatened the handsome stranger with her knife only last night. In retrospect, she thought she'd misjudged him, but she shook off her guilt. A rich man like him hardly needed her sympathy. Her survival and that of her grandmama depended on keeping her wits about her.

She slowed her step as she neared a large building. A well-dressed gentleman handed over his horse's reins to a groom. Lucy had heard of the Albany, the famous gentleman's quarters. It occurred to her that she might inquire about employment there. Surely a place designated for bachelors would require the services of maids. Now that she had a letter of character, she had a far better chance of finding decent employment. She told herself not to get her hopes up, but she had nothing to lose, so she rapped the knocker.

Two hours later, Lucy had passed muster with Mrs. Finkle, the head housekeeper. The rules were simple enough. All she had to do was clean until the rooms were spotless, and of course, she mustn't fraternize with the gentlemen residents. Lucy had no intention of jeopardizing her new position. She was thrilled that her pay would be twice what she made assisting Buckley. For the first time in three years, she dared to hope that she and Grandmama might improve their circumstances.

Mrs. Norcliffe's drawing room, that same afternoon

"I am exceedingly concerned about attendance at Almack's," Mrs. Norcliffe, the newest patroness, said. "The gentlemen are abandoning our fair temple of respectability in droves. Something must be done."

Lady Jersey sniffed. "One would think that the quadrille would entice the gentlemen."

Mrs. Norcliffe thought no such thing, but she kept silent. Everybody knew that Lady Jersey had introduced the quadrille to Almack's. "I will be honest, ladies. I have a personal concern in seeing Almack's returned to its former popularity with all of the beau monde."

Lady Cowper, whom everyone knew was having an affair de coeur with Lord Palmerstone, sighed. "I believe we must resort to stronger measures, but Mrs. Norcliffe, you speak of your own concerns. Does this perchance relate to Granfield?"

Mrs. Norcliffe set her dish of tea aside. "My son refuses to leave his shabby rooms at the Albany. I fear he will take after his bachelor uncle, God rest his soul. The dukedom is in jeopardy. I must find my son a bride, for he surely will not consider it."

Lady Castlereagh sniffed. "I've yet to meet a bachelor who did not resist marriage. My advice is to trap him."

"Oh, dear," Mrs. Norcliffe said. "I could not lower myself to such tactics." *Not yet, at any rate.*

Mrs. Drummond-Burrell, known as one of the highest sticklers, drew her quizzing glass to her eye. "You must find a way to entice Granfield. He will want someone young and pretty with at least five thousand for her marriage portion."

Princess Esterhazy's eyes twinkled. "Let us not forget that His Grace has already inherited a fortune. You need stronger inducement. I recommend an introduction to a beautiful young woman. If all goes well, he will conceive a grand passion for her."

Lady Jersey rolled her eyes. "The only thing that entices gentlemen is their clubs. They gamble, they drink, and they take snuff. How many lose and win fortunes every night? It is scandalous."

Mrs. Norcliffe applied her fan. "I had hoped that he would accept Lady Bellingham's invitation to dine. She had meant to invite Miss Lingley and her parents, but apparently my son begged off due to other commitments."

"Well, we all know what that means," Lady Sefton said.

Mrs. Norcliffe sighed. "Indeed, the clubs."

"I think they would live in them if possible," Lady Cowper said.

"Perish the thought," Countess Lieven said, "but truly

we must help Mrs. Norcliffe in her quest. A dukedom is too important to let fall to a distant cousin or worse. No one wants to find an American among one's relations."

Mrs. Norcliffe placed her hands primly in her lap. "Dancing is the mode of courtship, is it not? Do we not encourage our fair offspring to find their perfectly suitable partners for life at a ball?"

"Yes, of course," Lady Sefton said, "but you wish to make a point, do you not?"

"We need to make the experience exciting for the gentlemen," Mrs. Norcliffe said.

"No spirits," Mrs. Drummond-Burrell said. "The gentlemen will huddle around the sideboard all evening and overindulge."

"Mrs. Norcliffe, how do you propose to drum up excitement?" Lady Cowper said.

"It is rather daring," she said, "but one thing we know about gentlemen is that they cannot resist competing."

All of the ladies leaned the slightest bit forward.

"I propose a dancing competition, one that would stir up passions not only for the dancers, but for observers as well. Of course, I hope to find my dear son a wife in this manner."

"How can you be sure it will work?" Lady Castlereagh said.

Mrs. Norcliffe shrugged. "It is easy enough to tip off the scandal sheets. Imagine all of London anticipating the competition each week. News will circulate far and wide. Everyone who is anyone will not want to miss the weekly winners."

"Winners?" Lady Sefton said in a faint tone.

"Each week the couples will dance and compete to

stay in the competition another week," Mrs. Norcliffe said. "Some will be eliminated and others will remain until the very last."

"We are to judge them?" Lady Jersey asked.

"Of course," Mrs. Norcliffe said. "Who better than the patronesses to make the decisions?"

"I think we need an incentive for the gentlemen to participate," Lady Jersey said. "Otherwise, the gentlemen will return to their clubs."

"An incentive implies commerce." Lady Cowper fanned her face as if money were akin to devilment.

"In this case, it implies competition, and that is something no gentleman can resist," Mrs. Norcliffe said. "Imagine if you will how many will be envious of those who are able to participate or observe at close hand. Almack's will once again rise as the temple of exclusivity," Mrs. Norcliffe said. *And I will find my son a proper wife, so help me, God.*

"It is rather bold," Lady Jersey said, "but we are the patronesses. Who will dare criticize if we sanction the competition?"

"Indeed, it could result in the loss of one's voucher," Mrs. Norcliffe said.

"What will the prize be?" Lady Jersey asked. "It must be sufficient to draw the gentlemen away from their liquor, cards, and dice."

"Ladies, what do you say to five hundred pounds as the prize for the most elegant dancing couple? Are we prepared to contribute seventy-two pounds each?" Mrs. Norcliffe said.

"That leaves four pounds unaccounted for," Lady Sefton said.

"We will buy extra lemonade and buttered sandwiches," Mrs. Norcliffe said.

Everyone nodded their approval.

"Well, ladies, I believe we are all prepared for the first annual Almack's dancing competition," Mrs. Norcliffe said.

Lady Jersey observed Mrs. Norcliffe with a sly expression. "Pray tell, how do you propose to tempt your son into participating?"

Mrs. Norcliffe smiled. "What every mother resorts to when faced with an obstinate son. I will make him feel guilty."

THE DISH

Where Authors Give You the Inside Scoop

♥ ♥ ♥ ♥ ♥ ♥ ♥ ♥ ♥ ♥ ♥ ♥ ♥ ♥ ♥ ♥

From the desk of Vicky Dreiling

Dear Reader,

I had a lot of imaginary boyfriends when I was a kid. My friend Kim and I read *Tiger Beat* magazine and chose our loves. I "dated" David Cassidy, a yesteryear heartthrob from a TV show called *The Partridge Family*. Kim's "boyfriend" was Donny Osmond, although she might have had a brief crush on Barry Williams, better known as Greg from *The Brady Bunch*. I did a quick search online and discovered that *Tiger Beat* magazine still exists, but the stars for today's preteens are Justin Bieber, Taylor Lautner, and members of the boy band One Direction.

The idea of a big family and rock-star boyfriends really appealed to us. We traveled in imaginary tour buses to imaginary concerts. We listened to the music and sang along, pretending we were onstage, too. Of course, we invented drama, such as mean girls trying to steal our famous boyfriends backstage.

Recently, I realized that the seeds of the families I create in my novels were sown in my preteen years as Kim and I pretended to date our celebrity crushes. As I got older, imaginary boyfriends led to real-life boyfriends in high school and college. Eventually, marriage and kids led to an extended family, one that continues to grow.

In WHAT A RECKLESS ROGUE NEEDS, two close families meet once a year at a month-long house party. As in real life, much has changed for Colin and Angeline. While they were born only a week apart, they never really got along very well. An incident at Angeline's come-out ball didn't help matters, either. Many years have elapsed, and now Colin finds he needs Angeline's help to keep from losing a property that holds very deep emotional ties for him. Once they cross the threshold of Sommerall House, their lives are never the same again, but they will always have their families.

May the Magic Romance Fairies be with all of you and your families!

www.VickyDreiling.com
Twitter @VickyDreiling
Facebook.com/VickyDreilingHistoricalAuthor

♥ ♥ ♥ ♥ ♥ ♥ ♥ ♥ ♥ ♥ ♥ ♥ ♥ ♥

From the desk of Paula Quinn

Dear Reader,

As most of you know, I love dogs. I have six of them. I see your eyes bugging out. Six?? Yes, six precious tiny Chihuahuas and all together they weight approximately twenty-seven pounds. I've had dogs my whole life—big ones, little ones. So it's not surprising that I would want to write dogs into my books. This time I went big: 140 pounds of big.

In THE SEDUCTION OF MISS AMELIA BELL we meet Grendel, an Irish wolfhound mix, who along with our hero, Edmund MacGregor, wins the heart of our heroine, Amelia Bell. Grendel is the son of Aurelius, whom some of you might remember as the puppy Colin MacGregor gave to Edmund, his stepson, in *Conquered by a Highlander*. Since this series is called Highland Heirs, I figured why not include the family dog heirs as well?

I loved writing a dog as a secondary character, and Grendel is an important part of Edmund and Amelia's story. Now, really, what's better than a big, brawny, sexy Highlander? Right: a big, brawny, sexy Highlander with a dog. Or if you live in NYC, you can settle for a hunky guy playing with his dog in the park.

My six babies all have distinct personalities. For instance, Riley loves to bark and be an all-around pain in the neck. He's high-strung and loves it. Layla, my biggest girl, must "mother" all the others. She keeps them in line with a soft growl and a lick to the eyeball. Liam, my tiny three-pound boy, isn't sure if he's Don Juan or Napoleon. He'll drop and show you his package if you call him cute. They are all different and I wanted Grendel to have his own personality, too.

Much like his namesake, Grendel hates music and powdered periwigs. He's faithful and loyal, and he loves to chase smaller things…like people. Even though Edmund is his master and Grendel does, of course, love him best, it doesn't take Amelia long to win his heart, or for Grendel to win hers, and he soon finds himself following at her heels. Some of my favorite scenes involve the subtle interactions between Amelia and Grendel. This big, seemingly vicious dog is always close by when Amelia is sad or afraid. When things are going on all around them, Amelia just has to rest her hand on Grendel's head and it completely calms her. We witness a partial transformation of ownership in the small, telltale ways Grendel remains ever constant at Amelia's side.

Even when Grendel finds Gaza, his own love interest (hey, I'm a romance writer, what can I say?), he is still faithful to his human lady. We won't get into doggy love, but suffice it to say, there will be plenty of furry heirs living in Camlochlin for a long time to come. They might not be the prettiest dogs in Skye, but they are the most loyal.

This was my first foray into writing a dog as a secondary character and I must say I fell in love with a big, slobbering mutt named after a fiend who killed men for singing. I wasn't surprised that Grendel filled his place so well in Edmund and Amelia's story. Each of my dogs does the same in mine and my kids' stories. That's what dogs do. They run headlong into our lives barking, tail wagging, sharing wet, sloppy kisses. They love us with an almost supernatural, unconditional love. And we love them back.

I hope you get a chance to pick up THE SEDUCTION OF MISS AMELIA BELL and meet Edmund and Amelia and, of course, Grendel.

Happy reading!

Paula Quinn

♥ ♥ ♥ ♥ ♥ ♥ ♥ ♥ ♥ ♥ ♥ ♥ ♥ ♥ ♥ ♥

From the desk of Kristen Ashley

Dear Reader,

Years ago, I was walking to the local shops and, as usual, I had my headphones in. As I was walking, Bob Seger & The Silver Bullet Band's "You'll Accomp'ny Me" came on and somehow, even having heard this song dozens and dozens of times before, the lyrics suddenly hit me.

This isn't unusual. I have to be in a certain mood to absorb lyrics. But when I am, sometimes they'll seep into my soul, making me smile, or making me cry.

"You'll Accomp'ny Me" made me smile. It made me feel warm. And it made me feel happy because the lyrics are beautiful, the message of love and devotion is strong, the passion is palpable, and the way it's written states that Bob definitely has Kristen Ashley alpha traits.

I loved it. I've always loved that song, but then I loved it even more. It was like one of my books in song form. How could I not love that?

At the time, however, I didn't consider it for a book, not inspiring one or not to be used in a scene. For a long time, it was just mine, giving me that warm feeling and a smile on my face at the thought that there is musical proof out there that these men exist.

Better, they wield guitars.

Now, from the very moment I introduced Hop in *Motorcycle Man*, he intrigued me. And as we learned more about him in that book, my knowing why he was doing what he was doing, I knew he'd have to be redeemed in my readers' eyes by sharing his whole story. I just didn't know who was going to give him the kind of epic happy ending I felt he deserved.

Therefore, I didn't know that Lanie would be the woman of his dreams. Truth be told, I didn't even expect Lanie to have her own book. But her story as told in *Motorcycle Man* was just too heartbreaking to leave her hanging. I just had no idea what to do with her.

But I didn't think a stylish, professional, accomplished "lady" and a biker would jibe, so I never considered these two together. Or, in fact, Lanie with any of the Chaos brothers at all.

That is, until this song came up on shuffle again and I knew that was how Hop would consider his relationship with Lanie. Even as she pushed him away due to her past, he'd do what he could to convince her that, someday, she'd accompany him.

I mean, just those words—how cool are they? "You'll accompany me." Brilliant.

But Bob, his Silver Bullet Band, and their music did

quadruple duty in FIRE INSIDE. Not only did they give me "You'll Accomp'ny Me," which was the perfect way for Hop to express his feelings to Lanie; they also gave me Hop's nickname for Lanie: "lady". And they gave me "We've Got Tonight," yet another perfect song to fit what was happening between Lanie and Hop. And last, the way Bob sings is also the way I hear Hop in my head.

I interweave music in my books all the time and my selections are always emotional and, to me, perfect.

But I've never had a song, or artist, so beautifully help me tell my tale than when I utilized the extraordinary storytelling abilities of Bob Seger in my novel FIRE INSIDE.

It's a pleasure listening to his music.

It's a gift to be inspired by it.

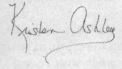

♥ ♥ ♥ ♥ ♥ ♥ ♥ ♥ ♥ ♥ ♥ ♥ ♥ ♥

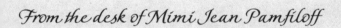

Dear Reader,

When it came time to decide which god or goddess in my Accidentally Yours series would get their HEA in book four, I sat back and looked at who was most in need of salvation. Hands down, the winner was Ixtab, the Goddess of Suicide. Before you judge the title, however, I'd like to explain why this goddess is not the dreary soul you might imagine. Fact is she's more like the Goddess of Anti-Suicide, with the ability to drain dark feelings from one person and redeploy them to another. Naturally, being a deity, she tends to help those who are down on their luck and punish those who are truly deserving.

However, every now and again, someone bumps into her while she's not looking. The results are fatal. So after thousands of years and thousands of accidental deaths, she's determined to keep everyone away. Who could blame her?

But fate has other plans for this antisocial goddess with a kind streak. His name is Dr. Antonio Acero, and this sexy Spaniard has just become the lynchpin in the gods' plans for saving the planet from destruction. He's also in need of a little therapy, and Ixtab is the only one who can help him.

When these two meet, they quickly realize there are forces greater than them both, trying to pull them apart and push them together. Which force will win?

♥ ♥ ♥ ♥ ♥ ♥ ♥ ♥ ♥ ♥ ♥ ♥ ♥ ♥

From the desk of Katie Lane

Dear Reader,

As some of you may already know, the idea for my fictional town of Bramble, Texas, came from the hours I spent watching *The Andy Griffith Show*. When Barney, Aunt Bee, and Opie were on, my mom couldn't peel me away from our console television. The townsfolk's antics held me spellbound. Which is probably why I made my characters a little crazy, too. (Okay, so I made them a lot crazy.) But while the people of Mayberry had levelheaded Sheriff Andy Taylor to keep them in line, the townsfolk of Bramble have been allowed to run wild.

Until now.

I'm pleased as punch to introduce Sheriff Dusty Hicks, the hero of my newest Deep in the Heart of Texas novel, A MATCH MADE IN TEXAS. Like Andy, he's a dedicated lawman who loves his job and the people of his community. Unlike Andy, he carries a gun, has a wee bit of a temper, and is blessed with the kind of looks and hard body that can make a good girl turn bad. And after just one glimpse of Dusty's shiny handcuffs, Brianne Cates wants to turn bad. Real bad.

But it won't be easy for Brianne to seduce a little lawman lovin' out of my hero. Dusty has his hands full trying to regain joint custody of his precocious three-year-old daughter and, at the same time, deal with a con-artist television evangelist and a vengeful cartel drug lord. Not to mention the townsfolk of Bramble, who have suddenly gone wa-a-ay off their rockers.

All I can say is, what started out as a desire to give Bramble its very own Sheriff Taylor quickly turned into a fast-paced joyride that left my hair standing on end and my heart as warm and gooey as a toaster strudel. I hope it will do the same for you. :o)

Much love,

Katie Lane

♥ ♥ ♥ ♥ ♥ ♥ ♥ ♥ ♥ ♥ ♥ ♥ ♥ ♥

From the desk of Jessica Lemmon

Dear Reader,

I love a scruffy-faced, tattooed, motorcycle-riding bad boy as much as the next girl, so when it came time to write HARD TO HANDLE, I knew what qualities I wanted Aiden Downey to possess.

For inspiration, I needed to look no further than Charlie Hunnam from the famed TV show *Sons of Anarchy*. I remember watching Season 1 on Netflix, mouth agape and eyes wide. When Charlie's character, Jax Teller, finished his first scene, I looked over at my husband and said, "*That's Aiden!*"

In HARD TO HANDLE, Aiden may have been crafted with a bad-boy starter kit: He has the scruff, the tattoo, the knee-weakening dimples that make him look like sin on a stick, and yeah, a custom Harley-Davidson to boot. But Aiden also has something extra special that derails his bad-boy image: a heart of near-solid gold.

When we first met Aiden and Sadie in *Tempting the Billionaire* (and again in the e-novella *Can't Let Go*), there wasn't much hope for these two hurting hearts to work out their differences. Aiden had been saddled with devastating news and familial responsibilities, and Sadie (poor Sadie!) had just opened up her heart to Aiden, who stomped on it, broke it into pieces, and set it on fire for good measure. How could they forgive each other after things had gone so horribly, terribly wrong?

Aiden has suffered a lot of loss, but in HARD TO HANDLE, he's on a mission to get his life *back*. A very large piece of that puzzle is winning back the woman he never meant to hurt, the woman he loved. Sadie, with her walled-up heart, smart, sassy mouth, and fiery attitude isn't going to be an easy nut to crack. Especially after she vowed to never, ever get hurt again. That goes *double* for the blond Adonis with the unforgettable mouth and ability to turn her brain into Silly Putty.

The best part about this good "bad" boy? Aiden's determination is as rock-hard as his abs. He's not going to let Sadie walk away, not now that he sees how much she still cares for him. Having been to hell and back, Aiden isn't intimidated by her. Not even a little bit. Sadie is his Achilles' heel, and Aiden accepts that it's going to take time (and plenty of seduction!) to win her over. He also knows that she's worth it.

Think you're up for a ride around the block with a bad-boy-done-good? I have to say, Aiden left a pretty deep mark on my heart and I'm still a little in love with him! He may change your mind about scruffy, motorcycle-riding hotties...He certainly managed to change Sadie's.

Happy reading!

Jessica Lemmon

www.jessicalemmon.com

Find out more about Forever Romance!

Visit us at
www.hachettebookgroup.com/publishing_forever.aspx

Find us on Facebook
http://www.facebook.com/ForeverRomance

Follow us on Twitter
http://twitter.com/ForeverRomance

NEW AND UPCOMING TITLES

Each month we feature our new titles
and reader favorites.

CONTESTS AND GIVEAWAYS

We give away galleys, autographed copies,
and all kinds of exclusive items.

AUTHOR INFO

You'll find bios, articles, and links to personal websites
for all your favorite authors—and so much more.

GET SOCIAL

Connect with your favorite authors, editors, and
other Forever fans, and share what's important to you.

THE BUZZ

Sign up for our monthly romance newsletter,
and be the first to read all about it.

VISIT US ONLINE AT

WWW.HACHETTEBOOKGROUP.COM

FEATURES:

OPENBOOK BROWSE AND
SEARCH EXCERPTS
•
AUDIOBOOK EXCERPTS AND PODCASTS
•
AUTHOR ARTICLES AND INTERVIEWS
•
BESTSELLER AND PUBLISHING
GROUP NEWS
•
SIGN UP FOR E-NEWSLETTERS
•
AUTHOR APPEARANCES AND TOUR
INFORMATION
•
SOCIAL MEDIA FEEDS AND WIDGETS
•
DOWNLOAD FREE APPS

BOOKMARK HACHETTE BOOK GROUP
@ WWW.HACHETTEBOOKGROUP.COM